PENGUIN BOOKS

## THUNDER FROM JERUSALEM

Bodie & Brock Thoene, with degrees in creative writing and history, respectively, are the authors of thirty-six novels, including the bestselling series *The Zion Chronicles* and *The Zion Covenant*. Together they have won eight Evangelical Christian Publishers Gold Medallion awards. The Thoenes live in Nevada and in London, England.

BODIE AND BROCK THOENE

# THUNDER FROM JERUSALEM

## THE ZION LEGACY

### Book II

PENGUIN BOOKS

PENGUIN BOOKS
Published by the Penguin Group
Penguin Putnam Inc., 375 Hudson Street,
New York, New York 10014, U.S.A.
Penguin Books Ltd, 27 Wrights Lane, London W8 5TZ, England
Penguin Books Australia Ltd, Ringwood, Victoria, Australia
Penguin Books Canada Ltd, 10 Alcorn Avenue,
Toronto, Ontario, Canada M4V 3B2
Penguin Books (N.Z.) Ltd, 182–190 Wairau Road,
Auckland 10, New Zealand

Penguin Books Ltd, Registered Offices:
Harmondsworth, Middlesex, England

First published in the United States of America by Viking Penguin,
a member of Penguin Putnam Inc., 2000
Published in Penguin Books 2001

1   3   5   7   9   10   8   6   4   2

Map illustration by James Sinclair

THE LIBRARY OF CONGRESS HAS CATALOGED
THE HARDCOVER EDITION AS FOLLOWS:
Thoene, Bodie.
Thunder from Jerusalem / by Bodie and Brock Thoene.
p.   cm.—(Book 2 of the Zion legacy series)
ISBN 0-670-89206-8 (hc.)
ISBN 0 14 10.0218 2 (pbk.)
1. Israel-Arab War, 1948–1949—Fiction.   2. Jews—Palestine—Fiction.
I. Thoene, Brock.   II. Title.
PS3570.H46 T49 2000
00–028994

Printed in the United States of America
Set in Minion

To Chance, Jessie, Ian, and Titan
with love from Bubbe and Potsy

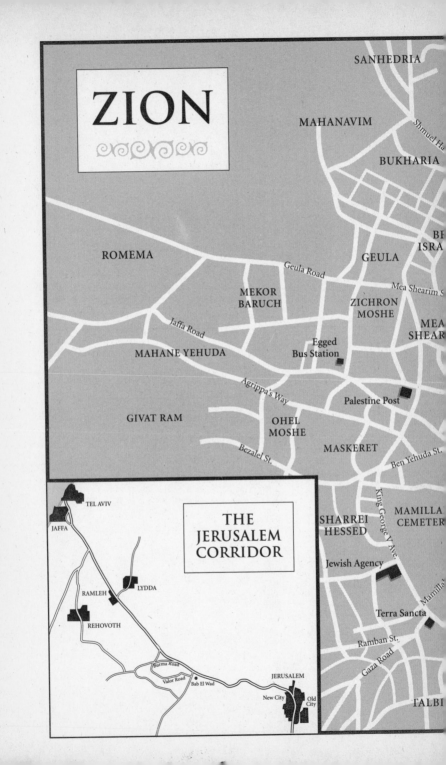

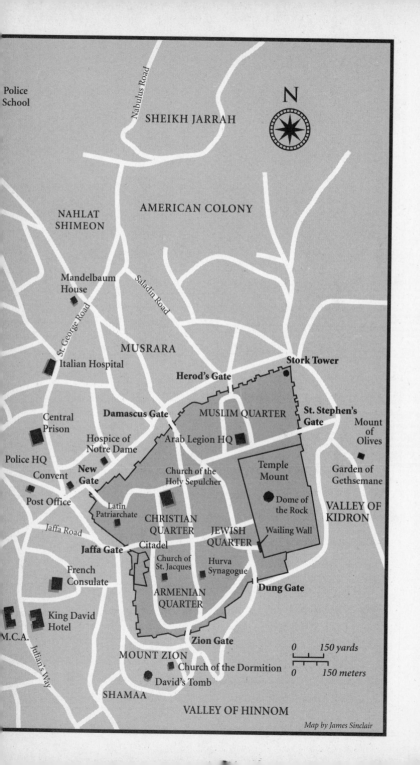

Police
School

Nabulus Road

SHEIKH JARRAH

**N**

NAHLAT
SHIMEON

AMERICAN COLONY

Mandelbaum
House

Saladin Road

St. George Road

MUSRARA

Stork Tower

Italian Hospital

**Herod's Gate**

**Damascus Gate**

MUSLIM QUARTER

**St. Stephen's
Gate**

Central
Prison

Hospice of
Notre Dame

Arab Legion HQ

Mount
of
Olives

Police HQ

Convent

**New
Gate**

Church of the
Holy Sepulcher

Temple
Mount

Garden of
Gethsemane

Post Office

Latin
Patriarchate

CHRISTIAN
QUARTER

Dome of
the Rock

**VALLEY OF
KIDRON**

Jaffa Road

JEWISH
QUARTER

Wailing Wall

**Jaffa Gate**

Citadel

Church of
St. Jacques

Hurva
Synagogue

French
Consulate

ARMENIAN
QUARTER

**Dung Gate**

King David
Hotel

M.C.A.

Julian's Way

**Zion Gate**

MOUNT ZION

Church of the Dormition

0      150 yards

David's Tomb

0      150 meters

SHAMAA

**VALLEY OF HINNOM**

Map by James Sinclair

# WEDNESDAY

*May 19, 1948*

*Sound a great shofar for our freedom,*
*and lift up a banner to gather our exiles,*
*and gather us together from the four corners*
*of the earth. Blessed are you, Adonai, who*
*gathers the dispersed among his People Israel.*

*The Amidah—The Tenth Prayer*
*"Kibbutz Galuyot" (Gathering of the Exiles)*

Rejoice, Jerusalem! Be glad for her, you who love her; rejoice with her, you who mourned for her, and you shall find contentment. . . .

*Isaiah 66:10–11*

"I am the Alpha and Omega, the beginning and the end. I will give unto him that is athirst of the fountain of the water of life freely. He that overcometh shall inherit all things; and I will be his God, and he shall be my son."

*Revelation 21:6–7*

# CHAPTER 1

The DC-4 had been flying in total blackness for hours. American Colonel Michael Stone was in the copilot's seat. Square jaw tense, head aching, the forty-five-year-old Stone did his best not to sound nervous.

He asked, "So how do you know where we are?"

With a grin that could be seen by the orange glow of the instrument panel, pilot David Meyer replied, "Doesn't really matter. We've been over water almost the whole time since picking you up on Corsica. One hunk of the Mediterranean is as wet as another."

Michael Stone was returning to Israel as military advisor to David Ben-Gurion. He had been a U.S. Army officer in the Second World War, in the ground war. He knew flyboys were easygoing in the discipline department, but this was over the top. "Then how do you know when we're there?" he demanded.

"Easy," Meyer said, gesturing toward the side window with a nod of his tousled blond head. "I know how long it should take. When I see the lighthouse in Haifa, we're there."

"And if you miss it?"

"Then we're delivering this plane and its cargo to King Abdullah in Jordan. Relax, Colonel. We've hit every checkpoint over Italy, Crete, and Cyprus . . . the last two while you were sleeping." David checked his bulky metal wristwatch. "Eleven hours now. Another half hour or less to go."

The cargo was a disassembled Messerschmitt fighter plane. Nucleus of the Israeli air force, the German aircraft was hitching a ride to its new home . . . Israel! Wings, fuselage, and prop nearly filled the back of the transport.

Ammunition and spare parts were crammed into the remaining space, except for the crevices occupied by two Czech mechanics and

David's copilot, Bobby Milkin. The three men in the cargo bay were fast asleep. Milkin, an unlit cigar clamped between his teeth, was curled around a Thompson machine gun.

The flight continued for a time in silence; then Colonel Stone noted, "I heard you and Milkin were bringing in Messerschmitts directly. In one piece, I mean. Flying. So how come you're driving the bus?"

"You're right," David agreed. "We tried. The Messer is only good for an hour or two in the air before refueling. We got as far as Athens. Had a little run-in. To make a long story short, sabotage took out the first two 109s when me and Bobby tried to short-hop 'em into the country. We were lucky. You know? Anyway, we hitched a ride back to Czechoslovakia to pick this baby up."

"In pieces. How many days to reassemble?"

"Too many."

"And what happens after we arrive? I mean, what do you do then?"

"Me? I've got a wife and a bath waiting for me in Tel Aviv." Sniffing the air David corrected, "Probably in the other order. Got the Boss's permission to take one day off before we make the hop back to Zebra . . . that's Czechoslovakia . . . for another plane." David's voice took on a hopeful note when he said, "If they get the first 109 put together while I'm gone I'm gonna trade in this bucket for a fighter." In a harder tone he added, "The Egyptians have got British Spitfires. Ellie . . . that's my wife . . . wrote the story for *The Times.* About the Egyptian Spits that beat up our people on the docks in Tel Aviv. Anyway, I'd like to meet those guys one on one."

■ ■ ■ ■

At twenty-nine minutes into David Meyer's half hour he blithely announced, "There it is." Swinging the transport plane in a wide turn, he dropped the port wing so Stone could see the beacon of Haifa Harbor. The rest of the port city and the countryside around was blacked out. "Glad to see the Boss doesn't believe in giving the Egyptians an easy target," he said, swinging the craft back toward the south. "Eighty miles to go. Better roust Bobby . . . if he isn't too drunk."

Bobby Milkin had not had anything to drink, but he was grumpy at being awakened. "Can't you do this without my help, Tin Man?" he groused. "Just 'cause we're comin' into an unknown field, over hostile territory, in the middle of the night. Sheesh, what a amatoor."

Stone did not stay in the cargo bay but instead took the unoccupied navigator's jumpseat. David hooked his thumb over his shoulder at the colonel. "Just making it look regulation for the brass."

A few minutes later the outline of Tel Aviv and neighboring Jaffa Harbor appeared in the moonlight. "That's it," Milkin crooned. "Come to Papa, baby."

"What say we let 'em know we made it?" David suggested. He dialed up the frequency monitored by the Jewish Agency and keyed the microphone. "Morning, boys. This is Israeli Airways flight number one bringing home the goodies."

After the Agency acknowledged, Milkin said, "Man, that sounds good. I hated havin' to be Panama Airways to fool the limeys."

They were over the middle of Tel Aviv and making the turn toward the southeast approach to the airstrip when the gunfire started. First one line of tracers floated up toward them, then a second, and a third. "Hey!" Milkin yelled at the ground. "We told you it was us!"

"Somebody forgot to tell our gunners that we have planes too," David said. "They think we're Egyptians." He jinked the craft left. Sideslipping to lose altitude before the lines of fire intersected the path of the plane, he added, "Either that, or the Boss is mad we're late, eh, Milkin?"

An even colder reception awaited them.

With the Arab capture of Lydda Airfield, Israeli operations were shifted to a strip carved out of the Judean hills about twenty miles southeast of Tel Aviv. Code-named *Oklahoma,* the destination had a control tower and barrels of flaming kerosene for runway lights.

"Fog," David said tersely. "Clear weather for a couple thousand miles and now this. Tell the passengers to buckle up, Colonel, then you do the same."

Raising the airfield tower, Bobby Milkin reported their arrival. "Ceiling zero, visibility zero," the tower responded, then suggested they circle out to sea until a break in the mist presented itself.

Studying the fuel gauges, David nodded grimly and headed the plane back toward the west. There were no longer quips in the cockpit, no horseplay. Colonel Stone needed no explanation as to the change in mood.

They completed two circles without any improvement in the visibility. On the third pass Milkin said, "Got it!" He pointed right of the center line where a break in the fog showed a double row of flaming markers.

"Call out the altitude for me, Bobby," David said tersely. "Keep it coming. Okay. Gear down. Set the flaps."

"One thousand," Milkin said. His cigar hung like an appendage from his lip. "Nine hundred. Eight. Seven-fifty."

At seven hundred feet the fog swirled in around them.

"Six-fifty. Six."

It was so thick David could no longer see the blinking wingtip lights.

At Milkin's call of "Four hundred," David shook his head and said, "We're pulling up." Tugging on the yoke, he urged the transport skyward and once again circled toward the sea. "How much fuel we got?"

Quietly Milkin said, "Enough for one more pass. Want to ditch?"

"How about you, Colonel?" David asked. "Think the Boss'd be sore if I messed up his transport and another of his fighters?"

"I never learned to swim," Stone replied.

"Good enough," David said. "Let's try again."

Moments later they were back in line with the runway, as nearly as David could tell. Once again Milkin reeled off the declining altitude figures. "Six hundred. Five. Four-fifty. I see the runway. Right. Little more right. Three. Two-fifty."

Suddenly out of the eddying vapor loomed a hill, dead in front of them and scarcely fifty feet below.

Despite Milkin's cry of "Pull up!" David resisted the impulse. If they did so now, they would have to ditch in the sea . . . if they could even make it back that far. Instead he jerked the plane hard to the right. He was trusting that the slope fell off more sharply on the side nearest the runway.

The ground raced past, looking close enough to touch. The nearness of the hill threw the roar of their engines back at them. Without lift and at reduced airspeed, the transport was sluggish in David's hands. It resisted him when he tried to correct its position. They were slipping sideways toward the ground.

"Gun it!" he shouted.

They came in at a slant above the first two barrels on the left side of the airstrip. A guard flung himself to the ground. David fought to realign the plane with the runway. "Cut 'em!" David bellowed.

The DC-4 bounced, vaulted back toward the sky, then bounced again. David and Bobby Milkin wrestled with the control yokes.

At last the transport settled. It rolled out sweetly and was braked to a stop, dead even with the last pair of marker barrels.

Turning to Stone, David wiped his brow and said, "Don't get the wrong idea, Colonel. We always do it like this."

■ ■ ■ ■

At twenty minutes after two o'clock on the morning of May 19, 1948, salvation came to the besieged Jewish Quarter of Old City Jerusalem.

The last blazing green line of a flare split the sky in an arch over the city, then died away. The image of it lingered in Haganah Commander Moshe Sachar's vision. He and his wife, Rachel, held out their hands in welcome to eighty Palmach troops. Carrying medical supplies and ammunition, the Jewish soldiers had broken into the Old City through Zion Gate from Mount Zion.

Behind Moshe, Jewish civilians, trapped for months in the Jewish Quarter, swarmed out of their shelters in the cellars of Nissan Bek, the Hurva, and Porat Yoseph Synagogues.

Fifteen hundred men, women, children, rabbis, Yeshiva students, and exhausted Haganah defenders packed the narrow lanes to cheer the arrival of fresh reinforcements. The shouts of jubilation were heard by the retreating Irregular troops of the Mufti as they withdrew from their positions. Laughing for the first time in weeks, Moshe kissed Rachel. "It sounds like we are cheering a football match!"

He could not hear Rachel's reply over the tumult. She squeezed his hand and mouthed the words "I love you" and "hospital." No further explanation was needed. She took a supply-laden soldier by the arm and led the way to Misgav Ladakh, the dilapidated hospital the Rothschilds built in 1854 and named "Refuge of the Downtrodden." Moshe had taken to calling the place simply "Downtrodden." These days of war had crowded the musty, vaulted rooms with wounded, all of whom urgently needed the medicine in the packs of the Palmach soldiers. One could find the place in the dark, Moshe thought, by following the stench. A stack of shrouded dead lay awaiting burial in a shed behind the building. The facility had one doctor and two trained nurses. It was staffed and run almost entirely by volunteers.

Moshe spotted Rachel's brother, ten-year-old Yacov, perched on the

shoulders of one very large Palmachnik. Yacov was singing "Hatikva,"
The Hope, and waving a homemade Israeli flag as his bony dog barked
at the soldier's heels.

"We are saved!"

"Blessed be the Eternal!"

It was plain that the Jewish inhabitants of the Old City believed
their war was over. Their joy made Moshe uneasy.

"It is a miracle! A miracle!"

"Praise be to Him who has been merciful and allowed us to live to
see . . ."

" . . . to see this day of our salvation!"

Kisses mingled with tears of rejoicing. The Palmach reinforcements
were swallowed up by the crowd of well-wishers.

Moshe knew the battle was far from won.

Jacob Kalner, the stocky, sunburned corporal who had first breached
the wall and opened Zion Gate, stood at the edge of the crowd beside his
wife, Lori. She was crying, her head against his chest. He patted her awkwardly, kissed her forehead, caressed her face in his hands, and then they
parted. With one longing look back at him, she ran after Rachel and the
Palmachnik. The trio vanished into the blackness of the street.

Jacob glanced up and caught Moshe's eye. He worked his way
through a gaggle of schoolchildren to Moshe's side.

He shouted to be heard over the din. "There are a handful of
my men holding Zion Gate and the corridor through the Armenian
Quarter."

Moshe guided him away from the noise. "The Irregulars may regroup and attack again. Get back to Zion Gate. We hold the tower of St.
Jacques, which overlooks the route through the Armenian Quarter to
your position. If you hear gunfire from there, you will know the Irregulars are advancing again."

■ ■ ■ ■

The voices of celebration surrounded Rachel Sachar and Lori Kalner as
they pushed through the human tide that clogged the twisted lanes of
the Old City.

Nathan Cohen, teenage grandson of the woman who ran the soup
kitchen at the Hurva Synagogue, called to Rachel, "Your grandfather,
Reb Lebowitz, is looking for you, Rachel! He said if I saw you. . . ." His

voice was drowned by cheering as a newly arrived Palmachnik was hoisted to the shoulders of the young men.

"Where is he?" Rachel shouted.

"Home," Nathan replied, sweeping by in a current of fifteen young Hasidim. "He said . . ." The rest of the communication was lost.

Lori took Rachel's hand. "Go to him," she instructed. "He'll be worried."

Rachel nodded. "I won't be long."

The two women parted. Lori headed up the sloping road toward Misgav Ladakh Hospital. Rachel turned toward the bulk of the Hurva. Grandfather lived across the lane from the synagogue in a cramped basement room with Yacov and his shaggy mongrel dog named Shaul.

The old man had hardly slept since Rachel arrived in the Jewish Quarter. He spent his days helping Hannah Cohen supervise the feeding of five hundred women and children in the soup kitchen. His nights were passed in study and prayer.

Rachel clambered down the steps to his quarters. The door was ajar. Soft light from a single candle illuminated the sparsely furnished room. The rabbi sat at a table where two rows of photographs were fanned out before him like playing cards.

He did not look up as she entered but said her name. "Rachel. Praise be to the Eternal."

She closed the door behind her. "The Palmach has opened the corridor. We are free."

At this he studied her briefly and then returned his gaze to the photographs. "You found Moshe?"

"He is at Zion Gate. The people have packed the streets of the quarter. They hinder the movement of supplies."

Grandfather nodded. "Yacov and the dog have gone. I kept the boy with me all night. But who can hold him back with such good news, *nu?*"

The aged man's voice was burdened with weariness. Or was it sadness? There was something here Rachel could not understand. Why, when the whole Jewish Quarter had turned out to celebrate, did he appear so subdued?

"Are you well, Grandfather?" She sat down in the chair opposite him. He was gazing at photographs of Rachel's mother and father. Of her brothers.

He raised his eyes to search her face. "You look so very much like her."

"I am glad for it." Rachel touched his arm. "She would have loved to see this. Wouldn't she?"

He inhaled deeply. "I have been thinking what possessions I have which must be saved."

"Everything . . . everyone . . . is safe now."

He inclined his head in a posture of doubt, then gathered the photographs and placed them in an envelope. He slid it across the rough tabletop to Rachel. "They are just memories. But one day you will want to show them to your children, *nu?* Show them that your mama and papa were real people. More than names. More than numbers among six million."

"You keep them," she urged. "You can show our children, yes?"

"It is better you take them. I have nothing else of value to leave you."

"Leave me? Don't talk like this. . . ."

Raising his hand to halt her objection, the old man rose with difficulty. He opened the door, letting the night into the room. The flame of the candle flickered. The cheering of Jewish voices echoed from Zion Gate. He whispered hoarsely, "A Lamedvovnik has come among us tonight."

What was he rambling about? Trying to hide her concern, Rachel turned back his bed. "You should sleep. You have not slept in days. Hannah Cohen says you are wearing yourself out."

He faced her, his eyes burning beneath heavy gray brows. "The Lamedvov. The thirty-six righteous ones. Do you understand what I am saying, Rachel?"

"Papa used to speak of it. A famous legend," she said cheerfully. "Now sleep."

"No legend. Lamedvov. Thirty-six righteous souls who live upon the earth in each generation. It is the Lamedvov who hold back God's judgment on the world." He cast a long look out into the night. "Tonight one of them has come among us. I felt his presence."

"Then the Jews of Jerusalem are safe. True?"

The elderly man did not reply. He sighed. Clearly she did not understand. She had missed his point altogether. Wearily he replied, "I am glad you are well. And Moshe. Moshe will send the people back to the shelters?"

"Yes."

"Good. Morning will come too soon for all of us. The children . . . morning."

"You must sleep, Grandfather."

He assented, hobbling to the bed. He lay down with his shoes still on. "I will rest an hour. Morning will come," he said, closing his eyes and falling into a deep slumber.

■ ■ ■ ■

The seventy-four-year-old Mother Superior of Soeurs Réparatrices Convent sat alone in the lightless bedchamber at the Latin Patriarchate.

With Dr. Baruch, Lori Kalner, Rachel Sachar, and the sisters of her order, Mère Supérieure had entered the Old City and taken refuge here in the Christian Quarter.

Replete with dignity, imperious and stern in her demeanor, it was rare for her to show emotion.

Tonight she wept with joy as the sound of singing drifted from the Jewish Quarter. The Arab boy Daoud had returned with news that Rachel and Lori were alive and well. Dr. Baruch was a ministering angel in the Jewish Hospital. The prayers of the sisters on their behalf had been answered.

Mother Superior's doors were open to a pinched balcony overlooking the ancient street.

From her chair she had prayed and listened, unmoving, as the battle raged. She had heard the roar of explosions and the rattle of machine-gun fire. The flares had illuminated her room so much that she could read the text of her Bible. Her finger held the page of the prophecy she found in Jeremiah 30.

> This is what the LORD, says:
> "I will restore the fortunes of
>    Jacob's tents
>    and have compassion on his
>    dwellings;
>    the city will be rebuilt on her ruins,
>    and the palace will stand in its
>    proper place.
>    From them will come songs of thanksgiving
>    and the sound of rejoicing."

■ ■ ■ ■

Something holy and magnificent had happened, and she was witness to it. Wiping her tears she whispered, "You have let me live to see this promise fulfilled, O Lord. Two thousand years have passed while Jews and Christians waited for this hour. Israel reborn and Jerusalem her capital! Christ has died. Christ is risen. Now Christ will come again." She held the sacred text to her as she began to bargain with the Lord. "And now, a simple request. I want to be back home in the convent when You return. I have lived and served a lifetime at Soeurs Réparatrices. This You know, Lord. In the place where we prayed daily for the peace of Jerusalem, men have made war. Where we prayed for healing, men have killed one another in our garden. We were driven from our sanctuary so this promise might come true. But enough is enough. Sweet Jesus, Savior, I wish only to go home. Back to Soeurs Réparatrices."

Mother Superior knew the facts. The convent was a tactical prize in the game of Jerusalem tug-of-war. It had traded hands a half-dozen times in the last few days. The most recent communiqué indicated it was occupied by Jewish forces. It flanked the Hospice of Notre Dame, which had become the bulwark of Jewish resistance. The granite mountain of Notre Dame and the smaller hill of Soeurs Réparatrices were the prizes each side wanted.

To go home? To return to the convent? It was a bleak and unpromising scenario. And yet . . . Mother Superior reasoned that she had a direct line to the same God who parted the Red Sea for Moses and who tonight opened Zion Gate to resupply the Jewish Quarter. With those examples fresh in her thoughts, she spoke aloud, "There are more who are with us than those who are against us."

# CHAPTER 2

North of the Old City's Damascus Gate, at the New City corner of St. George Road and Hanevi Avenue, stood the home of a wealthy merchant named Mandelbaum. The house was now occupied by Jewish defense forces and their commander, Peter Wallich.

Behind Mandelbaum House was the settlement of Hasidic Jews known as *Mea Shearim*. Across the intersection to the east was Arab-held Musrara. It was by machine guns mounted in Musrara that the Mandelbaum house was regularly sprayed with bullets. Elsewhere in the Holy City the battle shifted from street to street, but this one building was truly on the front line of the battle for Jerusalem.

Peter Wallich peered cautiously around the bullet-riddled frame of one of Mandelbaum's shattered second-story windows. His attention was fixed one-half mile to the northeast, on a dark promontory. It was the Arab village known as *Sheikh Jarrah*. "When the next attack comes," he was warned, "that will be the jumping-off point."

Stretching his sinewy six feet of height, Peter rubbed his eyes, as if that action would enable him to see in the pitch-black night. Another Arab mortar shell screamed overhead, and Wallich flinched. The explosion that followed was behind him, among the tenements of Mea Shearim, but it was still close. The fact that the Arab barrage was being used against the first Jewish community below the hill confirmed what Wallich had been told. He and his Gadna Jewish Youth Brigade were directly in the path of the Arab onslaught.

Six months earlier, Wallich had been a teacher of agriculture in Galilee's kibbutz Degania. His curly hair was bleached to a strawberry-blond while his once-freckled face had burned to a leathery brown. He looked much older than his twenty-five years, despite his easy smile and shy manner.

Then had come the United Nations vote to partition Palestine into

Arab and Jewish states and the Arab riot in Jerusalem's commercial district. Suddenly Wallich, former student of Haganah trainer Samuel Orde and former Night Squad commando, found his defense force commission reactivated. His command: teenagers with Molotov cocktails, pipe bombs, and bolt-action Italian rifles of First World War manufacture.

He ran his fingers through his tangled mop of hair in a gesture that had become synonymous with worried thoughts and turned back toward the map spread out on a card table. To the left of his location, Haganah troops held the Jewish suburb of Sanhedria, while an advance force of Irgun were posted nearer Sheikh Jarrah. But to Peter's right there was nothing, nothing but Arabs. "If they get past you," he had been told, "the Legion will be able to drive straight to Zion Square. They will split the New City in two, and Jerusalem will be lost."

■ ■ ■ ■

Naomi Snow, sixteen-year-old member of the Gadna Youth Brigade, sat alongside her sleeping comrades in the basement of Mandelbaum House.

She was French. Small and perpetually thin from the days of malnourishment, she was, nonetheless, pretty in a boyish way. Brown-eyed, bronzed by the sun, her brown hair cropped short, she looked younger than her sixteen years. But she had lived through enough to last a lifetime and then some.

By the yellow light of a candle she sketched a crude map of the city in her diary. Jerusalem was a clock face divided straight down the center.

Twelve o'clock was north of the walled Old City.

Six o'clock was Mount Zion in the south.

Muslims held the eastern half of the city. Jews retained the west. The Jewish Quarter of the Old City was positioned near the center of the circle but within Arab territory.

The Mandelbaum house was in the New City on the Jewish side of twelve o'clock. Only a road separated it from Muslim territory. Arabs, also young and poorly equipped, occupied the house across the street.

*I am here,* Naomi wrote, circling the spot. And then another circle across a penciled line. *Arabs there.*

Occasionally the two opposing groups took potshots at one another, but there had been no all-out attacks.

The nineteen members of the Gadna Youth had been placed here to keep the Arabs from venturing out from the Muslim side of noon.

While more experienced soldiers of the Haganah and Palmach had been busy capturing Arab positions, Naomi and the Gadna Youth had simply plugged a hole and held the line. *Like the little Dutch boy with his finger in the dike,* Naomi thought. It was not a rigorous duty. A shout and a few strategically placed bullets fired from Jewish windows kept Arabs under cover. Naomi doubted if anyone in her Gadna Youth Brigade had actually shot anyone. She certainly had not.

It was enough they were there, explained Peter Wallich, their commander. It made the Jihad Moquades think twice before wandering out.

But tonight momentous things were happening.

Jerusalem, its outer boundaries round, like a wheel, was in motion. In the darkness of the early-morning hours an imperceptible groaning could be sensed more than heard. Uri Tabken, round-faced, scholarly, and serious, had come back with the day's ration of water and a copy of the *Palestine Post.* The Palmach had captured Mount Zion!

Then the night skies over the Old City had been alight with flares and explosions. Word had come only an hour ago that the Palmach had broken in to relieve the Old City through Zion Gate. The Jihad Moquades were on the run!

Naomi wanted to remember the event. Was it a victory? Or simply a prelude to something fierce and terrible? She scribbled notes in the tattered journal.

*All week we watched Arab civilians go.*
*Mothers. Children. Old ones. Where are the men?*
*Carts and automobiles loaded up with household goods.*
*People stacked on top of things.*
*They are leaving. Leaving their houses.*
*Locking doors like they are going on holiday.*
*No sooner gone than Arab mercenaries break in.*
*Take up sniper positions in someone's bedroom window.*
*Plant a mortar where the flowers bloomed in window boxes. Who*
*    planted the flowers?*
*No one plants a garden unless they hope to smell the flowers on a*
*    summer night.*
*I am sorry to see them go. Real people. Are they afraid?*

*Uri says they have been told to leave by their leaders.*
*Get out of the way. Something big is coming.*
*Peter Wallich says they expect to come back.*
*They expect to be in their houses, picking their flowers, one day*
  *soon.*

■ ■ ■ ■

Despite the retreat of the Jihad Moquades, the life of the five-day-old state of Israel hung by a thread.

In the New City of Jerusalem, untrained and badly armed Jewish soldiers guarded the British Ophthalmic Hospital. These troopers, gathered on the hill south of Mount Zion, were unnerved by the silence. After days of sporadic fighting and eight hours of continuous battle, the southern approach to Jerusalem's Old City wall was hushed. "This is *meshugge*," Major Luke Thomas heard one of them say. "An hour with no gunfire, no mortars, no flares . . . nothing!"

"Maybe the Arabs have gone back to their tents?" suggested a second. "Maybe they gave up and went home?"

"And maybe they are out there right now, with knives in their teeth, crawling up this hill," a member of the seasoned Palmach force retorted. "Keep your mouths shut and your eyes open. This isn't over."

Major Thomas reconcentrated his attention on the wireless. "I say again," he repeated, enunciating each word with a clipped precision that matched the trim of his handlebar mustache, "we are in! Zion Gate is ours! When will more reinforcements arrive? Over."

The voice of Haganah Commander David Shaltiel replied, "Hold on . . . conferring . . . minutes, over."

The Palmach leader of the Mount Zion strike force, Commander Nachasch, poked his head into the radio room. "So?" he asked, loading the single syllable with skepticism. "What did he say?"

"He said he was conferring with other commanders, and he'd get back to me."

Nachasch snarled, "I can only spare twenty-two soldiers to guard the route into the Old City . . . *twenty-two!* And that leaves just forty Palmach holding Mount Zion," he said. "Where are my reinforcements? How can I move men and supplies into the Old City and defend against an Arab counterattack at the same time? Does Shaltiel understand how few of us are holding open the route into the Jewish Quarter?"

"Shall I broadcast that information on an open channel? That Haganah headquarters was not prepared?" Thomas paused, and an apologetic note entered his voice. "*We* were not prepared for the Palmach to succeed in the breakthrough."

The historic bad blood between the elite Palmachniks and Haganah rose to the surface, and Nachasch exploded. "So you were merely sacrificing us to no purpose? Blood and glory means Palmach blood and Haganah glory?"

Thomas said sternly, "The Arabs deserting the tower above Zion Gate was unexpected. No one could have foreseen that. Now we have an unbroken line of supply. From here in the New City to Mount Zion to Zion Gate! On into the Old City. Supplies of food and ammunition are moving into the Jewish Quarter. Reinforcements are on the way."

With an emphatic *harrumph*, Nachasch said, "I was not blaming you. You may be British, Thomas, but you have always spoken straight. Now do so with the High Command. Tell Shaltiel to send me fighting men if he expects us to hold!"

■ ■ ■ ■

The Jewish hospital in the Old City of Jerusalem was packed with wounded. Fourteen members of the Haganah lay bleeding in the corridors. A score of citizens, women and children with cuts from shattered glass, huddled together in the waiting room, where they were bandaged by volunteers and sent scurrying to the shelter of the Hurva Synagogue.

Dr. Hiram Baruch made a first pass through the seriously injured.

He noted five among the soldiers who would not survive. Two head wounds, skulls partially shot away, bullets lodged in brains. A seventeen-year-old with exposed intestines shredded from a hand grenade. A middle-aged man struggling to breathe as his lungs filled with blood. A young Yeshiva student shot through the spine. No feeling from the chest down. Hopeless! Hopeless!

There was no time to waste on those who would surely slip away before the sun rose. There was no morphine to spare for the dying. Mercifully these five were beyond the reach of pain. Baruch instructed the nurses to isolate them in a room next to the makeshift morgue while he attended the nine who had a chance at life.

Of these, four required urgent attention if they were to be saved.

The other five, all with serious but not immediately life-threatening wounds, would have to wait.

Pain made sixteen-year-old Daniel Caan a whimpering boy again. Rachel Sachar gripped his hand as he lay on a cot in the corridor of the hospital. He was covered with gray dust from the explosion that had trapped his leg beneath a quarter-ton of stone. His short-cropped hair was spiked in clumps. The pallid monochrome of his complexion and wild eyes gave him the look of a gargoyle that had come to life to writhe in agony.

Lori Kalner cut at the boot that encased Daniel's crushed foot. He cried out in agony and lunged to stop her. She was unmerciful. Stern. Stepping back from her task she glared into Rachel's worried blue eyes. It was clear that the foot was a shattered mass encased within the leather. Though the entire leg had been trapped beneath a stone block, it remained intact. The foot, however, had taken the full weight of the blow. A jagged anklebone protruded from the skin above the blood-soaked boot top. The foot was turned inward at an impossible angle.

Rachel Sachar was physically sickened by the sight. Beads of sweat stood out on her brow. Her complexion was ashen. Dark hair was damp with perspiration. She winced at the sight of the injury and looked away.

Lori scolded the patient. "In London I've seen women and children crushed beneath a house who behaved more bravely than you! Lie still!"

He cursed, then spit at her. "Bloody English butcher!"

She shoved him back hard on the mat. "Don't let the accent fool you. I'm a bloody goy from Berlin. A *shiksa* butcher from Deutschland. Tougher than you. Now lie still and shut up so we can take this off."

"*Das Boot oder der Füss?*" he demanded through clenched teeth and wiped his tear-streaked cheek with the back of his hand.

"Please, Daniel Caan. The boot must come off," Rachel chided gently. "Dr. Baruch cannot tend to your wound if he cannot examine it."

"Then let *him* get the boot off!" Daniel growled.

Lori shrugged and took Rachel aside.

Daniel shouted after her. "Good! Get out of here! Leave me alone!"

Lori ignored his taunts. She held Rachel's gaze. "Look, I'm cutting the leather away but . . . his foot has mostly come off inside the boot. You hear me? There's not much left of it in there. I've seen enough to know. There is a nursery rhyme in England. My little boy used to like it. Humpty Dumpty. About a chap who sits on a wall and falls off. Breaks into a million pieces . . . And all the King's horses and all the King's men can't put Humpty together again . . . You know what I'm saying? There's no putting his foot together again. I know what Doctor Baruch will have to do."

Rachel groped to steady herself against the wall. Pregnancy made her weak. "He is so young . . ."

"War made us grow old too soon . . . Are you going to throw up?"

"I . . . do not think so . . . Yes. Perhaps . . ."

"In the loo, if you please. I need someone strong here. He will fight."

"Morphine?" Rachel queried hopefully.

"He'll need it for the amputation. This is only the preliminary."

Rachel put a hand to her stomach. "Oh."

"Rachel. Go on. Get out of here. Send someone who can help me hold him down."

■ ■ ■ ■

All of Jerusalem was eerily quiet and dark. The Old City civilians had been sent back to the shelters. The shouting had stopped, and Alfie Halder was glad for it. Was everyone asleep behind the barricades? the big man wondered. Were Jewish defenders and the Arab Mufti's Holy Strugglers too tired to shoot each other? Never mind. It was a good time to be delivering supplies to the Old City.

Alfie was not tired in spite of days without sleep. The stars gleamed overhead, and it was cool. It was like a dream he had had when he was a boy confined to the sanitarium in Berlin. He had dreamed of running and running with no tall fences or guards to keep him in. In the dream, his friend, Werner, the boy who could not walk or speak, rode on Alfie's back as they escaped.

Tonight Alfie looked up at the stars and remembered when the orderlies came and took Werner and the other sick boys in the ward to gas them because of Hitler's edict that they were "useless mouths." That night Alfie had climbed the wall and had run away as fast as he could. He had run through the graveyard and had hidden in his mother's tomb beside the church. Like the dream. Except Werner was not with him.

Alfie remembered it all and said aloud as he jogged, "I bet you can see me, Werner. Huh? I am in Jerusalem, see? You are riding on my back, Werner." The thought pleased Alfie. He did not worry so much about the war when he pretended Werner was riding on his back.

Carrying one hundred and twenty pounds of medical supplies pilfered from the Ophthalmic Hospital, Alfie ran through the tombstones, up Jewish-held Mount Zion, then on toward Zion Gate and the Old City.

Approaching Zion Gate, he shouted up to his old friend Jacob Kalner, who, with twenty-two other volunteers, guarded the ramparts and the route into the Jewish Quarter. "Jacob! It's me. Alfie. I got stuff in here for the hospital where Daniel is. You there, Jacob?"

"Alfie. Come on," Jacob called back to him, his words slurred with exhaustion. "Is anyone behind you? Coming? Bringing ammunition?"

"They said they got no more to send."

"Nobody else?"

A second voice cursed. "What're they waiting for? Hospital stuff! How about ammo here? How long do they think we can hold this gate and keep the corridor open with six rounds each? If the Irregulars charge us one more time . . . What are those guys waiting for? They promised reinforcements."

Alfie did not linger to hear Jacob's reply. This was his sixth trip bringing supplies into the besieged Quarter. Mostly food. Not enough. Some ammunition. Not nearly enough. This was his first pack for the hospital. A small amount of morphine. Antiseptic. Important stuff, he was told. Breakable stuff. He must be careful not to fall on the pack or get shot at. Every other trip he had been shot at, but not this time. He was glad no one was shooting at him because the bottles of antiseptic would arrive unbroken. He jogged through the gate, entering the constricted lanes of the Old City.

As Alfie moved through the shadows of Ararat Road beside a gutted tinsmith's shop, a voice called urgently in German, "*Bitte!* You! Stop, will you?"

Alfie obeyed. Peering into the blackness of the ruined building he whispered, "Who's there?"

"You are Palmach?"

"Sure. I got stuff here for the hospital. Nothing broken. Who are you?"

"My name is Dieter Wottrich. I am no soldier, but they made me come here. By gunpoint they made me carry this pack. I stopped to relieve myself here. I fell behind the others. I am lost."

"I know the way. I will show you, *ja?*"

"The way in? Or the way out?"

"In. I got stuff here for the hospital. Nothing broken. I am careful."

There was a stirring in the shadow. "It's you. The *dummkopf!*"

Alfie was used to being called all sorts of things. He did not mind so very much. The bottles of medicine on his back were intact. His mission was to carry them to the hospital. He would see Daniel. The importance of his task overcame the unkind remarks of Dieter Wottrich.

The voice inside the hiding place complained, "Oh God, now You send me the idiot."

"I am not lost," Alfie said.

"But I am. Is that what you are saying?" Wottrich's words were barbed with anger. "Are you calling me a *dummkopf,* then?"

"I am not lost," Alfie repeated. "But I got to hurry. Daniel needs me."

"Get out of here," Wottrich ordered. "Why would I trust an idiot to lead me out of here? Someone with half a brain will pass by. Go on!"

"Sure." Alfie smiled and saluted. "I'll come back for you if you like."

"I'll be gone by then, please God."

"Sure. *Auf wiedersehen.*"

# CHAPTER 3

In the Arab-held sector of the Old City, Ahkmed al-Malik and Hassan el-Hassan welcomed the newcomer to Najid's coffeehouse.

Robert Brandenburg, German-born former SS lieutenant, eyed them with disinterest. His hard blue eyes glinted with disdain from his leathery face.

Serving as a volunteer with the Arab Legion, Brandenburg was commander of fifty mercenaries from Yugoslavia, Germany, and Great Britain. They were, indeed, strange bedfellows. In the case of the English and the Germans, they had fought against one another in the last war. But they were unified by one great passion: a hatred of Jews. This, and the promise of good payment for their services, had brought them together.

Brandenburg served with the Croat Ustase regime during the Second World War. He had himself supervised rounding up Jews, Serbs, and Gypsies, lining them up in front of mass graves and mowing them down. At least such executions—half a million that Brandenburg knew of—were over speedily, of no more consequence than shooting an animal. But these Croats! How they enjoyed killing Jews slowly, performing torture which had, at times, turned Brandenburg's stomach.

Ah, well. The Croats were efficient soldiers who took orders. Now they wore the red-and-white-checked keffiyehs of the Arab Legion. Brandenburg's fifty had been sent ahead of the Arab Legion Infantry to secure and hold positions in the Old City Muslim Quarter against the advance of the Jews.

Brandenburg's soldiers slipped in through St. Stephen's Gate on the east wall of the Old City. It was Brandenburg's intention to recapture Zion Gate from the Jewish Palmach and prevent the Muslim Quarter from toppling entirely to the Zionists. What the Mufti's Jerusalem

Commander, Ahkmed al-Malik, had failed to do with thousands, Brandenburg would accomplish with fifty.

Brandenburg had all this in mind as al-Malik and his assistant, Hassan, faced him.

The Najid coffeehouse was empty except for these three. Brandenburg sipped the Turkish coffee and waited for al-Malik to speak.

"You have seen how strong the Jews are." Al-Malik's opening sentence was an excuse for the cowardice of his men.

Brandenburg did not disguise his expression of disgust. "You will see what fifty well-trained and -disciplined troops can do."

"Precisely! These fellows sent to us by the Mufti in Damascus are untrained! I have told the Grand Mufti, Haj Amin, this very thing. We cannot hope to hold out here with such fellows. They are here only to loot, I told him. But . . ."

Brandenburg's lip curled slightly. "So, you called King Abdullah in Amman. You request the help of the Arab Legion to accomplish what you fail to accomplish."

"That is true. As Allah wills . . ."

"Allah has nothing to do with this. It is clear the matter is now out of your hands and the hands of the Mufti."

"Yes. Yes. *Insh'Allah.* Haj Amin is no longer a factor. I wish to serve King Abdullah of Jordan. To remain at my post here in the Old City and share in the victory of His Highness and the glorious army of Jordan."

Brandenburg replied with a snort of derision, "And for such . . . wisdom . . . what do you want from me?"

"To fight beside you. To share in the favor of the King when the Old City is captured, and the holy places are rescued from the Jews."

"And whom will you command?"

"There are one thousand of my Jihad Moquades who did not run. You have brought ammunition with you. These are truehearted, brave fellows. They have no loyalty to Haj Amin. Haj Amin has been hiding in Syria too long, they say. Give us Abdullah, a King who can conquer the whole of Palestine and save us from this Jewish state."

"And what will be your role in this new Jerusalem, this Jerusalem free from Jews?"

"I wish only to wait on the favor of the King. Let him judge me fairly. I am the one who called his palace in Amman. I am he who begged for his help to save Jerusalem. I remained at my post while the others fled. I am a loyal servant to King Abdullah and will serve you well as the fight progresses."

"And the Mufti? Your master, Haj Amin? He is the sworn enemy of the Kingdom of the Hashemites; of the House of King Abdullah."

Al-Malik raised his hand. "May Allah do with him as Allah wills. What is it to me?"

Brandenburg considered him for a long moment. He had seen this type of fellow often as the Wehrmacht progressed across Europe. Resourceful. Collaborators who could turn on the head of a pin. King Abdullah might have a use for such an insect.

"You held back the Jewish attack at Jaffa Gate," Brandenburg commented.

"I did. And at New Gate. The Jews were very strong."

Brandenburg nodded. "The King will find you a useful ally. Soon the armored column and the infantry of the Arab Legion will be here. Then it is only a matter of time until Jewish Jerusalem collapses. We will have a place for you."

■ ■ ■ ■

Daoud, Arab street urchin of the souks of the Holy City, son of Baruch the Jew, slept slumped forward in a chair with his head upon the sickbed of his younger brother, Gawan.

The sweet songs of the Catholic sisters floated through the corridors of the Latin Patriarchate, where hundreds of Christian and Muslim Arabs had taken refuge.

Four times an hour Sister Marie Claire, one of the virgin exiles of Soeurs Réparatrices, came into the ward to check Gawan's pulse and temperature. Sometimes she laid a hand gently on Daoud's head, and he was filled with a sense of well-being. He did not want to move.

Pleasant thoughts flowed through his brain as he dozed. Gawan would recover. *Insh'Allah!* They would spend their youth safely in the orphanage of the Christian infidels. Allah be praised, they would go to school and learn to read and cipher. One day they would open a stall in the Triple Bazaar for the selling of tobacco and narghiles. Or perhaps they would sell Players cigarettes to English tourists and become wealthy men like Samson the Turk, who was killed last week at Jaffa Gate. Everyone knew how the English loved their cigarettes. The Turk had always charged the English triple the price, and they paid it too. Daoud and Gawan would charge them four times as much and buy a fine house to live in.

All these things were on his mind as he slept and dreamed and listened to the praises of the old nuns.

The Mother Superior of the order glided into the ward at the side of a sister. Daoud recognized Mother by her scent. She smelled clean, like disinfectant, soap, and lavender water. He stirred but kept his eyes closed.

Mother touched Gawan and then stroked Daoud's forehead.

"The child will recover?" Mother whispered.

"Doctor Baruch expressed optimism."

The fabric of Mother's garment rustled as she moved to the foot of the bed. "Give thanks to the Lord for He is good. For His mercy endures forever."

"Amen," Sister Marie Claire said. "Daoud has expressed a desire to remain here, in the boys' school, with Gawan."

"I cannot doubt that it was the Lord's will that we helped Doctor Baruch enter the Old City. This child surely would have died had Baruch not been here." She paused as her voice quaked with emotion. "What men intended for evil God has turned to the salvation of these boys. And with the skill of Baruch no doubt many others in the Jewish Quarter will be saved. We have been soldiers of Christ's kingdom in this matter, Sister Marie Claire."

The sister spoke. "But what of us? How long will we stay here, Mother?"

"I have been praying on the matter. As yet I have received no clear answer. But it is my intention to return to the convent very soon, God willing."

"There are rumors. Some of the Muslim women say King Abdullah is coming to rescue the grave of his father. They say he has tanks."

Yes! The Arab Legion would come! Fully awake behind his closed lids, Daoud thought what a crazy old lady the Mother was to think she could go back to the convent. Al-Malik simmered with hatred for all things Christian. He would happily kill the nuns and be done with the bother of their presence. Then the convent would be fair game. Daoud had seen the place from the walls of New Gate: the convent pocked with shrapnel holes, the blasted windows blocked by sandbags.

He was tempted to tell her as much, but he held his peace. If they knew he was awake, maybe they would make him leave Gawan's bedside.

Mother continued, "We Christians are neutrals and the Archbishop has promised to telephone the Vatican about our situation. When word reaches the Holy Father in Rome, he will make his protest known."

Daoud was not sure who this Holy Father in Rome was.

The King of Italy?

Neither King Abdullah nor the Mufti would be impressed by an Italian. Nobody thought much of Italians. When the Nazis conquered Europe the Italians conquered Ethiopia. Why would anybody want Ethiopia? Mussolini had bragged about his victory against spears and slingshots. The brave men of Islam still talked about what a coward Mussolini was. The sentiment in the souks was that the Italians were idiots.

King Abdullah would scoff at a protest from this Italian Holy Father King.

Phone call from Rome or not, the convent would remain on the front line until the matter of who ruled Jerusalem was finally settled between men of courage. The Jews and the followers of Islam. Not Italians.

If the old Mother took her flock of sisters back to the convent, they would be blown up. It was that simple.

The two women still talked nonsense as they left the room.

Daoud raised his head and inhaled deeply. Gawan slept on, pale and fragile beneath his bandages.

"They saved your life, Gawan," Daoud murmured. "Allah would not be pleased if I let this kindness go unrewarded. Muhammad his Prophet has written it in the Koran. At least I think it is written . . . somewhere I heard it. So now I must repay these crazy old ladies. *Insh'Allah!*"

■ ■ ■ ■

An unmarked Jewish Agency car carried Colonel Michael Stone in the front seat, David Meyer and Bobby Milkin in the rear. The dirt road from the airfield to Tel Aviv was protected by three roadblocks guarded by stern-faced soldiers brandishing Sten guns.

"Just like home, eh? Jewish Mafia," Milkin quipped.

The city of Tel Aviv was blacked out. Towering hotels were silhouetted against a moonlit sky. A broad, four-lane avenue curved to follow the course of the beachfront.

"Miami." Bobby Milkin lit a cigar and tossed the match out the window. "Right, Tin Man?" he asked, addressing David Meyer.

"Yeah," David replied absently. "Sure. Just like Miami. Only we got no luggage. I could use a change of shorts."

The Agency driver, also an American, snorted. "Just like Miami, except for Egyptian bombers and ten thousand Arabs out in the dark. Say, when are you flyboys going to get up in the air around here? Shoot at them for a change?"

David "Tin Man" Meyer, a fighter ace who had won his reputation fighting the Luftwaffe over London during the Blitz and then in North Africa, replied, "Two more transports coming in tomorrow night with Messers. We're going back to Czechoslovakia to pick up another one. Soon as somebody puts them together we'll fly them."

Milkin added through clouds of smoke, "Meantime we're lookin' for a good woman, a bath, and a bed. Been a while, right, Tin Man?"

"Pilots and ground crew are billeted at the Yarden Hotel. Bath included. Find your own girls," said the driver, snorting. "Women aren't in the contract."

"My wife is at the Park Hotel." David snapped his fingers as the posh structure appeared at the curve in the boulevard. "Drop me off."

"Wife? You got a wife?" questioned the driver.

"Yeah. He got tired of bein' told it ain't in the contract, see?" Milkin drawled.

David explained, "Reporter."

"Park Hotel. Expensive. News correspondent's digs, huh?" The driver slowed and pulled to the curb. "So you're sleeping on somebody else's expense account, I hope?"

David leapt from the car as Milkin commented, "They won't be sleepin' tonight."

■ ■ ■ ■

In the kitchen of Misgav Ladakh, Dr. Baruch gathered a dozen of his staff to issue orders. Lori and Rachel were among them.

Lori leaned heavily against the cool plaster of the wall. She closed her eyes and pressed her fingers against her aching temples. She thought of Jacob, standing watch on Zion Gate a few hundred yards from her. There was so much she wanted to say to him. The words they'd exchanged had been so sparse compared to what she had rehearsed.

*I love you. I have never loved anyone but you. What I meant to say when I sent you away in Tel Aviv . . . when I said I was leaving you, going back to London . . . what I meant . . . was just that I want to have a life. An ordinary life. To live someplace where we can make love on Sunday morning and have babies and go for walks in the park . . . where there aren't bombs or hungry children or the fear that maybe this is the last hour we will be alive . . . I didn't mean I didn't love you. Oh, Jacob!*

Would there ever be time enough to say it all?

Lori looked up, sensing Rachel Sachar's sympathetic gaze upon her. *Eyes so full of sadness . . . knowing everything about me somehow without being told.* Rachel's hair was pulled back from her aquiline features. She gave a slight smile, then turned her attention to Baruch. The strain of long days and nights with little sleep showed in her blue eyes. She was, Lori thought, so beautiful and fragile-seeming, yet so unafraid. A woman with such courage would have been handy to have on a medical team in London during the Blitz. How many times had Lori risked her life in those days? Not because she was brave, but simply because she had nothing to lose, nothing to live for. Finding Jacob alive after the war had changed everything. Suddenly Lori *wanted* to live.

And what was the understanding between Rachel and Baruch? He watched after her with the gruff concern of an elder brother. She trusted him implicitly.

"As long as we hold Zion Gate and the corridor open, there is a way of escape," Baruch addressed Rachel as though no one else were in the room. "Here are my suggestions. Take this message to Moshe at the Hurva: beginning in the morning we will evacuate the more seriously wounded as well as noncombatants. Women and children. Rations in the Quarter are nine hundred calories a day. Two hundred calories more than the daily rations at Auschwitz. Signs of malnourishment are extreme. What amounts of food have come in are not enough. Sewers are backed up. Water supplies nearly depleted. The dead are unburied. An outbreak of typhoid is a matter of time. The elderly who will consent must leave the Quarter at first light. There is a better chance they can be cared for outside the Quarter. As for our little hospital? This facility will serve as an emergency-care center only. We can stabilize those with severe injuries and carry them out. Patch up those who aren't able to return to duty."

■ ■ ■ ■

Singing echoed from the basement of the Hurva in spite of the hour. The baritone voice of a soldier on guard in the dome of the sanctuary greeted Rachel as she entered the synagogue.

Her grandfather took her arm to lead her to the stairs. "They do not know if it is night or day any longer," he said. "Too many days underground. And it is safer to sleep in the daylight and go about one's business after dark, *nu?*"

A few candles illuminated the cavernous basement. Four hundred residents were crowded together in family groups—old and young couples and children too young to fight or serve as messengers. A girl with wild brown hair sat on a soup kitchen table and played the concertina. Babies slept or played on mattresses. Mothers and *bubbes* looked on. An elderly man with a cane hobbled around from group to group, offering a liquorless toast to life. They had endured the worst of the siege, months of privation, and they had survived!

Hannah Cohen, helped by her grandson Nathan, was on duty beside her stove, organizing the delivery of foodstuffs. She flashed a grin. With a broad wave she called Grandfather and Rachel to her.

Embracing Rachel she said, "It is wonderful, *nu?* Potatoes! Onions! What can I do with potatoes and onions! Manna from heaven. Again we are spared. By the hand of the Eternal!" Pinching Rachel's cheek she remarked, "And that fellow of yours! Moshe is there. In the pantry, studying maps with Rabbi Vultch and a Palmach fellow. I do not know his name. Tell Moshe he should get some sleep. His wife can make him listen, *nu?* He is going to drop dead if he does not sleep."

She pointed Rachel toward the storage room off the kitchen, then took Grandfather by the arm and began to explain that the children of the Quarter needed sunlight as much as they needed food.

Rachel took Dr. Baruch's message from her waistband. Reluctant to interrupt, she stood outside the unpainted door, which was open enough for her to see Moshe bent over an open map. He had not shaved in days. His uncombed hair fell over his forehead.

"The weakest point is to the north on that plateau," he said, his voice hoarse from exhaustion. "Look: the road from Ramallah passes directly between the Police School and the Hadassah Hospital. The Arab forces hold all that. Everything to the north and east. We hold the west."

"Our men . . . the Irgun . . . hold the Police School. If the Arab Legion comes . . . ," said a British voice.

Moshe was insistent. "They will enter Jerusalem from the north. They will either drive through Sheikh Jarrah, then south through Mea Shearim, or directly toward Damascus Gate, where they will enter the Old City in force."

"How can you be sure of it?"

Moshe straightened himself and sighed loudly. "Captain Alexander, it has always been as I have said. Every army that has invaded Jerusalem has come from that direction. The plateau is high ground. When the Romans laid siege to Jerusalem, the Twelfth Legion took positions on Mount Scopus, where Hadassah Hospital is now. The Tenth Legion held the Mount of Olives."

Rachel fingered Baruch's message. If the Arab Legion was moving on Jerusalem, perhaps it was more urgent that the Old City be evacuated.

"They could come from the west," argued Alexander.

"No. It will be here. It is the only way. The past shines a light on the future of Jerusalem. When Sennacherib besieged Jerusalem in 701 B.C., the Assyrians came down on Jerusalem from the north like the wolf on the fold. Then Titus. The Crusaders. Tancred's attack in 1099 came from here. The Arabs called the place *el-Meidan,* the site for horse racing, because the Turkish calvary held maneuvers here." Moshe slapped the map. "I tell you, the Irgun at the Police School must hold their ground in the north when the Legion arrives! I have had time to think it through. I do not dare put this out over the wireless. You must carry the message out to Luke Thomas and Nachasch."

"Military strategy taught by an archaeologist," said the Englishman, chuckling.

"In Jerusalem the past is the future; everything else is a matter of courage and ammunition. So tell them if the Legion breaks through in the north . . . if they get all the way to Damascus Gate and enter the Arab Quarter of the Old City, we will need a thousand well-armed soldiers here in the Jewish Quarter to hold out against them."

"*Oy!* There aren't a thousand well-armed Jewish soldiers in the whole of Israel," remarked Rabbi Vultch, his dark eyes burning as he glared at the map.

"And Jerusalem is not the only battlefront in Israel," Alexander reminded them. "The Syrians are across the Jordan in Galilee. The Egyptians are attacking Yad Mordechai in the south."

"Then we will need a miracle," Moshe replied.

"There are precedents, *nu?*" the rabbi said with a shrug.

"Let the miracle begin with our fellows holding the northern approach to Jerusalem," Moshe added. "We will tie up as many of the enemy here as we can."

"*Omaine,*" Rabbi Vultch said solemnly.

Captain Alexander scanned the map one last time. "We could use you on the outside, Sachar," he said crisply.

"I am needed here," Moshe explained. "These are my people. If the Legion breaks through . . . I will be needed here."

"As you say. Luke Thomas told me you were a bright fellow. At El Alamein with Field Marshal Montgomery, were you?"

"I was."

"That was a day." Alexander basked in the British victory over Germany's panzer units. "Thrashed Rommel. Turned the war around."

"That it did," Moshe said somberly. "We had tanks and artillery to fight the German Afrika Korps. Now the Arab Legion is equipped with those same British armored cars and artillery pieces. The Arabs have what we had. We Jews are left with . . . courage."

The meeting was at an end. Rachel stepped back into the shadows. The three men shook hands and parted. The Englishman rolled up his chart. He and Rabbi Vultch strode past Rachel without seeing her.

Rachel waited for a long moment before she spoke. "Moshe?"

He peered at her in the shadow as though he could not comprehend she was there. "I have been trying to remember if I merely dreamed that you were here."

"No dream." Rachel moved toward him.

They did not embrace. He inclined his head toward half a hundred faces that suddenly turned to stare at the couple.

She held out the note for him and said, "A message from Doctor Baruch. He . . . asked . . . he wanted me to come here . . . to find you."

He opened the letter, scanned the contents, and said, "Yes. Evacuate. Yes. We have already given the orders."

"Then . . . I should get back. Tell him."

Nathan Cohen said loudly, "What are you waiting for? So kiss her, Moshe!"

Moshe pretended to ignore him. He muttered under his breath. "A good idea. In here." He motioned to the map room, stepped aside for her to pass, then followed her in, closing the door behind himself.

Outside there was laughter and applause.

Rachel searched his eyes, then melted into his embrace. He kissed her and buried his face in her neck. She stroked the back of his head and whispered his name again and again. He pulled her down to sit beside him on the stone floor.

Touching her face in wonder, he said, "There was no time to talk. How did you get here?"

She recounted the story of the bombing of the refugee buses in Tel Aviv, of the nurses who were taken from the Jerusalem-bound convoy to help with the wounded. She told him how she and Lori Kalner had come up on the women's buses through the pass of Bab el Wad to Jerusalem on the first night of statehood and then had entered the Old City with the nuns of Soeurs Réparatrices. Their baby girl, Tikvah, was sheltered in the infant care center in Tel Aviv, and Rachel felt it was her duty to serve at Moshe's side among her people here in the Jewish Quarter.

"In the morning you must leave with the others," he said quietly.

She drew back. "Not while I have breath in my body will I abandon you or Grandfather or Yacov."

"You cannot stay in the Old City, Rachel. If the Arab Legion comes, it is certain we will face a much more dangerous enemy than the men of the Mufti's Jihad Moquades. The Legion is staffed with British officers. They are not fools. With you here I will not be able to concentrate. I will think of nothing but you. Of your safety."

"I will not leave you."

"I will not have it otherwise. There will be bloody battles ahead and . . . I am the commander here and . . . not just as my wife are you bound to honor my request, but . . . I am commander here and I say . . ."

"Do you remember the night we were married? I said, 'Entreat me not to leave thee' . . . we said not even death would part us. Do you remember, love? I have never spoken about the last time I saw my mother . . . my brothers . . . I have had to live with the shame of living . . . and I lived a life of shame because I was afraid to die . . . so I went on living when they died. I could not survive if I was parted from you now."

"The baby?"

"Safe in Tel Aviv. Paula Ben-Gurion told me that if anything happened . . . you know . . . if the Arabs . . . she said that the babies would be airlifted to safety first. I cannot ask for more."

"And the baby you carry . . . our baby . . . Rachel . . ." He was so tired. He laid his head against her shoulder. "Rachel . . . please . . . I cannot . . . too tired to . . . you should listen."

"When you walk out through the gates of the Old City, Moshe . . . only then will I go."

He did not argue. He was asleep.

# CHAPTER 4

Colonel Michael Stone nursed a cup of coffee in David Ben-Gurion's office in Tel Aviv. He showed no sign of weariness despite his long trip from America.

His round face was a pleasant contrast to Ben-Gurion's tense, preoccupied expression.

Stone twisted the West Point class ring on his finger. The Israeli Prime Minister, dressed in a worn-out bathrobe, paced the cluttered room.

"And what about America?" Ben-Gurion's eyes burned. "What does President Truman say? And the Joint Chiefs of Staff?"

"Officially you heard their reply. The whole world heard it. The United States of America is proud to be the first to recognize the State of Israel. And you gave them the reason. A nation based on the principles of liberty, justice, and peace as conceived by the prophets of Israel. Your words. An independent Israeli democracy in the middle of a Muslim stronghold. Israel . . . providing there is an Israel . . . could be the one stable influence in an area that could easily swing toward right-wing religious fanaticism. It makes good political sense. True?"

"So? Unofficially?"

Stone gave a wry smile. "Personally? No one thinks you will survive the week."

Within hours of Israel's declaring independence five days earlier, Tel Aviv had been bombed by Egyptian Spitfires. Egyptian tanks moved inexorably across the rocky soil of the Negev in the south. From the east the armored Legions of Transjordan and Iraq had swarmed over the border. The Syrians and the Lebanese joined together to strike to the north.

The settlements of kibbutz Kfar Etzion, eight miles from Jerusalem, had fallen. Its residents had been butchered. The road from Tel Aviv to

Jerusalem was in Arab hands. The Holy City was cut off, deep in Arab territory. Jews in the walled Old City had been surrounded by Arab Irregulars for months. Jews in the western half of the New City continued to hold back the Arab noose that threatened to strangle them.

These were facts.

Ben-Gurion ran his stubby fingers through his white hair in frustrated acknowledgment of the accuracy of the American assessment. "But will America support us? Help to equip us?"

"They have sent me back as a military advisor." Stone grinned and spread his arms wide as if to ask if his presence was not enough.

"The British have loaned Sir John Glubb to King Abdullah of Jordan. They have also left Abdullah armored cars. Tanks. Artillery. Ammunition."

"And thirty-eight crack British officers to command Abdullah's army," Stone replied. "Private opinion from the Joint Chiefs to the Oval Office is that you don't have a prayer."

Ben-Gurion leaned against his desk. "That is all we do have for the moment. So? You are here to advise."

"I spent several months advising your officers this spring. Unify your forces, I said. Bring the Haganah, the Palmach, and the Irgun together under one command." Stone extended his hand, fingers splayed to illustrate what he was saying: "So far you are like this. Without unity. Palmach hates Haganah. They are both hated by the Irgun." Stone closed his hand to make a fist. "You can't strike the Arabs effectively unless you unify the forces you have . . . and then . . ." He slammed his fist against the desk. "The training manuals I wrote for you before I left in March remain out there on your secretary's desk. Under a heap of . . ."

Ben-Gurion conceded. "Yes. Yes. You are right. Of course." He picked up a dispatch and passed it to Stone. "This news just came through. In Jerusalem Haganah and Palmach are fighting side by side. This morning Palmach troops broke through Zion Gate to relieve the Haganah in the Old City."

"Bring me up to speed," Stone encouraged.

Ben-Gurion recounted the latest transmissions. The attack on Jaffa Gate and New Gate. The capture of Mount Zion. The early-morning breakthrough to the Jewish Quarter.

"Once more into the breach, dear friends . . ." Stone recalled the scene from Shakespeare's *Henry V*.

"Reports say that the Mufti's forces are deserting en masse," Ben-Gurion concluded.

Stone leaned forward, listening intently. "King Abdullah will take the news badly. His father is buried at the Mosque of Omar. I read the intelligence reports. There is a rivalry between King Abdullah of Jordan and the Mufti. Both want to be king in Jerusalem." He reached again for his coffee, sipping the liquid thoughtfully. "The worst threat to the survival of Israel is Abdullah's army . . . the Arab Legion. If Jewish Jerusalem can hold out long enough . . ."

Ben-Gurion said eagerly, "Then we can break through to the city!"

Stone shook his head from side to side. "Jerusalem is indefensible. It is bait floating on a sea full of sharks. If we're lucky the sharks will smell blood and swim to supper."

"No!" Ben-Gurion protested.

"If the defenders of Jerusalem can hold on long enough, then maybe . . . just maybe . . . the rest of Israel can arm itself! Defend itself long enough to survive."

"But Jerusalem!" Ben-Gurion paled. "There is no Israel without Jerusalem! We must break through! Open the pass! Send all our resources to Jerusalem!"

Stone eyed him coldly. "I am here to advise. If you do that, there will be no Israel. Our one hope here is that Abdullah will be sentimental enough to want to visit his daddy's grave at the Mosque in Jerusalem. If he is, the rest of Jewish territory must be reinforced and defended while King Abdullah and the Arab Legion are occupied with capturing Jerusalem."

"You are advising—"

"That you fight the Egyptians in the Negev. Fight the Syrians and Lebanese in Galilee. Let the Arab Legion guard the pass to Jerusalem until the cows come home."

"And let Jewish Jerusalem fight alone?"

"Ever heard of a place in Texas called the Alamo?"

■ ■ ■ ■

Reclining against the stone wall, Rachel cradled Moshe's head in her lap and closed her eyes. The flame of the candle guttered, then flickered out. How long had it been since they had slept together in a bed? She tried to focus her thoughts, tried to pray. Prayers for Tikvah's life were interrupted by thoughts about Moshe's safety, then layered with fears about Grandfather and her little brother, Yacov. Strangely, she could not pray for herself. It was as though her own life were an insignificant thing when weighed against the importance of those she loved.

Moshe stirred and turned his face against the slight bulge where their baby grew inside her. It was unaware of anything but the warmth and shelter of her womb. When the distant rumble of Arab mortar shells quickened Rachel's heartbeat, did the baby notice her fear? She remembered her mother at the Umschlagplatz in Warsaw as they waited for the Nazi trains to take them away.

Mama had said farewell to her baby boy; to tiny Yacov. That day she had placed him in a basket like the mother of Moses had done.

Etta Lubetkin had given him to the Polish woman and had begged her with a look: *Have compassion! Take care of my child!*

To give him to strangers!

To board that train, knowing death waited at the other end of the tracks!

To die, never knowing what became of him!

Would it not have been easier to hold that baby in her arms and walk with him into the gas chamber and wake up together in heaven?

Easier to die together. But Etta Lubetkin had chosen a chance at life for her son, a life without her. Like the mother of Moses, she had trusted God to care for him, to see him safely on his journey here to Jerusalem, to be raised by Grandfather.

A question came to Rachel's mind: *Lord of heaven and earth, could we have survived so much, only to die here?*

As if Moshe heard her thoughts, he spoke. "I will not ask you to leave me again, Rachel. But our enemies are so many and so strong. We are so few. I would protect you from everything if I could . . . if you would let me."

Rachel tenderly stroked Moshe's dark hair. In the coolness of that small room, the image of her father came to her mind. How did he comfort her the day Warsaw fell to the Nazis? What was it he said that eased her fears?

"In Warsaw, when the city was surrounded and being shelled, I was afraid. It was my papa who gave me courage. He said this to me and my brothers." Rachel whispered in Yiddish: " 'Do not forget the prophet Elisha. The story in the sixth chapter of the second book of Kings? Remember him always! Surrounded by his enemies and alone except for his fearful servant, and yet he was unafraid. Do remember always, children, no matter what befalls us . . . Elisha said to his servant, "*Don't be afraid . . . Those who are with us are more than those who are with them.*" And then the Lord opened the eyes of the young man and he saw a sight of immense wonder! The Eternal had arrayed an invisible army of horses and chariots of fire around Elisha, ready to protect the Israelites from the Syrian army! And the enemy army came down the road in overwhelming force toward him, and Elisha prayed, *Strike these people with blindness.*" The Lord answered his prayer. Elisha told his enemies, "*This is not the road and this is not the city.*" And they followed him away in the wrong direction . . . It was a miracle, you see?' "

Moshe reached up to touch her cheek. "If only I could see with the eyes of Elisha."

She gave a laugh. "My brother David said the same thing. And then Papa said, 'Though we cannot always see the Almighty's hand of protection with our eyes, we must look with our hearts, *nu?* That is called faith. Even when the battle we face seems so great that we will be defeated, we must still trust in the Lord.' "

"The battle we face here in Jerusalem *is* great, Rachel. This patch of earth is the last toehold of the Jewish people on the face of the earth. There is no other place we can call home. Six million dead in Europe. Only six hundred thousand of us survive here in Palestine. Unless God sends us an army of angels in flaming chariots. . . ."

She laid a finger across his lips to quell his fears. "Papa also said, as long as one Jew remains alive, God's promise to Abraham is unbroken. And Papa said, as for the rest of us, who may perish before Messiah comes to rule in Jerusalem? For us, the victory we will have against Satan is that we continue to believe God. Have faith. It is a mighty weapon against the powers of darkness! Call on the name of our Messiah. Satan hates it when we trust God in spite of terrible trials. It means that he has lost his battle to destroy our souls. Satan first said when he tempted Eve in the garden, '*Did God really say . . . ?*' He called God a liar. She agreed. She doubted God. This is the first sin. . . . Faith in God is what the true eternal battle is about. Trust that God loves us is the key that will open heaven's gate to us. Remember what Job said? '*Though He slay me, yet shall I trust Him. I know that in the latter day I shall stand upon the earth and see my redeemer.'* "

Moshe kissed her finger and struggled to sit up. "I would have liked to know your papa."

"You will, one day."

"Yes. I believe that." He pressed her hand for several heartbeats. "How long have I slept?"

"A quarter of an hour."

"I feel . . . I have slept a complete night's sleep. I am glad you came, thankful beyond words that you are here with me. What would I do without you? My little rabbi."

"I will go back to the hospital. And . . ." She swallowed hard, trying to say what she had been thinking. "If . . . if we are ever parted in this lifetime . . . I believe, Moshe . . . that we will not be parted forever."

He held her tightly in his arms. "I am not afraid," he said at last. "Though He slay me . . ."

■ ■ ■ ■

The terrace doors of the hotel room were open. The rhythmic rushing of waves was a counterpoint to Ellie's breath against David's shoulder. The ocean breeze was soft, like a silk scarf brushing his skin. Like Ellie's fingers stroking his body.

David lay beneath her, his arms around her.

He had surprised her when he arrived, champagne in hand. A good surprise. The water remained in the bath. The empty bottle of champagne was on the table by the window. They had played all night until at last she fell asleep across him. He dozed and woke again, not sure if he was simply dreaming about her.

No dream, this. He sighed with contentment. Her long auburn hair smelled like flowers in a garden.

Too soon the sun would be up. Through the frame of the doorway, moonlight bloomed over the water and rolled into the room. Ellie's smooth, fair skin reflected the light as if she were part of the ocean and the sky.

It was times like this he wished they were not in Tel Aviv, but in Miami.

Days lying on the beach. Nights lying in her arms.

Someday . . . when this war was over, he was going to get a contract flying cigars from Havana to Florida. Or transporting silver-haired ladies to the Bahamas, maybe. Two days on, three days off. And Ellie could write travel articles.

Someday when this war was over he would bring her back to Tel Aviv, to this hotel. It would be the honeymoon they never had. They would make love for a month straight. Order room service. Never get dressed. Never go out. The thought was delicious. Better than food. He kissed her neck and stroked her back.

She stirred and nuzzled him. "Hmmm. What's up?" she asked in a sleepy voice.

"Guess," he replied.

■ ■ ■ ■

Outside the medieval walls the New City of Jerusalem was subdued. Glimmers of torches bobbed along streets in the Arab sectors of the New City, marking a renewed exodus among the Arab population.

"Yet another wave of them," said Peter Wallich to Naomi as they sat on the roof of Mandelbaum House. "These are on foot."

It was the poor Arabs who were leaving. Finally even the ones who had nowhere to go and not much to take away were going.

"It means something," Peter said, staring at the moving lights.

"Fireflies," Naomi remarked.

"What?"

"They look like fireflies," she repeated. He did not respond and she flushed at the stupidity of her comment. How could she think of fireflies in the garden of her childhood home in France at such a time? But the memory had come to her. The roses in the garden. Tiny, living, fairy-lights weaving and winking among the blossoms. Mama and Papa sipping a glass of wine and talking quietly about things Naomi could not understand. It was not their exact words she remembered, but the urgent humming of their voices. *They cannot hold back the Boche forever . . . and then what? The children. Naomi. Monique. Jacques . . .*

And the fireflies. Beautiful. Dancing. What did it mean?

*They are coming! Run, Naomi! Hide!*

Clearly Peter was troubled by what he saw. Brave Peter. He was never afraid. Nothing seemed to ruffle him. But he stood rooted, wondering what it meant.

His arm brushed against hers. She looked up at him, wishing he felt for her what she felt for him. He did not see anything but the swaying lights of the departing Muslim populace.

At last he said, as if to himself, "They will come from the north. Come to us first. We must be ready."

Who were "they"? she wondered.

# CHAPTER 5

The British generator that powered the pitiful string of electric lights in the Jewish hospital of Misgav Ladakh coughed, sputtered, and died, taking the last modern illumination with it.

A moan rose up from patients and staff alike.

In the surgery Dr. Baruch, examining the still-booted foot of Daniel Caan, called for a kerosene lantern, then said to Lori Kalner, "We will have light here in a moment. Never mind cutting away the leather. I will take it off myself."

To this, Daniel exclaimed bitterly from his darkness, "Bravo! Wise doctor! I told her to leave it! The shrew! She tortured me."

Lori remained silent, understanding the physician's meaning: leave the boot on during the amputation.

"He is shocky," she said, noting that Daniel was trembling uncontrollably. "What about anesthetic?"

"There is no more. Not even morphine," Baruch said as in the corridor a lantern hissed to life, spilling a brownish light over the scene.

"Yes. Yes there is," seventeen-year-old Yehudit Avram interrupted, bringing the lamp and Alfie into the surgery.

The pack of precious supplies in his arms, the big man, filthy and stinking from days without a bath, hung back in the doorway. "Hello, Daniel. Antiseptic and morphine. Other stuff. Nothing broken."

Daniel's teeth chattered. "Only my ankle, eh, Doctor? But he's going to fix that, yes, Doctor?"

Baruch did not reply to the boy's forced cheerfulness. "Did they send anesthetic?"

"I am not sure," Alfie answered.

Baruch dug through the pack, sighed, then glanced at Lori with a look that told her this was going to be rough. His smock covered in blood from four previous surgeries, he eyed Alfie. "I need an orderly. Someone strong. I need the help now. Go wash. Wash all over. There is soap, a bucket of fresh water, a towel, and clean surgical clothes in there. The shower room. *Schnell!* You want to help your friend here, don't you?"

Alfie nodded slowly, his eyes fixed on the mangled thing on the end of Daniel's leg, the protruding bone. He understood and moved to obey Baruch's orders. The doctor meant that Alfie would have to hold Daniel down while they cut off Daniel's foot above the ankle.

"Sulfa powder. Antiseptic. That much at least to help us fight infection. Aspirin. No antibiotics. No anesthetic," Baruch explained in a low voice to Lori. "A few dozen ampoules of morphine. That's it. Morphine will deaden the pain some, but he may still be conscious enough to fight us."

■ ■ ■ ■

"Where are the others?" Moshe demanded, scanning the bulwark of stone that crowned Zion Gate. Bundles of supplies lay against the wall.

Jacob Kalner stood watch alone at the outpost. At his feet rested a partially reassembled machine gun that the Muslim defenders had abandoned in their flight. He explained, "They're asleep." He indicated the six curled-up troopers Moshe had taken for heaps of supplies. "I can't keep them awake." To demonstrate, Jacob nudged a figure with his foot and commanded gruffly, "Wake up!" The exhausted soldier, a woman Palmachnik, moaned but did not stir. "Three days since any of us slept."

A mere handful of Palmachniks remained on their feet, lugging food, ammunition, and medical supplies into the beleaguered Jewish district from the Jewish-held position of Mount Zion outside the Old City.

"The Arabs are sleeping too," Moshe remarked. "But when daylight comes, and they see how few of us there are . . ."

"They will attack. Daylight."

"Let's hope your commanders send us fresh reinforcements by then."

"Besides the twenty-two of us here in the Old City, there are forty holding Mount Zion. We attacked across the Hinnom Valley from the British Ophthalmic Hospital. None of us believed we would take Zion Gate. I heard someone say . . . you know . . . there were four hundred in this unit last week."

"We can take the entire Old City and hold it, too, if they send us men and ammunition."

"The other Palmach were pulled back to guard the eastern flank outside the walls. It was just Kevel and me awake up here, and then somebody called him to tote another load." Shrugging, Jacob concluded, "Here I am: the Jewish army guarding the Gates of Zion."

"This is the first time since the wars of Judah Maccabee that a Jewish army has stormed the walls of Jerusalem and succeeded. *Mazel tov* and Happy Hanukkah," Moshe said wryly.

"Maybe they'll name a holiday after us, huh? Declare a day of rest. We could use it. Well, I'm not going anywhere. My wife is in the Jewish Quarter. Lori Kalner."

"She is working with my wife. Reason enough for both of us to stay awake."

Jacob scanned the darkness. "I couldn't sleep if I wanted to. She said good-bye in Tel Aviv. I thought she was going back to London. Didn't expect to find her here. The two minutes we spoke she said that the one thing worse than loving me is trying to pretend she doesn't love me. So, whatever that means . . . I want to find out what she means. She's in the Jewish Quarter working as a medic. Déjà vu. London in the Blitz. I haven't seen much of her, thanks to one war or another, and I don't intend to be separated from her again."

"Good reason to hold the gate open."

Jacob laughed without humor as he added, "I can always throw stones, eh? They kindly left me extra ammo: three clips and two grenades. The Palmachnik who took Kevel away did say, 'Oh, and Kalner, put that Arab machine gun back together.' "

"There's a chap at the Hurva who knows machine guns. I'll send him out."

"Have him bring food," Jacob suggested as his stomach growled.

Footsteps in the darkness stopped the conversation in midsentence. Jacob checked the bolt on his Sten gun and Moshe slid a rifle off his shoulder and across a groove in the stone to point it toward the sound.

"*Shalom* the gate," a female voice called from near the heap of collapsed cornice that had nearly claimed Daniel Caan's life.

"Yehudit?" Moshe returned. "Have you brought us a bazooka?"

Yehudit Avram replied, "No, just a Sherman tank, coffee, and sandwiches. And I am helping one lost Palmachnik find his way back out of the Quarter." Two people climbed the steps of the tower to join Moshe and Jacob.

Ibrahim Saleh, the Ethiopian porter, greeted Jacob with embarrassment. "I found the Hurva Synagogue with my delivery," he said. "But only when this young woman came to my assistance."

Handing Jacob a steaming mug, Yehudit said brightly, "Of course the coffee grounds have been used five times and the sandwich contains only one thin slice of very old cheese, but you can't complain about the service."

"Have you been to the hospital?" Jacob asked, his mouthful of stale bread making it tough to understand his words. "My wife is there. Lori Kalner."

"*Oy.* She is in the thick of it. I would rather be out here facing Arabs than patching those chaps up." Then Yehudit shared the news with Moshe. "The generator—the one that powers the lights in Misgav Ladakh—it just died. Dov says it is out of petrol, and the hospital has no more. Can the next relay of supply carriers bring some cans of petrol?"

Moshe apologized to Jacob. "I must go back to the tower of Saint Jacques." To Ibrahim he said, "Take the message about the petrol, will you? And tell the commanders what you have seen firsthand. Tell them to send reinforcements, preferably troops who are awake."

Jacob asked, "Just where is this tower in case I need to call for help?"

Outlined by the Judean stars, the spire of the Church of St. Jacques was silhouetted against the rest of the Armenian Quarter. From that vantage point every lane that led to Zion Gate could be protected by Jewish snipers. "There," Moshe said, pointing north. "Just—"

There was a shrill whistling overhead. A flash of light followed. Thunder boomed. The shock wave from the blast brushed Moshe's hair back from his face. Jacob's coffee spilled. Yehudit crouched and covered her head. Sleeping Palmachniks bolted upright and groped for their weapons.

The second of the Arab artillery shells landed farther away to the north. Its flash showed the tower of St. Jacques was demolished.

The soldiers on Zion's rampart hunched below the rim.

A third round fell outside the walls of the Old City, close enough to make shrapnel ricochet off the stones of Zion Gate.

"Too big for mortars!" Moshe said. "Artillery. It means the Arab Legion is shelling our positions." He spared one final glance for the ruined

Church of St. Jacques. There was nothing there, and no one to go back to now. "I have to return to the Jewish Quarter. Yehudit, come with me. Jacob! Ibrahim! The rest of you! Hold the gate as long as you can!"

■ ■ ■ ■

The hallways of the Jewish hospital were illuminated by votive candles, which had been pilfered from deserted sanctuaries in the Armenian and Christian Quarters.

Lori Kalner adjusted the lantern as Dr. Baruch proceeded with the operation on Daniel Caan's leg. Alfie Halder held the young patient down on the stainless-steel operating table.

The still-booted foot was discarded in a tin bucket beside the door. "It is a pity we could not save the ankle," Baruch muttered to himself. "Still, it is a clean job and when this is over . . . a well-fitted prosthetic . . ."

"He is lucky," Lori said. "I thought it would be much worse."

The *whoosh* of the artillery shells sounded over the roof of Misgav Ladakh. An explosion rocked the building. Conversations were silenced. Every eye looked up apprehensively.

"That was close," Lori said.

"Artillery," Daniel Caan slurred from his morphine-induced haze as Alfie pinned him harder against the table. "Run! . . . Run, Suzannah . . . The Legion is . . . they are . . ."

Dr. Baruch returned to his task, filing the sharp bone fragment to a smoothly rounded knob just above the ankle. "The Arab Legion is here," he said without emotion.

Lori remarked, "In London, we used to say if you can hear the shell you needn't worry . . . At least not too much." She managed a smile. "It's the ones you can't hear . . ."

"Hide . . . Suzannah . . . please . . . run . . . I have hurt my . . . foot, and I can't . . . help . . ." Daniel jerked in a spasm as he tried to sit up.

"Hold him," Baruch warned, cutting away damaged flesh, then measuring to wrap muscle and skin from the calf of the leg around the stub as a kind of fleshy pad.

Alfie, tears of pity brimming, averted his gaze. He whispered, "Alfie will carry you, Daniel. Don't worry. I can run fast for the two of us. Nobody is going to catch us, Daniel," he crooned.

Lori wiped sweat from Baruch's brow. Yet another barrage passed overhead. Thankfully, the concussions were much farther away.

"No-o-o-o," Daniel moaned. "Let me . . . die. Me . . . not her . . . not Suzannah . . ."

Baruch said loudly to the patient, "You are not going to die, Daniel. You may feel like it, but you will not."

Daniel said through clenched teeth, "Let me . . . I am a coward . . . Suzannah . . . Mama said . . ." A racking sob interrupted his string of words.

"Almost finished . . . you are no coward, Daniel. You have been a brave fellow." Then the doctor addressed Alfie. "Do you know who he is talking about? Suzannah?"

The big man licked his lips nervously as Daniel gritted his teeth and tried to rise. "His sister, I think. The two of them . . . Daniel ran away from Kfar Etzion. Him and his sister came here from Deutschland . . . left on a train . . ." He did not finish the story. The name of kibbutz Kfar Etzion was explanation enough.

■ ■ ■ ■

More Arab shells screamed overhead. They pounded the Jewish positions on Mount Zion. Orange explosions blossomed in the sky. There were no weapons in all of Jewish-held Jerusalem that could reply to artillery shells launched from the Mount of Olives.

The hammering was preliminary to an attack on Zion Gate. The Arab Legion was coming from both directions at once.

"Get ready!" Jacob warned the others. But which way to aim?

Ibrahim did not have a weapon. "Keep down!" Jacob urged.

"Shall I not go out for the petrol?"

Even in the middle of an artillery barrage, Ibrahim was prepared to follow orders without question. "No!" Jacob said. "Wait!"

By the light of another detonation, Jacob saw Moshe Sachar and Yehudit. They hugged the wall of the street leading into the Jewish Quarter, toward Lori, while Jacob was stuck outside. Not for long, he vowed.

There was a lull in the bombardment. "Now!" he ordered Ibrahim. "Find Nachasch. Tell him we need those reinforcements. We can't hold here five minutes against the Legion."

"At once!" Ibrahim said, saluting, then plunging down the steps.

There was no need for Ibrahim to hunt for Commander Nachasch. The Palmach officer himself dashed down the slope toward the gate.

Nachasch grabbed Ibrahim and shoved him in the direction of Mount Zion. "Get out! Get out!" Nachasch said. "Everybody, back behind the Dormition Abbey."

"Where are the reinforcements?" Jacob called from atop the wall.

"There won't be any!" Nachasch spat. "If you want to die, then stay! Otherwise, get out now!"

The Palmach troops shouldered their weapons and ran.

"We have to warn the Jewish Quarter!" Jacob bellowed. "They won't know we're gone!"

Outside the wall another salvo of artillery shells bracketed the slope beside David's Tomb. The female Palmachnik was tossed into the air like a scrap of cloth.

A line of machine-gun bullets zipped over Jacob's head. Firing came from behind him, from inside the Old City.

The Arab counterattack had begun.

"I said, we have to—" he repeated, only to discover that the road outside the walls was empty.

Jacob was alone on Zion Gate.

■ ■ ■ ■

More Palmachnik pack mules retreated out of the Jewish Quarter. Yelling, Jacob called to them to help hold the gate. "No weapons!" one shouted back.

When another spurt of enemy machine-gun bullets urged their exit, Jacob found himself still alone, covering their escape. He was determined to stay in the Old City, to fight his way back to the Jewish Quarter and Lori.

The first wave of Arab attackers came toward his location along Armenian Patriarchate Road. Jacob saw at once that these fighters were no rabble. They moved with discipline and economy, shooting from behind cover and advancing leapfrog-fashion on both sides of the street.

Firing a burst, Jacob ducked and moved at once to another embrasure. Rifle bullets spattered into the stones where he had just been. Thrusting the muzzle of his Sten gun around a block, Jacob loosed another rasping volley and rolled to another place.

How long would it take them to know that merely a single man opposed them?

"Avram!" he bellowed to a fictitious comrade. "Aim left with the first mortar!" He had no idea what the Arabic was for mortar, but he hoped these enemy soldiers knew enough English to get the idea. From a pouch he hurled a grenade in the direction of the smoking hulk of St. Jacques. The weapon exploded short of the oncoming Legionnaires but momentarily checked their advance.

*Please let them believe it's a mortar,* he silently prayed.

Stifling the impulse to unleash his ammunition in one long, dangerously wasteful salvo, he forced himself to fire three shots at a time.

"Chaim!" he yelled again. "Ready with mortar number two!"

Another grenade sailed over the wall, its flash allowing Jacob to bring down a Muslim trooper caught in the glare.

Then the bolt of Jacob's Sten gun chattered on empty. He had used the last clip.

Scooping up the pouch of grenades, he also grabbed the Arab machine gun. If he survived to make it into the Quarter, it would be useful for the defense.

Running feet pattered toward the tower even as Jacob descended and emerged beside it. Pulling the pin from another explosive, Jacob gritted his teeth as he deliberately released the handle and counted to three before throwing it. On the count of four he was back behind a sheltering column. On the count of five, it detonated.

Screams and anguished outcries followed, but Jacob was already dodging across the open space toward the rubble-strewn corner of the Armenian Preceptor's house.

Bullets dogged his flight, slapping into the wall.

How far was the trench that sheltered the southern approach to the Jewish Quarter? Would he make it, and if so, would its defenders not take him for an Arab and shoot him down even as he reached safety?

Jacob Kalner rounded the corner of Ararat Road beside the ruins of the Armenian Preceptor's house. The belt of machine-gun ammunition hanging from his shoulder swung in a wide arc and scraped into the stones. Sparks jetted in the darkness as a pair of voices called out warnings. One voice, speaking Arabic, yelled from behind him. The other, in Hebrew, called out from up ahead in the blackness.

A moment later, bullets from both directions zinged over Jacob's head.

Leaping the tumbled heap of building blocks, he rolled headfirst into a body. It was the corpse of the bomber who had been killed just before he could harm Lori and the others.

Could that instant of terror have been just a few hours before?

"Don't shoot!" he yelled in English to the Jewish barricade a hundred yards away.

This drew a rifle volley from the Jews and a burst of fire from the Arabs. Ducking his head, Jacob cradled the machine gun and the last two grenades.

He pleaded again, this time in his native German, "*Nicht schiessen!*" hoping that a Yiddish speaker at the trench would recognize the phrase and tell the others to hold their fire.

It worked, but not as he expected. A Jewish defender, blasting away into the night, was heard to yell, "*Nit gloiben!*" Close enough to the German for Jacob to recognize, "Don't believe it! It's a trick!"

Wanting to weep with despair, he closed his hands around one of the remaining grenades.

Arab voices called from the gloom that stretched up Ararat Road. The Muslims were advancing from two directions; Jacob would soon be surrounded.

*I can't rush the barricade,* he thought, *it's suicide. But if I stay here I'll be cut down in the cross fire. Back is into the Arab advance.*

Only the last choice offered any chance of survival. *Besides,* he reflected, *at least Lori won't have to see my dead body carried into her hospital.*

Jacob was startled when the body next to him jerked suddenly and then again.

The bullets that were striking the corpse were that close to hitting him. No time for thought remained.

Thrusting the machine gun through the ammo belts, he held a grenade in each hand and pulled the pins with his teeth, then spat them into the rubble. No turning back now.

Crouching, Jacob readied himself for the rush.

■ ■ ■ ■

Two blocks away, up Ararat Road, a firefight broke out. A homemade petrol bomb detonated. Rifle fire erupted, responded to by return fire.

Panicked Arabic followed: the Jews had sprung a trap. It was the advancing Muslims who were caught.

The Jews had a momentary advantage at best. A volley of shots came from the Arab side. The oncoming enemy was stronger in number than the Jewish defenders.

Jumping to his feet, Jacob raced back toward Zion Gate.

The way was clear. There were no opponents between him and the exit.

Then when he had a mere hundred feet to go, forms moved in shadows beyond the gate, in the direction of the Armenian Library.

Without slackening his pace, Jacob put all his force into throwing the first grenade. It sailed high in the air and exploded just as it hit the ground. A burst of flame displayed a trio of uniformed Arab Legion soldiers. Shrapnel scattered them, and the surprise illumination dazzled them.

Their shots went wild, buzzing over Jacob's head and splatting behind him against the stones of Sultan Suleiman's wall.

With one grenade left, Jacob was nearly at Zion Gate.

Ducking into the opening, he ran headlong into someone blocking his path.

An arm clamped around his neck.

If he dropped the grenade they would both be killed.

"Grenade!" he warned.

A wiry fist closed around Jacob's hand, weapon and all. "Kalner?" said Commander Nachasch. "Let's get out of here."

Taking the explosive device, the Palmach leader shoved Jacob ahead of him up Mount Zion and tossed the bomb back into the courtyard of Zion Gate.

The detonation drove the advancing Legionnaires away. By the time the Arabs cautiously probed forward again, Jacob and Nachasch were far outside the Old City walls and behind the shelter of the Dormition Abbey.

# CHAPTER 6

Inside the Old City walls and just two blocks east of Zion Gate, the defenders of the Jewish Quarter waited in anxious impatience for the coming of day. The Arab shelling had stopped. The last skirmish ended in total darkness and lingering confusion. There had been no further movement between their position and Ararat Road.

Ehud Schiff, sheltering his bearlike frame behind a stone pillar of the Church of the Holy Archangels, hissed to Dov Avram, "Where are those *farblondjet* Palmachniks? Did they get lost between here and Mount Zion?"

"Gently, Ehud," his comrade cautioned. "Don't talk so loud. We don't even know who was doing the shooting and where they are now. When the Palmach can send someone to link up with us, they will."

Turning sideways put more of Ehud's bulk behind the pillar, but left his brushy beard wagging beyond it. He gauged the distance from their advanced position to Zion Gate and back to the sandbag barricade at the bottom of the Street of the Jews. "If they don't still hold the gate . . . ," he began.

"*Tscha!*" Dov responded. "We have a lifeline to the outside, *nu?* That's what everyone in the Quarter celebrated last night, remember?"

As the sun rose over the Mount of Olives, it spilled its rays across the Temple Mount. The Old City was still veiled in night, but stray beams picked out church towers and minarets and the stones on the top of the all-important Zion Gate.

The lightening skies also revealed the column of smoke rising from where the Church of St. Jacques had stood. Ehud flicked a stubby thumb toward the fumes. "If the Arabs want to, they can drop more bombs on us, like they did Benny and the others . . . any time they want to."

Running from doorway to doorway, dodging in and out of shadows, Yacov Lubetkin arrived behind Ehud. "Moshe says the hospital is ready to evacuate the wounded," he said. "I am to find out if the Palmach guarding the corridor are ready for us." With that he took a step out of the portico toward Zion Gate.

Ehud's beefy hand shot out and grabbed him by the collar. The boy was jerked off his feet and yanked bodily backwards. "*Meshugge!* Do not even think about moving farther forward until we know it is safe! Look!"

Yacov's chin was forcibly swung toward the west, and he was held like an extension of Ehud's arm. The light, gradually seeping downward from the turrets, revealed heaps of rubble . . . and bodies. There was not enough illumination to distinguish uniforms, clothing, or features, but Ehud said harshly, "Some of those are ours! But by the Eternal, you will not become one of them yet!"

"Ehud!" Dov called out. "Look at the gate!"

Outlined at the top of the rampart was the head of a man walking guard duty . . . and on his head was a splash of red. "Palmach scarf or Legion keffiyeh?" Ehud wondered aloud. "I do not propose getting shot to find out!"

Then a second sentry joined the first, and then a third. All three wore the unmistakable red-and-white-checked headgear of the Arab Legion. "Go!" Ehud urged Yacov. "Go tell Moshe not to move any wounded! The corridor is closed; we no longer hold the gate!"

As a wide-eyed Yacov slipped away and sprinted back toward the Jewish district, the Arab guards came to life. A shot was fired after the retreating boy, then Ehud and Dov returned the fire, making the Legionnaires duck. From behind the protection of the battlements they blasted away again, but Yacov had already scampered to safety.

Another volley clipped the column next to Ehud's face. White dust and stone chips flew into his beard.

The doorframe screening Dov was also subjected to a hail of bullets. "This is no good," he said. "We have to get back. From that height they can shoot down on anything moving here, and we cannot touch them."

"You go first," Ehud said. "I will at least keep them worried. Go!" Without waiting for Dov to agree, Ehud fired at the first embrasure. Jumping to the other side of the column, he fired at the second opening at the top of the wall.

From shop entry to pillar, from pillar to mound of rubble, Dov's every dash across an opening drew a bullet. When the sandbagged trench was close enough, he made a last sprint and dove behind the barricade.

"*Oy!*" Ehud said to himself. "If I wait maybe they'll forget I'm here?" Another round zipped across the morning, and the acrid smell of burning hair filled Ehud's nostrils. "They have clipped my beard!" He waved toward the Jewish-held position. "Shoot!" he bellowed.

Bullets chasing him, Ehud lumbered toward safety. His Haganah comrades fired over his head toward the Arabs, but it was the lingering shade that frustrated the Legionnaires' aim. His goal was the center of the sandbagged barrier, but at the last moment he angled toward the far corner instead. At that same instant, three Arab bullets splatted like heavy raindrops into the central portion of the rampart.

Ehud dropped, wheezing, into the trench. "Are you hit, my old friend?" Dov asked with concern.

"No, by the Eternal," Ehud said between gasps for breath. "But if they make me run like that again I might as well be!"

■ ■ ■ ■

The slap of his shoes against the cobblestones echoed behind Yacov as he ran, as if his own footsteps pursued him up the deserted alleyway. He felt the terror of one being chased, although he knew Ehud and Dov held the Arab Legionnaires at bay behind him. His heart pounded more from panic than from exertion as he scrambled over the sandbags surrounding Nissan Bek Synagogue. The boy hurled himself into the sanctuary, where a crowd of five hundred civilians waited with their belongings for the signal to escape from the Old City.

The chatter stilled at the sight of him, pale and shaken, in the doorway. He stood panting, his hands extended toward them.

"The Arab Legion!" he cried. "They have recaptured Zion Gate!"

Silence. Disbelief. The crowd looked sullen; not frightened, but skeptical, as if they suspected Yacov of a mean-spirited practical joke.

"How can this be? We were told to assemble in the square. The Arab Irregulars have fled in terror, we were told," asserted the mayor of the Old City, Rabbi Akiva. A group of evacuees swarmed around him. Everyone talked at once.

A woman took Yacov's arm furiously and accused him of lying. He shook himself free and climbed onto a chair. "It was a short miracle, *nu?* You must not go outside! Ehud Schiff sent me to warn you! Do not go into the square! They have snipers on the rooftops."

"But the Palmach holds Zion Gate open for us!" cried an elderly *bubbe,* pulling her trio of small grandchildren into her skirts. "My daughter is due to give birth any day!" She inclined her head to where a pregnant woman sat on a heap of bedding. "We are going out this morning. They promised!"

Portly, pompous Akiva, leader of those who wanted to make peace with the Arabs, asserted his authority. "Thanks to your Haganah and their war, we are being driven from our homes. Is this new story a trick of the Haganah's, or were they lying to us before about the evacuation?"

Yacov shook his head. "All I know is that we saw the Legionnaires up on the gate. Their red keffiyehs . . . plain as anything. They shot at us! At me and Dov and Ehud! They have a clear line of fire up the street into the Old City! We had to pull back!"

"It cannot be," shouted a young woman cradling an infant. "They promised! They said we civilians must go! That we civilians are in the way! This cannot be."

"Whatever they said last night means nothing. The Legion is making the rules. At least for now."

Some wept. Others sank, dejected, onto the floor. Exultation and hope had given way to despair and bitterness in a matter of minutes.

Akiva grasped the lapels of his suit coat and glowered at Yacov. He demanded to know if Yacov was aware of the penalty for bearing a false report. "I know you are lying," he said, "because the soldiers of the Legion are honorable. They would not shoot civilians."

"It is no lie," Yacov said through gritted teeth. "If you do not believe me, walk to Zion Gate yourself."

■ ■ ■ ■

Yacov left the despair of Nissan Bek and made his way toward the dome of the Great Hurva Synagogue. The people gathered there were mostly Polish Jews, members of Yacov's congregation. They came from Warsaw and from Lodz. They spoke the same dialect of Yiddish, and everyone had lost relatives to the Nazi death camps during the war. At the Hurva, Grandfather was a respected rabbi.

"I will find Grandfather," Yacov said to his dog, Shaul, as they jogged along. "He can tell the people about the Arab Legion. They will not question what he says to them."

The dome above the sanctuary was hung with scaffolding, festooned with four Palmach men peering out the high windows. Several black-coated Yeshiva students made their way solemnly here and there on errands for the military men. A minyan of ten rabbis, heads covered with tallisim, stood together to offer morning prayers.

Grandfather was among them. Yacov stood to the side and waited.

From the stairway leading down to the basement, music from a concertina floated up in a sad song. People sang of the children on the trains, leaving their families forever. Then came the refrain about the village left behind on Sabbath eve, *erev Shabbos,* when the candles were lit and there were prayer services in the synagogue.

> *Fleygt di Mama bentshen*
> *Tate fleygt in Beis Hamidrash . . .*
>
> *Mother used to bless the Sabbath candles,*
> *Father used to go to Beth Hamidrash . . .*

The song was a sad one. It brought tears to Yacov's eyes. Though he had been too young, when they were taken, to remember his own parents, the lyrics never failed to make him yearn for what he had never known. With the melody came images of a mother lighting candles at a table spread with a white linen tablecloth and adorned with fresh-baked loaves of challah; of a father walking through the streets to the Beth Hamidrash, the house used for study of the Torah.

Yacov felt certain that with such a tune the members of the congregation were saying farewell to the old Hurva this morning. Perhaps since they were so sad to leave it they would not mind being forced to stay instead.

Grandfather said the final "*Omaine.*" He lowered the tallith from his head and caught sight of Yacov. Parting from the other rabbis, he shuffled to the boy. His expression was grim and almost angry.

"So! Where have you been? I have had the Krepske brothers looking for you all over!"

"I was with Dov and Ehud. Near Zion Gate."

"*Meshuggener!* Did you not know? *Gevalt!* The Arab Legion holds Zion Gate now! You might have been killed!"

"They sent me to tell you that very thing. How did you know?"

Grandfather raised his eyes to the scaffolding. "Those fellows . . . the ones praying up there? They have spotted the red keffiyehs everywhere beyond our perimeter."

"Does Moshe know?"

"Does he know! Yehudit found him and brought him to the radio room. So he gets the bad news from the commanders in the New City. They have to pull back. But they will come again later, thank you . . . and Moshe gives this news to everyone here while they are all deciding if they should eat a slice of bread for breakfast or leave it for the soldiers. They figure that once they are safe in the New City, probably there will be eggs and butter and jam for our bread! The moan that went up! *Gevalt!* So everyone ate the bread. What's the use of sacrifice? No one is leaving the Quarter this morning," the old man continued. "Listen to this!" He gestured with disgust toward the sound of singing. "*Fleygt di Mama bentshen!* The people torture themselves with songs about challah! You would think we were on the way to Treblinka!"

"In Nissan Bek it is worse." Yacov scratched his cheek thoughtfully. "Rabbi Akiva's people are not happy, I can tell you. I thought they would beat me for telling them the news."

The old rabbi stuck out his lower lip. "Akiva will not be happy until he sits down to eat at the table of the commander of the Arab Legion!" He waved a gnarled hand before his nose as though brushing away a fly. "Moshe asked me to carry the news to the hospital. You will go with me."

■ ■ ■ ■

"I want to go home, Alfie," Daniel whispered hoarsely in German. The effects of the morphine lingered. His voice was pleasant and drowsy, but he did not sleep. "To see Mutti."

"*Ja.* Me too." Alfie lit a single votive candle and placed it on a shelf in the small hospital library where Daniel and seven others lay. "I also miss my mother."

"Where are you from, Alfie?"

"Berlin."

"I am from Dresden. It is *sehr schön.* Beautiful, Dresden is. Old buildings, very old. Medieval. Four hundred years old, some of the buildings. There is a famous church there . . . Kreuzkirche on the Old Market Square." He rambled. "My papa owns a shop across the road, where the trolley stops. So many tourists, you see. He sells them post-cards and little . . . little things. *Kitsch*. Cups and saucers with pictures of the church. Spoons. Plates. Religious medals. Pocket knives. Very old church . . . old prayers linger there, he used to say . . . And some uh . . . lace things. Souvenirs. I had a toy trolley that played music. Mozart. I brought it with me to the kibbutz." Something pushed at his memory for an instant. "The kibbutz . . ." He paused and then began again. "Mama works in the shop. Just where the trolley . . . Do you know it? Have you been to Dresden, Alfie?"

Alfie towered over the young man's cot. He shook his head no. He had never been to Dresden.

Dresden was no more.

"Just Berlin."

Berlin was no more.

The Germany that had been home was gone. And those who loved the land were gone as well. The little shop across from the church. The little Jewish shopkeeper and his wife who sold souvenirs of the church on the Old Market Square . . .

Vanished.

"I told Suzannah we would go back home someday. She does not re-member any of it. She was so small when we left. I said . . . I told her . . . someday we will go home. I know right where the shop is. Where the trolley stops beside the cathedral. I will take her hand and jump off the trolley, and we will walk straight through the door. There is a little bell above the door."

"Sure." Alfie placed his hand on Daniel's head. "*Grüss Gott*, Daniel." He blessed him. "Someday we are all going home to see our mamas, *ja?*" He stooped and kissed the young man's forehead, then brushed his fin-gers across Daniel's eyes. "But now you sleep. Doctor Baruch says you got to sleep awhile now."

"It stinks here, Alfie."

"*Ja.*"

"Like a dead cow."

"*Ja.* It stinks real bad. Soon I will carry you out of this place. There is a garden where I will carry you. There are roses. They said everybody who cannot fight is getting out."

"I can . . . fight."

"No. I will carry you out."

Daniel sighed. "Home?"

"Sure," Alfie said quietly.

"Alfie?"

"*Ja?*"

"My foot is cold. Would you cover it up?"

"Sure, Daniel." Alfie stirred the sheet over the bandaged stump. "How is that?"

"Good. Better. *Danke.*"

Then Daniel drifted off to sleep.

# CHAPTER 7

Ramallah, a town eight miles due north of Jerusalem, was the staging location for King Abdullah's Arab Legion. It was in the hill country of Judea, high enough to have pines and cool nights. The adjoining village of El Bireh stood on the site of the Benjamite city of Beeroth, where the Holy Family rested one day's journey out of Jerusalem. It was there they missed twelve-year-old Yeshua when he stayed behind at the gleaming temple.

Outside the immodestly and misleadingly named Grand Hotel, King Abdullah himself walked the dusty lane with his military commander, Sir John Glubb. As if the visit were strictly for pleasure, Jordan's monarch pointed out the sights. "There, you see? That low stone wall in front of the Church of England school? It is from the days of King Herod the Great. And that walled-up cave, just there? It is one of the many rock tombs hewn into this mountainside for the noble families of Jerusalem. I suspect that after sweltering their whole lives in Jerusalem summers they wanted to be buried where sweet breezes blow."

Glubb, ramrod-straight in khaki uniform, Sam Browne belt, and sidearm, surreptitiously wiped away some of the sweat that the breezes of Ramallah had not relieved. "Very interesting, Your Majesty," he said. "Now, about the situation in Jerusalem—"

"Peace, Sir John," the King urged, placing two fingers against his lips. "I have just arrived."

"With respect, Majesty, the question I have will not wait."

"Very well, Sir John," Abdullah said with a sigh. "I was thinking how much I would like to have a palace here when this is part of my kingdom. Instead you remind me of the practical matters that must be addressed first."

"Your Majesty recalls I am afraid of committing our armored cars in the narrow lanes of Jerusalem where they cannot maneuver."

"What is your question, Sir John?"

"Let me withdraw the armor and all but one company of infantry. Let me use the vehicles in open country as they were intended. After we have established ourselves in firm control of the road from Jerusalem to the sea, we can starve the city into submission without taking any casualties."

"And what of the Old City in the meantime?"

Glubb knew that gaining sole possession of the Old City was uppermost in Abdullah's mind. That consideration alone had caused the King to break a promise to his British allies and order the thrust of men and machines into Jerusalem. Cautiously, Glubb suggested, "Does it really matter if Jerusalem falls in two days or two weeks? Ultimately we will possess it."

Stopping beside a trickling spring, Abdullah turned to face Glubb. The short-statured ruler tilted his egg-shaped head back. He examined the officer's eyes before replying. "You know that the tomb of my father is there," he said. "You likewise know that if the Jews should hold the Dome of the Rock—however briefly—I would be branded a traitor throughout the Muslim world if I did nothing to prevent it."

Sensing he was losing the argument, Glubb said rashly, "And if we continue to throw away lives and equipment to conquer Jerusalem and in so doing lose the war? What then?"

The king pointed to the water that came from the rock face. "From here," he said, as if renewing the travelogue, "some drops of water flow west. They flow into the Mediterranean." He touched the thin stream with his finger and showed the moisture to Glubb. "But the rest? It runs to the Jordan, and the Jordan flows to the Dead Sea. Does the water have a choice in its destiny? No . . . and neither do I. *Insh'Allah*, we will possess Jerusalem," he said piously. "And we will have shown the world that it is our highest priority. Use all our force. Use artillery. Use men. Spare no one. It is a matter of honor. Besides," Abdullah added, "the twenty-sixth is the two-year anniversary of my coronation. I must worship in Jerusalem by Wednesday, the twenty-sixth—one week away."

"Majesty," Glubb said, touching his cap brim and lowering his eyes in submission.

"Now," the King said, "since I have made this journey from Amman, come and hear me exhort our troops."

A wooden reviewing stand stood at the edge of Ramallah. A Legion sentry, taller than either King or general, stamped his feet and slapped his rifle to port arms. Men lying in the shade of olive trees jumped up and hastily buttoned their tunics. Their officers prodded them into lines as the King mounted the platform.

He beamed at them with pride. "My dear children," he said.

A howling wind swept up the wadi from the sea. As it reached the summit it clashed with a blast of scorching air from the desert. Together the two gales swirled and spiraled, flooding the air with dust, sending caps spinning, blinding the soldiers and drowning Abdullah's speech.

The ruler of Transjordan gamely continued his address for five minutes, then stopped when his notes blew away. He saluted and waved, but the smile on his face might have been carved in chalk-colored stone.

Abdullah's car roared up to retrieve the King and return him across the Jordan River to Amman.

On the walk back to the Grand Hotel, John Glubb idly noted that the spring had stopped flowing. It was entirely choked with dirt.

■ ■ ■ ■

In the north of Israel the Palmach captured the fort of Nebi Yusha from the Lebanese. Two Jewish settlements in Galilee were evacuated because of the Syrian advance, but a daring Palmach raid across the Jordan destroyed Syrian armored cars and an ammunition dump.

In the center of the fledging nation, the Arab Legion advance that should have cut Israel in two was redirected and concentrated on Jerusalem.

The cannons on the Mount of Olives each lobbed five rounds per gun into the Jewish Quarter. A brief respite followed this salvo before the next twenty rounds hammered the Old City.

When the lull in the firing came, Lori, carrying fresh bandages, took the opportunity to dash from the Hurva toward the hospital. Every living creature had gone to ground except one woman, followed by five small children. Lori spotted them as she rounded the corner of the compound of Nissan Bek Synagogue.

Mrs. Ada Kurtzman, a short round woman with an enormous voice, called to Lori. "Can you help me get my children back to the Hurva? We were caught in the shelling!"

Lori gestured toward Nissan Bek. "Here is a shelter. Closer than the Hurva."

Mrs. Kurtzman, holding the arm of an unruly three-year-old boy, shook her head in disagreement. "We will not be welcome there. It is Akiva's synagogue. I am Sephardi. From Holland. And this . . . *Abe! Abraham! Ab-ra-ham Kurtz-man!*" She rolled her eyes as the child squealed and yanked hard to escape her grasp. "He is a good boy, *nu?* A lot of energy, true? But he is a sweet child. 'Abe the obnoxious,' Rabbi Akiva has called him. The women of Nissan Bek have said things in the souks. So you see, they will not welcome us."

Lori shot an irritated glance at the woman and then the synagogue. "There's a war on. I have to get to the hospital. I've no time to take you back to the Hurva. We've got about three minutes before they start shelling again. Take shelter here until you can move, eh?"

Reluctantly the woman concurred. Lori scooped up the boy and carried him on her hip as she snagged the hand of an older brother and led the way into the towering edifice of Nissan Bek.

■ ■ ■ ■

It was after noon on Wednesday.

The road back to the airstrip was dirty and bumpy. Bobby Milkin's driving consisted of a string of swerves, near-misses with boulders, and rapid-fire expletives. Finally he managed to drop both front and rear axles into potholes at the same time. The vehicle almost became airborne.

"Milkin," David Meyer observed from the passenger seat, "if you drove a plane as badly as you pilot this jeep, I'd wish you were flying for the Arabs."

"Ha!" Milkin retorted. "I bet they would show me some respect. Warriors of the air, and like that. Riskin' our lives on hazardous missions. Here we fly into Israel at night. They put us up in a hotel, promise us a whole two days off, then call us up on a minute's notice. What's the point? I mean, what's the good of such a short stay in a hotel room?"

Despite the sidearm David Meyer wore on his hip, he looked the picture of relaxation. He was slumped in the seat. His hat was raked low over his forehead, and the smile plastered on his boyish features reeked of contentment.

Milkin scrutinized him as David pushed the cap brim up. "Don't answer that," he said.

"What's this hazardous-mission stuff? Everything is going great.

The jaunt to the kibbutz will be a milk run . . . a milk run. We hop into Galilee, drop off a jeep and the gunnery guys with their mortars, and cruise right on back to Zatec for the next load."

"Yeah, yeah," Milkin growled, a trail of cigar smoke streaming aft. "We don't know why they wanted us back here early, don't forget. Besides, last time somebody said milk run to me, it was over Cherbourg. 109s comin' outta the sun, double-A so thick I coulda walked across the Channel. . . ."

"This is different," David returned. "But hey, you said the magic word. By the time we get back we'll swap outta buckets and into a 109. Or I will. Then you get the second one."

"How about we shoot craps for it?"

"With your dice?"

Milkin waved one hand dismissively, then had to jerk the steering wheel to avoid a goat. "What a country," he said. "Draw straws?"

"Nix, buddy. I'm up first on Boss's orders."

The jeep rounded the last curve before the airstrip. There, in a tin building open at both ends to the sweltering breeze, lay the spread-out pieces of the Messerschmitt that had arrived with David and Bobby. Disassembled into even more components than before, it seemed to have disintegrated.

"There's your ride," Milkin commented with a snicker.

"What's up with this? Hey, Zoltan," David said, hailing the Czech engineer with the greatest command of English. "What gives?"

"Ah, Meyer. Everything is jake, yes?"

"No, everything is not jake! How come you took the landing gear apart? And why is that turbo off the manifold? You are supposed to build a plane, not open a spare-parts store."

"Spare-parts store? I cannot tell what is spare—"

"Never mind," David interrupted impatiently. Speaking in evenly spaced, staccato syllables he asked, "What . . . are . . . you . . . doing?"

"Ah! Czech copy of 109 is heavy in nose, yes? And underpowered, so is not—what is word? *Bezpecnost*? Is not safety for takeoffs."

Fuming, David responded, "We know about that! We practiced with these, remember?"

"But I can fix—"

"Don't fix! Put together! When I get back from Zatec I want a real plane to fly, and this is supposed to be it!"

"Okay, Meyer!" Zoltan returned with a smile. "I fix. Right now Mr. Stone wishes to see you."

"Stone, eh? All right, but remember: two days! I'll be back! Come on, Bobby. You go see if they took the compass out of the DC-4 or anything else helpful like that before they send us off with empty fuel tanks. I'll check on what Stone wants. Probably claiming a refund on his fare for that teeny jolt of a landing."

"Milk run," Milkin commented. "You said milk run, remember? Keep that thought in mind." Then to another of the Czech ground crew he asked, "Hey, what is that in the stew pot? Lamb and rice? Mind if I have some? Thanks! A big bowl? Yeah, terrific. See?" he said to David, "everything is going great."

■ ■ ■ ■

David found Michael Stone in another of the tin-roofed sheds. Instead of being surrounded by pieces of Messerschmitt, Stone was encircled with hundred-pound bombs. Each of the stubby-finned, fat-bellied cylinders of explosive was enclosed by a wooden frame that resembled a chicken coop. The American officer was seated on one of them.

Snapping a salute, David said, "Waiting for something to hatch?"

"Meyer," Stone said without preamble. "Do you know the Negev?"

"Negev, as in desert?"

"That's the one."

"Sure. A whole lot of nothing between here and Egypt. Why?"

"I want you to fly there and find this. Stone's finger jabbed downward at a map spread across two of the crated bombs.

Leaning next to Stone, David read the name underlined by the colonel's fingernail. "*Bir Asluj?*" Eyeballing the scale of the chart and the coordinates of the indicated village, he commented, "Twenty miles south of Beersheba and seventy inland from Gaza? Any reason I should?"

"About ten thousand reasons. The Egyptian army is coming north in two columns. One will have to fight its way up the coast, but the other is heading through the Negev. We don't have anything there to stop them."

"So you want me to fly a recon and locate them?"

Stone laughed, but David did not understand what was funny until the American colonel said, "Locate and bomb them!"

Making an exaggerated survey of the premises, David said, "Did I miss something? Did we get a B-17 when I wasn't looking?"

"What's wrong with what we flew in on?"

Now it was David who laughed. "Nothing . . . except it has no bomb racks, no bomb-bay doors, no bombsight—"

"But we do have bombs," Stone argued, patting the one on which he sat. "What say we load a few of these babies and pay the Egyptians a visit?"

"You're serious."

"As death," Stone concluded. "And tonight's flight to Czechoslovakia is postponed . . . so you have plenty of free time."

■ ■ ■ ■

Flying at seven thousand feet, David spotted the Egyptian column from several miles' distance. Even foreshortened by the angle, the row of troop carriers, armored cars, and tanks appeared to stretch clear back to Sinai.

Whistling softly, David remarked to Colonel Stone in the copilot's seat, "I see what you mean. If something doesn't get in the way of this juggernaut it'll be in Jerusalem by the day after tomorrow."

"And that is exactly what must not happen. I'm going back with Milkin to get ready."

"Colonel," David said, "if Egyptian Spitfires are around, I'll be making this baby do fancy footwork, and I won't have time to say please."

"Right," Stone acknowledged. "Get over the target and don't worry about us."

Dropping out of the afternoon sun, David leveled off at three thousand feet. Higher would be safer but would spoil any chance of hitting anything. Lower meant that even rifle fire could hit the DC-4.

The speed was reduced until the transport was dangerously near stalling. Over his shoulder David yelled, "Target . . . thirty seconds."

"Help me with this," Stone said, stooping low and shoving the first of the still-crated bombs toward the open cargo door. Together he and Milkin pushed the explosive device till it was poised on the lip of the hatch.

"Who gets to do the honors?" Milkin shouted over the roar of wind and the drone of the engines.

Eyeing Milkin's burly shoulders and forearms, Stone said, "You! You are hereby appointed bomb-chucker first-class."

"Gee, a promotion!"

Grasping a handful of secured cargo net with one hand and the back of Milkin's belt with the other, Stone instructed, "Pull the pin!"

Milkin did so. Like an oversized grenade, the weapon was now live and set to detonate at any impact to its nose.

"Five . . . four . . . three . . . ," David shouted.

The DC-4 swept over the column. Looking out and down, Milkin saw the Egyptian soldiers squinting into the glare and waving.

"Hello right back," Milkin said, and he muscled the bomb, crate and all, out the opening.

The plane swooped away as the explosion rocked them.

"Another," Stone said. "Make them think we got too many bombs to even worry about aiming."

The second weapon hurtled downward and exploded.

"Let's see how we did!" David yelled. Urging the plane steeply up, he yanked it to starboard, then dove to gain speed and frustrate any machine gunners.

The column was a mass of confusion. The attack destroyed any coordination of vehicles even though neither bomb hit anything but sand.

Dust clouds engulfed the first third of the procession. A trio of armored cars, racing ahead to escape, collided with others that had stopped in the middle of the track. Tanks, diverting off the roadway, crushed hapless jeeps. Riflemen in the column fired wildly into the air, missing the plane.

"Again!" Stone said with satisfaction. "Back to front this time!"

"Roger that!" David acknowledged. Banking sunward, David's turn brought the DC-4 in over the last third of the Egyptian vehicles; a line of fuel trucks. "Oh, man!" David exulted. "Ten seconds!"

"Go! Go!" Stone said, heaving at the third crate.

"Bombs away!"

An immense fireball towered skyward. The exploding fuel truck showered flaming diesel over a hundred yards of road. Egyptian drivers abandoned their lorries and took to their heels.

Bomb number four hung up on the lip of the hatch. Milkin shoved, and the crate refused to budge. He lowered his shoulder and heaved.

The extra force combined with a lurch of the aircraft broke Stone's hold on Milkin's trousers. The bomb shot out the opening. Milkin would have followed except that the colonel seized his knees and dragged him back.

When he recovered his breath, Milkin said, "I don't want to hog all the fun. Maybe you should take a turn?"

The Egyptian column, effectively cut into three parts and in total disarray, no longer looked like an efficient fighting machine. A pillar of smoke rose above the road.

Stone exulted, "It'll take them a whole day to unsnarl. They won't be as cocky after this either." He stood and muscled the remaining crate toward the doorway, then removed the safety pin and tossed it out. "One more time!" he shouted.

Sweeping around to attack from the front again, David twice jinked the plane to avoid streams of tracers coming up. The Egyptians had been caught with their pants down, but they still had anti-aircraft capability.

"Any time," he called out.

A stream of bullets slashed into the post-side wing—from above. A Spitfire, diving on the DC-4, flashed past. A second later his wingman likewise barreled by David's view.

Shoving forward on the control stick David put the transport into a tight right-hand turn. He dove to gain speed. He could hear the jabber of the Egyptian pilots on his radio.

The armed bomb slid away from the hatch. Its wooden crate bumped over the rivets of the cargo bay's floor.

"Grab it!" Milkin yelled. Then, "Keep her steady, Tin Man!"

Stone threw himself between the bomb and the fuselage. His breath exploded as a hundred pounds crashed into his ribs.

When David banked sharply the other way, the bomb skated toward the port side, dragging Michael Stone with it.

The pair of Spits surged past again, machine guns blazing.

In an evasive maneuver David headed for the cover of the nearby hills.

The bomb crate reared up against Stone's resistance, then bounced down with a thump.

The deck was tilted, requiring Milkin and Colonel Stone to push uphill. They managed to shove the last crate out the doorway.

It exploded on top of a sand dune, half a mile from the Egyptian column.

David keyed the microphone and pretended to give orders. "Second element!" he said briskly. "Attack from south while I decoy the fighter escort away. Repeat: attack from south!"

Whether because of his ruse, or because they were low on fuel, the Egyptian fighters did not pursue them. Even so, David stayed wound up tight all the way back to the Tel Aviv airstrip.

"Milkin," he said as they circled for landing, "if I ever say bomb jockeys have it easy, kick me, will you?"

# THURSDAY

*May 20, 1948*

*Return to Jerusalem your city in
compassion, and dwell in its midst
as You promised You would, and
rebuild it soon in our day into an eternal
structure, and quickly establish
David's throne within it. Blessed are You,
Adonai, who rebuilds Jerusalem.*

*The Amidah—The Fourteenth Prayer
"Y'rushalayim"*

*Our God has appeared on earth, and lived among men.*

*Baruch 3:38*

*When the Lord had been baptized, the heavens opened, and the
Spirit came down like a dove to rest on him. The voice of the father thundered: This is my beloved Son, with him I am well
pleased.*

*Matthew 3:16–17*

*"And I heard a great voice out of heaven saying, Behold, the
tabernacle of God is with men, and he will dwell with them,
and they shall be his people . . ."*

*Revelation 21:3*

# CHAPTER 8

It was a dusty journey for the Arab Legion up from the Jordan River Valley. Most of Major Tariq Athani's men kept folds of red-and-white-checked keffiyehs over their faces in order to breathe. Armored cars roared by all night long, forcing the infantry to scurry aside into the thorn brush and stones to avoid being crushed. Victims of puncture wounds and twisted ankles, six of Major Athani's men limped up the road from Jericho and Debir and on toward the Mount of Olives, but he was pleased none of them fell out or lagged behind.

Once the order came to move out, once they were truly committed to the battle of Jerusalem, everyone was in a hurry to see it. Tariq felt the hairs of his neck bristle yet again with anticipation.

The sky was dark and still, but it had been illuminated earlier with flares, exploding mortar rounds, and streaking tracers. On the whole of the march from Jordan a festival of fireworks seemed to welcome the soldiers of the Arab Legion. They came as the defenders of El Kuds, the Holy City, third most sacred site in Islam.

The bald, stony knob up which Athani and his troop struggled was no mountain. At twenty-five hundred feet above sea level, it was the highest hill in the vicinity but its importance lay in the fact that it dominated the eastern skyline of Jerusalem, looming over the Temple Mount and the surrounding countryside.

Seizing the high ground was part of Athani's military training. As the fourth son of a Bedouin sheik, Athani might have been a desert tribesman rather than an officer. Fortunately, Athani's father and grandfather had done good service for the British in the war against the Turks and the English had reciprocated by training him at Sandhurst. Because of his family's hereditary conflict with the royal house of Ibn Saud, Athani went into his military career not with Saudi Arabia, but with Abdullah's Arab Legion.

Stopping to wipe his brow, Athani reviewed what lay ahead. To his left was the Mount of Offense that hung over the Kidron Valley. To the right, north, and yet out of sight was Mount Scopus.

And beneath his feet was the dust of the Mount of Olives.

Both as an educated man and as a good Muslim, Athani knew the religious significance of the hill. It was here that the prophet Jesus of Nazareth had spoken about the end of the world, and it was from here that he was said to have returned to heaven. A good man whose followers had evilly corrupted him into godhood.

Athani started forward again. They were hiking alongside cemeteries. Christian, Jewish, Muslim, segregated according to their humanity but commingled in their mortality.

Sergeant Khatibi, the leader of the advance scouts, approached and saluted. "Sir," he said. "The artillery park is just ahead. I have identified our positions, and the commander of the guns knows we are moving into place."

"Well done, Sergeant," Athani said. "Send the squads to their assigned locations, then send the squad leaders to me. I'll be with the artillery."

The row of hunched forms, a battery of six-inch howitzers, loomed ominously in the darkness. Athani conjured up an image from his desert boyhood: sleeping camels, kneeling in a row.

But these camels carried death on their backs, the ability to rain twenty-five-pound projectiles on the Jews. The barrages of two- and three-inch mortar shells that they had suffered would be nothing compared to the destruction to follow when these were unleashed.

Athani found the commander of the gun battery, an Iraqi, and introduced himself. "But come," the artillery officer offered. "You should see what you are fighting for," and he led Athani forward to the brow of the hill.

Even by starlight the City of David gleamed. The Temple Mount, with the bulbous form of the Dome of the Rock perfectly silhouetted against the blacked-out city, lay spread like a model, a holy replica, seemingly just below his feet.

Athani dropped to his knees and prostrated himself on the earth, kissing the dust of the Mount of Olives. When he rose again he vowed, "We will gather it in, under our protection, and we will never let it go."

In this prophecy he was unconsciously echoing the longing spoken by the prophet Jesus from very nearly the same spot. But he forgot the warning delivered at the same time: *Jerusalem, the city that kills prophets.*

■ ■ ■ ■

It was in the early hours of Thursday morning that Lori and Rachel left the hospital for the Hurva. The floor of the shelter was packed with people lying side by side. The long dining tables of Tipat Chalev provided a sort of bunk arrangement for the more fortunate families. Adults slept on the tabletops, children beneath.

The two women picked their way across the basement and found a space, not big enough to stretch out in, but with a bit of wall to lean against.

The loss of Zion Gate and one more day of captivity had drained hope from those who sheltered beneath the Hurva. Tonight there were no songs. Hunger settled over them like a hand across their mouths, dulling their senses into silence. Even babies, who received only a slight ration of canned milk, cried halfheartedly.

What was said had been said before.

*When would help come again from the outside?*

*Would their rations be enough to last until Zion Gate was recaptured and the supply route was open?*

*How many men could the Jewish army spare?*

*How many bullets?*

*Would the Arab Legion camped on the Mount of Olives turn its cannon on the very visible dome of the building where they sought refuge?*

*Could the structure withstand the impact of even one shell or would everyone here be trapped, crushed, or burned to death?*

*Now that the Legion was here, what would the morning bring?*

These were questions without answers. Such conversations were murmured quietly in corners.

Rachel and Lori sat numbly, their backs against the stones. Lori's legs and neck ached. She realized that she had hardly stopped to sit down in the last twenty-four hours. She glanced at Rachel. Rachel's eyes were already closed.

The smell of too many unwashed humans in too close a space was, nonetheless, ten thousand times better than the smell of death that permeated every bit of mortar at street level.

*Another day passed without burial! How long until sickness took hold among the inhabitants?*

Lori tried to conjure a memory to compare with what these inhabitants of Jerusalem were living through. She remembered the packed Underground stations in London during the Blitz. Whole clans claiming space on the platforms . . . latecomers sleeping on flights of steps. They had been one family in those days. The bombs had fallen. Perfect strangers had comforted one another, turned their eyes heavenward and prayed for mercy, prayed for the defeat of Hitler and the liberation of his prisoners.

How she had come to love the courage and generosity of the English people!

Could they know, back home in London, the truth about what was taking place under the direction of British officers commanding Arab soldiers? Or were the correspondents of *The Times* traveling with Jordan's English commander, Sir John Glubb, reporting his exploits against the Jews as if he were Lawrence of Arabia fighting the Turks in World War I?

Did anyone realize the brutality of the siege against this minuscule community of religious Jews? Could they imagine the hunger of the children? The absolute absence of medical supplies, of basic necessities, like water to wash with? Could they dream of the hope for salvation, the prayers for the Messiah to return and rescue his people?

She thought not. The British civilians who hid from German bombs in 1940, the English soldiers who liberated the concentration camps in 1945 could not know the truth of the plight of the women and children here in the Jewish Quarter. They could not be aware that British cannons pummeled the Holy City from the Mount of Olives. Destruction of God's Chosen People from the place where the Jewish Messiah commanded His Jewish disciples to carry the message of love and hope to the world before He ascended into heaven. If the Londoners she knew could only see, Lori thought, the outcry from Great Britain would be so loud that King Abdullah would hear it in Jordan, and John Glubb would be returned to England and locked in the Tower!

Rachel's rusty voice startled her from her reverie. "They are hungry."

"Yes," Lori agreed.

"An odd thing, is it not? That the world hates us. The image of Jews is fat and full and greedy, *nu?* Look at them. These are so poor and hungry and wretched. The world's picture is so false! We were all poor in Poland. The Germans thought differently. You are from Germany, so you know. Was it that way in England?"

Lori frowned, remembering the Cockney rhyming slang for "Yid" was *Front Wheel Skid.* Someone had used the term about her husband. She had not understood its meaning for a long time. "Most people in England are . . . not . . ."

"Neither were most people in Germany either, I think." Rachel sighed. "But there were enough."

Lori said, "People in power. All it takes is one."

"If good people are silent." Rachel smiled sadly. "My papa used to say that. He used to say . . . truly good people are not quiet in the face of evil, *nu?* It is written in the Talmud: whoever has the opportunity to protest the misdeeds of his household and does not, shares in the misdeeds. Whoever has the opportunity to protest the misdeeds of his city and does not, shares in the misdeeds. And whoever has the opportunity to protest the misdeeds of the world and does not do so, shares in the misdeeds. . . ."

"My father protested in Germany and died for it."

"Then his reward is great in heaven. So many good people died for what was right. My grandfather says there are still thirty-six righteous left in the world. But I wonder sometimes, are all the righteous martyred, do you think? Is there anyone left with a voice who will protest the things that are evil?"

"Perhaps they are afraid to speak out."

"Afraid. Yes. I can understand that. The most eloquent righteousness is not a word at all, but a righteous deed done quietly. Without anyone knowing but God."

Lori thought of Jacob, fighting for a hopeless cause. She thought of her resentment about his commitment to Israel. "Maybe sometimes a person has to think about his family first. Hitler had the law of family guilt. I was guilty for what my father did. You see? Anyone helping a Jew was subject to death. His family was also considered guilty."

"It makes their silence understandable, at least. Perhaps." Rachel considered that fact.

"What the Nazis did to my father made weaker men afraid."

"And will their failure to protect the innocent lead to their own judgment? Papa used to say, better to die for righteousness than to live in acceptance of evil. Christian people . . . Polish Catholics . . . took my baby brother, Yacov, and saved him. I do not know what became of them. But if they could do such a brave thing, why did others not do the same?"

"Yes," Lori concurred. "And now, after everything . . . after I thought it was over . . . here we are crammed into the basement of a synagogue waiting for . . ." She turned her eyes to the vaulted ceiling. "I have been afraid to be underground since . . . since the bombs fell on London."

Rachel embraced her. "Yet here you are."

"There is a wonderful old store in London on Brompton Road. Toward the end of the war, when the Germans were sending the V-1 rockets to bomb London—*doodlebugs* we called them—the waiters at Harrods continued to serve high tea to very brave ladies who chose to stay put. Right now I would rather be in Harrods having tea during a doodlebug attack."

"So would I. But here I am," Rachel said. "Let's go upstairs. I am certain there is no tea, but we can sleep someplace where we are not so . . . protected, *nu?*"

■ ■ ■ ■

The Jerusalem night was still and hot.

Mothers carried young children from the safety of the Hurva basement into the auditorium of the synagogue in search of relief from the oppressive heat. Despite the half-sleep of exhausted misery, Lori was aware of their movements, of murmured words attempting to hush restless little ones.

She could not remember where she was. In the hold of the refugee ship plying the waters of the North Sea in search of the safety of England? Or was she dozing in the tunnels of the London Underground that first summer of 1940 when the German bombs pummeled the city?

Somewhere in the vast hall a baby cried, "I am thirsty, Mama!"

". . . no . . . no water . . . till morning . . ."

Would it ever cool off?

Then Lori heard the voice of her own child calling for her to come. *"Mama! The garden! Read me!" Little Alfie was two years old, but al-*

ready he loved to be read to. They would sit for hours in the shade of the plane tree and turn pages of the dog-eared volumes of Beatrix Potter.

"It's cool in the garden, little Al." She took his tiny hand and led him down the steps from the sitting room into the walled square of sunlit garden behind the Georgian white stucco house near Primrose Hill Park. In this quiet place the aberrations of wartime London were invisible. Anti-aircraft batteries at the top of Primrose Hill and sandbagged slit trenches across the road in Regent's Park seemed as remote from their lives as memories of Brown Shirts marching through Berlin.

Sunlight shone through the limbs and leaves of the tree to dance brightly on the grass in a hundred shades of dappled green. Rosebushes adorned the raised flowerbeds.

Al reached for a pink bloom.

"Be careful of thorns!" Lori warned him. He drew his hand back at her warning.

How well he minds!

Sunlight on his fine blond hair made a halo round his head. He raised his chin skyward and stretched his arms toward the light.

Lori sat with her back against the wide, strong trunk and drew him to her. He laughed and struggled to escape. She wrestled him onto her lap and blew kisses against his belly until he squealed with joy.

"Mama! Mama! Read me! Mama! Read me Benermin Bunny! Read me. . . ."

"Yes. The tale of Benjamin Bunny. . . ."

Lori reached for the book, but found she was holding a slip of paper with the heading CASUALTY LISTS. She strained to read the names but could not make her eyes focus because she was crying.

Little Alfie reached up and touched her face. "Mama. Mama? Don't cry. It be awright in the mornin'. . . ."

"No!" Lori said, remembering why she was crying. "No! It will never be all right again!"

Suddenly Lori was standing alone where the garden had been.

Where was little Alfie? "Where are you?" she tried to call but could not make her voice heard.

The plane tree was a charred stump; a tangle of splintered branches. The white stucco house was gutted, collapsed upon itself in a heap of broken stone and fragments of what her life had been. The garden wall spilled *out onto Prince Albert Road. The spire of St. Mark's church blazed while firefighters tried to save it.*

*"Over here!" Lori cried, but they could not hear her.*

*She could see the anti-aircraft guns crowning Primrose Hill. Trenches marred the once-beautiful expanse of Regent's Park.*

*"Somebody help me!" she called again. "My child is trapped! My mother! My mother! My baby boy is. . . ."*

*A voice, not her own, replied solemnly, "They were trying to hit the canal, you see. The Regent Canal across the road. The first bomb hit Saint Mark's. The second hit your house. The others in the stick—"*

*"But we were in the garden," Lori protested. "I was reading to him, you see. He can't be . . . can't be . . ."*

*Wedged between the jagged stones Lori saw something familiar. The breeze stirred, moving the pages of a half-burned volume of Beatrix Potter.*

*Lori stooped to retrieve it, and it crumbled in her hands.*

*She opened her mouth to scream. But a deafening explosion drowned out her voice.*

"Wake up!"

Who was it? Where was she? Women were shouting. Children were crying.

"Lori! Wake up!" It was Rachel Sachar, shaking her. "We should get below! The Arabs are shelling from the Mount of Olives!"

Lori said, "Jerusalem."

"We should take shelter!"

"No." Lori stood stiffly as the second shell roared overhead. "I will stay aboveground. They'll need us at the hospital."

■ ■ ■ ■

The Church of the Dormition, outside the Old City walls on Mount Zion, was crowded with soldiers inside and out. Exhausted Palmach-niks rested against stone pillars and slept until kicked awake and forced to go on watch.

In the cemetery behind the building, sitting on ground over which he had fought mere hours before, was Jacob Kalner. Commander Nachasch wasted no time in delivering his orders. "You are being reassigned to the Haganah forces on the northern front in the New City."

Despite his fatigue, Jacob shot bolt-upright at the news. "Leave!" he repeated with angry disbelief. "Why? My wife is in the Old City. My best friend is in the Old City. I want to be here when we make the next breakthrough."

Commander Nachasch shook his head. "Shaltiel is not sending any reinforcements. Without them, there won't *be* any counterattack. We can barely hold on here on Mount Zion."

"Yeah?" Jacob demanded. "Well, I can hold on here too! I'm not leaving without my wife!"

Nachasch drew his 1945 U.S. Colt and cocked the hammer, then pointed the pistol at Jacob's head. "I am too tired to argue," he said. "I saved your life, but I have no time to baby a prisoner. So make up your mind."

Major Luke Thomas stepped between the two men. "This is not necessary," he said, pushing Nachasch's gun hand down and smoothly drawing Jacob aside. "Corporal Kalner, I asked for you in particular. After watching you in action at Jaffa Gate and hearing about your exploits here at Zion, I requested you be assigned to me. We have no time, so I'll make this quick. We have received information that the Arab Legion will attack the New City today." Thomas waved his arm at the exploding Arab artillery rounds visible to the north. "Our armored force—such as it is—is desperately needed to stop their assault."

"But my wife—"

"Try to understand," Major Thomas said. "If the Legion drives into the New City, then the Old City is lost anyway. We have to first stop the Arabs outside the walls before we can rescue our people inside."

■ ■ ■ ■

The sun was just rising over Jerusalem.

Naomi Snow and Uri Tabken carried empty tin water pails down the sloping street from Mea Shearim. It was their turn to fetch the water ration for the members of the Gadna Youth holding Mandelbaum House.

The usual procession of Orthodox Jews on their daily quest for a water ration was nowhere to be seen. Only a few stragglers hurried through the streets.

Naomi and Uri were nearly alone on the walled lane. The arrival of Arab artillery on the Mount of Olives had driven everyone into courtyards and cellars. Naomi knew it would be only a matter of time before people's thirst overcame their terror of exploding shells. By high noon there would be long queues for water at Sokolow School, headquarters of Mishmar Ha'am Civil Defense.

Scarcity of water created a battle between hygiene and thirst. The first casualty in the war was the elegant public toilet installed by the English government at number 5 Harav Kook Street off Jaffa Road. In the ladies' room were a number of tile-lined stalls with porcelain toilets. The flushing mechanism was activated by pulling a handle on the end of a chain. This released water in the tank, known as the *Niagara*. Alas, the famous Niagara had gone dry. The useless toilets were like tombstones marking the death of British influence in Jerusalem.

In this one thing Naomi regretted the English departure.

For several weeks the main task of Mishmar Ha'am Civil Defense was feeding and watering one hundred thousand Jews cut off in Jerusalem. The quota of water for each person was a mere one-fourth of a bucket a day.

The entire sixteen members of the Gadna Youth brigade stationed at Mandelbaum House were allotted four buckets a day. Each morning the trip to the collection point was made on foot by two members of the brigade. The precious liquid was then hauled back to be evenly doled out, dipper by dipper.

The closest distribution center for Mandelbaum House and Mea Shearim was at the Sokolow School.

Waiting in line, Naomi gleaned the best, most accurate military intelligence from the gossip of prostitutes who came to the same collection point.

Today the water truck was in place as usual in the courtyard of the Sokolow School. A mere handful of Hasidim from Mea Shearim stood in line for their portion. Naomi and Uri took their places behind a gaggle of bedraggled prostitutes.

Uri, looking as embarrassed as the stern-faced Hasidim, studied the budding leaves of a pepper tree. Naomi inched closer to the women and tuned her ear to the babble of their conversation.

Naomi heard that business was off. What men there were to be had since the English soldiers marched away were halfhearted, scared spitless, and preoccupied with death.

The ladies were taking rations in trade for "the goods."

"So who needs money? If I'm going to die, I want to die clean and well-fed, right?"

"Everybody's going to die if Haganah and Palmach don't kiss and make up!"

"Fat chance! They're more jealous of each other than a wife and a mistress!"

"My date said that the entire Old City could have been taken from the Arabs. If the chaps in the Haganah had bothered to send a few soldiers to help the Palmach over on Mount Zion. You know?"

"It's Commander Shaltiel! His plan to take Jaffa Gate fails, and he can't take it that the Palmach takes Mount Zion and breaks into the Old City."

"All that blood for nothing!"

"And now that the Arab Legion has parked its cannons on the Mount of Olives it's a sure thing King Abdullah will be sending armored cars."

"And infantry."

"My date said . . . he heard . . . that the Legion has already diverted half of its force from attacking a kibbutz in the north to hit Jerusalem. By tomorrow."

"*Where* will they attack?"

"My date said it's a sure thing . . . from the north. First Sheikh Jarrah, then probably through Mea Shearim." She inclined her head meaningfully toward the group of Orthodox residents of Mea Shearim.

"That's the gossip."

"I think it's gospel. He got it from somebody who knows. That's the way Jerusalem is always attacked."

At this, Uri turned his attention from the pepper tree. He paled and mouthed to Naomi, *Mea Shearim! That means us!*

The hooker continued. "The Legion . . . and their British officers, huh? They'll be heading this way. Where? Zion Square? What's your date say?"

"He says if they get past Mandelbaum House it's a clear route into the New City."

Uri blurted, "Your date actually said *Mandelbaum House?* But that's where we are!"

A peroxide blonde with three inches of brown roots caressed Uri's face. "You can always come to my house, sweetie."

He blanched and backed away. The women chortled loudly.

"Naomi"—he gulped—"we've got to get back. Got to tell Peter!"

"It's gossip," Naomi hissed. "The water—"

He shoved his buckets into her arms with a clatter. "Can you manage?"

"No!" she replied angrily.

But Uri bolted, heading back to Mandelbaum House at a jog.

■ ■ ■ ■

A broomstick yoke was threaded through the handles of four full water buckets. Fuming, Naomi shouldered the burden for the long trek uphill to Mandelbaum House.

She emerged from the bustling courtyard of the Sokolow School onto the deserted street. She hesitated, resisting the urge to return to the school, to the companionship of other humans. Lifting her chin, she began to walk deliberately toward Ethiopia Street, the safe way back to Mandelbaum House.

But was it safe?

An eerie silence was punctuated by small-arms fire from the Old City. The blasted remains of *The Palestine Post* newspaper were plainly visible. Naomi was acutely aware that four people had died in that bombing. She stared at what was left of the building and thought about being alive one minute, sipping a cup of coffee, typing a story, then the next minute being blown to pieces.

Behind her were the remains of Ben Yehuda Street. Fifty-four Jewish civilians had died in that bombing. Little children. Mothers. Fathers. Old people. Sleeping, dreaming, but never waking up. Some of them had not yet been dug out from beneath stone and mortar. As the city warmed, the still-undiscovered dead made their presence known.

Naomi shuddered and quickened her pace, careful not to spill the water.

Up the slope she passed the bakery where the Haganah had hidden weapons in the dough as British soldiers searched the building. It was here that students and staff waiting for transportation to Hebrew University and Hadassah Hospital had gathered for coffee and pastry one month ago. Minutes after boarding the buses they were ambushed by Arab Jihad Moquades. More than seventy doctors, nurses, and students were massacred while the British soldiers in armored cars simply looked on.

This morning the bakery was shuttered. A sign in Hebrew, German, and English read: CLOSED. PRAY FOR FLOUR AND SUGAR! PRAY FOR PEACE!

Where was everyone? It was as though Naomi had been left alone in Jerusalem.

*Left alone! No one else alive! Where is Mother? There! Her finger cut off! They cut off her finger to take her wedding ring!*

Naomi gasped and looked up at the cloudless sky as she had that morning in the farm fields of France. Remembered terrors replayed in her mind. She cursed Uri Tabken for leaving her to manage the buckets and navigate the ghostly streets by herself. She tried to imagine what she would do to him when she got back to Mandelbaum House.

She muttered, "You will wish . . . wish . . . you will . . . that the Arabs got you when I am finished." She pictured grabbing him by his thick, curly mop of hair and shaking him until his glasses fell off.

Fury somehow helped to calm her fears. She hurried on, aware that she was walking too fast. Water sloshed in the pails, spilling on the cobbled street.

Surely Peter would not be angry with her if a little water was lost along the way. It was Uri who was to blame. Wait until she got her hands on him!

■ ■ ■ ■

Tears of rage streamed down Naomi's cheeks as she banged through the back door of Mandelbaum House into the kitchen. Three inches of precious water had been spilled from each pail in her struggle to carry them back.

Uri Tabken, flustered, shamefaced, sat at the table across from Peter Wallich. They looked up in surprise as she entered.

"*Farshtinkener! Putz! Momzer!*" she cursed at Uri as Peter jumped to his feet and helped Naomi carry the ration to the counter.

With a sidelong glance Uri bolted from the kitchen.

A string of French expletives followed his flight.

Naomi was sobbing. "It's spilled! I couldn't carry it! I've spilled the water! Everyone's gone!" she cried. "Peter! There's no one left between Zion Square and us! Everyone is gone! Jerusalem is empty! We are the only ones left!" Every step between Sokolow School and here had increased her terror.

Peter took her by the shoulders. "You did well, Naomi," he soothed. "There's enough for us. You brought it yourself. You did well."

"Uri left me! I tried not to spill it, Peter."

His expression stern, Peter said, "Uri is on latrine duty." This punishment meant carrying the chamber pots out to the garden to be dumped and contents buried. "He will use his water ration to wash the pissoirs."

This news soothed her. "Good," she spat. "Then I will not have to kill him."

"No." Peter almost smiled at her comment. But what was that in his eyes? Sadness? Resignation maybe? Maybe the Arab Legion would kill Uri. Maybe they would kill all the Gadna Youth in Mandelbaum House.

She wiped her tears with the back of her hand. "I was crying because I am angry," she blurted.

"I am angry too," Peter said. Then he repeated, "Uri panicked. He brought nothing with him I didn't already know."

"What about the things the prostitutes said? What about it? Is the Arab Legion coming?"

"Arab Legion Infantry is in the Old City. The Mufti's men are flocking back into the Arab Quarter through Saint Stephen's Gate."

"Armored cars?"

"Yes. They will come."

Her brow furrowed. "Here? Mandelbaum House?"

"Most likely."

"But where is everyone? Our people? The Haganah? I didn't see a soul on the way back."

"Hiding. And waiting. Like us. The Legion will begin shelling again soon. Wear us down. It's the way it's done."

"The whores at Sokolow School said . . . they said that the Jerusalem Command did not help the Palmach soldiers hold the Old City. Will anyone send soldiers to help us, Peter? Real soldiers, I mean? And machine guns and . . . and the rest?"

"I have radioed Shaltiel at High Command. They know we need reinforcements if we are to hold." He put a firm hand on her shoulder. "Look. With fighters like you in my command, I know we will do what we have to do."

Naomi blushed. Suddenly it was not so terrible that Uri had left her to complete the task alone. She had won Peter's approval. "What should we do?"

"The boys are breaking up furniture to use in the stove. No more kerosene for cooking. Right? The girls are in the basement mixing Molotov cocktails. Go on. Help them. We'll have a surprise for King Abdullah if he rides into Jerusalem on our street, yes?"

As if in reply, the boom of Legion artillery resounded from the Mount of Olives.

The two raised their heads in unison as the distant *crrr-ump!* echoed against the hills.

Naomi paled. Had the attack come so soon? "We aren't ready," she cried.

Peter stood as a second and third boom were followed by a fourth. "Not us," he said. "Not Mea Shearim. They're hitting the Old City again! It's the Jewish Quarter! They're blasting the Old City!"

■ ■ ■ ■

In the south of Israel the battle for Yad Mordechai continued. An Egyptian artillery barrage was followed by four armored car attacks, all of which were repulsed. The cost to the Jewish defenders was eighteen dead and twenty wounded.

Near the Sea of Galilee, the Syrian army battered a pair of Jewish settlements named Degania A and Degania B. A handful of Haganah defenders turned back the assaults.

Five Arab nations, capable of bringing overwhelming force to bear against Israel, were incapable of coordinating their offensives. Looking to Jordan's Arab Legion for leadership, they found King Abdullah's forces committed to a single spot on the map—Jerusalem.

In Jerusalem the resounding thud of artillery shells drowned out the songs of the Sisters of Soeurs Réparatrices in the chapel of the Latin Patriarchate.

Mother Superior rose from her knees, crossed herself, and said to Sister Marie Claire, "Enough is quite enough. These English guns! They are killing people and placing the Holy Shrines in jeopardy. We shall make an end to this!"

"But Mother," the nun protested. "We have prayed for peace. What can we do to stop cannons?"

Mother gazed at the crucifix. "Sometimes it is not enough to pray."

"Then what?"

"If God had a telephone, He would ring the Pope. He would ring the small little American President, Harry Truman! Then perhaps he would ring the English Prime Minister whose guns these are and whose British officers command them."

"But God does not have a telephone, Mère!"

"But!" The old woman raised her finger in warning. "Our archbishop has! And I shall insist he use it this instant!"

■ ■ ■ ■

Lori was on duty at Misgav Ladakh when the shelling of the Old City stopped. The sound of crumbling masonry continued like waves breaking against a rocky shoreline. Then silence, intense and somehow terrifying.

Crouched in the central corridor of the building, away from the windows, Lori raised her head. The score of patients and the twelve volunteer staff members who had taken shelter there scanned the ceiling as if waiting for it to fall.

Moments passed. Lori and Dr. Baruch looked at one another, expecting thunder to boom again. Nothing. Was it over, then? Had the Legion artillery gunners paused to rest awhile?

"Everyone all right?" Baruch asked.

"Don't forget to breathe," Lori instructed.

Thirty-two deep sighs replied. Nervous laughter followed. They had survived.

Baruch issued orders to the staff. There would be wounded to tend. Suddenly the hallway was a flurry of activity.

"Lori!" he barked. "Take Alfie with you. Round up a crew of stretcher-bearers. See what damage has been done."

The scent of smoke seeped into the hospital. Lori knew well what that meant. Had the synagogues been hit? What about all the civilians who had taken shelter in the cellar of the Hurva?

Alfie at her heels, she ran from the hospital.

Beyond the confines of Misgav Ladakh Hospital the domes of the Hurva and Nissan Bek remained intact. Everywhere Lori looked, however, the quarter bloomed with crimson flames and dense fumes.

The domed roofs of little houses collapsed. Walls toppled outward, blocking streets.

Alfie clenched his fists and screwed up his face. "See what they done," he muttered. "See, Lori. Look what they done."

Cries for help resounded in the alleyways. Bewildered, frightened, Yacov and the Krepske brothers stumbled toward Lori and Alfie.

"The Kurtzman house is hit!"

Lori remembered Mrs. Kurtzman. Small woman, loud voice. Five children clinging to her skirts.

Yacov shouted, "It's Mrs. Kurtzman! The children! They are trapped!"

From behind her a man's voice called. Two Palmach soldiers were down. Caught in the open, they lay wounded and stunned.

To the right, down the slope of Misgav Ladakh Street, came a woman's wail, *"Somebody help me! They've killed him! Killed him!"*

Alfie spun round at each new plea. "Which way, Lori?" Tears streamed down his cheeks. "Which one?"

Yacov Lubetkin shrilled, "Please! It's the Kurtzman house. I hear the little boy beneath! The little boy is crying!"

*London. Primrose Hill. The crump of heavy bombs. What was it the fireman was saying? "They were aiming for Regent's Canal, you see. Off just a bit. Missed the canal, you see. Hit the church of Saint Mark. Then your house and . . . your little boy? Your mother . . ."*

Alfie followed Lori as she scrambled over a pile of debris to Yacov.

"You heard someone?" she demanded.

Yacov Lubetkin was trembling. "I think it's Abe. The smallest one. They were turned away from Nissan Bek and returned home." He raised his arm to point toward a mass of stone and plaster that had been a house. Flames licked skyward. "There."

■ ■ ■ ■

*Fire!*

The faint whimpering of a child seeped out with the smoke from between the tumbled stones.

*"Mama!"*

Was anyone else alive in there? If the fire did not roast them, the fumes would suffocate them.

"*Mama!*"

Lori commanded that sand be brought from the barricades to quench the flames.

"*Mama! Wake up!*"

Carrying sandbags on his back, Alfie brought a troop of rescuers with him. Help came from twenty directions in the Jewish Quarter. Hasidim and Palmach, newcomers who did not know Mrs. Kurtzman, smothered the fires, then clawed at granite blocks.

Alfie pointed to an enormous stone. "He is scared, Lori. I heard him behind that. Meowing like a kitten."

"*Mama! It's dark!*"

"Do you recognize the voice?" Lori asked Yacov.

"There is Lucia, Sadie, Isabelle, Allenby, and Abraham. This is Abraham, I think. But no one calls him that. Too small for such an important name. Missus Kurtzman calls him Abe. The youngest. Also the loudest, like her."

"How old?"

"Three almost. He is the mean one."

Lori nodded, remembering Abe Kurtzman clearly. Large brown eyes. Towheaded. Husky with square hands. Clutching a square of worn-out blue blanket and laughing over his shoulder, he had fled from the wrath of his mother to hide beneath a table at Nissan Bek when Lori led them to shelter.

Abe the Obnoxious, the women at Nissan Bek dubbed him. A boy in need of frequent spanking and a father.

"Abe?" Lori crooned. "Are you there?"

Silence from below. Ominous.

A few feet away, workers uncovered the first of the Kurtzman children. A girl. Ten years old. Staring skyward. Smiling gently at nothing. She was dead.

Yacov Lubetkin, stricken at the sight of her limp body, cried out, "Lucia!" Covering his face with his hands, he fled the scene.

■ ■ ■ ■

Stunned by the day of shelling, those who gathered in the basement shelter of the Hurva were unnaturally subdued. In somber tones they talked about the situation. Two hundred rounds had been fired into the Jewish Quarter, yet the synagogues where the people sheltered remained standing. It was a sort of miracle perhaps. Or maybe the Arab High Command was conscious of what the world would say if English artillery officers in the employment of the King of Jordan destroyed places sacred to the Jewish faith, not to mention the killing of civilians. The congregation of the Hurva was deafened, not dead. Perhaps there was reason to hope.

Rachel and Grandfather ladled Hannah Cohen's soup into tin cans and cups for the children of Tipat Chalev. Then Yacov, weeping, brought word about the Kurtzman house and the discovery of Lucia's body.

Grandfather closed his eyes and bowed his head as grief swept over the assembly. "So. Mourning has come to us," the old man said hoarsely.

Suddenly Rachel understood what he had been talking about when she had gone to his room after the liberation. *Mourning will come!* She had thought he meant dawn would arrive, bringing good news. Instead, he had been speaking of the dark night of the soul. *Mourning!* Of loss and grief. Of children killed, familiar voices stilled, and innocent faces gone forever.

Hannah Cohen covered her face with her hands, as though trying to block the image of the Kurtzman youngsters.

Just then three teenage Hasidim burst through the door at the top of the stairs. Rachel recognized them as students of her grandfather's. Heedless of the stunned expressions on the faces of the crowd, one shouted from the landing, "Reb Lebowitz! Nathan Cohen is wounded! We have taken him to Misgav Ladakh. He calls for you!"

Hannah Cohen, Nathan's grandmother, gasped and sank to one knee. "But Nathan is no soldier! He does not carry a gun! True? How could it be? How?"

Rachel rushed to steady her, to help her to a chair.

*Mourning!*

Grandfather placed a hand on the woman's shoulder. "Stay here, Hannah," he said. "I will see to him, *nu?*"

■ ■ ■ ■

Misgav Ladakh overflowed with those who were wounded by the shelling.

Dr. Baruch spoke softly to Rabbi Lebowitz outside the curtained cubicle where Nathan Cohen lay. "An hour at most. A bullet in the spine. He is fully conscious, yet feels no pain."

"A mercy."

"The sole mercy for us here, Rabbi, is that the shelling has stopped. I do not let myself grieve for the dead. The Kurtzmans? There is no time. But for the living . . . We need an hour's peace to bury our dead, or they will kill the living."

"If the devil himself has given us this moment I will thank him for it."

"If we could evacuate the wounded and the civilians. We have used the last of the morphine. I have only aspirin to give those in agony. You are of more use here than I." He held back the curtain for the old man to enter.

The color had drained from Nathan's face. The youth lay on a blood-soaked cot. His eyes moved when his teacher, Reb Lebowitz, came to his side.

As the only surviving son of a rabbi in Warsaw who had perished in the war, Nathan had always meant a great deal to the old man. So now Rabbi Lebowitz took his limp hand. "Nathan Cohen, what are you do-ing here?"

"Reb Lebowitz," the young man gasped. "Bubbe will be angry at me. She will say I did not keep my word."

"What word?"

"I went to help at the Kurtzman house. To find . . . children. I promised her I would not get hurt. Then Arabs attacked the barricade and . . . I went . . . to help. A skirmish . . ."

"I will tell her you are not at fault."

"Papa will not be pleased to see me so soon."

"No."

The wide-set brown eyes pleaded with the rabbi. "I killed no one."

"Then your father will not be displeased, Nathan. You are a good son of a *kohen*. A fine Jew. Your father, blessed be his memory, is proud of you."

"Yes . . . see . . . I do not have blood on my hands."

Nathan was soaked with his own blood, hair matted, clothing satu-rated. His unfeeling fingers were caked with congealing blood.

"What is this?" Nathan glanced wildly at his hand, locked in the grasp of the rabbi. "Whose blood?"

"Yours, Nathan. Not that of another."

He blinked at the ceiling, relieved. "I feel nothing."

"Blessed be He."

"I saw the one who shot me. I was on the barricade beside Ehud and Dov. A sandbag—"

"Yes. Yes. Save your strength."

"Slipping . . . someone pushing . . . they were coming . . . shrieking . . . I rose up. On the other side it was my friend . . . Muhammad. The greengrocer's son from the souk. . . ."

"Muhammad Tankiz?"

"We . . . were startled. I think I shouted his name. He was afraid . . . he . . . shot me . . . Then Dov shot off his face. It . . . his face . . . vanished as I fell. But he has killed me."

"You must forgive him. *Nu?*"

"*Omaine.* I do. With all my heart." Tears trickled from the corners of his eyes. "I did not kill my friend, Reb Lebowitz. Not . . . kill . . . anyone . . . Help me say kaddish. Help . . . one last time."

The rabbi nodded, touched Nathan's fingertips to his lips, and began. "Magnified and sanctified be His great name in the world which He created according to His will."

"*Omaine.*" The voice was a mere vapor.

"May He establish His kingdom during your life and during your days, and during the life of all the house of Israel, speedily and in the near future and say—"

"*Omaine.* Rebbe? Is this . . . is it . . . the beginning? His kingdom?"

"You have lived to see the beginning. The Messiah will come now. This is the beginning of the ancient promise to Israel. The Messiah will come."

Nathan smiled faintly. "*Omaine,*" he repeated softly.

He was slipping away. The aged rabbi bent close to his ear and continued the prayer. "And when He comes to Jerusalem we will say, Blessed, praised and glorified, exalted, extolled and honored, adored, lauded, be the name of the Holy One. Blessed be He who is beyond all blessings and hymns, praises and songs that are uttered in the world; and say . . ."

"*Omaine* . . . I am . . . going to . . . see Messiah . . . ?"

"Yes, Nathan . . . my boy . . . I do not doubt it . . . And your papa too . . . and mama . . . and your sisters and . . . all . . . of the House of Israel who waited for deliverance. . . . May there be abundant peace from heaven, and life for us and for all Israel and say . . ."

This time there was no *Omaine*. A long sigh escaped from the parted lips of Nathan Cohen, followed by a rattle from deep within his throat. His eyes fixed upon some distant place and glazed over.

Rabbi Lebowitz bowed his head briefly, then continued haltingly, "Ah. Dear boy . . . Then, *Omaine*. May He who maketh peace in the heavens, make peace for us and for all Israel; and say . . . *Omaine*."

# CHAPTER 9

*H*ouses smashed! Children dead! This was the fault of Moshe Sachar!

Rubbing his pudgy hands together with agitation, Rabbi Akiva scowled at the cup on his desk blotter as if the porcelain had offended him. His stores of food—his private property—had been commandeered by the Haganah gangsters. They had not located every cache, of course, so the mayor still possessed tea and sugar, but he limited himself to two weak cups per day. Because money carried authority, even in the middle of a war, Akiva had arranged a black-market supply of drinking water. It was an outrageous price per quart—equal to a whole carton of cigarettes—but at least he was spared the indignity of standing in line for a water ration!

Picking up the receiver of the lone telephone in the Old City's Jewish Quarter, the mayor placed a call to a familiar number. "Yes, who is it?" he heard Taj Khalidi's voice inquire in Arabic.

"*Salaam,*" Akiva said to his counterpart among the Old City Arabs. "Once again I find I must come to you, old friend, in order to separate truth from Zionist lies." Akiva was convinced that no nation of Israel could be established until the Messiah returned. Until then, a secular Jewish nation was not only doomed to failure; it would interrupt previously harmonious relations between Jews and Muslims. Besides, Akiva did not like the recent Jewish immigrants from Europe. They were entirely too secular to suit his ultra-Orthodox spirit, and they had proved unwilling to submit to his authority.

"*Salaam,* my friend Akiva," Khalidi returned. "You are well?" he asked solicitously.

Nodding toward the phone, while grimacing at his teacup, Akiva murmured that he was well enough. "We understand that the Arab Legion is in control of the Old City."

There was silence at the other end of the line; then Khalidi responded primly, "It is even as I said to you earlier. The combined forces of the League of Arab States are everywhere victorious, sweeping away resistance."

"And the Jihad Moquades have fled?"

Chuckling heartily, Khalidi corrected, "You *have* been listening to the Zionists, haven't you? I'm sorry to disappoint the optimists in the Haganah, but no Arab soldiers have run away! By no means! There has been a change of command and the valiant Holy Strugglers have been withdrawn for a well-earned rest." After pausing to let that bit of news sink in, Khalidi continued, "Surely you are aware that the Legion has brought its artillery to the Mount of Olives. My friend, they are battering the entire city from there! From now on, I fear, the only blood being spilled will be Jewish blood. . . . Not willingly," he added, allowing an ominous note to creep into his words. "But this ill-advised grasping at Arab land by the Zionists! Surely you see that continued insurgency must have dire consequences." Lowering his voice as if to lend confidentiality to his next phrase, Khalidi added, "I have heard that certain mercenaries have arrived in Jerusalem—certain men who were devoted followers of the late German dictator."

"Nazis?"

"Naturally," Khalidi said smoothly, "I and all men of goodwill oppose the employment of such animals. They are hardened killers who have no respect for Allah—or for life. I tell you this in hopes that you may yet encourage a speedy conclusion to the fighting."

"What about a cease-fire?" Akiva suggested eagerly. "Now that we could surrender to the Legion and not to the Mufti's rabble, I feel certain I can sway a majority of the Quarter to agree to surrender."

"Including the Haganah?"

Khalidi's voice betrayed a touch too much impatience, and Akiva was struck with a fear that made him circumspect. "I can only speak for the civilians," he corrected. "Moshe Sachar commands the others, but I know I can lead the noncombatants out of the Quarter tomorrow if the Legion will guarantee safe passage."

For the first time in the conversation Akiva was aware that Khalidi had not been alone in his home. The phone was suddenly muffled, and the mayor could hear Khalidi speaking to someone else. But Akiva could not make out the words.

"I will get back to you shortly," Khalidi said next, and he rang off.

■ ■ ■ ■

Taj Khalidi hung up the telephone and turned in the alcove of his office. He addressed himself first to Robert Brandenburg. "I trust you did not find my words too offensive," he said.

Plucking a bit of cigarette tobacco from his lower lip, Brandenburg replied with a smile. "Not at all. I value the effective use of propaganda, as any good commander should. The question, as I understand it, is what to do with the Jewish civilians who want to surrender."

Ahkmed al-Malik, taking long, relaxed pulls on Khalidi's narghile, aimed an acrid stream of blue smoke at the ceiling and said, "We should let them come out! We can always kill them once they are in our hands."

Looking at al-Malik with disgust, Major Tariq Athani said, "It would certainly bolster our credentials with the United Nations if we allowed white-haired rabbis and the rest to walk to safety. The artillery battering of which you spoke will not apply to the Old City much longer. The United States and others are pressuring King Abdullah to spare the holy places."

"In any case," Brandenburg pointed out, "letting noncombatants surrender peacefully does not bring you closer to victory in the Old City. In fact, not having to feed and protect the civilian population would actually prolong the fighting. It is my opinion that you should refuse to deal. It must be a total capitulation or nothing. No truce."

"I agree," Athani said. Addressing Khalidi, the Arab Legion officer requested, "Call the rabbi back and tell him what we have said. Tell him we will offer safe passage to the residents of the Quarter, whenever *all* opposition stops. Our armored units will soon attack the Jewish outpost on the edge of Sheikh Jarrah. Then Mea Shearim . . . Mandelbaum House . . . why should we bargain?" He added, "But tell him, as a mark of our good faith, we offer a temporary suspension of the shelling. It may deceive them while we go ahead with our *other* plans."

"In the meantime," Brandenburg suggested, "tell me what you know about this Moshe Sachar I keep hearing about. Is he truly so indispensable to the Jewish Quarter?"

■ ■ ■ ■

"Something's moving up there!" fifteen-year-old Uri Tabken called from the sandbagged rooftop of Mandelbaum House in the New City.

Peter Wallich left his maps and hurried to look. "Where?" he demanded, peering up the road toward Sheikh Jarrah. Scanning past whitewashed two-story houses and over red tile roofs, he could find nothing in sight on the road. Everything appeared unchanged. "Where are you looking?"

Uri pointed toward a barren hillside that flanked the Nablus Road between Sheikh Jarrah and the Jewish community of Sanhedria. Out of sight from Peter's location, but in that same direction, was the advance Jewish defensive outpost manned by the Irgun. It was well protected by buildings that had housed the academy of the Palestine Police. It was a critical position because the Irgun could attack the flank of any Arab advance down the hill. Also, the defensive line from Peter's post to Sanhedria was extremely weak. That Police School was the forward rampart protecting the northern approach to Jerusalem.

Something *was* moving up there.

A single figure appeared, running down the hill. Then a pair of men could be seen, likewise moving so rapidly as to be almost tumbling on the slope. Then another lone man, this one carrying an object . . .

Snatching up his field glasses, Peter focused the lenses. "They are Irgun," he said bitterly. "They are already abandoning the school!"

Yelling "Cover me!" to his adolescent soldiers, Peter grabbed a rifle and charged out of the house. One hundred yards up Hanavi Road he climbed over a mound of tumbled stones that had been a home until hit by Arab artillery fire. On the far side of the destruction he met the first of the fleeing Irgunists.

"Stop!" he shouted, waving his arm.

The first terror-stricken deserter did not even pause. Over his shoulder the man called, "They have tanks! Cannons! Run for your life!"

When the next two defectors reached him, Peter was ready for them. Raising his rifle, he aimed it at one man's chest and said, "Halt or I'll shoot."

Both men skidded to a stop. Through gasps for breath the taller of the two reported, "We cannot hold them! It is an armored column coming straight for us."

"How long did the fight last?" Peter demanded.

The two men exchanged a look but said nothing.

Nodding grimly, Peter decided it was what he had expected; there had been no battle. The Irgun had seen the advancing armored cars and taken to their heels. "Turn around!" he ordered. "We are going back there." By this time six more frightened members of the Irgun had collected in front of Peter's rifle muzzle. One of them had a grenade launcher and the others possessed grenades and Sten guns.

"But we can't—"

"How far off is the column?"

One Irgunist finally admitted, "Perhaps a half-mile. We saw the lead car only."

"Time enough!" Peter said. "Turn around and march!"

■ ■ ■ ■

The armored command car lurched and bounced over rutted and uneven roads. Jacob Kalner hung on as Major Luke Thomas's driver spun the wheel, and the oversized jeep came dangerously near to upsetting.

The butt of the reassembled Arab machine gun rested between Jacob's feet. From his flight through Zion Gate, up Mount Zion, and on to this frenzied drive around the perimeter of the New City en route to a clash with the Arab Legion, Jacob never relinquished his hold on the weapon. It had become a kind of talisman for him; it was bound to be useful wherever he ended up.

The hurry was due to the recent reports from Mea Shearim: the Arab Legion had been spotted beyond Sheikh Jarrah. They were coming with armored cars.

"This is a move by the Legion," Thomas explained. "They had infantry and artillery here. Their armored thrust was probing well to the north. Now, it seems, Jerusalem has become their primary target." Over the roar of the engine and the howling screech of wind he continued, "We have no antitank weapons to speak of. We need time to prepare for this. You are in charge of building barricades on Saint George Road. Dynamite houses to slow their advance. You will see what needs to be done. Can you use that?" he asked, indicating the automatic weapon.

"I think so," Jacob replied, grabbing at a leather strap as a particularly violent bounce threatened to throw him out of the vehicle. "It wasn't broken, just jammed."

"Time," Luke Thomas repeated. "That's what this is about: buying time. We have arms arriving at Tel Aviv and men waiting to use them . . . provided we hang on here long enough to let them prepare." The command car screeched to a stop behind Mandelbaum House. "Do what you can," he said. "I have to see if we have any armored cars of our own running after the attacks at Jaffa Gate." Looking Jacob squarely in the eyes, he promised, "I'll get them to you as fast as I can."

■ ■ ■ ■

Captain Hakeem of the Arab Legion's Third Regiment turned in the turret of his armored car. Parked on the side of the highway to Ramallah, Hakeem noticed himself swelling with pride. Their fat tires churning, car after armored car of his unit sped past. Every commander, every driver, every gunner was grinning. To be chosen from all the Arab world to save the Holy City from the Zionists, it was amazing.

Hakeem's column raced ahead of the infantry that followed. Over one thousand Arab Legionnaires had been diverted toward Jerusalem, but it was Hakeem's personal goal that his unit would win the battle, thrash the Jews so quickly and completely that only mopping up would be left for the others. To be the conqueror of Jerusalem! Would not Hakeem's name be inscribed next to Saladin's and those of the other warrior-heroes?

British military doctrine regarding the use of armor required that no advance be made without accompanying infantry support. Hakeem knew this. Glubb Pasha knew this. But everyone from Glubb Pasha on down to Hakeem's regimental commander said the same thing: the Jews have no armor of their own and no antitank weapons. With speed, the Arabs would be unstoppable.

The command circuit radio buzzed. "Sheikh Jarrah in sight," he heard.

"Opposition?"

"Light rifle fire coming from Police School buildings on the right flank. Nothing from the left or center. No barricades visible."

"Straight ahead, then," Hakeem ordered. "Down the slope to Jerusalem!"

■ ■ ■ ■

The training school for the Palestine Police was a series of low-slung stone buildings, partly barracks and partly classrooms, surrounded by open fields. The walls provided ready-made ramparts for defense, and there was a clear field of fire toward the Nablus Road and Sheikh Jarrah.

The school was occupied by members of the Jewish Irgun Zvai Leumi, the so-called National Military Organization: terrorists who burned movie theaters in retaliation for Arab riots; assassins who slaughtered British soldiers; extremists who wanted Palestine without Arabs and had proven at Deir Yassin that they had the will to carry out their bloody plans. These were the defenders driven back to their post at gunpoint by Peter Wallich.

While the rest of the column had stopped farther back, the first probing wave of two Arab Legion armored cars neared the crest of the hill at Sheikh Jarrah. In a matter of moments they would sweep around the curve unhindered. That would be the signal for the rest of the force to descend on Jerusalem like ravening wolves. "Give me that grenade launcher!" Peter ordered.

It was merely a rifle-mounted device, designed to throw a signal flare but modified to propel a grenade. It had no sizable range and was neither accurate nor safe, but it was the sole artillery available to combat armored vehicles.

Eyeballing the range and angle of trajectory, Peter loaded the first explosive and ordered: "Everyone start shooting as soon as this explodes." Then he pulled the trigger.

There was a sharp crack, and the grenade was thrown in a high arc. It landed short of the advancing Arabs, but squarely on top of a low stone wall. The resulting concussion added flying stone fragments to the metal shrapnel. Peter saw the commander of the lead car throw up his arm as if to ward off a swarm of bees and drop from sight into the hatch.

The Irgunists opened up with their Sten guns and the other armored car hatches slammed shut. Then the two vehicles stopped moving and pivoted toward the school. Machine-gun fire from the turrets of the armored cars sliced into the Police School walls and windows.

Peter launched another grenade, which landed between the two Legion vehicles. The car in front of the detonation sagged backwards to the right as one of its rear tires was blown out. Dragging its hindquarters like a wounded animal, the armored car lumbered off the road toward the school.

While readying another round, Peter interpreted the indecision racking the Arabs by the contrary movements of the remaining vehicle. The second car started forward, then reversed onto the road, back toward the main body of the Legion force. "That's it!" Peter encouraged the other defenders. "They don't know what they are facing. It makes them hesitate." With that he launched another grenade.

It was more a result of chance than of Peter's skill that the weapon hit the crippled leading armored car on its rear deck, directly on top of a pair of spare fuel cans. The containers ignited with a *whoosh*, throwing flaming liquid out on both sides. Seconds later, two men jumped from the rear door to escape the pyre and were cut down by Irgun gunfire.

"We've stopped them!" a young Irgunist exulted.

"We were lucky," Peter corrected. "Mostly these grenades bounce off. But yes, we've made them stop and reconsider."

# CHAPTER 10

The Gadna Youth Brigade sentry, Uri Tabken, had just come off his rooftop position at the Mandelbaum house when Jacob Kalner arrived. On the second floor Jacob finally relinquished the Arab machine gun, allowing it to be added to the meager arsenal of defense. It was set up in a window, commanding the approach from Sheikh Jarrah.

"Come with me," Jacob ordered Uri, handing the boy a twenty-five-pound pack of explosives and settling the straps of its twin around his own shoulders. He set off at a brisk pace up the road toward Sheikh Jarrah. The sound of rifle fire and the deeper rasp of machine guns echoed down the slope.

The farther he moved up the road, the more of Jerusalem Jacob could see over his shoulder. The battlements of the Old City walls appeared. Beyond them was the Jewish Quarter . . . and Lori.

It was all so close! Such an insignificant bit of distance between where he stood and where she was. How pitiful the Jewish defense seemed. Like a wave's surge up on a beach, how could the rush of the Arab Legion be prevented?

Worry about her fueled his eagerness. Save Jerusalem, yes, but it was determination to rescue Lori that drove him on.

Below the brow of the hill, Jacob found exactly what he was seeking. At a spot where the highway made a turn to the right sat an ugly stone building that had once housed minor functionaries of the British Mandatory Government. It was two floors in height but, more important, the second story projected over the first.

"This is it," Jacob said, indicating that Uri should remove the backpack. Two pillars supported the weight of the front half of the building. If they were blown, the structure should collapse across the road, blocking it with rubble.

"How did you learn?" Uri asked as Jacob fitted detonators to the explosives and cut a length of fuse for each.

"I had to do it at Zion Gate," Jacob said.

"You did this once only?" Uri asked, backing away from Jacob's side.

When the fuses were lit, Jacob and Uri raced down toward the Mandelbaum house. Before they reached it, the dynamite exploded, one parcel two seconds before the other. The concussion of the first blast knocked them to the ground, and while they were hunched over, covering their heads, the sky rained fist-sized bits of stone. Jacob and Uri were pummeled with flying debris and gravel, but neither was hurt.

"Is that how you were taught?" Uri asked.

Turning to look at his handiwork, Jacob saw a four-foot-high heap of debris blockading the road. Would it be enough? Had he done what he could to shield Lori from what was about to happen? "That will buy us time," he said. "Come on. We're not done yet."

■ ■ ■ ■

"Lead vehicle destroyed!" Captain Hakeem heard over his radio. "The Jews must have mortars!" This news came from the surviving armored car roaring back toward him at top speed.

Engines rumbling like growling tigers impatient to be at their prey, Hakeem's column remained halted on the road. By standing on top of his turret Hakeem could make out the Police School off to the right, and the gutted, smoldering remains of his scout car.

No one had told him anything about mortars.

If the Jews had mortars, perhaps they also possessed bazookas or even antitank guns. The armored skin of his Daimler car was thick enough to stop rifle bullets, even the shrapnel from grenades. But rockets and mortar bombs and cannonfire . . . it was too risky to proceed unsupported.

Nor had the infantry come up. When they did he could divide his force, outflank and surround the school position, and drive out the Jews.

Waiting for the infantry would mean sharing the glory of capturing Jerusalem.

Hakeem decided to call for artillery instead.

Clicking his radio over to the frequency he shared with the battery on the Mount of Olives, Hakeem requested an immediate barrage to drop on the Police School.

Mortars!

Let the Jews cope with twenty-five-pound shells and see how they liked it!

■ ■ ■ ■

As the first Arab artillery rounds dropped on the Irgun and Peter Wallich at their post in the Palestine Police training academy, word came that the road below the hill was blocked and that reinforcements had arrived at Mandelbaum House with dynamite and automatic weapons. What the message did not make clear was that the reinforcements consisted of one man and one machine gun.

Another shell shrieked overhead, bursting on the athletic field behind the school. The building in which Peter crouched rocked with the impact and plaster fell from the ceiling.

The next explosion hit directly on top of the barracks, one structure away from Peter's location. The walls blew out and the tiled roof lifted straight up in the air. Then, having nothing to support it, the roof broke into chunks the size of automobiles, crushing everyone inside.

"Now we go!" Peter ordered.

The classroom cleared before he had even rebuckled his cartridge belt.

■ ■ ■ ■

Captain Hakeem viewed the results of the shelling with delight. The Jews were retreating! As Hakeem watched, a bare handful of men ran from the Police School. Another shell added its emphasis to their departure by striking the last of the intact buildings, destroying an end wall and half of the front.

There was no longer a threat to his right flank and whatever mortar or other weapons the Jews had possessed were now eliminated.

"Radio the battery to cease firing!" Hakeem yelled to his gunner. Pumping his clenched fist up and down in the age-old signal for a cavalry advance, the eager officer urged his column forward.

There was nothing to stop him!

Sweeping by the ruins of the school, Hakeem's armored car passed a mosque and a Muslim seminary and dropped over the crest of the last hill separating him from Jerusalem.

It lay before him, spread out and glistening. From his vantage point Hakeem could see the heights of the Temple Mount to his left, Jewish-held outposts such as the tower of the YMCA building to the right.

Straight ahead lay Jewish-held Mea Shearim and the road that led directly to the Damascus Gate and mastery of the city.

"Go! GO!" he urged his driver as another shell fell beside the road between Sheikh Jarrah and the Mandelbaum house.

The armored car rounded a hairpin turn in its descent from the plateau of the Arab village. It slued sideways as the driver stomped on the brakes to avoid the pile of debris blocking the road. The barricade was solid in the middle but diminished toward the right shoulder. On that side, the way could be cleared by moving blocks and broken timbers.

Cursing the delay that disrupted his ride to glory and honored memory, Hakeem leapt from the vehicle. With his own hands he tore at the broken masonry. Without even waiting for his gunner to join him, Hakeem struggled with another slab, rolling it a few inches at a time toward the side of the road.

Another Arab cannon shell whistled overhead. It sailed over the Arab suburb of Musrara and exploded barely fifty yards from the Nablus Road. "Did you not—"

Hakeem never managed to finish his question for the gunner as to whether radio contact with the Arab battery had been made, for the arrival of the next shell answered it.

The detonation was on the other side of the heap of stone. Hakeem's armored car was obliterated.

The gunner, his body shredded, ceased to exist.

Captain Hakeem, his back and legs bleeding from a score of shrapnel wounds, was picked up by the second armored vehicle in the column.

He was carried to the rear as the Arab armored thrust into Jerusalem retreated up the hill behind Sheikh Jarrah.

■ ■ ■ ■

Of the eighteen Irgunists who had been assigned to hold the Palestine Police School, six returned uninjured. Of the rest, four were dead, four were seriously wounded, and the others had minor wounds.

Their early desertion from their post had nearly cost Israel the loss of Jerusalem, but they had paid dearly for their victory.

Peter Wallich returned to his teenage soldiers, who would scarcely let him catch his breath in their desire to hear his story. "So you have saved Jerusalem," Naomi Snow exulted.

"I wish it were that easy," Peter corrected. "What we have accomplished is to gain several hours to get ready for the next attack. And for that we must thank the Arab gunners for blowing up their own men . . . and whoever caused the obstruction in the road, of course."

Uri Tabken brought Jacob over to Peter. "Here he is," Uri said, struggling with his divided loyalty to the two heroes. "He came from nowhere yelling orders, but he seems to know his business."

"But I know you," Peter said, studying Jacob's crooked nose and wrestler's build.

Jacob returned the stare without any show of recognition. "I'm sorry," he said. "I don't—"

"You're Jacob Kalner," Peter added as proof. "Don't you remember? We came into Palestine together on that tramp steamer with the Hayedid. You and that big fellow . . . what was his name? Alfie? I'm Peter Wallich."

"Wallich? But the night of the British raid . . . I never saw you on Cyprus. I thought you were dead."

Peter's lined face split into a smile. "I escaped. Hid out in Haifa and got smuggled into Galilee. Within a week I had a new identity card and a new life. But enough of ancient history. So you are the one responsible for saving our necks from the Arab armored brigade?"

"The barricade worked, but I can't take credit for the cannon."

"A miracle."

Jacob nodded. "Yes, but a brief one. They will come again this afternoon."

Disagreeing, Peter suggested, "Perhaps we'll have another small miracle. British doctrine says: 'Advance in the morning. Consolidate in the afternoon.' I should know; I have spent ten years evading their patrols. And this Legion thinks with the heart of an Arab but the head of an Englishman."

Jacob thought about that concept. He did not know if it made the Arab Legion sound more formidable or less. "Either way, since they hold Sheikh Jarrah and can come down on us at will, there is no time to waste."

■ ■ ■ ■

Even though he was awaiting the call, Rabbi Akiva jumped when the telephone rang. For the length of three rings, he regarded the device as if it might be a poisonous snake. Finally he answered and said hopefully, "I know we can be ready to leave by noon tomorrow. Shall we go out via the Armenian Quarter or the Street of the Chain?"

"Alas," Khalidi said sorrowfully, "I am distressed to tell you that such a truce is not possible. The commander of the Arab Legion . . . a gallant officer . . . advises me that he himself recently proposed a cease-fire for the purpose of rescuing wounded soldiers. This humane proposal the Haganah gangsters denied."

"But we are noncombatants!" Akiva protested, his voice growing shrill. "If we stay here we will be killed . . . religious scholars like myself . . . women and children!"

Khalidi's words dripped with sympathy when he said, "I truly regret that Moshe Sachar and the Haganah have so little regard for you and for innocent human life. They are forcing you to remain in a precarious position. If only Sachar could be convinced that he is responsible for the needless shedding of innocent blood."

"Sachar," Akiva repeated harshly. "If only he had never come back."

"Do what you can to arouse the sensible ones in the Old Quarter," Khalidi advised. "For our part, we will halt the shelling of your district . . . for twenty-four hours. Perhaps you can make the Haganah commander see reason. But this is final: no truce, no evacuation of civilians unless soldiers surrender. All arms must be laid down. Call me again tomorrow, if you can."

"Yes, yes!" Akiva agreed, pathetically eager to grasp this one slim chance. "Thank you! Thank you! But ask the Legion commander to hold off shelling our district for one more day . . . just one more!"

■ ■ ■ ■

Mandelbaum's neighbors along St. George Road were a mixture of the wealthy and the impoverished. Single-family manor houses, with high ceilings, quarters for servants, and polished marble floors, balanced against the ill-favored, gray, flat-sided three-story tenements that composed much of Mea Shearim.

Jacob had already rigged explosives in a Hasidic apartment building on one side of the Mandelbaum house. He was busily implanting them in the home of a wealthy spice merchant three doors down, on the other side of the Gadna outpost, when a disturbance in the street caught his attention.

Major Luke Thomas, in his command car, arrived at the head of a procession of three armored vehicles. Two of them had crudely drawn stars of David decorating their turrets; the third displayed the insignia of the British unit from whom it had been stolen.

More surprising than the appearance of the cavalry was the caravan of civilians that accompanied it. Around the column capered a hundred residents of the neighborhood. Many still in nightshirts, they had fled Mea Shearim before dawn when the first Arab artillery shells rained down. Now, carrying the same meager belongings that they hoped to save, they were returning as if Luke Thomas were Moses leading them into the Promised Land. They cheered the retreat of the Arab Legion, banging pots and pans and waving feather pillows like palm branches.

An elderly Hasidic rabbi, aided by four of his followers almost as aged as he, approached Jacob. Their beards wagged and the fringes of their prayer shawls twirled in the breeze that spun down off the heights of Mount Scopus.

At the same time, a short, fat man with slick, greasy hair and wearing an expensive three-piece suit bustled importantly ahead of the Hasidim. Behind the obviously well-to-do, obviously non-Hasidic figure labored a line of servants toting trunks and a portable phonograph. "This is my house!" he said in a challenging tone. "You must leave at once."

"I'm sorry," Jacob said. "This house is already mined. When I blow it up it will block—"

"Blow it up!" the man protested. "Do you know who I am?"

Jacob shrugged. "No, and it doesn't matter. The Legion turned back today, but they will come again. We need barricades all along here."

Feeling a tug at his sleeve, Jacob found one of the wizened rabbi's assistants. "Please," the man said. "A young fellow with a gun would not let us into our block. The Rebbe wishes to know why."

Repeating words of apology, Jacob again explained that the tenement building was about to be turned into rubble.

"But it is home to thirty families!" the earlocked and fur-hatted Hasid argued.

In a hoarse voice faint as a desert wind sifting a handful of sand against a windowpane, Rabbi Matthias Krebnik stilled the debate when he said, "Peace, Yochanan. Did not the Almighty preserve us in Poland? and in the camps? and on the seas? And did He not bring us to Eretz-Israel? If He now demands of us a bit of brick and plaster, what is that?" Then he addressed Jacob, who bent nearer to hear. "Sir, may we have time to collect some of our belongings? They will be needed to share with others who lost everything to the Arab bombs."

After Jacob assured them there was time to gather their possessions, the Hasidim, unlike the wealthy businessman, moved off to do so without further comment.

Waiting until the ultra-Orthodox covey was out of earshot, the rich man winked and said with unctuous certainty, "Of course, now that you can blow up a whole apartment block, there is no need to dynamite my home today."

"I do not intend to blow up this house today," Jacob said.

"Ah!"

"After the first of the Arab armored cars has passed this point, I will blow it up behind them to trap them in the middle. Now you must leave so I can finish. If as much as a single spark lands here—let alone a Legion shell—all that will be left of this house and us will be a handful of dust."

■ ■ ■ ■

Daoud left the Latin Patriarchate through a back entrance. The melodious chant of the sisters followed him like leaves dancing on a breeze above the filth and uncollected rubbish of the Old City.

Emerging from an alley into the Christian Quarter, he noted that the twisting street was devoid of life. He looked to the right and left, where the lane wound away beneath the shadows of overhanging buildings. Not even a cat crossed the cobbles. The Christians had all gone away. Had Muslim snipers taken watchful positions within the deserted buildings?

Daoud stepped into a patch of sunlight. Across the lane, in the doorway of a shuttered souvenir shop, he saw movement. Who was there? Who stood observing him? He was tempted to turn back. If he returned now, the old Mother would not ever suspect that he had been gone. He would have something to eat, spend the day helping with Gawan.

He raised his head as if to catch the scent of danger.

He called to the figure, "You and I are the only ones out today."

In reply a man stepped out from the alcove. It was the gardener, the man who had carried Gawan to the haven of the Patriarchate.

"I have been waiting for you, Daoud," said the old man. "Tell me news of your brother."

"He is alive."

The man smiled, revealing a patchwork of missing teeth. "All is well with you, then, boy?"

"I did not thank you for carrying Gawan to this place."

"You are leaving the sanctuary?" He extended a hand to Daoud as though to welcome him.

"The Mother, she is a foolish woman, with a will like a mule. She says she will go back to the convent. I wish to see if it is safe for her to return." Daoud went to the man's side and gazed into his cloudy eyes.

"It is not," said the old man plainly. "Will you go back and tell her so?"

Daoud considered the information offered by the gardener. How could he know what was safe and what was not? "I must know this thing for myself."

"Al-Malik and Hassan el-Hassan prowl the walls of the Old City. There is danger for you if you go back. The Arab Legion has retaken Zion Gate. How will you answer if they ask where you have been?"

Daoud shrugged. Perhaps al-Malik would think Daoud had been a deserter. What story would Daoud tell if he was asked? The boy frowned. "Where is your wheelbarrow?"

"Full of roses to plant upon the grave of the Jewish children. I left it near the garden of Gal'ed."

Daoud nodded thoughtfully. He knew the sheltered square in the Jewish Quarter. What was the old man doing there? Nothing made sense anymore. Why should he expect the actions of the ancient Arab to be understandable?

"I must go to Jaffa Gate. I must find out what will happen."

"I will walk with you," said the old man.

Daoud pressed on. The footfalls of the gardener echoed behind him as he made his way toward the Muslim barricades in the Citadel of Jaffa Gate.

"Did you see how many men in King Abdullah's Legion?" Daoud inquired.

No reply.

Daoud asked once again, then turned and saw that he was alone. The old man had not followed him after all.

# CHAPTER 11

Former SS Lieutenant Robert Brandenburg examined the Arab-held section of the Old City with the eye of a military historian. Studying the Citadel of David that protected Jaffa Gate, he marveled at how close the Jewish forces had come to breaking through.

There were three ways the walls of Jerusalem could be breached: extended siege and starvation of the inhabitants, stupidity of the defenders, or treachery from within.

In the case of the Jewish Quarter, starvation and treachery were chipping away at the Jews. But the leader of the Haganah, this Moshe Sachar, was no fool. His lines of defense moved like the waves against the seashore. Ebbing, flowing, changing hourly from one strongpoint to another, from housetop to basement.

This strategy reminded Brandenburg of the defense of the Warsaw Ghetto. A handful of Jews had held a panzer regiment at bay for over fifty days. In the end the only way to defeat them was to level the entire section of the city. Even then Jewish fighters escaped through the sewers like rats. No doubt they had resurfaced here to fight again.

The German officer pondered the problem he faced.

He carried with him the writings of Flavius Josephus and was familiar with the bloody history of the Holy City. Josephus, like Rabbi Akiva, was both a Jew and a collaborator. Born Yosef ben Mattityahu, Josephus had been the governor of Galilee when the great rebellion against Rome began in 66 A.D. Believing the revolt was doomed, he switched his loyalty to the Romans. He accepted Roman dominion over his nation without apology. Like Akiva, perhaps Josephus believed that peace at any cost was better than the alternative.

Brandenburg knew Josephus had been right. In the end, Jerusalem had been utterly destroyed. Not one stone was left upon another, as Jesus of Nazareth had predicted forty years before the siege.

Would that happen again? Indiscriminate shelling from the batteries on the Mount of Olives had already damaged several irreplaceable structures. A call from the Armenian Patriarch to King Abdullah in protest of the destruction of the tower of St. Jacques had sent a tremor through the Arab Legion forces.

The King's words were repeated from man to man. "You are sent to protect the holy places of Jerusalem, not to destroy them!"

Warsaw was Warsaw. But Jerusalem! The world would not approve the leveling of Jerusalem to root out the Jews. It would take a bold move to bring this conflict to a rapid conclusion. By someone within the Jewish camp.

He walked briskly across the court of the Citadel, reflecting on its history. Josephus had written:

*Jerusalem was defended by three walls except where it was shut in by impassable ravines. It was built on two hills facing each other and separated by a central ravine. . . . Of these two hills the one was occupied by the Upper City. This western hill was much stronger and straighter along in length; being so strong it was called the Stronghold by King David.*

This was the position Brandenburg's men held in the Old City. No one would break through from the outside. And as for the Old City Jews? The Jewish Quarter was once again virtually an island, cut off from the rest of the city. There was no way out for them except through Brandenburg and the Legion mercenaries. Theirs was a hopeless situation. But what would it take to make them believe it?

A bullet in the brain of Moshe Sachar would end their resistance. Rabbi Akiva was right about that.

Brandenburg considered the problem as he walked through the streets.

The newly arrived troops of the Arab Legion made their barracks in a building called the *Kishleh.* Built in 1838 in the shadow of the Citadel of David, glowered over Jaffa Gate, it first housed Turkish troops. Next, it housed the British soldiers of the Mandatory Government, then the Holy Strugglers of the Mufti's army, and now the mercenaries of the King of Jordan.

Before all that, it had been the site of Herod the Great's palace, the place where the three Magi had come in search of the newborn King of the Jews.

*There were ceilings remarkable for the length of the beams and the splendor of the ornamentation, and rooms without number, no two designed alike, and all their contents being of gold and silver. . . . The open spaces between them were all green lawns and coppices of different trees traversed by long walks. These were edged with deep canals and cisterns everywhere adorned with bronze statues through which the water poured out. . . .*

Josephus had watched it burning from the Mount of Olives. The Roman general had been furious at its destruction. He had wanted the treasures intact for himself, as King Abdullah did now. But the rage of the Roman soldiers could not be contained. Along with the torching there had been a slaughter of the Jews such as Jerusalem had never seen.

Brandenburg mopped his brow. The heat was intense even in the early morning. He glanced up as al-Malik came toward him.

"Lieutenant! Hassan has captured a Jew! He is a prisoner at the Rawdah School. He knows much. He was trapped behind our lines but came out to surrender when his thirst became unbearable."

"Water," Brandenburg said aloud as he looked up into the merciless sky. "And there is the difference. There are no fountains in the Jewish Quarter. The Jews have no water."

■ ■ ■ ■

The prisoner, dressed in a pair of shorts, sat tied to a chair in the cloakroom of the Rawdah School. His face was bruised and swollen, eyes swollen shut, front teeth broken. His shoulders and chest were covered with cigarette burns. His brown hair was matted with blood.

"You will talk, Jew!" Hassan el-Hassan jerked the man's head back and spat in his face.

The man sobbed. "I know nothing, I tell you! Nothing! My name is Dieter Wottrich. I came here on a ship. To Tel Aviv. I get off the ship, and they bring me here on a bus! I am told to fight! Told to carry this pack into the Jewish Quarter. I get lost and you capture me! I am nobody!"

Lieutenant Brandenburg, arms crossed, leaned against the frame of the door and watched the interrogation.

Another slap. A hard punch to the man's ribs. Then a long drag on a Turkish cigarette. Hassan twirled it, blowing smoke into the captive's face in prelude to pressing the glowing butt into his flesh.

"Don't! I beg of you! Mercy!"

Brandenburg intervened. "Stop it," he said, commanding Hassan.

Hassan shot a furious glance at the German lieutenant. "He admits he came up Bab el Wad from the sea!"

"So what?"

"He had to be at Deir Yassin! Had to be among them!"

"*Bitte* . . . Please! I don't know this place! I got off the ship and they—"

"*Ja.*" Brandenburg put a hand gently on Wottrich's head. "I believe you."

Wottrich sobbed convulsively. "Make him . . . stop . . . I cannot tell . . . I do not know. . . ."

Hassan drew his knife. "I will cut the truth out of the dog!"

"You will go." Brandenburg drew his Lüger. "Or you will find you have suddenly lost your mind."

Hassan stared at the weapon, inclined his head in acquiescence, then backed from the room. "I let you deal with the dog."

"You must believe me," Wottrich cried.

"*Ja.*" Brandenburg's voice was soothing. "I believe you, friend. There," Brandenburg said. "You see? He is gone. Gone." He stooped to look into the mangled face of the Jew. "*Besser a hunt in friden vi a zelner in krig, eh?* Better a dog in peacetime than a soldier in war. So you see . . . I know Yiddish. You can speak to me."

"*Ja, ja,*" gasped Wottrich. "I swear to you. I come here not by choice. I get off the ship—"

"What ship?"

"*Joshua Reynolds* . . . from Marseilles."

"You are a German Jew. From where?"

"Hamburg."

"And who did you come with? To Palestine?"

"No one! I swear! I came alone! Alone! There is no one left!"

"There was no one else on the ship?" Brandenburg mocked him.

"Yes. Many . . . Many others from the D.P. camps. No one I know."

Brandenburg shrugged as if it did not matter. "You were caught carrying medical supplies. Are you a medic? Why did you come to Palestine?"

"I came to . . . I wanted to work here. Schoolteacher. Nobody . . . Just to live."

"You have heard . . . *Nochen toit vert men choshev?*"

"*Ja.* But how do you know Yiddish?"

"Say it. Say what it means."

"After . . . death . . . one becomes important."

Brandenburg smiled and patted the prisoner on the back. "This is a true saying. So much wisdom in the *mamaloschen,* true? No need to be afraid. It is painless." At that he held the Lüger to Wottrich's head and pulled the trigger.

■ ■ ■ ■

Former SS Lieutenant Robert Brandenburg dressed in the clothes of Dieter Wottrich. Light blue, long-sleeved cotton shirt, blue wool trousers worn thin in the seat, holes in the pockets, leather braces, brown summer-weight jacket with the insignia of the Haganah pinned to the shoulder, reading glasses in the pocket; identification card for a D.P. camp in Italy. Brandenburg stared hard at the photo and tore up the paper. The backpack filled with medical supplies bound for the Jewish hospital finished the disguise.

The Arab boy called Daoud said with admiration, "Lieutenant Brandenburg, I cannot tell you are not a Jew."

"Neither will they be able to." Brandenburg jammed a Greek fisherman's cap onto his head and tucked his Lüger into his waistband.

"Hassan says you were speaking Yiddish to the fellow. How did you come to know their language?" asked the boy.

"Jewish prisoners. The camps in Croatia. It is much like German. I picked up enough to converse."

Al-Malik shoved the child aside. "Your skill will be useful. The Jews of the Old City speak nothing else."

"I will blend in. I have done so before when it was necessary. And Moshe Sachar?"

Al-Malik replied, "Taj Khalidi says he was born here. He is an educated Jew. English schools. Fought with English soldiers at El Alamein. Taj Khalidi has known him his whole lifetime. He sent this picture."

In the dim light two teenage boys, one Arab, one Jewish, looked back at Brandenburg from a faded black-and-white photograph. Their arms were linked. They were friends. The tall, dark-eyed Jewish boy had an expression of hope and joy on his thin face. His smile was warm and genuine. Brandenburg tapped the photo. "Khalidi kept this?"

"They were boys together in the Old City. Khalidi says this Moshe Sachar left as a young man. He speaks like an Englishman. Khalidi has sworn by the Prophet that they are mortal enemies for many years. He saw Sachar in the Jewish Quarter from the roof of his house on the Street of the Chain."

"Sachar is the chain that binds the Jewish Quarter."

"Khalidi could tell you more."

"The Jews have a saying: *Brecht zich a ring, tsefalt di gantseh kait:* One link snaps, and the whole chain falls apart." Brandenburg shouldered the pack. "So, I am nobody. Dieter Wottrich. A schoolteacher from Hamburg, *nu?* Conscripted right off the ship. Made to work. Forced to fight. Separated and lost from the Jewish Palmachniks when I entered the Old City with these supplies. Trapped in the cellar of a bombed-out house until thirst drove me to the open. . . ."

Brandenburg, confident in his deception, warned al-Malik, "I will leave our territory through the Armenian Quarter from Saint James Road. Hear me now. I will kill Moshe Sachar, and the chain will be broken. Then I will return across the Jewish barricade from the same direction. You must see that the sentries know I am behind the lines."

■ ■ ■ ■

Near the southwestern corner of the Old City Jewish district was a group of four Sephardic synagogues. Interconnected, these sanctuaries, the Ben Zakkai, the Central Synagogue, the Stambuli, and the Eliyahu Hanavi Synagogue, were between the Great Hurva and the Old City wall. The Central Synagogue had once been an entrance hall to the Zakkai and Eliyahu, until being roofed and turned into another place of worship.

Moshe was standing with Rabbi Vultch on the balcony of the women's gallery inside the Central Synagogue. The two men were discussing the defensive perimeter of the Quarter and how much longer it could be held at its present size and shape.

"It is a question of supplies," Moshe said. "If reinforcements get in through Zion Gate soon, then we can hold the Quarter indefinitely. Every day we hang on gives the rest of the Yishuv time to bolster defenses, receive shipments of weapons . . . come to our rescue . . ."

"And otherwise?"

Moshe said, "I do not think the Arab Legion will fritter away its men in headlong, uncoordinated attacks. Up to now the Jihad Moquades would hit us along the Street of the Chain, and we would send more men there to fight them off. Then they would attack from the Armenian Quarter, but leaving us enough time to reinforce that side." Moshe shook his head. "I think the Legion commander, whoever he is, is smarter. He will encircle our area and squeeze it from all sides at once. We must think about falling back to a smaller and more easily defended perimeter."

"What would the new boundaries be?"

Above the synagogue's balcony were a pair of windows. Through the nearer one a beam of light shone on the dusty floor. With the toe of his boot, Moshe made three marks on the pavement in a rough triangle. Touching the topmost point he said, "This is the Hurva. On the right, Nissan Bek. The third, the complex we are in right here."

Stroking his beard Vultch observed, "That would be about a third of the area we presently hold, *nu?*"

"Less than that," Moshe said. "But it—"

"Sachar!" Akiva's booming voice called from the ground floor of the synagogue. "I need to speak with you. Where are you?"

Vultch raised his eyebrows, offered Moshe a sympathetic grin, and made as if to leave. "Don't go!" Moshe said softly. Then replied, "Up here, Rabbi."

Panting and sweating after climbing the steps, Akiva appeared cross and accusatory. He seemed to suspect Moshe of having deliberately chosen the place so as to inconvenience him.

"Sachar," he repeated. "The Haganah has failed to reinforce the Quarter. You must agree that further resistance is futile and suicidal."

The words were inflammatory and treasonous, but Moshe recognized that Akiva had a large, loyal following in the Old City. He attempted to respond reasonably. "They have not stopped trying to break through," he corrected. "They succeeded once; they can do so again."

"But there is no cause!" Akiva argued. Clasping his hands behind his back, he strode about the gallery, heedless of Moshe's impromptu map. "You told my people that they would be in danger if they surrendered to the Jihad Moquades. Very well! But now the Legion has arrived, so surely there can be no further objection to an honorable—"

"Every day we hold out, every Legionnaire who cannot fight elsewhere because we keep him occupied here, makes the existence of Israel more certain."

"Bah!" Akiva grumped. "If you are determined to get killed, you should not force peaceful civilians to die with you! Like the Kurtzman family!"

Vultch spoke up. "Rabbi Akiva, you are being unfair! The Arabs will never allow noncombatants to be evacuated. You and your people are hostages until we either win or lose."

His face wrinkling as if at the taste of something sour, Akiva retorted, "Sachar, you have twenty-four hours to come to your senses and order a complete surrender. I have arranged a one-day cease-fire . . . at least as far as artillery shelling is concerned. After that the blood of every innocent resident of this community is on your hands."

"You have arranged . . . How did you do that?"

Smugly, Akiva replied, "That is my business, the same as the welfare of my people is my business. One day! Can you live with the guilt if you do not agree?"

His bulk swaying as he moved down the steps, Akiva neither responded to any more queries nor turned back again as he left the synagogue.

"What do you make of that?" Moshe asked Vultch. "What can he mean?"

"Does it matter?" Vultch replied, tapping his shoe on Moshe's diagram, scuffed by Akiva's pacing. "We will not surrender while we have a defensible perimeter, eh?"

"No . . . no, of course not. But he knows more than he is telling."

"So?" Vultch said. "Maybe we have secrets of our own? Have you heard the reason why this synagogue is sometimes called *Kehal Zion?*"

Watching Akiva's retreating form and lost in thought, Moshe muttered, "Hmmm?"

"It's just an old story, of course," Vultch volunteered. "But it is said that a hidden tunnel connects this place with David's Tomb, clear out there on Mount Zion, beyond the walls. Wouldn't that be a secret indeed?"

# CHAPTER 12

The Krepske brothers, tousled and breathless, burst into the lobby of Misgav Ladakh Hospital. Rachel, mopping the floor of the corridor, heard them before she saw them. Their words tumbled out.

Leo, who had dropped several pounds, was no longer round and jovial-looking. Thin and worried, he demanded, "Get the doctor!"

". . . the doctor! Get him!" echoed Mendel, his olive complexion darker than usual for lack of washing.

"Hurry!"

"Hurry up! It's the mayor!"

". . . It's Mayor Akiva! Get Doctor Baruch!"

". . . Baruch!"

Rachel propped the mop against the wall and hurried toward the boys. The brothers were Yacov's age and known for overexcitement. But why were they shouting? Had Akiva been wounded?

"What is it?" Rachel asked.

"Rabbi Akiva!" blurted the first of the red-haired siblings.

"He has to see Doctor Baruch! Right away!"

Yehudit Avram, the mayor's estranged daughter, emerged from a ward. At the mention of her father, her complexion became ashen.

"Is my father hurt?" she asked anxiously.

Leo Krepske stopped short at the sight of Yehudit. "No."

"Hurt?" Mendel sniffed uncomfortably. "No."

Yehudit seemed relieved. "Then what is this about?" She turned to Rachel as though Rachel might know what was going on.

Rachel shrugged. "I know as much as you," she said. Then, turning to Mendel, she asked, "What's all the excitement?"

Mendel blinked uncomfortably at the floor beside Rachel. "He has to see Doctor Baruch. That's all."

"That's all," Leo agreed.

"Where is my father?" Yehudit pressed. "Is he hurt or ill?"

"He's outside," Leo explained. "Not hurt."

"Not sick. He won't come in," Mendel amplified.

"Won't come in?" Rachel glanced toward the door. "Why not?"

Mendel squirmed. "Because—"

Yehudit took Mendel by the shoulder. "Say it! What is this about? Why won't he come in?"

Mendel looked to Leo for assistance. Leo, his face a mask of terror, sputtered, "He says . . . the mayor says . . . Rabbi Akiva says . . ."

"Yes? Yes?" Rachel stopped to gaze directly into the boy's eyes. "He says?"

Leo pulled away from Yehudit and blurted, "Rabbi Akiva says Rachel Sachar is a whore. A whore for Nazis. He says he won't come in here because she is in here and she is a filthy—"

Yehudit grabbed the boy by his lapels and gave him a shake. "Shut up! Shut up, you little *momzer!* Repeating such gossip! Such terrible rumors!"

Mendel cried, "Don't hit him! He didn't say it!"

"I don't think she is," Leo shouted. "It's him! Rabbi Akiva! Your father! He's the one who says it! Not me!"

"Not us!" Mendel concurred. "He says she burned off the tattoo on her arm. The one that marked her for the officers. He says he won't come into the hospital, see? But he has to talk to Doctor Baruch about the surrender!"

Rachel felt the color drain from her cheeks. Involuntarily she touched her forearm where the words, *Nur für Offizere* had once been. She stepped back as though she had been struck. She felt the stares of everyone in the lobby. The silence was palpable, and then she heard the hum of whispered voices among the other volunteers.

Dr. Baruch, his expression icy, appeared at the end of the hallway. He stood rooted, glaring at the scene in the lobby. Baruch knew the full truth about Rachel. She turned toward him. Their eyes met. He shook his head from side to side, then raised his chin as an unspoken cue for her to regain her composure.

"Rachel . . . ," Yehudit faltered sympathetically. Then her eyes flashed. "Go on. I'll take care of this." To the Krepske brothers Yehudit fumed, "*Oy!* You two! You're such liars even the devil won't believe you!"

Don't ever come in here again like this unless you have important news! Like the King of England has arrived with the President of America to stop the war!" She shoved them toward the exit.

Leo argued, "Rabbi Akiva says he doesn't want to see you either, Yehudit."

"Is that a fact?" Yehudit spat. "Tell my father the mayor that if he wants to see Doctor Baruch he had better have a good reason. Like a head wound! *Nu?* And he can crawl in through the front door like everybody else! Now get out!"

The brothers, hammering on one another for position, banged out the door.

Yehudit opened her mouth to speak to Rachel, who seemed unable to move.

Nothing.

Yehudit's gaze flitted to Rachel's arm. The scar was covered, but still Yehudit saw it. Everyone in Misgav Ladakh knew it was there.

Rachel tried to smile, to shrug off the confrontation. Dr. Baruch laid a hand on her shoulder.

"Trouble?" he asked, though he had seen enough to know.

"My father," Yehudit muttered. "Trouble. Always."

Comforted by Baruch's touch, Rachel drew a ragged breath. She said quietly, "Rabbi Akiva . . . the mayor . . . wants to talk with you. He is outside."

Baruch nodded curtly. "When he wants to talk to me, he knows where he will find me."

In that same instant the door burst open. Akiva, flanked by two other rabbis from Nissan Bek, stood glowering at Baruch.

Akiva's face was flushed with anger. "Doctor Baruch!" He spoke the name as if it were a command to come to attention.

Baruch stepped between Akiva and Rachel. He whispered to her, "Go, quickly." She obeyed, hurrying into an adjoining room. She stood at the door and watched Baruch. "Keep your voice down," Baruch replied to Akiva. "This is a hospital, not the bema of a synagogue."

Akiva blustered, "There will be no hospital or synagogue left standing in the Jewish Quarter unless you listen to me."

Yehudit approached her father. "Papa . . . ," she protested.

Akiva ignored her. His eyes narrowed obstinately at the sound of her voice. His face hardened. He addressed Baruch alone. "I have spoken with Sachar. Told him there is a chance. If we in the Jewish Quarter will surrender to the Arab Legion . . . They have promised . . . twenty-four hours . . . in good faith they have promised not to shell the Quarter. If we will lay down our arms and surrender, all will be well."

Baruch held up his hand to interrupt the rabbi. "And what was Commander Sachar's reply?"

"He will not listen to reason. A stubborn, foolish man! He will get us killed! We will lose everything! You know the truth. No medicine. Your wounded need more than this! We will all perish. Women. Children. I have forbidden the young men of my congregation to fight. But peace-loving though they are, they will die with the rest of the youth in the Quarter unless we . . . men of goodwill . . . make an end to this trumped-up war. If everyone simply refuses to fight . . . If the civilians en masse refuse to help . . . what will Sachar do? It will be finished."

Baruch considered the words of Akiva for what seemed like a long time. Raising his eyes, he sighed. "You are right."

Yehudit gasped. Baruch shot her a look demanding silence.

Akiva softened. He almost smiled. "I knew you were the man to talk to."

Baruch queried, "How many young men of fighting age do you have in your congregation, Rabbi?"

"Forty-two. Moshe Sachar has tried to recruit them and failed. There are a handful who have gone over to his side to fight without my permission. I do not consider them part of my congregation any longer. Some"—he stared at Yehudit—"some traitors. They will get their just reward. *Omaine.*"

Baruch eyed him bitterly. "There are twenty persons on the hospital grounds who cannot walk away. They cannot leave without help. I need strong men. Stretcher-bearers to carry them to a better place."

Akiva smiled broadly. He had won. "Of course! Of course! I will send the young men of my congregation to help."

Baruch nodded. "Tonight. At dusk."

"Just as you say! *Nu?*" Akiva puffed happily. "Dusk it is! They will be proud to assist in any way!"

"So," Baruch concluded. "It is settled."

"Well done!"

"And now . . . I have work to do." The interview was at an end. Baruch turned on his heel and strode back toward the surgery.

Akiva and his companions left the building.

Yehudit trailed after Baruch.

Rachel emerged from the ward and called after him. "Please! Doctor Baruch!"

He paused, rubbed a hand over his aching neck, and then explained wearily, "We have a truce tonight, thanks to the good rabbi. There are twenty dead lying in the shed out back. They cannot leave us unless they are carried. And buried. Forty strong young men should be able to manage the job tonight, eh?" There was a glint in his eye as he addressed Yehudit. "What do you think, Yehudit?"

■ ■ ■ ■

Moshe hurried his pace. Did a tunnel lead from the Old City beneath the Sephardi synagogue outside to Mount Zion and David's Tomb?

Grandfather would know if the legend was fact or fiction. The old man had guided, or rather misguided, the archaeologists of the Parker Mission through the labyrinth beneath the hill of Ophel just after the turn of the century.

In 1908 an eccentric European named Juvelius claimed to have deciphered secrets from the Book of Ezekiel. Among these messages was the location of temple treasures hidden just before the Babylonian destruction of Jerusalem in 586 B.C. The concealed trove was supposed to include the original manuscript of the Torah as well as the ark of the covenant.

The hefty sum of twenty-five thousand pounds sterling was raised under the direction of an English captain named Montague Parker.

One of the chief guides of the expedition was a young, robust Jewish scholar named Shlomo Lebowitz. Thanks to him, the search concentrated outside the walls of the Old City, around the Spring of Gihon. It continued for three unsuccessful years. When the money ran low, the leaders of the expedition spread rumors that treasure had been found. This was an abysmal lie. Valuable archaeological data was recorded, however, by a French scholar named Vincent. Because of this one Frenchman, the mission was at least a scientific success. Moshe was acquainted with Vincent's writings. They contained the most complete descriptions of the underground water systems beneath the hill of Ophel.

When Parker's search around the Spring of Gihon proved a failure,

Shlomo Lebowitz was dismissed. He had managed to keep the treasure hunters away from the Temple Mount and the true treasure of the Temple Library, which was concealed beneath it.

Dismissing Grandfather, the Parker Mission secretly began digging at night. The exploration shifted to the Temple Mount in an area known as Solomon's Stables and in certain tunnels to the north of the temple area. To gain access to the temple the English adventurers dressed in Arab garb. Grandfather followed them for nine nights and then informed the authorities of the illegal excavation. Word of their violation of the sacred Mount spread like fire through Jerusalem. It was the time of Muslim pilgrimage to the Holy City. Riots began, and the Englishmen were forced to flee for their lives onto a yacht moored in Jaffa.

Forty years later, Grandfather was still guiding curious treasure hunters and scholars away from the actual tunnel that led to the cache of priceless manuscripts stored beneath the Temple Mount.

Would he know if there was truly a means to escape underground from the Old City without violating his oath?

Moshe found the old man among the Torah scrolls of the boys' school of the Hurva compound.

Grandfather glanced up as Moshe entered. "*Shalom,*" he said in a distracted voice. "The Legion has stopped shelling for the day. What does it mean?"

Moshe answered truthfully. "I have just met with Akiva."

Grandfather scowled. "And what black news does the mayor have for us?"

"He has something to do with this . . . with the lull in the fighting. Somehow he has been in touch with the Legion. They have given a sort of ultimatum: twenty-four hours for us to surrender."

"And then?"

"Then they aim their artillery at the Jewish Quarter again."

"Will they let civilians pass in safety?"

"It is all or nothing."

"I see." The old man furrowed his brow. "And you have come to ask . . ."

"The legend about the tunnel from the Sephardi synagogue outside the Old City to David's Tomb?"

Grandfather sighed. "Not a legend. Very little in Jerusalem is legend. What wild tales we hear are at least partly rooted in truth."

"Then we could evacuate the civilians? The wounded?" Moshe felt the surge of hope.

"That tunnel was sealed when I was a boy. Did I not tell you? A friend of mine . . . we were children . . . he entered, fell down a shaft, and the tunnel was sealed."

"Sealed? Can it be opened?"

"It was dynamited. Blocked with tons of stone. That is one passage which will never be opened."

Moshe rubbed his cheek in thought. "Is there . . . any other way?"

Grandfather did not reply. He turned back to the Torah scroll open before him.

Moshe tried again. "I mean, is there any way of escape that would not violate your vow?"

"And *your* vow?"

"And mine. For the sake of saving lives."

"I will tell you something, Moshe. All of life is contained in one scroll of the Torah. The secret place I have shared with you—and you only—contains all the collected commentary on the Torah. God has given us a glimpse of Himself in the numbers and words He gave. He gave us everything. The Word is living, fluid. It quenches our thirst like pure cool water. There is nothing more precious in all the world than what God has hidden in His Word and what is hidden beneath the Temple Mount. I cannot risk losing what centuries of men have died to preserve. *Nu?*"

Moshe nodded. He studied the darkening sky. Akiva indeed had some influence on the Arab force. At least the Jewish defenders had been given time to regroup, to prepare.

"You are right. Yes. You are right," Moshe said. "I was hoping there was another way."

"We will have to hold them back. Hold them as long as we can."

"And will the Arab Legion come knocking on the door of the Hurva tomorrow, Moshe?" Rabbi Lubetkin asked as he sat down at a study table in the Torah school library.

"Today we were lucky," Moshe said to the old man.

"If your children and grandchildren are healthy, you are lucky. Ask Hannah Cohen, who lost young Nathan today. Or Mrs. Kurtzman, driven from the shelter of Nissan Bek with her children. Now those souls are but a little way above us. God rest them. We were not so lucky."

"Yes. Nathan. A fine lad. The Kurtzman children." Moshe, sobered by the thought of such loss, lowered his voice to a murmur. "And yet, the armored cars of the Arab Legion did not come to Damascus Gate. That is what I mean. Today they did not come ahead."

"And tomorrow?"

"We can hope for miracles, but don't rely on one."

"Is that all you have to say to me? Well, then . . . half an answer also says something, *nu?*"

"I am not trying to be obscure. I simply cannot say what stopped them from coming today or what tomorrow will bring."

The rabbi tugged his beard thoughtfully. "If it doesn't get better, depend on it, it will get worse."

Moshe agreed wearily. "Well spoken."

"How's this?" The rabbi held up his finger to punctuate the meaning. "When the toothache comes, you forget your headache."

Moshe grinned in spite of the seriousness of the situation. "Haj Amin and the Arab Irregulars were a headache."

"So the Arab Legion with its tanks and cannons and English officers has come all the way to Jerusalem from Jordan to become our toothache." Grandfather raised his bushy eyebrows in comprehension. "*Oy.*"

Moshe nodded and continued, "You know what Akiva is saying to his congregation. 'A bad peace is better than a good war.'"

"Corn will grow on a pile of manure!" The old man snorted. "He, who turned away Mrs. Kurtzman because she was Sephardi! On his word nothing will stand. With such a man as Akiva for our mayor, why should we worry about the Mufti or King Abdullah? I did not vote for him. *Pffeh!*"

"There is a new sentiment among the people of Nissan Bek," Moshe explained carefully. "Since the Arab Legion has arrived, they no longer fear a massacre. There is a strong feeling that perhaps the Quarter should surrender."

The rabbi's eyes blazed. "They sell Jerusalem at a cheap price! Their lives for Jerusalem! True? And you, Moshe, Commander Sachar . . . You who know what treasure we alone guard beneath the Jewish Quarter of Jerusalem . . . what do you say? Do we hand over even one Torah scroll to a Muslim *goniff* who tears up the Holy Scriptures to take to the privy with him?"

"You know my answer. As for myself I am prepared to die here. But

Rachel. The others. The children. I cannot say what will happen when the armored cars of the Legion reach Damascus Gate. When the artillery on Olivet turns on the Quarter again. It may be that I will die, and the Quarter will have no choice but to place itself in the hands of the enemy. You must be aware of the possibility. For the sake of the treasures you protect."

Grandfather rubbed his hand over his face as if to wake from a dream. "Yes. I can see where these thoughts come from and where they may lead. And I must tell you what I wished never to say. If we are driven from the Quarter . . . either by defeat or by surrender . . . then I have a sacred duty to protect the treasures beneath the Temple Mount."

"How can they be more protected?"

"The library vault will be sealed. From within. You understand?"

"From within the chamber?" Moshe struggled to grasp what the old man was saying plainly.

"And if I should die before I reach the vaults, then one must take my place and fulfill the vow to protect the sacred texts. Do you understand me, boy?"

Moshe nodded, imagining his own entombment far beneath Jerusalem. "There is a way that this could be accomplished?"

"The builders of the chambers were master masons supervised by Onias, the high priest of the temple. Their skill has made the sealing of the chamber a matter of knowing how. I will show you tonight. I must show you tonight!"

Moshe would gladly die to save such a wealth of knowledge for a future generation. He added, "I mean to warn you. If there is anything . . . any sacred text . . . here aboveground in the Old City . . . anything at all that needs to be concealed or protected . . . you see, don't you? You see what I am suggesting to you."

"You are saying that what we Jews face here in the shadow of Solomon's wall is the same annihilation we faced when the Babylonians came to destroy Jerusalem on the ninth of Av. When the Greeks desecrated the temple in the days of Judah Maccabee. When the Romans camped upon the hills round about and burned Jerusalem and the temple."

"Yes. That is what I am saying. This may be the same as those terrible days. The people are hungry. More than the matter of bread . . . the drinking water is low. A cup a day per person. We can eat weeds that grow in the cracks of pavement, but without water, how long will the people survive?"

"As long as one can move even a finger it is difficult to think of the grave. But destruction is . . . inevitable, then? Surrender?"

"Thirst is a greater enemy than all the Legion's bullets."

"And the temple library?"

"Has it ever been sealed before?"

"Never. Always one of us stayed behind to guard the passage from chance intruders. Always . . . ready to pluck out the keystone from its place and close the gate to wisdom until the coming King opens it again. But, God be praised, it has not been required."

"And let us hope it will not be. But if it is . . . rest easy, Grandfather. I would give my life to save what you have protected."

"So. You are a good boy, Moshe. You would have made a fine rabbi, *nu?*"

"My father thought as much."

"You father is spinning in his grave at the sight of you today," the old man teased.

"And my mother."

"God forbid she is looking down on this! There will be no peace in Paradise if she is watching!" He clapped Moshe on the back. His voice became grave. "I thought there would be more time. More . . . time." His eyes gazed sadly around the room. "The years I have spent in this place . . . ah, well. I cannot think about the past. No time. The future has burst upon us like a thief. The present is what we have. . . . There are indeed things we must conceal. A scroll. A shofar. I will need your help. And there are things I must reveal to you before the night ends, and the Arab Legion comes to the gates of Jerusalem."

# CHAPTER 13

The leaders of the Arab Legion gathered in the mosque of Sheikh Jarrah. The consolidation of Arab positions along the ridge above Mea Shearim was complete. Captain Hakeem stood stiffly upright. His bandaged wounds were too painfully inflexible to allow him to sit. He answered questions about the failure of the morning's attack.

"The pitiful blockades erected by the Jews would not have stopped my assault if it had not been for the shell that fell short," he said defensively. Hakeem knew that the morphine injection made him slur his words, so he chose each phrase carefully and delivered each syllable with precision.

To Legion Chief John Glubb, Hakeem sounded like a mechanical man. "Tomorrow they will have more barricades, better manned and with better weapons," he said. "Today's best hope was speed and surprise. Tomorrow will require more . . . tactical planning . . . and infantry support."

Major Tariq Athani, commanding the Legion infantry in Jerusalem, had been called away from his attack on the Old City to help plan the assault on the New. "My men are ready," he said.

"Now," Glubb said, "about the proper axis for the push. There are two possibilities: The first route is down Saint George Road into the center of Mea Shearim. This, while the most direct, would require fighting through the Jewish-held area. The second course is down the Nablus Road, through Arab-held Musrara to the Damascus Gate. Once there, we have an unbroken line of communication and supply from Ramallah to the Old City. We can then turn and drive west along the Old City wall to Zion Square."

"This will prolong the conquest of the New City," Hakeem argued.

"But will result in the fewest casualties," Glubb responded. "After today, I think we are agreed that another headlong rush will not succeed. And there is one more factor. His Majesty King Abdullah has expressed his concern that we secure the holy places before anything else. To do that, we must eliminate resistance in the Jewish district of the Old City. All right, here it is: Hakeem, you will send the main body of armor and infantry straight down the hill to the Damascus Gate. Shelling at oh-five-hundred hours will soften up the area for rollout at six-hundred hours. Questions? Comments?"

There was only one. "May I suggest," Hakeem said thickly, "that one of the first armored cars carry an experienced artillery spotter? From a vantage point in Musrara he can by radio correct the aim of the Olivet battery."

Glubb looked at Hakeem with sympathy. The man had been overeager, but he had no lack of courage. "Well thought of," Glubb said. "Just be certain that the driver in the lead car can follow orders explicitly as to which route to take."

■ ■ ■ ■

Major Luke Thomas, Peter Wallich, and Jacob Kalner stood on the roof of the Mandelbaum house. They were grouped around a T-shaped black handle that protruded from a dull green box. With Thomas's help, Jacob had rigged electric wires from that box to a mine that would destroy the spice merchant's house and trap part of the Arab Legion in an ambush.

From their lookout, the three men could see the minaret of Sheikh Jarrah's mosque. Built as a lean, six-sided structure, one sharp edge of the Muslim prayer tower faced directly toward Mea Shearim. In the afternoon light it looked like a sword blade slashing downward toward Jewish Jerusalem.

"There are just two routes once they get below the village," Thomas said, waving his arm and pointing as he spoke. "Straight down the Nablus Road to the Old City wall is the first possibility. But if they are coming at us, they will take Saint George Road where it forks to the right off the Nablus Road and be in our laps five minutes after leaving Sheikh Jarrah."

"And which do you think they will choose?" Peter asked.

"Before this morning's battle I would have said they would meet us head-on. But now I think they will use Arab Musrara as cover and go directly to link up with the Arab Quarter of the Old City," Thomas said. "There is nothing we can do about that route—nothing. Once they get past Kalner's roadblock below Sheikh Jarrah—and we cannot count on further cooperation from Arab artillery to stop them—once past that curve, it is direct to the Damascus Gate. All the time out of reach of our guns. Then the focus of our defense must become the Hospice of Notre Dame."

Link up with the Old City! Jacob tasted mingled frustration and fear, and the flavor was vile. His efforts had helped delay the Arabs for one day, but in so doing had he set them on the path that presented the most direct threat to Lori? It could not be!

Dominating the northern approach to the wall of the Old City, the French Hospice of Notre Dame appeared as a massive fortress. Fought over ever since Jewish independence was proclaimed, the building was now in Jewish hands, but young and inexperienced ones at that.

"Can it hold?" Jacob asked, turning to study the multistoried granite building.

"As with all things in this war," Thomas admitted, "it would be better if we had more time to reinforce it and prepare."

"Perhaps I can be reassigned there?" Jacob said hurriedly, thinking again of placing himself between the Arab Legion and his wife.

Major Thomas disagreed. "What if I'm wrong?" he said. "We cannot leave this route undefended, nor," he added, pointing at the detonator, "can we miss a chance to snare and destroy part of their vehicles. No, what we need is another miracle like this morning's misdirected cannonfire, something that sends them into our hands. But we cannot expect it."

■ ■ ■ ■

An hour into the flight north toward the kibbutz of Zorash, David Meyer noticed that Bobby Milkin seemed grumpier than normal. "What's up, Milkin?" he asked. "Worried? No fog reported in Galilee. Piece of cake. Drop off the jeep and the passengers. We're out again in half an hour, tops." All David received in reply was a groan. "What's with you?"

A colossal gurgling sound echoed in the cockpit and finally Milkin said, "I don't feel so good. Ever since that lamb and rice . . . I don't think that lamb was strictly lamb, you know? My guts are . . . how soon we gonna be there anyway?"

David laughed in spite of the pained expression on his friend's face. "Hold on, cowboy," he said. "Twenty minutes or less."

Another rumble from the copilot's chair convinced David of the necessity to make it "or less."

The airfield outside Zorash, code-named *Brooklyn*, was not even as regular a facility as *Oklahoma*. There was no airstrip, merely a smoothed field. There was no tower and no radio communication with the ground. The Haganah holding the area had been told to light their runway beacons at nine o'clock and David would find them.

True to the compass and the correct elapsed time, the yellow gleam of flames appeared on the horizon. David glanced again at Bobby Milkin. This was serious. There was no cigar clamped in Milkin's jaw. Instead he was holding it in his hands, shredding it into flakes. Beads of sweat were all over his brow. "Get us down, okay?" he asked plaintively. "Else I'm gonna have a problem, see?"

Knowing Bobby was not going to be of any use in the landing, David hammered on the door to the cargo bay and yelled, "Get ready! We're landing."

He circled the area marked by the flames. The strip was identified by only two bonfires, one at each end.

David muttered, "Gee, really went all out for us, didn't they?"

Even so, the landing would present no problem. Visibility was perfect. There was no moon, but the improvised signal fires marked the runway plainly enough. The windsock, beside a tin shed at the near end of the strip, hung straight down.

"Here we go, Milkin. Relief is in sight. Gear down, half flaps." He recited the litany of the landing routine to himself.

The DC-4 floated lazily toward the ground. When the wheels settled into the soft earth, the nose dipped from the drag, but not severely. David taxied the transport to a standstill about three quarters of the way along the length of the strip. His hand hovered over the switches to kill the engines while he listened momentarily to their rhythmic hum.

Milkin was already unstrapped from his harness and plunging toward the door.

One of the gunnery officers stood in the entry to the cockpit. "Nice landing," he offered.

"Get out of my way!" Milkin bellowed, sweeping the man aside.

The urgency in Milkin's manner was amusing, but David's attention was fixed on the nearby runway flare. Instead of a barrel containing kerosene-soaked sand, the flames shot up from a truck overturned in a ditch.

"Bobby, wait! Something's not right!"

A file of soldiers emerged from the dark halo ringing the burning lorry. They were wearing khaki uniforms and helmets, and their weapons were pointed at the DC-4.

*Arabs!*

"Hang on!" David said, grasping the throttles and sending full power to the engines.

Milkin and the gunnery officer tangled together and fell to the deck.

Sluggishly, reluctantly, the wheels revolved in the soil's embrace. The plane bumped across the furrows.

Gunfire popping, David cranked the control stick and stomped the rubber pedals. He sent the transport into a tight turn and aimed it at the other end of the runway. Bellowing from the back told him that the outside cargo hatch was open. "Close it!" he yelled. "We're getting out of here!"

More figures appeared, lining the strip. A bullet smacked into the windshield, grazed it, and shrieked off in the dark. Hammer blows rang along the hull.

*God, don't let them hit anything crucial! Come on, come on!*

He heard confused shouting from the back and knew that the hatch was not secured.

*Hope nobody falls out.*

David forced himself to watch the speed indicator even though he wanted to bodily yank the plane into the air right then!

*A third of the way to the opposite end.*

*Half.*

*Three quarters.*

*Feeling the moment when contact with the earth is lessening, weight coming off the gear and onto the wings.*

*A flurry of shots from the right.*

*A sudden tilt in that direction!*

*An uncontrollable shudder. Tire shot out!*

*Get up, you! This can't happen! We've already made it!*

*The landing gear dug into the soil, bent, crumpled.*

*The starboard wing dipped, touched the rocky field.*

Instantly the DC-4 slued around in a circle!

*More shouts from the back as unbelted men were tossed and tumbled. Louder crashes when crates of ammunition and equipment broke loose from their moorings and smashed about the cabin.*

*The wing snapped off.*

What was left of the plane launched at a tangent to its death spiral.

*Sparks from the metal dragging. Fuel smell! Thick and plentiful.*

Unasked, David's mind did the calculation: *capable of fifteen hours without refueling. Ninety minutes used. Enough go juice to light a pyre they could see in Jerusalem!*

The cockpit jerked forward as if trying to tear free from the rest of the fuselage.

The shattered airframe landed on the slope of a ditch, broadside to the runway, hatch on the side facing the darkness.

"Everybody out and run for it!" David shouted.

"Avi!" someone said. "He's under the jeep!"

"Take Milkin! I'll get Avi!"

*More gunshots from the Arabs, then miraculously, some in reply from the ditch.*

*A break at last!*

*The Israelis had thought to take their weapons with them.*

David reached down. He was wearing a holstered revolver. From the bulkhead behind the pilot's seat he grabbed a flare pistol loaded with one shell.

Pinned against the bulkhead by the vehicle, Avi was crushed, dead.

*Can't leave the Arabs a jeep, machine guns, mortar, ammo. Gotta torch this pile.*

Fuel pooled on the ground under the wreck.

"Get clear!" David yelled. "It's gonna blow!" As much as it was a warning to his comrades, he hoped the Arabs would be frightened into keeping away too.

Backing toward the mounded blackness of the ditch, David aimed the flare pistol and squeezed the trigger. The leaking fuel exploded with a roar, engulfing the remains of the DC-4 in flames.

■ ■ ■ ■

A hillside orchard loomed ahead, promising a place to hide. His long legs churning, David plunged across the ditch and up the bank on the other side. A bullet whined past him, then the DC-4 exploded. Mortar shells detonated in the flaming wreck. Machine-gun slugs heated by the fire rattled like a pan of supercharged popcorn. Chunks of the plane's aluminum skin whirred through the air like sawblades.

Flinging himself prone, David hugged the ground. A jagged piece of propeller spiked down like a javelin and buried half its length three feet from where he lay.

*You gonna die like this, Meyer?* The ground around him was pocked by a hale of debris. Nuts! After all he had survived, here he was observing the means of his own death. There was something unacceptable about just lying there waiting to die from a piece of carburetor falling on his head.

Half-running, half-stumbling, he scrambled toward the cover of the orange orchard. He plastered himself to a tree trunk as bullets whizzed past.

When the explosions subsided and the roar of the inferno diminished, angry Arab voices succeeded them. Even without being able to understand the words, David knew that the exploding shells had caused enemy casualties.

*Score a couple for us, anyway.*

So where was Milkin? David had not seen him since the crash. Had he escaped?

David was hidden among the trees now.

*Orange trees, thick-trunked and brushy with foliage. Mean thorny branches like the ones back home in L.A.*

He remembered the night he and a dozen fraternity pledges had been ordered to strip naked and climb the orange trees. When they came down the next morning the fraternity brothers had driven off, leaving thirteen naked guys hiding in the orchard. Climb another orange tree? Only if his life depended on it.

More loud shouts and gunshots from behind urged him on.

Dashing down an avenue formed by the neat rows of trees, David glanced over his shoulder to check for pursuit.

*This ain't L.A., buddy. Keep your head!*

A fallen branch tripped him, pitching him sideways.

Lunging for a handhold to keep from sprawling, his body swung round and his right foot encountered only air.

He clung to the last orange tree above a sheer drop.

*How deep is this hole?*

His hands pierced with two-inch-long spines, David wormed his way in toward the trunk and headed up. His cowboy boots slipped on the branches. Spiked in the shoulders and the top of his head, one thorn gouged a furrow in the back of his neck.

Then he heard two men approaching. He froze.

Had they heard him?

David's breathing sounded like the puffing of a steam locomotive. Gravel crunched under pairs of booted feet. The searchers argued vehemently about something. Their strident voices covered the boom of his thumping heart.

The steps came to a halt directly beside his tree.

*Don't breathe!*

One of the two Arabs chose that instant to step past David's tree. With a shriek and a string of oaths, the leading searcher nearly fell from the precipice. A clatter of metal followed as the man dropped his rifle and his helmet. The helmet rolled over the edge of the cliff. It was a long time before David heard it hit bottom.

More swearing, followed by nervous laughter.

David willed thoughts into their heads. *Nobody here, pal. No point looking. What kind of fool would climb an orange tree? Go home, have a beer! Relax!*

Moments later the pursuers retreated down the hill.

# CHAPTER 14

I t had been hours since the piping voice of tiny Abe Kurtzman had been heard. Except for Alfie Halder no one believed the child remained alive beneath the crushing weight of the broken house.

Four Kurtzman children lay side by side on the cobbled lane. Their lifeless bodies were covered with a tattered quilt and a tablecloth.

Alfie towered over them, his simple face a mask of grief, wide-set eyes seeing things no one else could see.

From a smashed bedstead in the ruins he rescued two pillows. He knelt and tenderly placed the pillows beneath the heads of the dead children. "You will wake up," he whispered, caressing each cheek. "And there won't be no more war. You'll see. It was a bad dream. Everything will be beautiful."

"Doesn't he know they are dead?" asked a Hasid bitterly.

"He knows . . . something." Lori could not explain about Alfie. How could she explain what she did not understand herself? She laid her hand on his shoulder. "Come on, then, Alfie."

Alfie glanced up, "This road to the Promised Land is a hard road, Lori."

She knew from his tone that he was not talking about the road, but about something else. Life.

"Yes," she said.

"They have gone ahead to the good place without him." Alfie turned his back on the four bodies. "Mama too. He will need you. You should sing to him. The way you and the baby used to sing in the garden." He resumed digging.

Lori stared at his broad back, resenting the reminder that she had once been able to sing. Had Alfie heard her speak of that quiet summer in the garden?

*The baby learned to walk in May, the same week England's sons were*

*dying on the beach at Dunkirk. In Primrose Hill I worried about every-*
*thing while I pruned the roses. The baby toddled to me, patted my back,*
*and began to sing. His words were not words, but simply praise and joy. He*
*did not know about the war, about the heartache that had brought us to*
*England. There were the roses in bloom. The plane tree was in leaf. Every*
*blade of grass was a miracle. I thought somehow that God must under-*
*stand why he was singing. Maybe the song of a baby was valued more in*
*heaven than all my prayers. I began to sing with him and was not afraid*
*anymore. . . .*

Alfie heaved a ponderous stone to the side, then turned fiercely on
Lori. "Did you hear? I told you! He is little. He is scared. Sing to him!"
He pointed to a triangular opening in the debris.

Everyone in the rescue crew paused a second. What was this half-
wit giant talking about? Lori felt their eyes resenting Alfie for his hope.
There was death here. How dare he expect life?

She nodded, then obeyed Alfie's command.

What if the boy was alive? Would singing keep him breathing long
enough? She knelt beside the opening.

What song would a Jewish baby know? Never mind. It was not the
words that mattered. Softly she began to sing the French lullaby her
baby had loved.

> *Drop down dew, you heavens above,*
> *let clouds rain on the Just,*
> *let the earth be opened*
> *and bud forth a Savior.*
> *Miracle of loving.*
> *Like roses blooming in a garden . . .*

■ ■ ■ ■

The moon looked like a slice of candied orange peel hanging above Jerusalem, thought Yacov. Tantalizing. Delicious. Enough for everyone. He
wanted to forget what he had seen at the Kurtzman house.

He would have liked to climb onto the spike of the minaret at the
far end of the Street of the Chain and pluck the moon out of the sky. He
was that hungry. "It is only the moon," he said to his dog, Shaul. "And if
it was a giant slice of orange peel? Why should you care? You rat catcher.
Stuff your belly with rats as if nothing has changed."

The dog padded beside him.

"Steal your supper from the Arabs in the souks like always. You know they feed you because they think you are a fine Muslim dog. *Insh'-Allah*. A true dog of Allah and his Prophet. They do not know you are a Jew, Shaul, or they would kill you."

The dog did not reply.

Yacov carried the bag of meager provisions to the front-line barricade where Dov and Ehud stood first watch.

*"Shalom!"* Yacov called as he approached the barricade.

"It is supper?" Ehud asked.

"It is something like supper," Yacov replied.

Dov laughed. "What has Hannah Cohen sent us tonight?"

Yacov sniffed the bag. "Pita bread. Stuffed with . . . something."

Dov replied in Yiddish, *"Fun loiter hofenung . . .* stuff yourself with hope, and you can go crazy."

Ehud added, "After last night I had such wind!"

"True," Dov agreed. "It was Ehud's wind alone that chased the Mufti's soldiers out of the Old City!"

"So," Yacov said, "we should pray for a favorable breeze again tonight, eh?"

"Any breeze." Ehud took the food from him. "The air is hot."

"Is there coffee?" Dov asked.

A canteen was slung around Yacov's shoulder. "Cold. Left from this morning."

"It is too hot for hot coffee anyway." Ehud sniffed the nameless stuffing inside the pita bread. "Onions? Is there anything else?"

At that, Shaul whined.

"Nothing for you!" Dov scolded the animal.

Shaul stiffened and bristled, staring out past the barricade into the deserted street.

Ehud and Dov came to attention. They snapped up their rifles and faced the void. "Get down!" Dov warned Yacov.

"What is it?" Ehud whispered.

Shaul barked and snarled menacingly.

"There's a good dog," Dov remarked. "Better than ten watchmen on the walls."

There was a stirring in the shadows. Yacov felt the skin on his neck tighten. "Someone is there," he said.

Shaul growled again.

Neither Dov nor Ehud would shoot until they had clear sight of the enemy. No use wasting one precious bullet on a stray cat.

"Halt!" Ehud bellowed, keeping low. "Halt, or you are dead!"

From the inky space a man's voice replied in Yiddish, "Don't shoot! My God! I am one of you! *Bitte!*"

"Who is there!" Ehud demanded.

"My name is Dieter. Dieter Wottrich! My God! I am one of you!" He said urgently, "Let me in! I got lost! Lost! I've been hiding in the basement of . . . my God! Let me pass!"

Ehud and Dov exchanged looks. Ehud kept his rifle ready. "*Got hit op di naronim!*" he said.

From the shadows the newcomer repeated, "Yes! *Oy!* God does indeed watch over fools! And I am the biggest fool of all! *Bitte!* Let me pass!"

"Come ahead, then," Dov said. "Remember, one false move, and you are a dead fool!"

■ ■ ■ ■

Concerned faces looked on as Dieter Wottrich sat against the sandbags and gulped down nearly a full canteen of precious water. A two-day ration went down his gullet and also down the front of his shirt.

Shaul whined and licked moisture from Wottrich's face. The man patted the dog, slopped a bit of water in his palm, and offered it to Shaul.

Ehud said gruffly, "The dog finds his own water." He took the empty canteen from the newcomer.

Ah well, Yacov thought, the fellow was half dead from thirst. No water since yesterday.

Ehud asked, "What did you see out there? Anything?"

Wottrich replied, "Much. Yes. The Arab Legion is here in force."

"How many did you see?"

"What sort of weapons?"

"Ammunition? Supplies?"

Wottrich looked up sharply. "Where is your commander?"

Dov replied, "You mean Moshe Sachar? He is at the Hurva, I think. On the radio. Begging the New City Jerusalem Command to send us reinforcements and supplies."

Ehud added, "From his mouth to God's ears, eh?"

Dov concluded, "From God's mouth to Shaltiel's ears along with a kick in the ass!"

Ehud said, "At least God has sent us one more defender. True, Dieter Wottrich? Better late than never. And what did you bring in that satchel of yours? A tank? A cannon?"

"A pot of strawberry jam is what I have been dreaming of." Dov pawed through Wottrich's pack.

"Medical supplies," Wottrich said.

"And not much at that," Dov noted. "At least did you bring information about Arab positions? What did you see out there?"

Wottrich stood stiffly. "I should first report to the commander. Commander Sachar, yes?"

Ehud shrugged. "You think he will be surprised to hear we are surrounded and outnumbered, eh?"

Dov instructed Yacov, "Take the man to Moshe at the Hurva, will you? Tell Hannah Cohen he needs something to eat. Tell Moshe to tell Shaltiel . . . bullets and strawberry jam." He mussed Yacov's hair affectionately.

Ehud passed the pack of medical gear to Wottrich. "Welcome to hell. Trade this in for a rifle if you can find one."

■ ■ ■ ■

Enmeshed in the clutches of an orange tree, David could not move hand or foot without impaling himself on a vicious thorn. Gritting his teeth against each jab, he wriggled as high up the tree as he could manage. It would take a dedicated Arab to drag him down from this perch. Of course, if they discovered him they could shoot him and leave him hanging as a warning to others. In David's youth his uncle had paid him a penny apiece for each mockingbird dispatched in such a way in the old plum tree. It was not a pleasant memory right then.

Located at the top of the hill and rising above the rest of the orchard, David's tree offered a view back to the airstrip.

What he saw by the flickers of the burning wreckage was the roundup of Israeli soldiers. First one was prodded at bayonet point into the circle of light. Clubbed with the butt of a rifle, he fell to his knees and rocked, holding his head in his hands.

The second and third were brought back minutes later and similarly knocked down. Fifty or sixty Arabs around three helpless Jews.

Some time passed.

*Where is Bobby Milkin?*

Even from a distance, David knew none of the captured men was Bobby. His gorilla-like build was instantly recognizable.

The fourth snared Israeli was dragged back to the airfield by a trio of Arab soldiers. The ring of captors obscured David's view.

*Is it Milkin?*

Apparently unable to walk, the last captive was dumped unceremoniously in a heap.

*Not Bobby!*

All the Jewish fighters were accounted for, except Bobby Milkin.

Then the torture began.

It seemed that the Arabs did not know how many men had been on the plane when it landed. Nor did they know how many survived the crash to escape into the hills.

But they intended to find out.

David saw one of the Haganah gunnery officers—it looked like the one named Carmi—whipped across the teeth with a pistol barrel. When that abuse did not produce results, the pistol muzzle was placed behind Carmi's ear.

Moments later, the Arabs split up into three squads, leaving a handful to guard the crippled prisoner. Each group of enemy soldiers took one prisoner, and the reason was soon apparent.

At the edge of the orchard Carmi called, "Meyer! Milkin! Give yourselves up. If you come in, you won't be hurt."

*Yeah, right,* David thought.

In the distance the other two Jews were made to do the same.

Good news! Carmi was calling both names. It meant Milkin had not been killed trying to escape.

Carmi's words were muffled and hoarse.

"Meyer! If they see you running, you'll be shot! Come in! Give yourself up."

An Arab voice, but speaking in English, demanded, "Again! Call them again."

"I told you," Carmi replied. "I think they died in the fire. I didn't see them after the crash."

"Again!"

"Meyer! Milkin!"

Gingerly, David let a screen of leaves fold over him. As much as he wanted to keep watch, he was afraid of light reflecting off his face.

The search went on and on.

David had a horrible cramp in his right leg, but could not stretch it out. He did not dare cause the slightest rustling sound, or he would be caught.

Footsteps passing below him made him hold his breath till his chest burned. When at last he had to either breathe or pass out, he gulped in a lungful of air that smelled of orange blossoms. The incongruity between the sweet, cloying scent and the smell of fear from his own body was immense.

"Meyer! These are Syrians. They are real soldiers. They respect the Geneva conventions. We'll be treated as prisoners of war. Come out! We'll get medical aid . . . water. Come on! Elazar has two broken legs! Meyer! Milkin!"

The voices retreated down the hill. David waited till he counted five minutes, then pushed aside the foliage.

The DC-4 was reduced to a charred, glowing skeleton. The flames were dying, but still gave off enough illumination for David to see the ring of Arabs around their captives.

All four Jews were lined up again on their knees, their hands tied behind their backs. The Syrian commander waved his men aside, leaving a space through which David could see what followed.

The officer walked briskly up to each prisoner in turn, leveled his pistol, and shot the man behind the left ear. The first man had no warning and made no attempt to move. The second, third, and fourth were killed as they writhed helplessly in their bonds.

The delay of the sound in reaching David's location made the reports sound like distant claps of thunder.

*Give yourselves up! You won't be harmed!*

# CHAPTER 15

Moshe followed Grandfather into the sanctuary of the Hurva. The old man muttered without looking at Moshe, "And so the Hurva will once again be as it is named."

Moshe recalled that the word *hurva* meant "ruin" in Hebrew. This ignoble title was earned on November 8, 1720, on the Shabbat when the Torah reading began with God telling Abraham, "Get thee out. . . ." On that day the Arabs broke into the Ashkenazi Synagogue, tore up the Torah scrolls, and burned the building. One hundred years passed before the "ruin" was rebuilt in its present Byzantine splendor. The large, dark hall where Moshe and the rabbi stood was almost square. Four massive arches supported the dome, ringed by the balcony where Haganah and Ashkenazi stood watch. The dome, a landmark on the city skyline, was also an obvious target for the Legion artillery on the Mount of Olives. Moshe did not know why today the Arabs hesitated to make the Hurva a ruin once more.

On the eastern wall of the sanctuary stood the two-story ark. It had come from Russia. It was so large that twelve camels had been required to carry it from the port of Jaffa, up the pass of Bab el Wad, to Jerusalem. A Baroque masterpiece of ornately carved flowers and birds, it was one of Jerusalem's treasures. Set on the top between the Ionic pillars were tablets of the Ten Commandments. Two enormous bronze candelabra were a gift from the Czar's court tailor in St. Petersburg. The bema stood on a base of pink marble.

Moshe knew the dread of helplessness as he and Grandfather approached the ark. One shell fired from Olivet would destroy it in an instant.

And what about the spirit of the place? There were several study houses: batei midrash, talmudei Torah, yeshivot where generations of boys had attended school and grown up to become like the stooped old rabbi Moshe followed. Grandfather was one of the committee of Wise Men, a member of the Beit Din Zedek, the religious court. What would his life become if the Jewish Quarter should fall? If the Hurva were once again a ruin?

Moshe sighed. Now the Hurva was a refuge for its congregation. Seven cisterns held the precious water supply of the Quarter. One command issued from King Abdullah in Jordan would bring everything to an end. It seemed somehow inevitable to Moshe.

What was it that Grandfather would attempt to save from among the artifacts in the synagogue?

Grandfather approached the towering ark without ceremony. He unlocked a small door, revealing a windowless room in the interior. Moshe entered after him. Altar cloths, silver candlesticks, beeswax candles, and prayer books were stored in cupboards.

The rabbi ignored the more valuable items.

He tugged a keyring from the deep pocket of his long black coat. He stood before a cupboard and with a slight bow whispered the words, "The circle has come round, Moshe. The end has come to its beginning . . . beginning again. Remember the circle . . ." And then, "Blessed art thou, Oh Lord, who hath given us life and sustenance and allowed us to see this day. . . ."

Moshe watched, saying nothing. Why was the rabbi thanking God for a day so clearly loaded with portents of a catastrophic end for the Jewish community in the Old City?

The doors opened to reveal a long, twisted ram's horn, a shofar. On the lower shelf in the corner was a clay pitcher sealed with lead and stamped with the emblem of a seven-branched candlestick, the temple menorah.

Quietly Moshe began, "There is a legend about a jug of sacred oil and a shofar—"

"It is no legend," Grandfather replied, removing the shofar from its place and passing it to Moshe. "These remain from the days of the temple. The shofar will be blown to announce the coming of Messiah. The oil will anoint him." He cradled the jug of oil. "Without this building Messiah still will come. That is what we must think of tonight. So we each carry one thing to safety, *nu?* Come with me."

By the light of a tin lantern Moshe followed the aged rabbi down the steep stone steps to the subbasement of the Hurva Synagogue. An invisible wall panel was concealed behind a stack of crates. Moshe knew that from here a labyrinth of five passageways fanned out like the fingers of a hand beneath Jerusalem.

The old man turned to Moshe and tapped his forehead. "As you enter, remember," he instructed. "This is the gate of the Lord. The righteous shall enter it and find wisdom. A wise man hears one word but understands two. Everything means something. Everything!"

Moshe nodded.

They moved steadily onward through the musty passage toward the cavern of Solomon's masons, which contained the secret library of the ancient temple. A chill of excitement coursed through Moshe.

■ ■ ■ ■

Brandenburg followed Yacov Lubetkin and the dog through the unlit streets of the Jewish Quarter. The houses were unoccupied, he knew. Windows had been shattered by the concussion of the earlier shelling.

"A ghost town," he said aloud as they passed under the archway of a building that was built above the thoroughfare.

Yacov replied, "Everyone is staying in the synagogues, *nu?* They are afraid to stay in their homes. Nobody likes to be alone when they are scared."

At least, Brandenburg thought, this gave the artillery spotters on the Mount of Olives easy targets. A few well-placed shells would provide a solution to the Jewish problem in the Old City.

Brandenburg touched the Lüger semiautomatic pistol concealed in the waistband of his trousers. One shot to the head, and Moshe Sachar's influence would be at an end. In the same way, one definitive barrage aimed at the dome of a synagogue, and the citizens would be clamoring for surrender.

"You know your way around here," Brandenburg complimented Yacov.

"All the shortcuts," Yacov boasted.

"Have you lived here always, then?"

"No," the boy replied in a matter-of-fact tone. "Warsaw first. I was born in Warsaw. So I am told. But I do not remember. My sister is also from Warsaw. She looks like pictures of my mother. Very pretty. And she is married to Moshe Sachar." He was proud of this fact.

Brandenburg recalled the beauty of young Jewish women in Poland. It was a fact that officers in the SS had often remarked on. The brothels of SS officers, known as "The Stables," were stocked with Jewish "mares." While on leave during the war Brandenburg had taken advantage of his rank and had visited SS Stables in Germany and Poland. In matters of sexual pleasure, as in music and art, Jews provided Brandenburg with much he could appreciate.

"Your sister is pretty, is she?" Brandenburg queried.

"Some think so. Moshe thinks so." The boy trudged on.

"Did she escape Warsaw before the war? With you?"

"No," Yacov answered. "I thought she was dead. Grandfather thought she was dead. But then . . . here she was. Looking just like the photograph of Mama."

"She is lucky she survived," Brandenburg said in feigned sympathy.

"They say it is good to talk about troubles that are past. But she doesn't talk about it. Rabbi Akiva, who is rabbi of Nissan Bek Synagogue, has said terrible things about her. I don't know all of it. Grandfather says Rabbi Akiva has an evil tongue. But maybe someday Rachel will tell me about Mama. How she died. And my father and brothers. But maybe it is too soon." Yacov did not reduce his pace as they climbed a set of steep stairs.

"Yes."

"Where are you from?"

"Germany," Brandenburg answered truthfully. He did not mention Dresden.

"Ah. Then you are not religious."

"Not at all."

"Many Jews came to Palestine from Germany. My grandfather is a rabbi. He says German Jews are not so interested in learning Torah as Jews from Poland. Some were baptized. But it made no difference. The Nazis arrested them too. Gassed them just the same. So, what city?"

Brandenburg recalled the details gleaned in the interrogation of the real Dieter Wottrich. "Hamburg."

"Did you work there?"

"I was a schoolteacher."

"Were you arrested? Put in a camp?"

"Yes."

"Which one?"

Brandenburg did not answer. Too much detail could trip him up. "You ask too many questions. When will we be there?"

"Soon." They progressed in silence for five minutes. Then Yacov blurted, "There is the entrance to the courtyard of the Hurva. We are Polish Jews here. Nissan Bek is where Akiva is the rabbi. He is also the mayor." This was announced in a dismissive tone. "He does not think much of the idea of Israel. He does not like Jews from Poland either. His daughter married Dov Avram. Dov is also from Warsaw. He is a hero. He killed a thousand Nazis in the Ghetto uprising, *nu?* A Polish Jew. When Akiva's daughter—her name is Yehudit—she is a *mensch,* a person! . . . So, when she married Dov, it was a scandal." Yacov took pleasure that Akiva was not happy with the match. It was plain the boy was not fond of the rabbi of Nissan Bek. "Maybe Moshe will put you on duty over there."

"First I must meet Moshe. Yes?"

"So!" Yacov stepped aside and gave a bow as Brandenburg entered the compound.

■ ■ ■ ■

"Here we are," Yacov announced as he led Robert Brandenburg toward the stairs leading to the basement of the Hurva Synagogue. "But first I have advice for you."

"Yes? and what is that?"

"Stay away from Hannah Cohen. She likes to make newcomers work in the kitchen. *Oy,* is she a slave driver! Tell her that you have important business with Commander Sachar."

That was exactly what he would do, Brandenburg thought.

The thick door opened to reveal a spectacle of babble and confusion. Except that these people were cheerful, it was not unlike the scenes at Croatian train stations. As an SS officer, Brandenburg had been in charge of rounding up *Untermenschen* and deporting them to concentration camps. Then as now, children were underfoot everywhere, some lost and crying, others making nuisances of themselves with games of tag, which the frightened adults failed to control. People tried to sleep, but how they could do it amid the noise was impossible to imagine. In a corner a group of elderly men prayed in a circle, their heads bobbing as if they were bearded marsh birds. In another corner a lone rabbi traced a page of a commentary with his finger, though his eyes looked into another world.

It gave Brandenburg an unpleasantly peculiar sense. It was like being inside the barbed wire with those about to learn the real truth about the showers.

The one exception to the sense of being among helpless victims was a group of young people. Seated in a circle on the floor, these preteens were turning old tins of cigarettes—Players was the brand—into grenades. Stuffed with explosives, sealed around a fuse, added to a growing pile, the homemade weapons accumulated.

"What is the matter, Dieter Wottrich?" Yacov asked. "Are you searching for someone?"

"How will we find Commander Sachar?" After killing a man in this crowd it would not be easy to make a getaway. Brandenburg's mind spun ways to lure Sachar outside, to a place in the night, near an escape route. Unconsciously he fingered the butt of the pistol.

"Moshe will be talking with Rabbi Vultch, or perhaps my grandfather," the boy replied. "In a study chamber. They use it for maps."

A more private spot. Perfect. Brandenburg had no objection to killing three or even more other Jews along with Sachar if it simplified things. His muscles tensed as he readied himself for combat.

As Yacov led the way toward a corner room, Brandenburg could hear muffled voices coming from just beyond the door. They were there. With one hand on the Lüger, Brandenburg reached toward the knob, then started back as a woman appeared in front of him.

"*Shalom,* Rachel," Yacov said importantly. "This is Dieter Wottrich. He escaped from the Arabs and needs to make a report to Moshe. Where is Moshe?"

Brandenburg's eyes took in Rachel's form and face, and he appreciated what he saw. Like classical music, she was another tribute to Jewish expression. When she caught Brandenburg staring at her, she became flustered. Grabbing her brother's shoulders, she drew him in front of her like a shield, but Yacov wriggled free. "Well?" he said impatiently. "Where is he?"

"I don't know," Rachel replied. "I was looking for him myself. Rabbi Vultch is in the map room. He says he saw Moshe and Grandfather here in the basement together, but we looked and they aren't here now."

"Is there another set of stairs out of the basement? Can they still be in the building?" Brandenburg inquired. "I really should tell the commander what I can remember of Arab positions while it's fresh in my mind."

"Moshe is often called away without warning," Rachel said, not knowing why this man made her feel uncomfortable and reticent. "You should make your report to Rabbi Vultch, and he can assign you to a position."

"I really think—"

"A new recruit?" Vultch said, emerging from the office. "Praise to the Eternal for unexpected blessings! We need a good man in the trench at the south end of the Street of the Jews. I'll take you there myself."

# CHAPTER 16

Gripping the precious shofar, Moshe followed Grandfather along the ragged course of the tunnel. One hundred and fifty yards were traversed beneath the houses and streets of Old City Jerusalem until the rabbi stooped to pass through the wall of what had been his own house.

"I would offer you a cup of tea if I had tea and time to drink it." He carefully placed the cruse of oil and the lantern on the floor. "Do you remember?" He raised his hands as if to offer a blessing. "Everything means something, *nu?*" He placed his palms on either side of a pillar of stone that formed part of the wall beneath the stairway. After a gentle pressure the column groaned and swung back easily at his touch.

Musty dampness invaded the cellar. Light from the lantern pooled beyond the secret portal. The light faded into the distance.

Grandfather lifted the container of oil, then held the index finger of his right hand aloft as though it were a candle. Moshe parroted the gesture, keeping his gaze riveted on the enormous stone blocks that lined the corridor.

"You have not forgotten," Grandfather said. "Can you find the way alone this time? I will hold on to your coattail, eh? You will lead me." He stepped aside, leaving the entry clear.

Moshe hesitated. "I . . . I don't know."

"I will give you the exact number of corridors that lead from here. I spoke in general terms before. You were not ready to think . . . to think . . . And so . . . Twenty-two branches from this entry. Many drop into cisterns. Others drop into oblivion. As in all things you must know where to begin, eh? At the beginning. There is one way to the gift that waits beneath this holy ground for the coming of Messiah. Only one way to find salvation for Israel. The narrow way. You must thread the eye of the needle with this." He jabbed his finger skyward.

"Yes." Moshe was perspiring. He stepped forward and felt the stone roof of the secret passage for three sets of grooves carved in stone by a master mason over two millennia before.

The first groove was three fingers' wide. The second had the breadth of two fingertips. The third slot was as wide as Moshe's index finger and as deep as his knuckle. This was the one true path into the cavern of scrolls.

Grandfather retrieved the jug of sacred oil, then with his free hand reached upward, checking the placement of Moshe's hand. "Good. Good. Twenty-two paths. Think! But only *alef* will lead you! What does *alef* mean? The beginning. One. And you must not trust anything but this one truth. Do not falter. Do not turn. Follow the way as I have shown you. As we walk let your heart hear the voice of the one who created you for this journey! Moshe! Moshe! Let faith be your candle, and you will find wisdom."

At that, the rabbi blew out the flame in the lantern. The dark pressed against them. Grandfather hooked his fingers in Moshe's belt.

The old man called out. His voice resounded down the corridor and echoed back like ten thousand voices calling them on. "Hear O Israel, the Lord our God, the Lord is One! *Alef!*"

"*Alef* . . . one. . . ." Moshe breathed and tried to clear his mind of everything but the tip of his finger. One! *Alef! First letter of the Hebrew alphabet. Its numerical value . . . one. Hebrew contains an alphabet of twenty-two elemental letters, each letter with a numerical value. Twenty-two paths from here but only one . . . alef . . . is the true point of beginning. Alef! Hear O Israel the Lord our God is . . . one Lord . . . I believe in one God, the Father, the Almighty, creator of heaven and earth, of all that is seen and unseen! One Creator! Everything means something!*

With that the two men began their journey.

■ ■ ■ ■

Neither the rabbi nor Moshe spoke as they descended into the inky depths of the Holy City. Moshe's finger slid easily along the track in the low roof of the passageway. Three times he experienced a blast of cool air as they bypassed secondary tunnels. As the old man instructed him, his footsteps were mincing, one foot in front of the other, as though measuring a distance.

Measuring a distance? Everything means something!

Moshe counted as he walked. 360. Sharp turn to the right. A switch-back descending yet another 314 paces, followed by a series of apparently insignificant numbers.

The process began again. 360. 314. 159. 265. 358. 97. 93. 238. At last of series of 7 short switchbacks contained 22 paces each.

What did it mean?

After a slow turning, 70 paces brought them to the end of the track.

"Here it ends," said the old man. "And here it begins."

Moshe remembered how they had entered for the Vigil of Pentecost. The thought of the seven thousand precious volumes contained within made his voice crack with eagerness. "The library chamber is beyond the wall. Yes? I kneel here, yes?"

"And raise your finger again. You will find the way."

Moshe dropped to his knees, the mouth of the chamber just before him. Grandfather followed. The two crept forward through an opening Moshe guessed to be about three feet high. On their knees they progressed seven paces along grooves worn smooth by centuries of other sojourners.

As it had on his first visit, the wind greeted Moshe with a blast that stung his eyes. In the oppressive dark why had he kept his eyes open? What was he searching for in the blackness?

The rabbi cloaked Moshe in the fabric of his prayer shawl.

"Everything is here," the old man whispered. "Waiting."

With that he struck a match and lit the lantern in a niche, then placed the lamp directly in front of Moshe. This time the light seemed too bright for Moshe. The glare blinded him to the awesome sight illuminated in the vast subterranean hall. Moshe shielded his eyes.

The rabbi took the shofar from Moshe, placing it and the jug of oil on a stone ledge in the wall above the door.

Then he spoke. "Stay on your knees. We will begin with a brief lesson. The knowledge you will find here is like this light, *nu?* If you stare at it too much, too close, it will blind you. Then you miss what the light illuminates." The rabbi swept his hand toward the cavernlike hall. The ceiling was thirty feet from the floor. The back wall was at least one hundred feet from the entrance. Four stone balconies were supported by twelve marble pillars and linked by steep steps. Upon the shelves were thousands of sealed clay jars. Three long wooden tables were in the center of the room. Carved into the cornice of the lower balcony was a phrase repeated in Hebrew, Greek, and Aramaic:

WHAT WAS—WHAT IS—WHAT SHALL BE

Grandfather continued in a quiet voice, "Knowledge never exists for its own sake; always it points to God. To His design."

Moshe nodded. "I understand."

"You do not have understanding. Not yet. Knowledge is not understanding. Knowledge is not wisdom unless it dwells in the heart of a wise man."

"I am not wise. Not worthy." Moshe possessed a sense of overwhelming shame. He knew so little!

"A wise and worthy answer. Empty yourself and become like a child, a slate that has no writing upon it. Hear everything for the first time. See everything for the first time. Let your heart ask questions, or you will never find the answers! Let the Eternal One draw His image upon you. Wisdom begins in the darkness of the womb with *Alef. El Shaddai. Elohim. Adonai.* Our Messiah . . . With the Holy One, blessed be He. . . ."

"If only . . . ," Moshe stammered. "If . . ."

"If there were not a war to fight?"

"Yes!" Moshe gasped. "To find this now! At this grim hour when I cannot say if we will hold the Old City for even another day!"

"The events of this age were recorded before you or I were ever born. The exact year and month of Israel's rebirth is predicted. . . . It has come true."

"But what of these things? The Old City? Jerusalem?"

"I have not found the answer for tomorrow, but this I am sure of: All is written in the Torah. Past. Present. Future."

"I read Torah. Five books of Moses. I read a history."

"Because you do not know what you are reading. In it is everything."

"Help me."

"The answer is at the root of the tree. You do not see the root, the life of the thing, unless you dig. Then the root burns and illuminates."

Moshe felt frustration. "I have no time for riddles."

"Yes. Time is short. So, you are a linguist. You know these things. One sample. Speak the letters *Tav* and *Resh* aloud. Say the word."

"Tor?"

"Meaning?"

"Tor is the root of Torah."

"But the root has a meaning, too, *nu?* How did you graduate from university and not know about such things?"

Moshe responded to the challenge. "Tor means an order, as in a well-ordered string of words. Yes?"

"Yes. We see where Torah comes from. But there is more. You think it is too small to matter, but it is a light! A blazing light! More! Say it!"

"Tor is also the word for a turtledove. And it is used as a term of endearment."

"Yes! Now cast your mind from the meaning of the word itself to revelations in the Scripture when the dove appears!"

"Ah!" Moshe cried, knowing instantly the references. Noah released a dove from the ark to search the waters of death that covered the earth. The dove never returned to the ark and was not seen again in Scripture until it appeared to alight upon the shoulder of Yeshua as he rose from the waters of his baptism.

Moshe saw it plainly:

*Noah, the ark, all humanity condemned! The waters over all the earth reeking with death! The dove, searching, searching the face of the deep for the one safe place to land! And then he finds Jesus coming up from the water of baptism! Here is life! He is the one! Resurrection! The embodiment of Torah! The Word made flesh!*

"Tor. A humble word," Grandfather instructed. "Neglected. But full of meaning, *nu?* Root of Torah. The Word of God. The Word written by His very finger."

"That is what you mean when you say that everything means something."

"And that is wisdom. To ask your heart, Why a dove? Why did God use the word *beloved* to describe Yeshua? What is God saying to those of us who stand on the riverbank and watch? I will leave it to you to ask and find your own answers, *nu?*"

"But can you tell . . . can you tell me what tomorrow will bring? The future?"

"Messiah will come. Jerusalem will be the capital of His kingdom."

"How can it be?"

"It is written plainly. We look for the light of His return to Jerusalem. Until then the Scripture teaches us that the heavens declare the glory of God. And yet we live in the world; we look up at the heavens and still men do not believe. Is it because they do not know what to look for? True? Of course, true! He has placed His seal upon everything! Every star is numbered. The hairs of your head are numbered. The Eternal is fond of numbering things. So we start with the One who created the heavens for His pleasure and glory. And say . . ." They repeated the *Shema* together.

"*Omaine*," Moshe said. Opening his eyes he saw that Grandfather had moved the lantern to a study table in the center of the cavern. On the table was a scroll, six pencils, and a pad of white writing paper.

Moshe raised his face to scan the vast repository containing thousands of ancient scrolls. A hunger to *know* consumed him.

"You can get up," Grandfather instructed. "I should have waited until you were forty years old to show you these mysteries. That would have been proper. Tradition tells us that a man cannot grasp these truths until he has lived forty years. A generation. Moshe and the children of Israel wandered forty years in the wilderness. Jesus fasted forty days in the desert. Perhaps you will ask, why forty, *nu?* But there is no time to wait for your fortieth birthday. Come. Sit. I will not take these things with me to the grave. I have great mysteries to show you before I go."

■ ■ ■ ■

In the midst of the lost temple library Moshe considered how easy it would be to study one scroll and then another and another until a lifetime had passed. It was his idea of what heaven would be: to learn! To know!

The desire to stay was almost overwhelming. During the Pentecost Vigil he had spent seven hours reading the memoirs of the daughter of Onias, high priest in the days of the Maccabee rebellion. This one scroll had changed his view of Jerusalem forever. Even the stones seemed to be living. At least memories of the dead existed within the stones. That night he had heard a voice—a woman's voice—calling his name!

The old man placed a hand on Moshe's shoulder. "You think I do not know what you are thinking? You are not the first who has dreamed of moving in, stocking up on several years' supply of sardines and tins of peaches and biscuits, eh? A cot over in the corner of the mathematics room. Biographies? Histories, maybe? Torah. The Law and the Prophets. Now there is a study!"

"When the war is finished, I may vanish for a month or two."

"That is why I bring you here. I hope you will not be required to stay longer than you wished. So. A few rules before we begin, *nu?*"

His matter-of-fact manner reminded Moshe of his first day at Oxford, when the porter had directed him to his quarters with a stern warning and a list of rules.

"Of course."

"If you want to live, you learn to tell time."

"Curfew. It's been years since I missed curfew at Magdalen College."

"Here you will find the punishment much harsher than at university. . . ." The old man guided Moshe to a shadowed alcove. Lifting the lantern, he revealed a circle of brightly polished lapis lazuli flecked with gold. It was hanging on the wall. About the size of a schoolroom clock face, it was marked off with each of the twenty-two letters of the Hebrew alphabet. A thick square peg of onyx was set in the center.

"What is it?"

"It is better to ask what it does." The old man glared at the thing.

"All right, then."

"Remove the rod from the circle, and the chamber will be sealed." He gestured meaningfully to the entrance at the opposite end of the cavern. "And yes, it is as it appears. He who does this thing will never leave here."

"A pleasant way to die."

"Maybe. But I think a man might go mad before he had a chance to read himself to death, *nu?*"

Moshe did not mention the voice of the woman he had heard the night of his first visit. Was that an indication that he, too, could go mad? "And the other rules?"

The old man eyed Moshe. "I know you heard her voice. The first night. You are not mad. You read about her life . . . as I did as a young man . . . and somehow she called to you."

Moshe colored. "But I . . . it was a dream, I thought."

"I heard her as well. I have heard her many times."

Sobered by the revelation, Moshe nodded. They would say no more about it.

The rabbi cleared his throat. "So, you counted your footsteps in the passage?"

"I did." Moshe frowned, remembering the sequence.

"Everything means something, eh?" The rabbi shoved pencil and paper across the table to Moshe. "Write, already. Before you forget the pattern."

"It is important, then?"

"The key to what is past and what will come. It points to He who holds all things together by His word." Grandfather shrugged. "Only a little important."

Moshe scribbled in silence. He showed his figures to the old man. 360. 314. 159. 265. 358. 97. 93. 238.

Grandfather scanned the numbers. "What of the last seven turnings? You forgot them?"

"Seven short links of twenty-two paces."

Grandfather wrote the information down. "So. The path first led you 360 steps. Think. What does that number mean to a Jew?"

Moshe's brow creased. "Three hundred and sixty days in a lunar year. The cycle of a year."

"Basic Torah school information, eh? Simple detail, you think? Maybe not so important? I will tell you. Remember the number when you study prophecy. Follow the calculations of years using this number, and everything will be plain to you. Remember too that the years are spoken of as 'sevens.'"

"Every seventh year being a sabbatical year," Moshe reasoned.

"Yes." The old man was pleased. He unrolled the scroll of the book of Daniel and pointed to the passage that Moshe recognized to be chapter nine. "So. Daniel writes the exact number of years from the command to rebuild the temple until the Anointed One would atone for wickedness and bring in everlasting righteousness and then be cut off. After that the city and the sanctuary would be destroyed." He smiled and scratched his beard. "You remember when the city and the temple were destroyed?"

"In the year 70 A.D."

"Remember always to calculate prophetic years as 360 days, Moshe.

And do you recall the date in Nehemiah in which the command was given to rebuild the temple?"

These were elemental dates that Moshe had committed to memory for classes in ancient history at Oxford. "445 B.C.?"

The old man seemed surprised by Moshe's quick response. "This will be easy for you, *nu?* From that date until the Messiah would accomplish righteousness and atone for sin and then be cut off? Sixtynine sevens. You may calculate the years yourself. It is written plainly, *nu?*"

Moshe calculated the number of years that would have to pass between the royal command recounted in Nehemiah and the time when the Anointed One would appear on the scene. He recalled the players and the events of that era.

Rome controlled the world from Palestine to Britain. In 12 B.C. Halley's comet appeared as a heavenly portent in the skies. The same year Caesar Augustus confirmed the right of Jews to pay their tithes to the temple in Jerusalem. Around this time Herod the Great, who was not a Jew, murdered his sons by Mariamne, thus ending the Jewish bloodline of the Maccabees.

From that time religious Jews believed the coming of the Anointed One was near. Bethlehem, City of David, was the appointed place of His birth. The exact date of the birth of Jesus was lost to history. But had Daniel fixed the time of the death of the Messiah?

Dating from the month of Nisan, 445 B.C., and adding sixty-nine sevens, 476 years of 365 days, brought Moshe to the year 31 A.D.! The year of the crucifixion?

"Close enough." Grandfather sighed with relief that Moshe was such a bright pupil. Moshe scratched his figures on the paper. "And what about the last seven years? The seventieth seven?"

"Last means last," the old man concluded. "The very last. We have not yet lived to see them. But this much I am certain of: those last seven years could not begin until there was once again a nation of Israel! Do you see? Israel and Jerusalem are the center of all end-time prophecy. The territory of ancient Rome must also become a power in the world again. Some thought it was Hitler's Reich, but I said, not without a nation of Israel, *nu?*"

Moshe stared at the numbers on the paper. It was clear! Jerusalem was destroyed in 70 A.D.! Two thousand years had come and gone since the first part of Daniel's prophecy was fulfilled. And now Israel was re-born! Only from that moment could they look up and know that the last seven years were possible!

The old man continued, "The last seven will not be years of peace for Israel or Jerusalem. Scripture teaches that there will be tribulation as the world has never seen! Some thought it was the Holocaust. But it could not be, I said. Not until Israel is a nation once again."

"And now?" Moshe asked.

"When the end comes, Messiah will rule in Jerusalem. And his kingdom will have no end."

"Is there more?" Moshe asked, eager to know.

"I meant this as an example only. So simple. So obvious. There are hundreds of fulfilled prophecies about Messiah. Isaiah 53. Psalms 22. Nearly three hundred on the surface. But *oy!* Thousands and myriads are entwined in the roots of Torah. On and on. We study accurately fulfilled prophecy, *nu?* And by these clear truths we can be sure that prophecies about the future will also come to pass. So, end of lesson one. You get the point, *nu?*"

Moshe, gulping down as much information as possible, whispered, "Is that all?"

"God's Word is as deep as the sea. We skim the surface of understanding."

"I would dive into it if I could."

"You want more." The rabbi gazed solemnly at Moshe's notes.

"As much as you will give me."

"Then I offer you this. There is more to the number 360 than prophetic years. And what else . . . what else do you think of when you see this number?"

Moshe stared at the paper. He shrugged. "A circle? Three hundred and sixty degrees?"

Grandfather slapped the table exultantly. "And the degrees of a compass by which we find our way, *nu?* The very voice of the Eternal God, a signpost for understanding is found here." Snatching up the pencil he drew three circles, each smaller than the one before. "How were your skills in mathematics at university?"

"Dismal."

"Doesn't matter. Do you remember the number the *goyim* call *pi* and we call *Archimedes' Constant?*"

"Measure the distance around a circle. Measure the distance across the circle and divide."

"And the number is always the same! Always! True? Of course, true! No matter how large or small your circle is, the answer is always the same." Grandfather hesitated and then asked, "Do you remember what it is?"

Moshe reached back into his memory of elementary arithmetic. "3.14159265 . . . something . . . and so on into infinity. And it goes on forever without repeating its pattern. No one has ever calculated to the end. No one ever will."

"Close enough." The rabbi pointed to the number of steps in the passageway that Moshe had written down. He erased the extra decimal points until the number read 3.141592653589793238.

Moshe let out a low whistle of astonishment. "Everything means something!" he cried. "The number of steps we walk to this place is . . . pi? The value for . . . well, for figuring out circles?"

With the joy of one who had kept a secret for too long, Grandfather laughed and stood to twirl around three times. He raised his hands in the air. "*Oy!* I have wanted to tell someone about this!" He gave a victory cry. "There's more. More!" He sat down across from Moshe again. His face was glowing with pleasure. "There is a less accurate figure than this used to convey pi, of course. Schoolboys know it." He wrote the figure like this: 22/7.

Moshe said in astonishment, "Seven switchbacks with twenty-two paces in each."

"Yes! Now think! Think, Moshe! What do these numbers mean to a Jew?"

"Twenty-two letters in the Hebrew alphabet."

"Yes! *Oy!* Such a *maven!* Such a bright boy my granddaughter has married!"

"And seven . . ."

"Remember . . . Think of the beginning . . . a hint . . . creation . . ."

"Seven days in creation. Seven days in a week. Seven . . . there are so many sevens in Scripture . . . which is important?"

"All of them! Seven colors in a rainbow. Seven notes in a musical scale! Language! the language of the Eternal! The heavens declare the glory of God! On and on in creation! All! All! Each of the twenty-two letters in the Hebrew language also has a numerical value, *nu?* The five books of Torah are written by the hand of God. Endless combinations of letters. Backwards and forwards. Twenty-two elemental letters in the Hebrew alphabet each written upon a circle. Wheels within wheels, you see."

Moshe nodded. He was reminded of the encoding machine called *Enigma,* which the Germans had used during the war for military transmissions. It contained wheels mounted within wheels which could be moved backwards and forwards to encode messages that were thought to be unbreakable. When the British secretly cracked the code, they were able to read the German radio traffic, and this achievement helped the Allies win the war.

Was the old man talking about something similar? It made sense. The fact that there were hidden messages in the Torah had been known for centuries. Jesus himself had declared that not one jot could be removed from the Scriptures until all things were fulfilled.

The rabbi continued. "The value of pi, Archimedes' Constant, is also written by the hand of God. The messages of Torah and pi are connected. . . . The two are connected, you see. The words of Torah are not merely backwards and forwards, up and down, but they are within the circle. Within the wheel. Like the wheels Ezekiel saw! Torah is a scroll, you see. A kind of circle . . . a sort of wheel. . . ."

Moshe drew back. This was too much of a leap. The value of pi was a quantity everyone knew was without explanation. It had no pattern and extended beyond what the human intellect could comprehend. To say this was a sort of key to unlocking secrets in the Torah was far-fetched.

Grandfather held up his finger. "Ah. He doubts. Ah well. I have worked on the formula for years. I have added my notes to others, *nu?*" He inclined his head toward a doorway that led to another room. "Mathematics. The numbering angel, the powerful Palmoni, who appeared to the prophet Daniel, has sometimes stooped to whisper in my ear. The message is this: In the time of the end it will become clear. Knowledge will increase."

"We are in the end times?"

"We are. The circle is almost complete."

"You believe this?"

The rabbi took Moshe's hand. "With my whole heart, my son. We are all—all of us—part of the greatest fulfillment of prophecy in two thousand years."

Moshe exhaled loudly. They had been in the library nearly three hours. "We will have to stay here longer than three hours for me to grasp this."

The enthusiasm of Grandfather faded into weariness. What he knew with a certainty was to remain a secret for a while longer, it seemed. "*Oy*. Yes. Of course we must go back to the real world. There is a war to fight. It is written. . . ."

"Do you know the outcome?" Moshe leaned forward, intensely curious.

"The ultimate outcome I have already shared with you. The Anointed One has come. He has atoned for our sin. He will come again to judge the living and the dead. But tomorrow? Next week? It depends on . . . many things. On you, on me. All of us, I think. And so we should go back, *nu?*"

■ ■ ■ ■

Mother Superior entered the study of the Catholic Archbishop with Daoud at her side.

The highest-ranking Roman Catholic cleric in Jerusalem, the Archbishop was a small unassuming man with a large nose and a ring of white hair like a sort of halo around his bald head.

Daoud spotted him instantly for what he was: an Italian!

Still, he was pleasant enough. He offered Mother and Daoud the fine big leather chairs and took an ordinary straight-backed chair for himself. He seated himself before Daoud and leaned forward to gaze intently with milk-chocolate-colored eyes into the boy's face.

In fluent Arabic he inquired, "Mother tells me you have been moving about among the Muslim soldiers, Daoud."

"Yes. It is easy for me. I was apprentice to the bomber Dajani. I helped to kill Jews. The men of the Jihad trust me. No one looks a second time as I pass by."

"You take a risk when you go among them. Why do you do this thing?"

"For my father, Baruch, who has given me the life of my brother, Gawan."

Mother elaborated, "He means the Jewish Doctor Baruch who entered the Old City with us."

The Archbishop nodded. "You have done what you have done. It is not wise to leave us again until this issue is settled. You understand?"

"I must help as I can. It is the will of Allah and his Prophet that I repay your kindness. Mother and the sisters are very kind to us."

The Archbishop sighed. "Mother says you brought information."

"Yes. *Insh'Allah.* I was nearby the leader of the Legion as he spoke with al-Malik. This new man is a lieutenant. A German fellow. Big. Strong, and smart. They say he learned Yiddish because the Jews he killed begged for their life in this tongue. He will pretend to be one of them."

"A Jew?" The Archbishop exchanged a look of surprise with Mother Superior.

"Yes. The German has gone into the Jewish Quarter. He will kill the leader of the Jewish defense, Moshe Sachar. Al-Malik says the assassination of Sachar will put an end to Jewish resistance. Without him, the rabbis say, no one in the Jewish Quarter will fight anymore."

"The end of the conflict would be a good thing," the Archbishop said.

"I do not care about the Sachar fellow. But for Baruch and the women who helped to save Gawan I owe the debt of my life. If the German kills the Jewish leader and the Jews give up, the Jihad will have them cut into pieces after they rape them! I must not stand by and remain silent."

The Archbishop rose and strode to a window overlooking a courtyard. "You have done the honorable thing. King Abdullah is also a man of honor. He will not hold with his soldiers acting in such a way to civilian prisoners."

"Abdullah the King is not here. The real soldiers of the Legion are not yet fighting in the Old City. The fellows who came here in advance are not Muslims. They are European . . . Christian men, I think. So I tell you what I have heard. Perhaps the Italian Holy Father King will call the King in Amman and tell him."

Mother Superior sat forward. "Indeed. The Holy Father telephoned the American President and the British Prime Minister and the King in Amman. He protested the shelling of the Jewish Quarter and it was stopped. Now the Arabs must take the Jewish district yard by yard instead of dropping bombs upon the people and the houses. World opinion does have some power. Perhaps it will be thus with this other plan to kill the Jewish commander. Assassination! Diabolical."

The Archbishop clasped his hands behind his back as if they were tied. "Artillery pieces shelling the Old City from the Mount of Olives is one thing, Mother. The shells fell near to Christian holy places as well. Of course the whole world protested such irresponsible actions! But what can be done about a lone German mercenary entering Jewish territory to kill one Jew?"

Daoud stood up. "Then you must tell someone . . . these Old City rabbis must not surrender until King Abdullah's army takes over Jerusalem! They come with tanks and armored cars. Real soldiers. The road to the sea is held by the Jihad, and the Jews will never win it back. The Legion will capture Jerusalem; of this I am certain. But for the Jews to surrender too soon to these Germans and the soldiers of al-Malik is to die."

The Archbishop returned his gaze to the courtyard. The staccato popping of gunfire penetrated the sanctuary. He nodded. "Perhaps it is already too late. But we shall do what we can do to send the Jewish Agency a message that surrender must only be to the proper authorities. You are a brave boy, Daoud. You have our thanks."

# FRIDAY

*May 21, 1948*

*Cause the progeny of David, your servant,*
*to blossom quickly. Let him shine in your*
*deliverance, for we await your salvation*
*every day. Blessed are You, Adonai,*
*who causes the light of salvation to blossom.*

*The Amidah—the Fifteenth Prayer*
*"David"*

*A light will shine on us this day, the Lord is born for us: he shall be called Wonderful God, Prince of Peace, Father of the world to come; and his kingship will never end.*

*Isaiah 9:2, 6; Luke 1:33*

*". . . And the Word became flesh and dwelt among us, and we beheld his glory . . ."*

*from John 1:1–18*

*"And the multitudes that went before, and that followed, cried, saying, Hosana to the son of David: Blessed is he that cometh in the name of the Lord . . ."*

*Matthew 21:9*

# CHAPTER 17

J ust after midnight on Friday, the bodies of the four Kurtzman children were carried to the morgue. Gunfire on the barricades drew
the rescuers back to the perimeters of the Jewish Quarter. Lori, Alfie,
and a handful of Hasidim remained, working without benefit of light.
Even the flicker of a candle would draw sniper fire.

The racket of the border skirmish ended. No soldiers returned to
dig. What was the use? There had been no sign of life for hours.

Rachel Sachar brought food. Yehudit Avram and Hannah Cohen
came to see the place where the house had stood. Others came to look.
They shook their heads in disbelief, leaned on one another, mourned,
and went away.

Alfie did not tire. He worked with a determination born of hope.

How many times since baby Al died had Lori dug with bloody
hands through London's ruins to find someone else's child beneath the
fallen bricks? Sometimes alive . . . sometimes.

But never was the child she rescued the one she looked for.

*It can't be! I went to market! He was playing on the rug when I left! He
must be there still!*

Tonight, once again, Lori fought the urge to hope. As the half-
witted giant at her side commanded, she sang lullabies to little Abe
Kurtzman and called the child's name as they cleared the rubble.

What was the use of it, she asked herself. "We should come back in
daylight," she suggested.

"No," Alfie insisted. "More bombs in the morning."

Lori lost track of time. Moonlight illuminated the site. At last Alfie
tossed a beam to the side, straightened himself, and said to Lori, "Down
there." He pointed to a hole, the top of which revealed a stone step.

On her knees, Lori probed the space. It was large enough for her to squeeze into. It descended into the cellar. "I'll need a torch when I get down."

Someone handed her a flashlight.

Alfie whispered, "Listen."

Lori paused, straining to hear. Nothing. She was half-sick, certain of what she would find.

Alfie patted her shoulder as she slipped into the space.

She inched downward, feet first, on her back, one step at a time. The collapsed floorboards of the upper story formed a sort of pipeline. Moonlight shone down the shaft. Five steps. Eight. Her feet touched something hard and unyielding. She could descend no farther.

"Take cover. I'm switching on the torch," she warned Alfie and the others.

The yellow glow of the flashlight lit up the internal wreckage. The splintered beams of the house were hung with the flotsam and jetsam of ordinary life. An upside-down cupboard spilled shattered dishes. One unbroken teacup perched on the open cupboard door. There, the remains of a rocking chair. A child's dress. The head of a blue-eyed doll stared back at her. An open book of nursery rhymes . . . *Dear God! Sweet Jesus!*

And then . . . a woman's bare foot protruded from beneath a tabletop and a mound of bricks two yards from where Lori lay.

"Missus Kurtzman." Lori spoke the name dully. It was not a question. There was nothing hopeful in her tone. Lori could not reach what was left of the woman. It would take days of labor to remove the body.

Lori kept the light fixed on the foot for a long moment. Then she moved the circle to the right. A wall. Nothing. Then to the left, back to the table.

Half the tabletop lay at an angle against a truss. Within this space Lori saw the arm and shoulder of the dead woman wrapped around the blond head of her child. And there was his square, little-boy hand, clutching a fragment of blue blanket.

The mother had died trying to shield her child from the blast.

Had she succeeded? There was no movement. Not a breath. No sign of life in the small form of Abe, wrapped in the death grip of his mother.

An overwhelming sense of grief welled up in Lori. She fought the urge to cry out, to beat her fist against the stones. *Oh God! Dear God! He's dead! Dead!* How many times had this scene been repeated, and yet she never got used to it.

Still, she waited, hoping for the dead to awaken. "Abe?" Lori spoke gently. "Can you hear me?" Her mind replayed the verse,

> *Each one whom Life exiled I named and called,*
> *But they were all too far, or dumbed, or thralled,*
> *And never one fared back to me or spoke. . . .*

From above, Alfie called to her, "Did you find the kitten, Lori?"

She groaned, then choked out the reply, "He's not . . . moving. Oh, Alfie . . ."

*All of them!*

She switched off the torch and lay in the darkness of the tomb, wishing she, too, had died with her child that day in Primrose Hill. Wishing she had not lived to learn how hard it was to go on living.

And then . . .

The trickle of a single stone falling from the heap.

The clatter of a teacup as it shifted and shattered.

A whimper.

The piping voice of Abe Kurtzman. "Mama?"

Lori gasped and fumbled with the flashlight. "Abe!"

The beam shone on his bewildered face. He raised his head and blinked back at her. He fought to loose himself from the cold embrace of his mother. *He doesn't know!*

"Come on, Abe," Lori urged, reaching out to him.

"Where is Mama?" he wailed.

Lori willed the child not to look down at the mangled corpse of his mother. Willed him to free himself from the unfamiliar grasp of death.

He kicked against the dead weight that held him fast.

"Come to me, Abe." Lori's arm strained through a triangle of splintered beams. Her fingertips stretched toward him.

"I want Mama!" He managed to scramble upright, snatch up his blood-soaked blanket and lunge toward the light. "I fell! I fell down and down! Where is my mama?"

"Abe! Abe! Come on, baby. Honey." *Not hurt! Oh God! Thank you!* "I'll take you out of here. Come to me, Abe!"

Up the shaft Alfie cried joyfully, "Lori! Lori! I hear him! Lori! He is alive, Lori!"

■ ■ ■ ■

Alfie left the site of the Kurtzman house sometime after Lori carried little Abe away. At the foot of Gal'ed Road he heard the angry voices of young men.

They had shovels. Alfie knew they were burying the dead.

The Kurtzman children lay among the stack of more than twenty awaiting burial. Alfie stepped into the shadowed portico of a deserted shop. His chest ached from sorrow. He covered his nose and watched for a time as the black-coated specters lined the grave with bodies, covered them with lime, shoved soil into the pit, then tamped the earth and fled back toward Nissan Bek.

He stayed in the darkness for a long time. He wished that someone had said a prayer or had sung a hymn. Why had they run away so fast?

Taking his hand from his nose, he inhaled. The air was better. He smelled roses.

He reached out in the direction of the sweet scent. His fingers brushed the leaves of a bush. "Roses," Alfie said as he knelt down beside a wheelbarrow containing three rosebushes. "I saw you on Pentecost when the nuns came into the Old City. Is you here, then?"

From behind Alfie a resonant, pleasant voice whispered like the rustle of curtains blowing in a window. *"I brought these for the little ones. They are safe."*

Alfie closed his eyes, afraid to look at the enormous Golden Being with eyes so kind and yet so sad. There were times before when Alfie had looked into the radiant face. *Beams of light shone from the forehead where the crown of thorns had been. And from the wounds in hands and feet and side. Warm, living, beautiful light!*

If the gardener had stayed too long, Alfie would have run to Him, gone away with Him.

"Will they have a long sleep?" Alfie asked.

*"Not so very long now."*

"When?"

*"When the world does not expect it. Then."*

"What should I do?" Alfie implored.

*"Plant the roses."*

"Is that all?"

"*Water them.*"

"What else can I do?"

Silence. Then the voice, fading . . . "*In Israel's battle the prayers of the saints stand like mighty towers of refuge for the Chosen of the Lord. For Israel.*"

"I will pray . . ."

"*I will bless those who bless my people and curse those who curse them . . .*"

"What about Jacob?" Alfie queried. "Lori and the boy? A-ber-a-ham? The people here? What about them? Will they live? Will we live to see it?"

There was no reply.

Alfie always wished the gardener would stay longer, but he never did. He was gone, leaving behind the rosebushes. And Alfie to plant and water.

■ ■ ■ ■

In the basement of the Mandelbaum house, Jacob Kalner and Peter Wallich reviewed the barricades and the planned demolition of the spice merchant's dwelling. Then Jacob brought up the subject of the teenage soldiers. Round-faced Uri Tabken snored, openmouthed, in one corner. His glasses were clutched in one hand. Naomi Snow busied herself dividing up and distributing rations to a score of other soldiers, the oldest no more than seventeen.

"Before Major Thomas brought me here," Jacob said, "I was with a cobbled-together bunch called the Spare Parts Platoon. Fresh off the boat, you know . . . barely knew which end of a rifle to point at the Arabs."

Peter nodded.

"But these . . ." Jacob said, jerking his head toward the young troopers. "They're just children."

"Hardly," Peter retorted. "Uri, there, is from Batina, near the Croat border with Hungary. He was ten when Croatian Nazis tortured and murdered his whole family. Hid in a haystack while they gouged out his father's eyes."

Peter fell silent as they both considered fifteen-year-old Uri.

Next, Peter indicated brown-eyed Naomi. The girl, trim and athletic, was not beautiful, but she was vivacious. "The Snows were French

Jews, living in Vichy, France, in a tiny village near Clermont. Thought they were safe till '43, when Laval's men wanted to curry favor with the Gestapo. Do you see that scar on her forehead?"

By the flickering light of an oil lamp Jacob could see a crooked white line that began over Naomi's left eye and ran up into her short-cropped, mousy-brown hair. He nodded.

Resuming his narrative, Peter said, "Grazed by a bullet and left for dead. Spent a night and a day buried under two sisters and twenty neighbors. Don't call any of my soldiers children . . . don't underestimate them."

Naomi brought Jacob Kalner his rations for the evening: a cup of water and three ounces of dried fish. He thanked her politely. As Jacob studied the unappetizing fare, Peter observed with a wry smile, "At least it's better than dried lentils and no water. That's what they gave us on the night we arrived here from the kibbutz."

Jacob shrugged. "I wasn't complaining," he explained. "I was wondering. If this is all we can manage out here in the New City, what must they be down to in the Old City?" Taking Peter's silence for encouragement, Jacob continued, "My wife is there." He gazed at the gray-painted bricks as if he could see Lori's face. Then, shaking off the personal reflection, he asked, "How about you? Are you married?"

"No," Peter replied. "Never the right time . . . or the right woman."

Naomi brought Peter a chunk of coarse bread as gray as the wall. "Here," she said. "I'm full already. You take it."

Despite Peter's protests, Naomi insisted until Peter accepted the offering with thanks. She went across the room to attend the bandaged arm wound of another Gadna youth, but she continued to steal glances back at Wallich.

"That girl loves you," Jacob observed.

"She's just a child, barely sixteen," Peter protested hurriedly, in total contradiction of his earlier warning. "Ten years younger than I am." The hasty response convinced Jacob that Naomi's adoration had not gone unnoticed.

Seeking to redirect the conversation, Peter admitted, "I was in love with an older woman once. Lucy, the Hayedid's wife . . . before she was his wife, I mean. I wanted to be her knight in shining armor and take care of her. You knew Captain Orde was killed in the war?"

Jacob acknowledged that he had heard of the Hayedid's fate.

"Lucy Orde lives in America," Peter said. "I got a letter from her last Hanukkah."

"And there's never been anyone else?"

Now it was Peter whose eyes lost their focus as his sight turned to memory. "There was a girl in Warsaw," he admitted. "A true raven-haired beauty. Rachel was her name. Of course, I don't know what became of her." He added wretchedly, "What a stupid thing to say! I don't know what became of my baby brother after I sent him off to England. I don't know what happened to the rest of my family, either."

"All of us lost people we cared about."

"It is why we must fight and we must win!" Peter said fiercely. "We must create a place where at least one generation of Jews can grow up with nothing but good, happy memories. Where children can really have a childhood."

# CHAPTER 18

Even as more dismantled fighter planes reached Israel, Michael Stone led jeep patrols in the Negev. "Hit fast, hit hard" was the American's motto. Harassing skirmishes on Egyptian tank columns were like fleas annoying elephants, but they forced Egypt to slow down its advance.

Elsewhere in Israel, the news was not as encouraging.

A few miles from Jerusalem, Arab artillery shelled the settlement of Ramat Rachel, and an Arab armored column reached Bethlehem.

The Iraqis assaulted a bridge over the Jordan near Gesher.

But the most potent Arab force—the Arab Legion—remained bogged down in the conquest of Jerusalem.

Robert Brandenburg joined the Haganah defenders at the south end of the Street of the Jews. When he asked where the commander, Moshe Sachar, was, they replied that he was everywhere, organizing everything from soup to the making of explosives.

Dov waved a stalk of something foul-smelling. "Here, Dieter, if you're hungry. The sandbag brigade . . . ten-year-old kids, but everybody helps, *nu?* They collect weeds from courtyards around the Quarter. These taste like garlic and fill out the empty space. Have some?"

Declining the offer and thrusting the noxious plant away from his face, Brandenburg turned toward Yehudit. "So, what's the drill?" he asked. "Who guards, who sleeps, and when does the watch change?"

"Were you in the army, Dieter?" Dov asked, seeking to assess the man and see if there was knowledge behind the words.

Brandenburg reminded himself that he must not sound too experienced about tactics or weapons. None of the Jews he had met so far, except for Dov, Ehud, and Rabbi Vultch, seemed to have any training. The real Dieter Wottrich probably had never carried a rifle in his life.

"I meant, how long do we have to stay out here?" Brandenburg asked. "All night?"

"First night on duty and already griping?" Dov said, with a lightness in his tone to show he was joking.

"Wait!" Yehudit said. "What's that?"

Atop the looming mass that was the tower above Zion Gate, a glowing orange dot appeared. "Cigarette," Dov commented. "Maybe the Legionnaires aren't so bright. I can pick him off from here." He raised his rifle as he spoke.

Silently cursing his senseless Arab Legion comrade, Brandenburg thought it would serve the idiot right to get his head shot off. Still, it might be one of his own company. Brandenburg would find out and punish the simpleton later. For now he had to save his life.

Grabbing a Sten gun out of Yehudit's hands, Brandenburg called, "I'll get him," and loosed a clip of bullets. The spray of lead went nowhere near the tower, but the gleam from the cigarette vanished and a fusillade of returning shots smacked around the Jewish trench.

"*Meshugge!*" Dov scolded, pouncing on Brandenburg's back. "We don't have enough bullets to waste like that! And you hit nowhere near him either!"

"I'm sorry," Brandenburg apologized, pleased he had saved the Legionnaire's life and cost the Haganah precious ammunition at the same time. His apparent lack of ability and good sense had also branded him as hopelessly unmilitary.

A hoarse whisper from the direction of Ben Zakkai Synagogue inquired, "Dov? It's Moshe. Is it an attack?"

Moshe! And he could make it look like an accident! With a feigned cry of alarm, Brandenburg rolled over onto his side in the trench, aimed the Sten gun in earnest this time, and squeezed the trigger.

Nothing happened. He had already used the entire clip.

"Give me that!" Dov said, taking the weapon from Dieter Wottrich. "You could have killed Commander Sachar! We do not shoot without thinking, and we never fire an entire clip, *nu?*" Then, to Moshe, Dov added, "It's nothing, Moshe. Our latest recruit has the jitters."

"Train him right," Moshe said without approaching any nearer to the barricade. "Good night."

■ ■ ■ ■

Clutching his blood-soaked blanket, little Abe Kurtzman clung to Lori's neck as she carried him to the hospital. In the blackness of Gal'ed Road, the stench of the dead was intense.

Lori shielded the eyes of the child as they passed the square where a crew of young men from Nissan Bek Synagogue were hard at work burying the dead. Among the corpses, Lori knew, were Abe's brothers and sisters.

*"We will not be welcome at Nissan Bek . . . Abe the Obnoxious, Rabbi Akiva called him. . . ."*

*"Let the little children come to me, . . . the kingdom of heaven belongs to such as these. . . ."*

*"Not welcome at Nissan Bek . . . Mrs. Kurtzman took them home. . . ."*

*"If anyone causes one of these little ones [harm] it would be better for him to have a large millstone hung around his neck and to be drowned in the depths of the sea. Whoever offers a cup of cold water to a little child has offered it to Me. . . ."*

*"My Abe, he is a good boy, nu? But full of energy. . . ."*

Tears of fury brimmed in Lori's eyes. The once lively child trembled all over. His breath came in short, wheezing gasps. He had not spoken a word since Lori extracted him from the tomb of his home and gathered him in her arms. Did he somehow know what had happened?

This much Lori was certain of: the unkind words of Akiva had been a knife in the heart of Mrs. Kurtzman. The unfeeling remarks about Abe from the women of Nissan Bek had ultimately resulted in five deaths.

She wanted to shout at the Nissan Bek grave diggers! To tell them that this tragedy was their fault! She longed to call down the curse of a millstone on their necks.

But she did not. She was certain that turning away Mrs. Kurtzman and the children had already caught the attention of heaven.

*Judging a child?*

*Gossip!*

A curse hovered above the lofty edifice, waiting to crack the arrogant walls and spill the unfeeling people into the street.

When Abe coughed and gagged at the odor, she tucked him closer against her and ran away from the frightful scene.

■ ■ ■ ■

Naomi found Peter on the roof of the Mandelbaum house. She brought him broth in a tin can and a slice of bread. He took it gratefully and nursed the soup, as though he knew it might be a long time before he tasted food again.

He alone was awake, watching, scanning the shadows of the city for signs of movement. Three other defenders, including Uri Tabken, lay sleeping within the ring of sandbags. They seemed to be a heap of lifeless marionettes waiting to be jerked into action. Rifles were propped at awkward angles against the sandbags like the controls of an absent puppet master.

Jerusalem stretched out before them, brooding, indistinct. The night sky, however, was radiant, a black-velvet dome frosted with starlight. The air was scrubbed clean by an east wind. In Paris on such a night, Naomi thought, lovers would be walking hand in hand along the Seine. *They would count the stars together and go home to make love.*

She whispered, "A beautiful night."

Peter replied, "My grandfather in Warsaw used to talk about the hour the Shekinah Glory left Jerusalem. He said that it comes back sometimes on *Shabbat*. On such a night you could almost believe it."

"He knew the history?"

"History? This is Jerusalem. Yesterday. Today. Forever the same."

"We live in the present and the past, I think. I wish I had paid more attention in your history class at the kibbutz."

"It's never too late."

"Teach me something new."

"I know about things that are old, I'm afraid."

"Tell me . . . about the Old City. I may never see it myself if what Uri says comes true."

He scratched his head and peered up at the stars. Then he pointed across the rooftops, beyond the wall of Suleiman to where the dome of the Hurva Synagogue glowed dully in the center of the Jewish Quarter. "The Hurva stands on the site of the palace of Agrippa II and Berenice," he said.

"Who were they?"

"Agrippa. Great-grandson of Herod." He shrugged. "At least I think that is the relationship."

"Never mind." Naomi sat down cross-legged beside him. "I'll never check. Tell me about them."

"Agrippa was a royal prince, but Rome pulled the strings. From his rooftop . . . from where the Hurva stands, he could have seen the crucifixion of Christ. The earth grew dark. There was an earthquake. Probably made an impression. Then, years later, when he was king, Agrippa interrogated the apostle Paul, who was in prison in Caesarea."

"Who was this Paul?"

"Paul. A Pharisee. Torah scholar. Killer of Christians. Converted after he saw a vision. He became a kind of mystic Hasid."

"Why did Agrippa care?"

"Paul became as strong in defense of Christianity and the Christians as he had been against them. It was quite a change. So Paul was on trial for his life and he taught the King from the writings of the prophets. Nearly converted him, too. Converted his wife, some say." He shrugged. "They lived right there. Where the Hurva stands."

"How do you know such things?"

"I am a treasure trove of useless information."

"More, please." She was enjoying the diversion. Enjoying the fact that he was looking at her, talking to her.

Peter pointed skyward to a faint cluster of stars directly overhead. "There. Where the stars look like a sort of comma? It is called 'Berenice's Hair.'"

"Named for her? For Agrippa's wife?"

"No, for his sister. More likely she was named for the constellation. I have been sitting here, thinking how extraordinary it is to see those stars and know that two thousand years ago she saw the same constellation. The sky has changed very little in two thousand years."

"Tell me." Naomi rested her head against the sandbags. "Talk to me about something besides the war. As if we were sitting out beneath the stars. As if . . . we were . . . back home. I mean on the kibbutz. And you were telling me things. Things you know about."

He chuckled. "There will be an examination on the material." It was the first time he had shown pleasure since they had arrived in Jerusalem. "In Greek the name Berenice means 'victory bearer.'"

"I like this already."

"In Egypt, in the time of Ptolemy III—"

"Never heard of him."

"A Greek king, ruling in Alexandria, in Egypt. A scholar like his father. He built a great library and a great kingdom. He was married to a woman named Berenice. A real beauty. Hair so thick and beautiful . . ." He touched Naomi's hair softly. "So beautiful it was . . . famous, I suppose. And they were in love."

"I like this."

"Yes. Well, Ptolemy went off to fight the Assyrians and Berenice vowed that she would sacrifice her hair at the altar of Aphrodite if he returned safely."

"And did he come home?"

"He came home. She kept her vow. You can imagine how disappointed he was that beautiful Berenice was bald. To make matters worse, the next morning the hair was missing from the altar."

"Someone stole it?"

"The King was not sure he could love a bald woman. He was cross with her. There was a Greek mathematician and astronomer who lived at court. He told Ptolemy that the goddess Aphrodite was so pleased with her sacrifice that Berenice's hair had been transferred to the heavens." Peter pointed up again. "There it is."

"A clever fellow, this mathematician."

"Victory-bearer. Glistening over our heads tonight, see? Over Jerusalem. Over the palace of Agrippa and Berenice. Over the Hurva." He paused. "Is this what people talk about under the stars?"

"Only you would know such . . . stories, Peter."

"I've had no practice teaching night courses."

"So finish." She wanted to add that there was much he could learn about night courses if only he would notice what she felt for him. His nearness warmed her. Her heart raced when his hand brushed her arm.

"Finish?"

She asked, "Did Berenice win back the love of Ptolemy?"

"Her hair grew back, and they lived happily ever after."

"Then I am content." She touched her fingers to her close-cropped hair. Would Peter look at her if she grew her hair long? If she put on a dress? Had Peter ever seen her in a dress?

Peter added, "And they built a large library."

"Then *you* are content?" she teased.

Silence. He kept his gaze fixed heavenward. He remarked sadly, "Must I be content?"

"Why not? Being discontented won't change anything."

She knew about being discontented. She had always loved Peter Wallich, her first teacher at the kibbutz. Lately her dreams had been obsessed with him. *His hands exploring her body. His mouth pressed hard against hers.* Wanting him so badly she ached had not changed anything.

He said, "But if I could, I would change everything. You kids . . . sixteen of you."

"I'm not a child anymore, Peter."

"I always thought of you as my kids. I've watched you grow up and now . . . what you must face . . . before you have even lived . . . I am concerned for your lives. Yours and . . . well . . . everyone else's here."

She wanted to hold his face and kiss his mouth. When he lay sleeping she wanted to lie next to him, wrap herself around him.

"I can't think about such things," she said quickly.

"I have to think about it," Peter replied. "Tomorrow this place . . . Mea Shearim . . . the Mandelbaum house? Will be the most obvious target in Jerusalem. . . . Everything here could vanish."

Naomi sighed. "My hair is too short to make an impression on anyone's altar."

He laughed again. "I hadn't noticed."

"But I intend to grow it long after the war. Think Aphrodite would take a promissory note? Keep you safe in exchange for my hair?"

"Aphrodite wouldn't believe a promise coming from a girl who would rather be driving a tractor than dancing."

"How about Uri's hair? All those curls. His is prettier than mine. I could say, you know . . . keep Peter Wallich safe. Here's the bargain. I'll seduce Uri and shave his head . . . like Delilah. Yes?"

"You always were a funny kid," Peter said, handing her the empty soup tin. "Now, go on. Get some sleep."

■ ■ ■ ■

The face of little Abe was frozen in a mask of tearless grief. Eyes wide, yet unseeing, he would not let go of his blanket. He would not release Lori's hand. He lay curled in a fetal position on the examination table at Misgav Ladakh.

"Nothing broken, Abe," remarked Dr. Baruch lightly as he palpated every bone. "No concussion." He smiled into the face of the child but received no response. To Lori he added, "Shock. You have seen this before. Bombing."

"Yes," she agreed, grateful the child was physically uninjured, but immeasurably concerned for his wounded soul.

"He will not let go of you?" Baruch asked.

Her reply was controlled. She could not let Baruch know how much she was affected by this boy. She had learned to harness her emotion, to keep grief hidden beneath the surface. "I will bathe him, then. Warm water does wonders for such cases. Clean clothes. I will take him to poor Hannah at Tipat Chalev. She will feed him soup. She will help. When he is with other children, perhaps . . ."

Baruch inhaled deeply, disagreeing. "I think the good God has given this matter into your hands, Lori Kalner."

"You need me here, and you know it . . . there is so much to be done. I can't—"

A knowing expression flitted across Baruch's lips. "Life often calls to us when there is so much to be done, eh? When did you last recognize it? Life, I mean? When did you last yield to it?"

"I . . . I don't understand. . . ."

"I have watched you. You are good with trauma, indeed. Self-controlled, steady and sure of yourself as you wade through blood. You would make a fine doctor, I think. And yet—"

"I can't hear this. Not tonight," she said, feeling as though she would break.

"There is nothing I can say that you do not already know." The kind doctor shrugged. He would not offer healing when it was not welcome. "So Lori . . . Bathe yourself. You are covered in blood. And bathe him then. Take him to Tipat Chalev. Hannah Cohen will welcome him, poor child. Hannah has lost her only family as well. Poor woman. She will need to spend her grief on compassion for someone who has lost even more than she. That is how grief takes wings and becomes love." His thin face overflowed with pity. "Yes. You are right. There is much to be done here. Two surgeries. Too much for you to be gone long."

■ ■ ■ ■

From David's vantage point in the orange tree he saw not only the executions but the aftermath. Syrian soldiers dragged more bodies out of the darkness and piled them on top of the gunners.

*Must be the guys who were supposed to meet the plane.*

The Arabs carefully gathered up any Haganah weapons. They prodded the edges of the glowing plane wreck. David wished for just one more unexploded mortar round to choose this instant to ignite.

As if in mocking reply, the flashes of artillery shells lit the night miles away to the west.

*Part of the Syrian offensive or a Jewish counterattack?*

Trucks roared up out of the darkness. The Syrians embarked, leaving the bodies of the Jewish soldiers where they lay.

The Arab commander, hands on hips, made one final visual sweep of the scene. For a moment it seemed that the man's eyes met David's, that he was looking directly at David's hiding place. Apparently satisfied, the officer climbed into the cab, and the column motored off eastward.

David's discomfort on his perch was agonizing, yet he was afraid to move.

*What if that commander left one squad strung out around the orchard? He must know we're Americans. What is the propaganda value of displaying captured Americans in Damascus?*

He was still thinking in plural terms. David believed that Bobby Milkin was out there somewhere, alive.

Realizing he could not let dawn arrive without putting some distance between him and the scene, David eased himself down one branch. He let the limb take his weight, then hesitated again, listening for any sign of a lurking sentry.

There was a gap between the lowest branch and the ground.

*Hit the ground running!*

He dropped the last few feet. No sign of an alerted guard.

At his first stride the pointed toe of a cowboy boot kicked something that clattered metallically over the pebbles.

His pistol.

David bent to retrieve it. It must have fallen when he climbed the tree. It had been lying on the ground the whole time, literally under the feet of the Arabs who were searching for him. He had been lucky.

No sounds except the whirring of insects and the wind. The distant shellfire had stopped. Breathing a trifle more easily, David was caught off guard when a rustling of leaves was followed by a nearby ponderous thud. The crash was succeeded by a groan.

Pistol in hand, David froze, aiming the muzzle in the direction of the sound.

Then came a curse in finest Brooklynese and a crunching noise in fallen leaves.

"Bobby?"

"David?"

"You all right?"

"Dropped my last cigar!"

Holstering the pistol, David advanced toward his friend. The shifting night wind swirled. "Milkin! Is that you? Man, you stink!"

"And you call that a landing? I told you I was gonna have a problem."

■ ■ ■ ■

The two pilots huddled in a ditch beside the orange grove.

"What are we gonna do?" Bobby Milkin asked. "Which way to our guys?"

Glancing up, David took in the Big Dipper and the North Star. Pointing south he replied, "That way, I guess. It's where the map showed a kibbutz."

"Yeah? And what if the Syrians paid it a social call before comin' here?"

"You got any better ideas?"

They followed the ditch until it dead-ended against a dirt track. The two men hunkered down behind a boulder. The air, at least the air upwind from Bobby, was scented with sweet orange blossoms and pungent sage. Crickets chirped. It reminded David of the foothills of California. All these things were deceptively friendly associations. Across the road was a field covered with waist-high grain stalks. David reminded himself that a few hundred yards in the other direction lay the bodies of men like himself, who happened to be on the wrong side of the Arab fence tonight.

"We waitin' for Christmas? Or what?" Bobby demanded.

"Hold it!" David warned, putting a hand on Bobby's arm. "I hear something."

*Engine noises, approaching from the west.*

A line of trucks, illuminated only by cat's-eye headlight slits, motored past. David watched the first lorry long enough to see that the markings were in Arabic script, not Hebrew.

Milkin swore under his breath.

They plastered themselves against the rock face.

"What is this, the whole Syrian army? How many more?" Bobby hissed when the count reached nine.

"Shut up!"

The last truck in the column lagged behind the others by a hundred yards. It coughed and sputtered. With an ominous clatter, it ground to a halt directly in front of the boulder.

"Back! Get back!" David urged. The toes of David's boots plowed furrows as he and Milkin scooted on their bellies away from the road.

Frustrated Arabic voices seemed to be scant inches from David's hiding place. The bonnet of the disabled lorry flew up with a crash that made David jump. He groped for his sidearm.

*One pistol. Eight shots. Bobby's got zip. How many Syrians are there? Fifteen? Twenty?*

More Arabic discussion was followed by a shouted order. The truck's starter ground endlessly, but the engine refused to catch. With a dismal dragging noise it revolved slower and slower.

*It's the carburetor! Idiots! Don't kill the battery! They're gonna kill the battery. Then they're gonna kill us!*

Footsteps approached the ditch. David held his breath. Beads of sweat dripped from his brow into his eyes. His hand on the pistol, he tensed, ready to kill the intruder if he got any closer.

*God, I don't want to die in a ditch beside the road!*

A stream of falling liquid spattered across the rocks as the Syrian relieved himself.

Then the truck motor caught with a reverberating bellow. The hood banged shut. Urgent words called the urinating trooper back. The truck moved forward before the soldier reached it, forcing him to catch the tailgate and swing himself aboard. There were laughter and taunts from the troops.

Engine racing, the lorry bounced away, intent on catching up to the convoy.

Bobby and David emerged from hiding.

"Okay. So now we both need a change of clothes," David said.

# CHAPTER 19

The child followed Lori's exit from the Hurva with his eyes. When she was gone, the glazed expression once again slipped over his features like a mask.

Hannah Cohen welcomed little Abe onto her ample lap as Rachel, Yehudit Avram, and old Shoshannah took over the duties of feeding the children and the refugees.

Abe leaned his head against Hannah's bosom and stared with a vacant expression at the bustle of the Tipat Chalev soup kitchen. He still would not release his blue blanket to be cleaned. He did not accept either food or even a drop of milk to drink.

Hannah rocked him and sang to him, but Abe did not seem to notice. His mind had drifted to a distant place and would not be called back. He would not close his eyes to sleep.

After a few hours Rachel took him from Hannah, who slipped away to rest awhile. Rachel sang to him, but he did not hear her voice. Again the offer of nourishment was made and rejected. Yehudit tried to coax the blanket from his hands. Tiny fists gripped it desperately. Knuckles whitened as he clung to the piece of fabric.

Old Shoshanna relieved Rachel. Her kindly voice and gentle hand upon the child's brow made no impression. Mothers brought their children to speak to him, to ask him to play. He did not acknowledge their presence.

Hannah came back and stood beside Rachel. The two women observed the child with pity.

"He has not slept?"

"No," Rachel replied. "Nor eaten. Nor had anything to drink."

"His little soul has decided to fly away," Hannah said in a wondering tone. "I have seen such with older folk. Never with one so tender in age. They let go, and there is no calling them back."

"There must be something to do. To reach him."

Hannah said, "He sees what we do not see. Look at his face."

Rachel replied, "When I was a child I found a little bird beneath the tree in our garden. It had fallen from the nest. The mother bird scolded me from the branches as I picked up the baby and carried it into my father's study. He told me it would die. Mama and I tried hard to feed it, but . . ."

Hannah took Abe into her arms again. He was limp and unresponsive. "If you will sleep awhile, little one," Hanna crooned, "morning will come and you can play with the other children, *nu?*"

He gave no sign that he heard her encouragement.

■ ■ ■ ■

David experienced the weight of weariness. How far had they traveled across the hilly terrain of Galilee? In two hours the sun would rise and they would be sitting ducks.

"Can't travel by day. We gotta hole up someplace," he said. "Sleep awhile. Travel again tomorrow night."

"Day or night, we gotta get out of these clothes," Bobby Milkin muttered.

"One whiff of you, camel driver, and they'll shoot us in self-defense."

"How long you think it'll take 'em to notice the cowboy boots?"

"They're good luck."

"Some good! Some luck! You gotta ditch the boots."

"Over my dead body." David bristled.

"Die with your boots on, Tin Man, but I ain't gonna be there to watch," Milkin grumbled.

"We walk another hour, then, but no more."

The allotted hour stretched into ninety minutes. Their hike took them down a long canyon. There was no sign of habitation. No kibbutz to welcome them.

They stumbled across the remains of an L-shaped stone fence with a crude shelter. It was overhung by a ledge that promised relief from the late-May sun. "Sheep pen?" David suggested. "What do you say we hang it up?"

"It ain't the Ritz, but under the circumstances . . ." Bobby sank down. "What I wouldn't give for a cigar."

No sooner had David selected a flat stone for a pillow and curled himself around another rock than Bobby said, "You hear somethin'?"

"Yeah. You. Shut up, why don't you?"

Bobby refused to be shushed. "There it is again. Hear it?"

"No, I—" David interrupted himself. "A bell?"

"Bicycle?" Bobby guessed. "There ain't any trolleys runnin' out here."

"Trolley! Geez, Milkin! Your mama never took you to see a Shirley Temple movie? Happy orphan kid sheepherding in Switzerland. Leaves her old grandfather. Heidi. You know? It's a cow . . . no, must be a goat's bell."

Milkin's brain was lagging. "Shirley Temple? Nah. My mama liked gangster pictures. George Raft. Bogart. Wild about Bogart. G-men. Tommyguns. We could sure use a tommygun."

David ignored him and sat up. "Come on." A bell around the neck of a goat meant a flock of the things were close. Goats? Sheep? That meant shepherds. Clothes. Maybe food.

Milkin followed reluctantly.

Beyond where the canyon's walls shrank in height and its mouth widened, David spotted a dark, oblong shape. It looked like an enormous coffin barring their progress.

"Bedouin tent," David remarked. "No lights. No sounds. Everybody's asleep. Let's see what we can pinch."

"I'll go," Bobby volunteered. "No sense both of us riskin' our necks."

True to Bobby's fondest wish, three striped robes hung across one of the guy ropes that supported the enclosure. He snapped up two and retreated back to where David waited.

A chained dog barked viciously.

Confused shouts erupted inside the tent. "Run for it!" Bobby yelled as he passed David.

A figure in flapping cloth loomed up. There was a snap and *whooshing* jet of flame as the pursuer shot an antique muzzle-loading rifle.

David fired one shot into the air in return.

The flapping sandals retreated toward the encampment.

Back at the abandoned sheepfold, Bobby and David donned the robes, then buried their clothing under a heap of stones. Except for David's lucky boots.

Milkin scowled, "So when's the last time those things brought you luck, Tin Man? I'm hangin' around you. I got no luck. Lost two Messers out of Athens. Nearly killed last night. Lost that plane. Shot at by Shirley Temple's grandfather . . . This is luck?"

"We're alive, ain't we?" The sky was beginning to lighten in the east. David suggested, "Let's get out of here, find a hole and sleep."

■ ■ ■ ■

As the world watched, Arab forces closed around Israel.

But what surprised the global observers was the lack of a conclusion.

Despite the confident predictions of Arab spokesmen that the conflict would last barely three days, it rolled to the end of the first week with no sign of a definitive Arab victory.

The Jewish settlement of Yad Mordechai, on the main coast highway to Egypt, still had not surrendered.

The Lebanese, after preserving their honor with a few skirmishes, settled into a defensive posture.

The Arab Legion, bowing at last to pressure from other Arab states, attacked a target outside Jerusalem—a power plant at Naharayim. Otherwise, the British-led and -equipped juggernaut of the Legion—which was supposed to split Israel in two and bring a speedy end to the war— was no nearer that goal than at the beginning of the contest.

In the Old City of Jerusalem, Daoud did not mean to eavesdrop on the conversation between Sister Marie Claire and Mother Superior. He sat on a bench behind a potted palm as they plotted their escape back into the convent. They did not see him. Sister Marie Claire spoke rapidly and in an urgent whisper. Just the sort of voice one could not help listening to. So it was that Daoud could not help hearing everything.

"But Mother," said Sister Marie Claire. "We prayed for peace. The Archbishop has telephoned everyone about our convent. The Americans! The English King! And poor Mister Churchill, who says he regrets very much that he is voted out of office and is not a political force any longer. Not even the Holy Father's direct plea to King Abdullah will make him order his fellows to stop shooting at our beloved home. Nor will Ben-Gurion make his soldiers give up Soeurs Réparatrices! They say they gave up the bell tower of Saint Jacques and the Arabs took it. They will not make such a mistake again!"

"Then *we* shall make them leave the convent," said Mother Superior in a determined voice.

"Make them. How can we make them do what the Holy Father and . . . and . . . Winston Churchill cannot do?"

"They are barbarians, but they would not kill servants of God. They will not fire upon the convent if we return to it."

"Shall we all go? Sister Angélique is so very frail . . ."

"No. You and I shall go, Sister Marie Claire. We shall leave when it is darkest night. I shall take with me the papal flag, and we shall hang it from the window of the upper floor for all the combatants to see. They will not blast the flag of the Holy Father. They would not dare!"

Sister Marie Claire quietly considered this proposal. "I am not certain I know my way back out of here. And in the dark, too?"

Daoud leapt to his feet and parted the potted palm. "I know the way!" he declared.

The women stared at him suspiciously, as if he were an intruder.

Sister Marie Claire, who liked him and fed him well, said, "It is a sin to eavesdrop on a private conversation."

Daoud replied, "Not for Muslims."

Mother Superior's expression changed from disapproval to canny appraisal. "You know the Old City, Daoud?"

"Very well, Mother."

The old woman said to Marie Claire, "He will be safe with us."

Daoud added, "I shall go with you! I know the way! There is a way out and the men of the Jihad will not even look up as you pass."

Mother Superior said firmly, "It is God's will the child was there behind the palm. He has heard us and offered to help and . . . I am certain it is the will of God!"

■ ■ ■ ■

Jacob Kalner slept in the cellar of the Mandelbaum house. For the first time in so many days that he could not count them he had allowed fatigue to drag him downward into unconsciousness. His last waking thoughts had been of Lori and worry over what the following day would bring, but his concern did not stop with slumber. He dreamed of

Arab Legionnaires swarming over the Old City defenses and overrunning the Jewish Quarter, shouting *"Deir Yassin!"*

He awoke to find himself, rifle in hand, standing in the middle of the basement floor. His befuddled brain could not fathom how he came to be there until the pavement again bounced under his feet as the second shell of the Arab pre-dawn barrage landed in Mea Shearim.

He groped for his cartridge belt and refilled his pouch of grenades.

Jacob's move toward the stairs was intercepted by Peter Wallich. "They won't attack until the barrage is lifted," Peter said. "Major Thomas has his three armored cars out of sight, but flanking Saint George Road, ready to trap the Legion if they come into Mea Shearim."

Three battered armored cars against the entire Arab Legion! And how much ammunition did Thomas's group have? And how much enemy armor would they face? Would the odds be five-to-one? Six? Worse?

Peter continued his instructions, unaware of Jacob's internal anxiety. "The major wants you and your machine gun here, but be ready to blow up the rigged house behind the Arab advance if they come this way."

If! What a singularly insignificant word to contain so much desperate thought!

Wanting so badly to protect Lori, Jacob willed all the Arab forces in the world to descend upon *him*.

"Twelve," Peter counted as another detonation rumbled through the New City. "Thirteen, fourteen." To Jacob he added, "Major Thomas says if the Arabs follow British doctrine they will use five shells per gun, and he thinks the battery is only four cannons. So . . . fifteen! Sixteen!" At the count of "Twenty!" the shellfire stopped. "God go with you," Peter said.

■ ■ ■ ■

From the sanctuary of the Hurva Synagogue, Yacov shouted, "Twenty!" as the last Arab artillery shell thundered from the cannons on the Mount of Olives to rip across the sky and explode outside the Old City walls in Jewish-held Mea Shearim.

Then, silence.

Rachel uncovered her ears.

"Are they finished?" Rachel asked.

Yacov grasped her hand. "With the barrage, yes. Moshe taught me how to count. Five shells from each gun. The English way. The way they did it at El Alamein against the Germans. They have softened up our positions on Mea Shearim so they can bring their armored cars and infantry down Nablus Road maybe to Damascus Gate. Or maybe turn down Saint George at the fork and try to take Mea Shearim. Come on. You want to see?"

"From where?"

Yacov pointed toward the dome of the Hurva. "Up there. With Moshe and Alfie and Ehud. The dome."

"It cannot be safe," Rachel said. "Moshe told me—"

"It is as safe as anywhere in the Jewish Quarter," the boy said brightly. "If they want to blast the Hurva we are dead inside or out. As for Arab snipers? They will also be watching what happens outside the walls. Like a cricket match. True? No one understands the rules but everyone shouts. Eventually someone wins, and no one knows how or why. . . . This morning we in the Jewish Quarter are forgotten. The Arab Legion is thinking of playing cricket against the Jewish-held New City. Otherwise they would have been pitching their bombs at us here and we would already be dead, *nu?* We will be able to see everything to the north and west. Mount Scopus. The Nablus Road, where they will come. You can see the Hospice of Notre Dame on the other side of the walls from there. Alfie says our chaps still hold it."

Rachel followed him.

Dashing across the sanctuary to the stairs that led up to the women's gallery and out to the roof he called, "Since the shelling is finished, the Arab Legion will advance against our positions in the New City. *Come on!* Maybe they will come straight into the Old City through Damascus Gate. *Hurry up!* Armored cars and infantry. Then we should run! But also maybe there will be a big fight in Mea Shearim. Maybe they will want to conquer the entire Jewish-held New City, *nu?* Then we will be an island here. Probably then we will have to surrender! But me and the Krepski brothers have vowed we will die fighting first."

"How do you seem to know everything?" asked Rachel, genuinely irritated with his prattle about dying.

"Moshe told me what they would do. It is the English way. He knows the English way. The battle for the New City will begin soon."

■ ■ ■ ■

Of the armored force cobbled together by Luke Thomas, a single car had weaponry more powerful than machine guns. The Daimler vehicle stolen from the British in the last days of the Mandate was equipped with a twenty-millimeter cannon, capable of firing incendiary cartridges or rounds that could pierce steel.

The major deployed the other two vehicles so that one was on Mea Shearim Road, ready to hit the Arabs in the flank and the other across St. George Road in an alleyway, positioned to do the same.

Electing to command the Daimler himself, Thomas placed it behind the roadblock that had been the Hasidic tenement building. The cannon had a clear field of fire up the length of St. George Road, all the way past the Mandelbaum house.

The location meant he would be exposed to enemy fire from the moment the Arab armor made the turn toward Mea Shearim, but Thomas gave that consequence of the post no thought. If the Legion did, God willing, turn away from the Old City and into Mea Shearim, stopping them would depend on an all-out first effort. The Haganah could not allow the Arabs time to maneuver.

Nor would the infantry be far behind. A regiment of Legionnaires charging with machine guns, grenades, and bazookas would finish any chance of resisting the armored vehicles.

Not merely one but a whole string of miracles would be required for Jewish Jerusalem to resist the assault for even one more day.

# CHAPTER 20

The seventeen engines of the Arab Legion's armored cars rumbled. It was one contingent out of the Arab Legion force, but more than enough to overwhelm the ragtag band of Jews.

The lead vehicle was driven by Gamel Azzam, a Jordanian soldier from a desert tribe more used to camels than motorcars. Azzam had never been to Jerusalem before.

"Let nothing delay you," he had been told. "Take the road straight down the hill and you will arrive at Damascus Gate and complete the link with the Old City."

Riding with Azzam at the front of the column was Lt. Negri Shufik. An artillery spotter attached to the Olivet battery, Shufik had never been to Jerusalem before, either. His orders were also clear: accompany Azzam into the Arab-held section of Jerusalem, locate a suitable observation post, and make radio contact with the Mount of Olives. The importance of his mission had been underlined for him. "Arab Musrara and Jewish Mea Shearim are separated only by the most winding of curving streets. From east of Jerusalem it is impossible to accurately place cannonfire on targets without a spotter to correct the aim. Under no circumstances are you to get involved in the battle. We need your reports to begin as soon as possible so we can shell Jewish positions without endangering our own advancing troops."

Both men understood their orders.

As soon as the barrage stopped, though it was half-past five in the morning, Shufik announced to Azzam, "Let's go!"

Azzam, pleased to have such a clear-minded officer with him, engaged the gears and moved the armored car forward. When he did so, the sixteen other vehicles followed.

Major Tariq Athani came out of the mosque where he had been at morning prayers. "Where are they going?" he asked his aide, who shrugged. "The attack is not scheduled for another half hour. Get our men into line!"

Once more, the armor was moving to attack without infantry support.

■ ■ ■ ■

From the roof of the Mandelbaum house, Uri Tabken saw a Legion armored car come over the crest of the hill at Sheikh Jarrah and begin its descent. "The Arab Legion is coming!" he yelled. "Everyone to your posts! They are coming!"

During the night Arab sappers had used the cover of darkness to slip beyond Sheikh Jarrah and clear Jacob's roadblock. The armored column moved without haste, but inexorably, along the road, flaunting their strength.

Hunched over his machine gun, Jacob slapped the receiver shut on a belt of ammunition and peered up the hill. For the second time that morning Jacob found himself among people who were counting. Three Arab vehicles followed the Nablus Road, then two more . . . then more . . . and still more. . . .

He spared a glance downward, reassuring himself that the wires leading from the detonator to the explosives at the spice merchant's house were intact.

In the other direction, back down St. George Road, and away from the advancing Arabs, hurried a mass of Jewish civilians. Mattresses over shoulders, carrying suitcases and pushing handcarts loaded with dishes, the nightgowned residents of Mea Shearim were fleeing again. Those who had returned in the wake of Luke Thomas's three armored cars were retreating at the first Arab barrage, even though it was not yet dawn.

Resuming the count, Jacob noted a total of seventeen armored cars advancing at such a methodical pace that it was terrifying in its self-assurance. Seventeen! The rolling machines, bristling with weapons, exuded confident superiority.

But which way would they go at the bottom of the hill?

Would they take the fork in the road that brought them toward Mea Shearim, or would they continue straight toward the Damascus Gate?

There was one positive thing to report: "They are coming without infantry," Jacob said aloud. To Naomi Snow, assigned to Jacob as a courier, he ordered, "Take this message to Major Thomas: Legion armored column moving. Seventeen armored cars headed down Nablus Road, destination not yet known. No infantry in sight."

The Mandelbaum house had no antitank weapons, no bazookas. Nothing but Jacob's machine gun, petrol bombs, and a few grenades. If the Legion turned toward Mea Shearim, it would be like facing a charging herd of bulls. Courage and determination were essential, but common sense said fortune favored the bulls!

And what was worse?

Seventeen Arab Legion armored cars moving unopposed to the Old City? All hope was lost! If it was as Major Thomas imagined and Jacob feared, the Arab Legion was going to go straight down the hill and arrive at the gates of Jerusalem uncontested.

Lori!

All the preparation that might stop the Arabs if they took the fork to the right on St. George Road toward Mea Shearim would come to nothing if they continued on.

If only they would veer right, Jacob thought. Luke Thomas's armored cars were ready, the blasting charges in place, the petrol bombs waiting, the trap set.

If only there were a way to make them turn toward Jacob's position at the Mandelbaum house.

Bring on the charging bulls!

■ ■ ■ ■

From the machine-gun nest atop the Hurva, the New City neighborhoods of Jewish-held Mea Shearim and Arab-held Sheikh Jarrah were plainly visible. Along with Moshe, Ehud, and Alfie, twenty other spectators had climbed onto the roof to watch. What happened next would decide the fate of the Old City Jewish Quarter.

Rachel settled in behind the sandbagged fortification between Moshe and Alfie. Moshe and Ehud observed through field glasses.

Smoke roiled up from Mea Shearim. The Nablus Road, winding down toward the Damascus Gate, was a black ribbon in the early-morning sunlight. St. George Avenue forked off the Nablus Road to the right and slashed through the center of Mea Shearim.

"I see them," Moshe announced. "I count seventeen armored cars moving down Nablus. Coming straight for us."

Ehud concurred. "*Oy!*" he said. "So many! If only they would turn right."

Moshe said to Rachel, then to Yacov, "Look toward the smoke. That is Mea Shearim. Our fellows hold that neighborhood. If the Legion takes the fork down Saint George Avenue toward Mea Shearim, we might have a chance. Another day at least to retake Zion Gate and get more men in here to defend against a frontal attack."

"And if they take the left fork?" Yacov asked. "If they come straight to Damascus Gate and into the Old City? We will still fight them, *nu?* We will still beat them, eh, Moshe?"

Moshe did not reply.

Rachel queried, "What happens if they break through our lines at Mea Shearim?"

Ehud replied, "They will be sipping tea in Zion Square before noon. Jewish-held Jerusalem will be finished, eh?"

Moshe's silence confirmed the big man's gruff honesty.

No one spoke as the vehicles crept like beetles down a branch.

Moshe muttered, "Infantry? Where are they? Come on. I don't see their infantry. Unusual for an armored column to advance without infantry."

Alfie blurted, "Look! I see them!" He rose up and pointed to the plateau. "Thousands. See? Look! Soldiers! Marching where Jacob is!"

Every eye strained to see. Someone commented that the idiot was seeing things again.

Rachel tried to calm Alfie. "We don't know where Jacob is."

"Yes. He is down there in the smoke. Down there where all the soldiers are going."

"Tell him to shut up," complained a Yeshiva defender. "We are trying to watch, *nu?*"

"It looks as though they mean to come straight to Damascus Gate." Moshe's tone was solemn. "Take us out here in the Old City first."

"There are more of us than there are of them," Alfie cried joyfully.

"Seventeen armored cars!" scoffed the Yeshiva student. "You call that more of us?"

Like Yacov, Alfie's enthusiasm and confidence had become an irritation in the face of the obvious.

"They are moving toward the fork," Moshe recounted. "Still no infantry. They are certainly coming to our positions, then."

Alfie responded by saying to Yacov, "The sun. The sun is so bright. The sun can make them blind."

"It would be nice, *nu?*" Yacov responded patiently.

Alfie, irrepressible, leapt to his feet as the column approached the fork in the road. He cupped his hands around his mouth and shouted, "This is not the way! This is not the city!"

■ ■ ■ ■

After the third sharp turn below Sheikh Jarrah, the Nablus Road aimed itself at the Damascus Gate. Gamel Azzam, his confidence growing as the bottom of the slope approached, gasped with astonishment. The rising sun illuminated the Temple Mount, previously buried in the shadow of the Mount of Olives.

Jerusalem revealed—reveled in—its splendor.

"But it is beautiful!" the driver exclaimed.

"And it is about to be ours," Lieutenant Shufik exulted. "Go on, speed up!"

Looming ahead on the left was the bulk of the Dominican church of St. Stephen the Martyr. It was within Arab-held territory and would make an excellent observation post for the artillery spotter.

To the right, its granite heights equally dominating the approach to the north wall, was the Jewish-held Hospice of Notre Dame. From the direction of their advance, Shufik could see the huge statue of Mary— Miriam as she was known to Muslims—holding aloft the infant prophet Jesus. The sun in its climb caused the gold-leaf adorning the brows of the two figures to gleam.

Shufik studied the sculpture, enrapt with its beauty.

Then the sun rose higher over the city and its rays beamed directly at the five hundred windows with which the edifice of Notre Dame was pierced. On such a brilliant, cloudless morning, every beam was reflected back, and all of them seemed to penetrate Shufik's visor, blinding him. "Ah!" he exclaimed. Then without thinking added, "Look!"

Azzam slowed and stared in the direction Shufik indicated. His eyes and senses were struck by a burst of light more powerful than he had ever experienced. "I cannot see!" he complained, coming to a halt and breaking into a sweat lest the car following behind crash into them.

A bullet clanged against the armor.

"Move this!" Shufik commanded.

"Yes, yes!" Azzam agreed. "But I cannot see. Which way is the road?"

"Keep going straight!" Shufik said, exasperated. "We were going straight before! Just keep on!"

One block ahead, the Nablus Road actually took the slightest of jogs to the left to accommodate the intersection with St. George Road.

Azzam, blinking away tears from his dazzled vision, turned the wheel to the left to follow the highway.

"What are you doing?" Shufik demanded. "Straight! Straight! Here, let me!" And he yanked the steering wheel to the right, sending the leading vehicle and the entire column of Arab armored cars in the wrong direction, down St. George Road toward Mea Shearim.

■ ■ ■ ■

Peering between the sights of his machine gun toward the far end of St. George Road, Jacob Kalner felt an electric charge run up his spine. The Arab Legion's armored cars, after stopping in the middle of the intersection, were turning toward him! Already the leading vehicle was lined up in the center of his sight picture. "They are coming!" he hissed. Then, louder, he repeated, "They are coming into the trap!"

Nervously he touched the plunger of the detonator. At the moment of contact he jerked his hand back, as if afraid that the tingle in his frame might set off the charge prematurely. The ambush was going to work! He was still standing between Lori and the Legion.

One floor below, Peter Wallich urged his teenage riflemen, "Wait for them! There is nothing your bullets can do to stop armor. Wait till they are close enough to use the Molotov cocktails."

■ ■ ■ ■

"I think I see a barricade," Azzam said, leaning forward to peer through his visor. "Up ahead, beyond that large house at the next corner."

"You are imagining things," Shufik corrected. "There cannot be any roadblocks on the way to the Damascus Gate. And we must be right because the Jews would never have let us come so far into Mea Shearim without shooting. It would be suicide for them."

The cavalcade motored along St. George. No one was in sight on the street, neither shooting nor cheering. "Where are the crowds?" Azzam wondered aloud. "I thought our people would turn out to welcome us as the saviors of Jerusalem."

"It is strange," Shufik noted, his vision clearing at last. "Perhaps they are afraid of the shellfire. All the more reason for me to find an observation post as soon as possible."

Debris from pervious Arab cannonfire littered part of the road, but Azzam was able to skirt it easily. They passed the large three-story house at the corner of St. George and Hanevi Avenue. Its windows were broken, but the rooftop was lined with sandbags.

"I do not understand," Azzam said, glancing up. "This is not the road."

Those were the last words he ever spoke.

■ ■ ■ ■

"Fire!" Luke Thomas yelled, even though he was himself pulling the trigger of the twenty-millimeter cannon. A steady drumbeat of pulsing thunder split the morning as round after round of armor-piercing shells zipped across the blocks that separated Jewish from Arab vehicles.

Thomas watched as his salvo ripped into the leading armored car. Part of the turret tore open like a tin can; then a hatch, ripped from its hinges, flew upward and away as if a giant wind had lifted it and tossed it aside. The car lurched sideways, then accelerated with a roar. Jumping the curb, the vehicle smashed into a stone water fountain, slued sideways, turned partially on its side, then slammed into a light pole, its underbelly exposed to the incoming cannonfire.

After the initial set of armor-piercing shells, Thomas had loaded the belt with incendiary rounds. At first these gave no evidence of causing any additional damage, but then they impacted the undercarriage of the armored car and it exploded.

The entire body of the vehicle lifted up on a fireball of exploding ammunition and fuel and was thrown over backwards, to land on top of the second armored car.

■ ■ ■ ■

Jacob opened up with his machine gun. Since the first two armored cars had already passed his position, he concentrated his fire on the third. Sweeping the machine-gun barrel back and forth in patient arcs and firing short bursts of five rounds each, Jacob aimed at the visor slits.

His target fired back, but his bullets sliced into the Mandelbaum house at ground level.

It was the fourth car in the line that elevated its sights. Beside Jacob's location a string of fifty-caliber slugs lacerated the sandbags, then tore into a Gadna Youth rifleman. The soldier, a boy of no more than fifteen, threw up his hands to his face, then toppled over the parapet.

From the next floor below, Jacob heard Peter Wallich yell, "Now! Now!" and glass bottles of petrol, their descent traced by the smoke of flaming rag fuses, arched toward the crippled vehicles. Two smashed directly on the enmeshed armored cars, showering them with flaming gasoline. Two more Molotov cocktails detonated in front of the third vehicle, which reversed and rammed into the fourth, spoiling the aim of its gunner.

From the alley and the side street, the other Jewish armored cars added their volleys to the carnage. Jacob could see that confusion reigned in the Arab column. They had not been expecting to be attacked at all! They were in close order, one behind the other, and had to maneuver sideways before they could even bring their guns to bear on their assailants.

One man jumped from the flaming wreckage of car number two and ran toward the rear. In the process of reloading, Jacob glanced to the side at Uri Tabken. The young man aimed his rifle, but then closed his eyes when jerking the trigger. A bullet struck the pavement beside the fleeing Arab, making him run even faster.

Jacob could see at the end of St. George Road that no more armored cars were coming in the direction of Mea Shearim. As he watched, the far end of the column began to move in reverse, back out of the trap. It was time to demolish the other building in order to catch as many of the Arab vehicles as possible.

Yanking upward on the black handle of the detonator, Jacob prepared to send the electric charge that would touch off the dynamite. Bracing himself against the stone parapet for the blast that would follow, he thrust the plunger downward.

Nothing happened.

No thunderous eruption followed.

Hurriedly tugging the handle up past the ratchets, he leaned into the downward stroke with all his weight.

Nothing.

Something had cut the wires leading to the charges.

They would have to be ignited another way if the trap was to succeed.

"Come with me!" Jacob yelled to Uri Tabken.

There was a chance the mines could be exploded using prima-cord fuses. Turning his machine gun over to another Gadna fighter, Jacob and his assistant descended to the first floor of the Mandelbaum house. The spice merchant's house was a half block away, and an alleyway gave cover from the bullets of the armored cars.

If only they could get there before the Arab Legion sent its infantry!

■ ■ ■ ■

Jacob and Uri dashed across Hanevi Avenue and reached the alley behind the spice merchant's house. A shell burst against the roof of the building as they entered. Slate roof tiles shattered, and fragments landed on the pavement behind them as they ducked inside.

Uri huddled against the wall inside the kitchen, struggling to catch his breath after the dash. Reaching up from his crouched position, Jacob yanked the boy to his knees. "Keep low!" he ordered.

Heavy-caliber slugs fired from St. George Road in front of the house slashed through the front windows, the dining room wall, and the hallway, to splinter copper pans hanging from the kitchen ceiling.

"The charges are in place," Jacob noted. Then, indicating the two coils of fuse, he added, "Help me string these to the back door. From there we'll splice them into one."

■ ■ ■ ■

Major Athani led the third company of his infantry at a run down Nablus Road toward the intersection with St. George. The fourth company followed farther behind, held in reserve until Athani decided where to commit them.

Reaching the stalled line of armored cars, he pounded on a hatch. "What's the situation?" he demanded.

The commander of the vehicle knew very little. "Seven of our column made the turn to the right, then the Jews attacked. You can hear our cannons returning the fire."

"This is the wrong road, anyway!" Athani bellowed. "You were supposed to go to Damascus Gate! Go past the turn and straight ahead."

The armored-car officer was shocked. "We cannot leave our comrades!" he argued. "We will advance and fight our way through!"

Half of the Arab column was trying to reverse its way out of the trap. The other half of the Legion force was trying to maneuver a way into St. George Road. There was a traffic jam caused by those trying to retreat while blocked by those still creeping forward.

A Davidka round, fired by Luke Thomas's men, whistled overhead and exploded across the street from the corner of Nablus and St. George. "Move!" Athani said urgently. "Make this thing climb a wall if you have to, but get it out of—"

The following Davidka round dropped just behind the eighth Legion vehicle, spun it around like a top, and blew out two of its tires. Now the intersection was completely obstructed. None of the trapped Arab armored cars could get out of St. George Road and none outside St. George could proceed to Damascus Gate until the way was cleared. "Back it up!" Athani ordered the rear half of the column. "Back to Sheikh Jarrah! My men will rescue the others. Get this armor out of here before we lose it entirely!"

# CHAPTER 21

Naomi Snow peered around the fractured stone tracery that had been one of Mandelbaum's second-floor windows and fired her rifle. With the practiced ease of a seasoned veteran, she ducked back behind shelter as Arab Legion bullets smacked the outside wall.

Peter Wallich's teenage troopers were doing well. Despite the disparity of weapons, they were more than holding their own against the armored cars. Car three had taken a direct hit from a petrol bomb, and its crew abandoned the vehicle. Car four was in a three-way duel with the remaining flanking Haganah armored cars and the Davidka mortar.

Up on the roof with Jacob's machine gun, Peter had managed to blow out one of car five's tires before the weapon jammed again. The Legion's armored cars, as powerful as they were, could not shoot in all directions at once. They had shown their vulnerability to Molotov cocktails and mortar shells. If Jacob could hurry up and destroy the building behind the remaining vehicles, the net would be closed, snaring more Arab machines.

Thinking about Jacob's mission caused Peter to look across the intervening rock walls to the alleyway behind the spice seller's house. He noted with satisfaction that Jacob and Uri were outside on the stoop, slicing the fuses. It would not be long now.

There was movement in the haze of cordite smoke three blocks farther toward Sheikh Jarrah. More than fifty Arab Legionnaires, their red-and-white headgear standing out even through the smoke-shrouded air, were approaching Jacob's position. He and Uri were concentrating on the coil of prima-cord. Keeping no lookout, they were unaware of the approach of the Arab infantry.

With his machine gun jammed, there was nothing Peter could do against so many from such a distance.

How to warn Jacob? No shouting carried above the din of gunfire and detonations. The obvious escape route from the soon-to-be-demolished building would carry Jacob and Uri across an open space where they were certain to be seen and shot to pieces.

Peter grabbed a rifle. Praying that the sights were true, he worked the bolt, aimed at the wall over Jacob's head, and fired.

He saw the streak of white smoke left by the bullet's impact with the wall, saw Uri look up with alarm.

Jacob flinched, but bent to his task again.

Furiously working the stubborn bolt, Peter ratcheted in another cartridge and fired again.

This time Jacob also ducked as he realized the shot had come from behind him. Cautiously he turned to look.

Careless of his own safety, Peter stood up above the sandbags and waved. In emphatic gestures he pointed toward the approaching Arab infantry. *Get out of there,* his signals insisted. *You are about to be surrounded!*

■ ■ ■ ■

Jacob saw Peter Wallich waving again from the rooftop fortress of the Mandelbaum house. Over his head Peter brandished the Arab machine gun.

"That's it," Jacob said with finality. "Peter is telling us that he will try to make the Arabs keep their heads down while you climb over the walls."

"And you also?" Uri asked.

Jacob declined. "No time to argue. You must go as soon as he fires, and get as far away as you can, while I light the fuse. Get ready!"

Signaling to Peter, Jacob knelt behind the teenager. At the first staccato yammering of Peter's weapon, Jacob shoved Uri and shouted, "Go! Don't look back! Run!"

Bounding away like a frightened rabbit, Uri threw himself up and over the first intervening stone wall without even drawing a shot from the Legionnaires.

Jacob reviewed his options. Now that Peter had fired on the Legionnaires, they were sure to be alerted. After igniting the cord, Jacob would have no more than a half-minute before the detonation. If he was not far enough away, or if he ran directly into Legion rifle fire, the result would be the same. His fingers trembling, an icy breath of fear blew through his thoughts. Perhaps he could stay where he was and surrender?

It seemed the only way to avoid certain death.

Jacob heard the grumbling engines of the Arab armored cars and the rattle of their machine guns. If he did not close the trap, they would escape; he knew it. Every Legion weapon that survived this ambush would be turned against the Old City, where the odds of continued resistance were already stretched to the breaking point.

His hands again perfectly steady, Jacob lit the fuse. He even made certain that it caught before he sprinted down the alleyway.

No time to climb over many walls. Only speed and distance from the explosion could save him.

At the end of the garden he jumped one partition and landed in an open area that led halfway to the Nablus Road. This must be the route along which the Legionnaires were advancing.

Jacob's stomach tightened with the expectation of meeting a bullet. None came. No shots were fired.

Racing toward the corner of the next building, he spared a glance over his shoulder. There was no enemy in sight, not one!

He barely had time to question what this meant when the earth rumbled under his feet and the speeding fist of the concussion wave tumbled him into a rubbish heap.

■ ■ ■ ■

The Arab Legion drive into the New City sputtered and failed, but for a time fierce fighting engulfed Mandelbaum House. Uri Tabken was down to his last grenade and Naomi Snow to her final petrol bomb before the Legionnaires pulled back.

Had the Legion's armor punched through Mea Shearim . . . had two of the four Legion infantry companies not disappeared in the middle of the battle . . . the outcome might have been vastly different.

As the Arab Legion broke off the engagement in the New City, things heated up again in the Jewish Quarter of the Old.

REHOV HAYEHUDIM read the faded letters painted on the fifth course of stones above the gutter. The Street of the Jews was hot and dirty. It had always been those things in a Jerusalem summer, reflected Moshe, but in his youth he had never seen it so deserted. Because Arab snipers on top of the Old City wall could shoot right down the length of the street it was not safe to move openly in daylight. Drawing near or leaving the barricade had to be done in a stealthy manner until the last few unprotected yards. At that point only a rush and a jump behind the sandbags would serve. Even violent movement did not always confer protection. Ephraim Solomon, a Yeshiva student, had been wounded by an Arab bullet that very morning. Fortunately, the injury was only a scratch and the boy would be back on duty that night.

Turning his head, Moshe studied the other defenders: Dov, Yehudit, Rabbi Vultch, and the new man, Dieter Wottrich. He also gazed up the road toward the Hurva Synagogue and thought about his brief tryst with Rachel. When would they again be alone together in a place free of danger?

The heat made him drowsy. Rabbi Akiva's promise of a break in the shelling was holding true so far, whatever that fact meant. Perhaps the lull would give the Palmachniks a chance to reorganize and launch another attack on Zion Gate. In any case the respite from explosions was welcome.

The combination of quiet and the dense, heated air encouraged Moshe to give in to childhood memory. It was a substitute for fretting about Rachel's safety.

How wonderful this dusty street had been to a young boy growing up in Jerusalem. Open-air stalls offered oranges and figs, watermelons piled higher than his head, pyramids of limes and lemons. The Street of the Jews was a blind man's paradise. The aroma of freshly ground coffee mingled with the pungency of green olives and the oily fragrance of pickled herring.

Blinking hard, Moshe tried to clear his head of images of abundant groceries. It was another kind of self-inflicted torment. There were no figs there now, no limes, just barren trays that mocked the hungry.

A single shop on the lower end of Rehov Hayehudim still had something to offer. A heap of lumpy yellow soap cakes occupied the soap maker's window. This at a time when there was precious little water for drinking and none at all for washing!

Moshe forced himself to re-create the thoroughfare as it had really been in his youth.

There had been sounds as well: the tinsmiths and the cobblers always seemed to be competing for his admiration. The cobblers' stubby hammers clattered and thumped more than they rang, so the metal workers had the advantage there. But the solder used to form drinking cups and pierced-tin lanterns made his eyes water. Besides, the ferocious recklessness with which the cobblers plucked sharp spikes from mouth to hand to boot heel was impressive.

There had been an order to life in those days: Grapes in the summer gave way to raisins in the winter. Food again! Maybe such thoughts were inescapable. Yeshiva School, older brother, Eli, cuffing him for his miserably smudged copybook. *Don't disgrace the Sachars!* A sigh escaped Moshe unnoticed by any except Wottrich, who always seemed to be watching him, as indeed he was right then. Probably the man felt guilty for having wasted the ammunition. He was observing what Moshe did so as to avoid additional mistakes. The so-called information offered by the penitent Wottrich had been useless; the man could not even tell the Church of the Holy Sepulchre from the Mosque of Omar! His descriptions of Arab Legionnaires had them possessing everything from bazookas to tanks. Clearly the man had been frightened out of his wits. He was trying to be useful, but nothing he had seen made any sense.

Returning to his daydream, Moshe attempted to slip back into the pleasant pond of reminiscence, but found he could not. His last recollection had been of his brother, Eli; Eli who had fallen in love with an Arab girl and been murdered in riots inspired by the Mufti. Moshe had not even been in Jerusalem when it happened, but he felt guilty about it just the same. He had heard the gruesome details. The killing had been instituted by Ibrahim el-Hassan, whose own younger brother was still around, killing Jews.

Why did his brother's martyrdom and the recollection of Ibrahim el-Hassan cause Moshe to stare at Dieter Wottrich? What an absurd connection to make!

Moshe shook off his drowsiness and confused thoughts. He concentrated instead on the Quarter's immediate problems of ammunition, food, and water.

■ ■ ■ ■

The rumors were flying among the Old City Jews.

The Arab Legion had been thwarted by an angelic host.

Lightning from heaven struck the Arab armored cars.

Robert Brandenburg knew better. The Legion armor had fallen into an ambush. Unable to maneuver in the cramped lanes, they must have been hemmed in and picked off.

A child could make better use of armored vehicles than that!

Clearly, the feeble Jews were not really so feeble. The Haganah commanders knew how to set a trap and how to spring one!

Brandenburg viewed Moshe through slitted eyes. An oppressive glare reflected off every surface.

Brandenburg was not happy with his lack of progress in eliminating the Haganah leader. He had hoped for a brilliant stroke. Yet here he was, stuck in a trench, dirty, hot, and thirsty. He might even get shot by one of his own men.

There had been plenty of opportunities to kill Sachar. The Jewish commander was only a few yards away, preoccupied and inattentive. The rest of the motley sentries kept a cursory watch. Brandenburg was armed with an obsolete bolt-action rifle, but at this distance he could hardly miss.

The difficulty was that although all were drowsy, at least one of the guards was always alert. Sachar would be dead in one shot. But before Brandenburg could work the bolt or run ten steps he would certainly be killed as well. He had no interest in dying for the Arab cause or any other cause. He would wait until he had a decent chance of escape, even if it meant delaying until nightfall again.

The problem with waiting was that he did not want to be caught when the Legion shelling resumed. The great killing power of artillery did not distinguish friend from foe. Nor did he want to expose the character of Dieter Wottrich to any more scrutiny than necessary.

Gunfire, the rattle of machine guns, and the louder bangs of exploding grenades reached his ears. The noise of fighting came from far to the north, probably outside the Old City walls. Perhaps it was a Legion attack on Mea Shearim or on the Jewish stronghold at the Hospice of Notre Dame.

A muffled explosion resounded from the same direction as the other shooting. Unlike the previous sounds of the New City battle, this concussion was a deeper rumble, and it came from nearby. The guards regained their vigilance.

The possibility of eliminating Sachar slipped away again.

■ ■ ■ ■

The reverberation concerned the defenders at the Street of the Jews barricade.

"What was that?" Dov questioned Moshe. "It sounded too big to be a hand grenade, but we heard no shell pass over."

"It must have been another bomb attack. But where?"

Yehudit asked, "Armenian Quarter?"

Tense moments passed while the defenders speculated. Then a larger explosion succeeded the first and the location of the new threat was clear. It came from behind them, in their own territory.

One block away, between the Jewish blockade and the Sephardic synagogues, the front of what had been the cobbler's shop burst outward in a shower of bricks. Chunks of masonry rained down. The defenders covered their heads, and the air was choked with smoke. The thick brown cloud was almost too full of plaster dust to be breathable.

"Look out!" Moshe cautioned, through hacking coughs. "Rabbi Vultch! Keep watching Zion Gate! They may hit from two directions at once."

When the atmosphere cleared, Moshe could see a gaping hole where the building had been. A new passageway from the Arab-held territory had been blasted into the Jewish district. The Arabs had dynamited two back-to-back houses. Their new entry point was behind the Jewish front line of defense.

Before Moshe could repeat his warning, Arab Legionnaires appeared in the gap. A dozen troopers, firing rifles and Sten guns from the hip and tossing grenades, swarmed onto the Street of the Jews.

The barricade was an island, isolated from the rest of the Jewish Quarter. It was surrounded by Arabs. Shots poured in from two directions. They were in a cross fire.

Moshe, Dov, and Yehudit concentrated on the Arabs entering the Quarter from the new opening. Rabbi Vultch, on the other side of Brandenburg, kept up a methodical peppering of the Legionnaires on Zion Gate. His shots were deliberate. Carefully spaced rounds kept a second attack at bay.

"Shoot! So, shoot already!" Vultch urged Brandenburg, who was holding his fire. "This is not the time to save bullets!"

The Haganah forces fought back aggressively. The rush of Legion troopers emerging from the cobbler's shop stalled. Four Arab soldiers went down and were dragged to shelter in the ruined building.

"How can we get to the Hurva?" Dov yelled.

"We can't unless we drive them off!" Moshe shouted in return. "Then we can make a run for it." He fired a three-shot burst from his Sten gun and two Legionnaires ducked.

Brandenburg glanced around. Vultch was occupied with the snipers atop Zion Gate. Brandenburg raised his rifle and pivoted the barrel toward Moshe.

"Here, you, Wottrich!" Vultch said. "Give me a hand. Shoot at the wall. You won't hit anyone, but you may spoil their aim."

Biting his lip with frustration, Brandenburg obliged. He fired at the Zion Gate parapet, worked the bolt, fired again.

An Arab mortar round burst thirty yards in front of him. A Legion machine gun set up in the ruined building unleashed a torrent of bullets. The slugs slashed the outer cover of the sandbags behind which Dov, Moshe, and Yehudit lay prone. The three were forced to aim their weapons through small gaps in the rampart.

From two blocks north came shouting and a renewed flurry of shots. A whole string of explosions rattled the street. Haganah troopers on the rooftops lining the Street of the Jews hurled grenades down on the Arab soldiers!

Bombs landing on the exposed Legion position made the Arabs jump up and run. Well-aimed fire from the synagogues and from the barricade cut them down. The Arab attack faltered.

Another mortar shell burst in the street, closer to the trench this time.

Vultch engaged three snipers atop the wall. He did not see Brandenburg turn away from Zion Gate.

The former SS officer chambered another round. For an instant Yehudit's form obscured Moshe's as the woman rose to squeeze off a cartridge. Then she sank back, and a line was clear from Brandenburg to Moshe.

Brandenburg raised the rifle.

"NO!" Vultch yelled.

Lunging to the side, Brandenburg fired at Vultch. Even though both men were crouching, Brandenburg's bullet angled up to strike Vultch in the chest.

Vultch's eyes widened, then faded just as quickly.

Moshe, Yehudit, and Dov were busy with the Legion breakthrough. They had not seen Brandenburg kill Vultch.

More grenade explosions pushed the Legionnaires back into the shattered cobbler's shop.

Working in another shell, Brandenburg faced Moshe again.

The third Arab mortar round dropped on the far side of the trench, past the corner of Rehov Hayehudim. The concussion tore Brandenburg's rifle from his grip. The weapon flew away like a flicked toothpick.

Brandenburg himself was tossed across the sandbags by the explosion. He was barely conscious enough to hear Moshe cry, "You two grab Rabbi Vultch. I'll take Wottrich. We can make it to our lines if we go now!" Brandenburg passed out as he was flung over Moshe's shoulder.

A run of two blocks through the whine of sniper fire brought Moshe, Yehudit, Dov, and the men they carried to the shelter of Ehud and the other Haganah troops.

Firing and throwing grenades as they backed away, the Jewish defenders kept the Legionnaires at bay. The Haganah forces that rushed to Moshe's rescue returned to their positions in the Sephardic synagogues and in houses north of the breakthrough.

Already another barricade was being formed to replace the one that had been lost. Books and furniture, washtubs and mattresses, thrown from second-story windows, were heaped in the middle of the Street of the Jews. The Arab breach had cost the Haganah one block of territory . . . and the life of Rabbi Vultch.

Moshe delivered Dieter Wottrich into the arms of Alfie, to be carried to Misgav Ladakh.

■ ■ ■ ■

Alfie carried the unconscious man in to Lori at Misgav Ladakh. He was a well-built, muscular fellow, large-framed, and difficult to manage. His complexion was fair, yet his arms were deeply bronzed.

"Alfie, help me get his trousers off."

Alfie obliged, tossing the ripped trousers into a basket of bloody bandages.

He had an old scar from a bullet wound in his right thigh: a soldier. And he was uncircumcised. "Not a Jew," Lori remarked. She did not question the issue of his Jewishness. She did not really belong there either. "Is he English, Alfie?"

"No. He says he is Wottrich. I passed him on the first night here. He did not want to be here. Not at all. Did not want to fight. He said he was lost. I do not remember him, but he called me bad names like he knew me." Alfie shrugged. "He says he is Wottrich."

The name sounded familiar. Someone from the ship, perhaps? There was a Wottrich. A bookish, shrunken chap who wore spectacles and kept his finger in a volume of poetry as he wandered around the deck.

Not the same man.

This fellow did not appear to be badly injured. A jagged tear in the flesh of his right hip and buttocks. There was a scalp wound. Lori could not tell if his skull was fractured and his brains scrambled. If that was the case, then maybe he would die and there was nothing to be done about it. Dr. Baruch had others to attend.

With Alfie standing by to hold Wottrich in case he awakened, Lori set to work cleaning the injury and fishing out a finger-sized sliver of metal.

"He won't fancy sitting on that side for a week or two," she noted, stitching him up and painting iodine over the patch.

He moaned and cursed in German. He opened his eyes and blinked at her.

She answered him in his mother tongue.

"So, Wottrich, is this a self-inflicted wound?"

He scowled. "Wottrich . . . no, I . . ." He hesitated, then, "I am . . . wounded?"

"Not seriously. But you will want to remain standing at supper. You slept through the worst of it."

"Where am I? Sarajevo? Field hospital?"

"Jerusalem. Old City."

"You . . . must forgive me. Fräulein . . . I cannot . . . I . . . it is unclear to me. You are German?"

"*Ja,*" Lori said with amusement. "Like you. What are you doing here?"

"I cannot remember." The patient put a hand to his forehead. "My head aches."

"Wait until tomorrow." She patted his hand and instructed Alfie to help him to a cot. "You will be fit for duty by then."

■ ■ ■ ■

David guessed the temperature among the arid rocks had topped a hundred degrees by noon and kept climbing.

There had been neither food nor water since the night before. Where were the Jewish lines? Had the entire country been conquered by the Arab armies before David had a chance to fight?

"Man, I'm thirsty," Milkin complained. "I been thinkin' about a cold beer, y'know?"

"You want to go back to the Bedouins and ask for a handout?"

"Don't they have some kinda rule about helpin' strangers?"

"That bullet last night was Arab for 'Welcome, friend. Come on in.'"

Vigorously scratching himself, Milkin added, "So maybe goin' back ain't such a good idea. But can we get movin' anyhow? I mean, there's somethin' livin' in these robes besides me."

Squinting at the disk of the sun, half obscured by the western hills, David nodded.

Skirting the valley floor in order to avoid roads, they kept to higher ground. The ruins of a Crusader castle topped a rocky peak. A splash of green grass colored the desolate hill, clearly identifying the source of a spring.

Taking the lead, David followed a goat track toward what he hoped was a watering hole.

At the base of the slope they found water. Cool, clear liquid bubbled out of a rock and chuckled into a natural basin about the size of a wash-tub. Dropping to his knees, Milkin plunged his face into the pool and slurped. David cupped a handful of water, but kept a watchful eye on the surroundings.

Falling water and the enclosed hollow of the hills made it tough to hear.

"This is more like it," Milkin said. "Tin Man, don't you figger we could stay here long enough to wash? I mean, what would a few minutes hurt?"

"Sure, Bobby, I—"

David froze in midsentence. Footsteps were coming up the trail.

Boots, not sandals. There were no boulders big enough to hide behind. No trees to climb.

"Put up your hood, Bobby," David said. "Brass it out . . . act like we got every right to be here. Follow my lead."

With that, David started walking toward the oncoming group of men, making no attempt at concealment.

There were five soldiers, wearing red-and-white-checked headgear. The point man tensed at the sight of David and swung his rifle to the ready.

David gave a friendly wave and, using what little Arabic he had picked up in the souks, said, "*Salaam.*" He pressed on, pointing in the direction of the Bedouin encampment, as if to say, "We're from there."

His pistol hung around his neck. It was concealed by the collar of the robe.

*Five of them. Can I take them all?*

The third man in the file—the squad leader?—rattled off a string of words David could not follow.

*Yara . . . Have you seen anyone?*

"*La!*" David said with an emphatic cutting gesture. *No!*

"*Yatzhab!*" the squad leader said.

*Yatzhab! The Arab equivalent of "Scram. Beat it."*

The leader had lost interest in what he thought to be two ignorant nomads. Drawing a crookneck flashlight from his web belt, he unfolded a map and gathered the squad around him. Gesturing toward the ruins of the castle, he then indicated his chosen route.

David and Bobby Milkin were ten yards past the patrol. Then fifteen.

The heel of David's cowboy boot clicked sharply on a flat stone. He stumbled and fell, the hem of his cloak catching on the top of his boot.

The squad leader's head jerked up. He spotted the unorthodox footgear.

"American! *Youqif!*" he barked.

*Halt!*

"Run for it!" David yelled, then promptly tangled his boot toe in the frayed hem of the robe and fell, sprawling. Milkin, close behind, plunged into him and likewise tumbled.

A rifle butt slammed into David's back as he tried to rise. An army brogan connected with his cheekbone.

In the next second the two men were jerked to their knees. Hoods were torn back to reveal their features. The Arab leader ripped David's pistol from around his neck and brandished it aloft.

He whipped David on the back of the neck. The world spun around. One soldier grabbed him from behind. A second began to pummel him.

Milkin, kicked in the stomach, retched. Two Arabs took turns pounding him. Through eyes already swelling shut, David saw Bobby's face covered with spattered blood.

The hammer of a pistol cocked back. The muzzle was roughly shoved against David's ear.

*This is it!*

Another line of figures loomed up in the twilight.

Half-conscious, David tried to follow the heated exchange.

The newcomer pushed aside the other soldiers and snatched the flashlight out of their leader's hand. Thrusting it forward, he turned it on David's face.

A voice speaking with a clipped British accent asked, "Well, well? What have we here? Spies? Take them to my headquarters."

Surrounded by twenty armed men, staggering from the beating, their hands tied behind their backs, David and Milkin made no attempt to escape.

After some time they came to a road that was bumper to bumper with troop transports. The two Americans were loaded in the back of a British-made army lorry. A brief drive took them to an encampment.

For an hour they lay beneath the muzzles of their guards. Milkin's nose was clearly broken. His swollen face was unrecognizable. From the pain in his side David guessed that he had sustained a fractured rib.

David's battered muscles had stiffened, making it difficult to walk when they were jerked to their feet and ordered to march to the commander's field tent.

Through the slits of swollen eyes, David stared at the English officer as the man finished his supper of lamb and potatoes. His uniform was decorated with campaign ribbons identifying his march through North Africa and then through Sicily with Montgomery.

Ironic, David thought. They had fought on the same side. David in the air and this man on the ground.

The officer sipped a glass of wine, then dabbed his neat mustache with a white linen napkin.

At last he looked up from his meal to study the two men before him.

"Gentlemen, I am Major Francis Burr of the Arab Legion. And you are . . . American flyers? Not ground troops, surely." He flicked his swagger stick toward David's telltale cowboy boots.

His words thick because of mangled lips, David ventured, "Americans, Major, but not combatants. Correspondents . . . newspaper correspondents. Dressed like this so we could live off the land . . . get close to the war . . . come up with a real desert nomad's-eye view."

"Oh, really?" Burr said with amusement, indicating Bobby. "Writers?"

"He's my photographer."

"Yeah, that's right," Milkin asserted. "I take the pictures. Tin Man writes the words."

"Enough charades," Burr ordered. "The boots . . . Tin Man . . . that would make you Meyer. David Meyer. Am I right? Rumors abound. Tin Man flying for the Yids!" When David said nothing he continued, "I was in North Africa in the last war. I doubt if there was a single officer in armored command who was not aware of the contribution made by the famous Tin Man in strafing Rommel's forces." The officer sucked his teeth. "So what is a brave fellow like you doing fighting in a war between Jews and Muslims?"

David raised his chin defiantly and replied coldly, "Seemed like the Christian thing to do."

"You're on the losing side this time," Burr argued. "My chaps would have killed you if I hadn't intervened. They have not quite grasped the Geneva Convention. Of course I could have you shot as spies."

"But you're gonna let us go, right?" Milkin blurted. "Gratitude, old times' sake—that sort of thing?"

"Unfortunately not. Eventually you will be delivered to Amman and turned over to the U.N. for safekeeping. Sent back to America, I should think, if they'll have you. I understand the U.S. government is revoking the citizenship of mercenaries fighting for Israel."

"Eventually?" David asked.

"For the moment you will accompany us. We are heading southwest. In a few days we will completely sever the Tel Aviv-to-Jerusalem road—effectively slicing the so-called State of Israel in two." Burr snapped his fingers, indicating the interview was at an end.

"Major," David said to Burr as the guards entered. "Seeing as how I'm on the wrong side and all . . . Mind if I ask you a question?"

"My pleasure."

"So how's it feel taking up where the Nazis left off?"

■ ■ ■ ■

Friday morning's victory in Mea Shearim was a tremendous boost to the Jewish defenders of the New City, but everyone knew there was more fighting to come.

With St. George Road blocked, the next Arab Legion attack on the New City came on Suleiman Road, in front of Damascus Gate.

The Hospice of Notre Dame was the focal point, the bastion of Jewish resistance.

From the slate roof atop the center wing of the hospice, Major Thomas, Jacob, Peter, Naomi, and Uri looked across Musrara toward the Damascus Gate. Built by the mingled contributions of schoolchildren and wealthy French industrialists, the five-floor-high hospice was practically solid granite. Since its construction in 1888, its five hundred cells had provided rest for thousands of travel-weary pilgrims. Its grandiose existence was also a testimony to the pride of nations.

The building, shaped like a block capital letter *E,* faced northeast, and the bottom stroke of the character rested on Suleiman Road. The hospice towered over both the Old City walls to the south and the onion-domed Russian Orthodox churches to the east. Notre Dame announced to all the world that Catholic France honored the Holy City, and demanded respect there, too. The French had few claims to property inside the ancient walls of Jerusalem, but the hostel was a ponderous presence outside them.

Aside from the political statement made by the structure, the hospice afforded the present occupants practical advantages. With row upon row of arched, round-topped windows, Notre Dame was a giant blockhouse dominating any approach to the New City of Jerusalem from the east. If the Old City was a wheel rolling toward the west, Notre Dame de France was the stone on which it would be halted.

The two sides in the weeklong conflict knew the value of this chunk of real estate. It had already changed hands three times, from Haganah to Jihad Moquades and back to Jewish possession again. Jacob and the others had come from Mandelbaum House to reinforce the defenders.

Jacob, looking down from the commanding height of the hospice and along the northern wall of the Old City, recognized the building's strategic importance. "There is no way the Arabs can move anything toward us from Damascus Gate without being under fire the whole way," he observed. Then, pivoting in place toward the Jewish positions to the west, he lowered his voice before continuing. "And if they held this," he said, "we would have to fall back across Jaffa Road—maybe back to the King David Hotel."

"You sum it up neatly," Thomas praised. "And if the trap on Saint George Road had not succeeded, we would have Arab armor breathing down our necks. As it is, they will be more cautious about committing what they have left."

"Where are the crack troops we are reinforcing?" Jacob asked. "So far I've seen Gadna youth and a handful of Irgun. Oh and some middle-aged Home Guards. Naomi had to show one of them how to load his gun."

Thomas waggled his finger for Peter Wallich to join them, and the three men moved out of earshot of the teenage sentries. "Bit of unfortunate news, I'm afraid," he said.

"Major," Peter commented, "when you return to sounding so British, it makes me nervous. Tell us quickly: how bad is it?"

"Our own remaining armor must guard the north flank of Mea Shearim to keep the Legion from pulling off an end run and getting behind us that way. That's where I will be." Thomas let that news sink in, then continued, "Renewed attempts to break through Zion Gate you already know about. Those attacks require manpower."

Jacob nodded. He wanted those efforts to continue. Communication with the Jewish Quarter had to be reestablished so evacuations—including Lori's—would be possible.

"Also," Thomas continued, "Haganah forces are being mustered in the region beyond Bab el Wad. We will attempt to secure the road to Tel Aviv. We need that link," the major hurriedly added, "because it is the sole source of supply." The pause following these words was saturated with portents. "What you do not know is that there is an Arab Legion column coming toward Bab el Wad from the north and a column of

Egyptian tanks approaching Jerusalem from the south. We can stop them, but it means . . . it means—"

"It means no reinforcements here," Jacob said, finishing the sentence.

"It means we are the 'crack troops' who will have to hold Notre Dame," Peter added, looking toward Naomi. She was staring at him and, as if reading his thoughts, nodded. "Well," he said at last, "I hope there is no quota on miracles this year, because I'd hate to run out now."

■ ■ ■ ■

Peter Wallich called for Jacob Kalner. A pair of Arab Legion armored cars had arrived at Damascus Gate. "So far it's only two," he said, "and a handful of infantry, but there will be more. What can we do about them?"

From the roof of the Hospice of Notre Dame, Jacob studied the terrain and shrugged. "Not much except throw petrol bombs. The open area in front of the Old City wall lets us watch their movements. It also works against us. There are no buildings along Suleiman Road that I can dynamite to block their route."

"What about that?" Peter asked, pointing behind them to the west. He indicated the Convent of Soeurs Réparatrices.

"The convent? But it's on the wrong side of us."

Peter agreed. "But if they get past us, there will be no stopping them from overrunning the New City. We should rig that building just in case."

Thinking about the dictatorial Mother Superior, Jacob said, "I would rather take on the Arab Legion's armored cars than tackle the lady that runs that place."

Arab armored cars rumbled forward along Suleiman Road. Two vehicles advanced in staggered formation, one ahead and on the left shoulder, the other back twenty-five yards and on the right. "Probing our defenses," Jacob noted. "Maybe we can convince them to leave us alone."

The leading car fired its turret cannon. The shell smacked into the second floor of the hospice with a crash. The impact, three floors below Jacob and Peter, was scarcely felt in the granite structure.

Naomi Snow appeared on the roof. "Get down," she sternly warned Peter. "Do you want to get shot?"

The roof was lined with sandbags, as Mandelbaum House had been. Peter and Jacob carefully aimed at the visor slits of the armored cars.

Both vehicles fired their cannons. Out of range of any Haganah weapon, the Arab cars each launched five rounds. Every shell exploded against the east face of Notre Dame. None of the Gadna Youth defenders were injured.

The armored cars ceased firing and rolled backwards toward Damascus Gate.

Naomi said, "Notre Dame is too big. They don't know where to begin, eh?"

Jacob said. "This was just a probe. Tomorrow they'll be back in force with infantry support. Then we're in trouble. We are spread too thin to defend this place if they get close. Petrol bombs aren't the answer. They will blast away from a distance and send in their infantry. What we need is a way to take them out farther away from us."

"Wishing for a bazooka?" Peter asked, referring to the American shoulder-fired antitank weapon. "You might as well wish for tanks or American bombers."

Jacob looked thoughtful. "I may know where we can get what we need."

■ ■ ■ ■

Haganah High Command agreed with Peter Wallich's assessment about the convent of Soeurs Réparatrices. The building was admirably placed to be blown to rubble and barricade Suleiman Road. Since the wall of the Old City was across a slender stretch of the road from the nunnery, the obstacle created would be impossible to circumvent. It would take the Arab Legion days to clear.

If Notre Dame failed to hold—if it even appeared to be endangered—the destruction of the convent would buy the Jewish-held portion of the New City time to regroup. They could then prepare a replacement line of defense.

Jacob had earlier been in the garden of Soeurs Réparatrices but was turned away from entering on that occasion by the imperious Mother Superior. Beginning belowground, he reviewed the construction of the building with Uri Tabken trailing along behind.

"This cellar," Jacob observed, patting the cold stone of the basement, "is a problem. We don't want the upper stories to collapse into it, because then the blocks won't tumble outward onto the road." He continued his circuit of the room's perimeter, stepping over a radio and around an oak armoire.

"Are these nuns rich?" Uri asked. The cellar was filled to capacity with furniture, clocks, locked trunks, and overstuffed suitcases.

"Look at the tags," Jacob said, indicating one of the carefully lettered slips of paper that dangled from each object.

"Fedderman," Uri read aloud from the tag on the radio. "Bagdikian, it says on the chest. Bin-Saled is written here on the hose of this narghile. Jewish names, Armenian names, Arab names . . . what can it mean?"

Jacob looked around the room once more, then headed for the steps without replying. "Come on," he said. "Let's see the ground floor."

"But all these belongings—"

"I did not see it, but I can guess," Jacob said quietly. "When the fighting broke out, everyone in this part of the New City recognized that their homes were on the front line. They brought their precious things here for safekeeping before they fled. Let's go. I want to get the dynamite placed before it gets any later."

Jacob found Naomi and Peter in the convent library. He paused at the door, mesmerized by the view. On three sides of the room the walls were covered from floor to arched ceiling with leather-bound volumes. It was an autumn forest planted thick with learning. The browns and tans, the ochers and greens of the bindings grew in harmonious profusion from the rich red of the cherrywood shelves.

Catching sight of Jacob, Naomi burst out, "You can't do it! There must be five thousand volumes here. Priceless, some of them." Stretching out her hand toward a section crammed with books written in French she removed one from the shelf and opened it. "Hugo. *Les Misérables*. This is a first edition."

"And these are just books," Uri added. "The basement is full of people's lives." He summarized what they had discovered in the cellar.

"You see?" Naomi asserted. "We can't do this. Peter, make him stop."

Jacob noted the load-bearing walls and the angle of the fireplace. At a study table he sketched the room on a scrap of paper while Peter looked on. "If we ignite these charges first," Jacob said, pointing to his scribbled drawing, "then these and lastly these, the building should fall outward into Suleiman Road."

"Peter," Naomi implored again. "Make him stop."

Jacob whirled around. "Do you think I like doing this? Haven't we had our lives torn to shreds and thrown up for the wind to scatter? But the Legion won't stop because we ask them to. Think, Naomi! If they get this far it will mean that Peter and you and I and Uri are either dead or captured. Do you want that to be for nothing because we didn't blow up this library or some furniture?"

Naomi was crying. She held Victor Hugo's novel in her hand. "Mama read to me from this. She said Hugo was one Gentile who understood what suffering and persecution was all about! It was the last book she read before . . . before . . ." She broke down into sobs.

Stepping between her and Jacob, Peter said, "That's enough. I'll take Naomi back to Notre Dame. You and Uri can manage here."

As Peter led the girl away, Jacob vowed, "I will rig the cables from here to Notre Dame. We will wait until it is absolutely necessary before we detonate. If the convent can be spared, it will be."

■ ■ ■ ■

"Good *Shabbos,* Rabbi Lebowitz. Good *Shabbos,* Yacov," Dov and Yehudit Avram said as they passed Rabbi Shlomo Lebowitz and Yacov. "Why are you out on the street?"

"We are going to Gal'ed Road."

"You should not be out. You should go back to the shelter."

Grandfather, his hand firmly around Yacov's shoulders, said, "We must say Kaddish for the four Kurtzman children and for their mother too, may they rest in peace."

"Say Kaddish at the Hurva, then. Not here."

"For seven days we sit shiva. This must be done," the rabbi said sternly, pressing on with the sad-faced boy at his side.

Dov called a warning: "You know the Englishmen on Olivet with their great cannons may begin firing soon. They do not care about our mourning. They do not know what it is to sit shiva. The dead are past hurting. But you are in danger. Do not stay long!"

The old man nodded in acknowledgment. Indeed the cannons would begin firing again soon. And then how would anyone go out to the graves of Gal'ed to remember the dead? Yet it was not for the sake of the dead that Grandfather led Yacov to the grave. It was for the sake of the living, for Yacov.

They ascended the lane. Grandfather struck a match above the blooming rosebushes. Intense color in a world coated with lime dust.

The old man paused, allowing Yacov to drink in the sight, then shook out the flickering light.

"Look! Grandfather!" he whispered in wonder. "Where did they come from?"

"Who knows?" replied the old man. "But there they are. *Nu?*"

From beneath the eaves of the building behind the grave a dove crooned.

"You knew they were here?"

"Rachel told me. I had to see for myself."

"Who planted them?"

"Count the roses," the old man instructed. "Bud and bloom."

Yacov obliged; touched each blossom. There were thirty-six in all.

"One for each of the Lamedvov," Grandfather replied in an awed tone. "One of the thirty-six righteous is here among us, child."

"How can you know this?" Yacov asked.

"I have felt the presence for some time."

"What does this mean? Is he a man? A Jew?"

"The Lamedvov may be man or woman. Jew or Gentile. It matters not. He knows the hearts of all. True? Of course, true. The Lord chose twelve to represent each of the tribes of Israel. Each of those taught two until there were thirty-six, and so on . . . Together the Lamedvov are the true remnant of righteousness which restrains the hand of the living God from judgment. For their sake the world goes on."

"What happens when one dies?" Yacov motioned toward the freshly turned earth.

"Like the roses, there is always a new bud to bloom when the petals fall. Sometimes there are more than thirty-six. Never less."

"Thirty-six roses! Why this number?" The boy clung to the old man's hand and gaped at the bushes.

"It is the number of life. Of the giving of blessing to the world. You must remember these roses when you are old."

At the cooing of the dove Yacov looked up. "I will remember."

Something sparked in the old man's memory. "You must remember, Yacov, the dove also. When you read the Scripture . . . Seventy-two servants were sent two-by-two to bring the Word of life to Israel. He told them to be as gentle as doves. Thirty-six teams—the Lamedvov—carrying healing and redemption. Offered to Israel. Like the pair of gentle doves a young woman brought to the temple for sacrifice to redeem her firstborn son, *nu?*"

Again the dove on the ledge cooed. An instant later, a second bird fluttered down to join it.

Yacov frowned in thought. "I wish I knew everything."

"Everything speaks to us if we listen. It is not the dove, but God's Word which is our redemption."

"I do not understand it, Grandfather."

"And I wish I had time to tell you what I have learned in a lifetime . . . You must find it yourself. And if you seek, you will find the answers. Know this. There is meaning . . . obvious and also hidden . . . to be searched out . . . in every word of the Law and the Prophets. In every word choice and number recorded there. That is the joy of studying Torah. In all things and each event written there, the holy wisdom of the living God is woven. A golden thread is within God's tapestry, always pointing to His love for us and His plan for our salvation." The old man put his hand on Yacov's cheek, then pulled the prayer shawl over his head. "Now we will say Kaddish, *nu?* Not for your friends, but for the sake of our own souls. Listen how they speak sweetly to you from beyond the grave . . . they sing like children running into the courtyard of the temple to greet Messiah as He enters! These innocent souls have seen the One we long to see. He has embraced them."

At that, man and boy began to pray.

"*. . . And when He comes to Jerusalem we will say, Blessed, praised and glorified be the name of the Holy One, Blessed be He; who is beyond all blessings and hymns, praises and songs that are uttered in the world. . . .*"

# CHAPTER 22

Late Friday night, a clump of bedraggled Arab Legionnaires huddled together outside Damascus Gate. They were all that remained of the infantry companies. Out of six hundred men who marched south from Ramallah, the total number who eventually reached the rendezvous was three hundred.

The surviving soldiers of the two companies that had vanished almost entirely were each examined for an explanation of their conduct. Where had they been? How could they have gotten lost? Were they totally ignorant?

Major Athani carried out a number of these interrogations himself. He knew he would have to give a report to Sir John Glubb, and he wanted to have his facts straight. The difficulty was that none of the stories made sense.

"We started marching west," one Bedouin trooper reported, "but after hiking for an hour, we found ourselves heading east. Most strange."

Some claimed that a man dressed as a Legion officer—a major, some said, while others maintained he was a colonel—had appeared and ordered them to follow him.

It was the narrative offered by a one-eyed desert tribesman that Athani found wholly believable. "My friend Jabaar," the man said, "told me that he did not wish to wander around an unknown city and be shot at by Jews. He said he was going home to his wife."

In the end, Athani made no attempt to explain any of this in his radio report to Sir John Glubb. He merely confirmed that the lead armored car had taken a wrong turn. When the armored column was hopelessly pinned down, the infantry went in to save them. The cost of the rescue had been fifty percent killed, wounded, or missing.

"We have received the strictest orders from His Majesty to carry on with the capture of Jerusalem," Glubb said in response. "Athani, I am placing you in overall command. Your objective is the Hospice of Notre Dame."

Athani's aide produced a map that reduced the square mile of the Holy City to an area as small as the palm of a man's hand. On it the fingernail-sized structure of Notre Dame did not look formidable at all.

Athani knew how deceiving that appearance was.

"I will plant our mortars here, outside Damascus Gate," Athani said. "Machine guns near the gate. Six-pounder cannons on the walls, here and here." He pointed to the jagged line that represented the Old City ramparts flanking the hospice's south face. "With our remaining armored cars to cover the infantry advance, that should do the trick."

■ ■ ■ ■

Lori worked methodically on a young Palmachnik. He lay on a wooden dining table that served for examination of the less seriously wounded patients. Baruch, overwhelmed by the volume of surgeries, left this duty to Lori.

Daniel Caan, his eyes full of bitterness, watched her. She sensed his hatred. It was a tangible thing, almost as though he blamed her for the loss of his foot.

The room, packed with fifteen other wounded men, smelled of antiseptic and blood. She cut the trousers from the patient.

"Superficial shrapnel wounds of the upper thighs and right calf. You'll be back on the barricade again in no time," she said encouragingly.

The man grunted.

She probed a laceration. He cursed.

"That hurt?" She held up a chunk of metal about the size of a fishing sinker.

"What do you think?" the patient snapped. "Why can't I be seen by a real doctor?"

"Because you are not really hurt. Merely stung a bit. The doctor has more serious cases to tend to. You have good blood. It coagulates nicely."

Lori was smiling until she looked up at the glare of Daniel Caan. Daniel remarked to the Palmachnik, "She enjoys her work, eh?"

The wounded man agreed. *"Ja!"*

After Lori was done probing wound after wound, tossing each metal shard into a tin container with a satisfying clank, Rachel appeared in the doorframe.

"Lori," Rachel said, her eyes darkened with worry, "I was looking for you. The little boy."

"Abe."

"He will not eat. Will not speak. His eyes are clouded over. Hour by hour he slips farther from life. I have spoken with Doctor Baruch. He says you must go with me. Tend to the child. He says the boy will most likely die if you cannot bring him round."

■ ■ ■ ■

Lori hurried with Rachel back toward the shelter where little Abe Kurtzman lay dying.

As they approached the garden on Gal'ed Road, Lori noted three rosebushes had been planted on the otherwise unmarked grave. A paradox in a world turned upside down. The earth at each base was damp. What fool had wasted precious water as if to somehow commemorate the spilled blood of children? Rosebushes blooming in the midst of destruction? She resented the intrusion of beauty into a world shattered and irreparable!

Rachel's eyes lingered on the sight as they passed. "Strange to see them there. Red, like perfect cups of new wine. A toast to life."

"Not life, I fear," Lori countered.

They hurried away from the place. Rachel explained, "You have heard what Akiva says about me. Now I will tell you . . . There was a bird that sang outside my window when I was a whore for the Nazi officers at Auschwitz. I thought the creature mocked me. But I think . . . if I had understood its language I might have found comfort in what it said. Things eternal wanting to speak to my heart as I grieved. To remind me of life, maybe?"

Lori tried not to stare at Rachel. So the rumors Akiva had spread were born in truth! The scar on Rachel's arm, her patient acceptance of sorrows: all this made sense. Dr. Baruch had been at Auschwitz. The two knew each other. Lori groped for a word to speak, but found herself mute in the face of such acute suffering.

Rachel spoke again. "The rosebuds sing to me of things eternal. If only we could hear."

"They are just roses."

"You and I see this life from different points of view, I think. I will always remember roses, in the middle of a war, blooming on the children's graves of Gal'ed. And I will bless the Lamedvovnik . . . the righteous one . . . who brought them and planted them here and watered them with his tears."

■ ■ ■ ■

Lori and Rachel came into the food pantry where a cot had been fixed for Abe. The child lay with his eyes fixed, staring at nothing.

"Has he slept yet?" Rachel whispered to Hannah.

The old woman replied with a shake of her head. "How can he stay awake? And nothing to drink. Not a drop. He will not swallow."

Lori slipped past the two and knelt beside the cot. She leaned her face close to his and searched his eyes for a sign of awareness. Stroking his hair, she said his name. "Abe? Abe? It is Lori, yes? You remember, Abe? I sang to you." She began to hum the melody of the French lullaby.

The blankness remained unchanged. What vision played behind his grieving brown eyes? What voice from beyond dulled his hearing?

"You were right, Rachel." Hannah rose from the chair. She waved her hand across her face in a motion that said she could take no more of this. "He is like the bird you found in your garden."

Yes. A small bird. Its heart beating wildly at first and then slower and slower as it let go of life! He could no longer cry out. He had stopped calling for his mother even as he lay in her cold embrace. Had he lain there in that tomb and realized his mommy could not answer him ever again?

Such a wound was as dangerous and potentially fatal as a bullet in the heart. Baruch had been right. The child needed her. As much as the life of any of the wounded soldiers at Misgav Ladakh, that of Abe Kurtzman hung by a thread.

"He knows what happened to his family," Lori murmured, pressing his hand to her cheek, kissing his fingers. "Sweet Jesus! He is a baby. Mercy, God. Please." And then, "Abe. Little Abe. Remember me? I came for you? Won't you speak to me?"

There was no flicker of response from him. No awareness that anyone at all was near.

The skin on his arms was dry and brittle. He was badly dehydrated. "We must try to get fluids into him," she instructed Rachel.

"We have tried for many hours. He will take nothing."

Lori nodded, comprehending. "Fetch broth from Hannah. We will try again."

# SATURDAY

*May 22, 1948*

"The spirit of the LORD God is upon me; because the LORD hath anointed me to preach good tidings unto the meek; he hath sent me to bind up the brokenhearted, to proclaim liberty to the captives, and the opening of the prison to them that are bound;

To proclaim the acceptable year of the LORD, and the day of vengeance of our God; to comfort all that mourn;

To appoint unto them that mourn in Zion, to give unto them beauty for ashes, the oil of joy for mourning, the garment of praise for the spirit of heaviness; that they might be called trees of righteousness, the planting of the LORD, that he might be glorified."

Isaiah 61:1–4

"And there was delivered unto him the book of the prophet Isaiah. And when he had opened the book, he found the place where it was written,

'The Spirit of the LORD is upon me, because he hath anointed me to preach good tidings unto the meek; he hath sent me to bind up the brokenhearted, to proclaim liberty to the captives and the opening of the prison to them that are bound . . .'

And he closed the book, and he gave it again to the minister, and sat down. And the eyes of all them that were in the synagogue were fastened on him.

And he said to them, 'This day the scripture is fulfilled in your ears.'"

Luke 4:17–21

# CHAPTER 23

Crouched in the debris-strewn shadows at the base of Mandelbaum House, Jacob said to Peter, "I'll go. The Legion has snipers in the buildings at Nablus Road. No reason for both of us to get shot on what may be a worthless expedition."

"I can watch your back," Peter said. "Besides, if we find something useful it may take two of us to carry it."

Jacob was grateful for the company. He had never seen a night so black as this. It was perfectly suited for a raid on the deserted Arab armored cars trapped on St. George Road. While two of the vehicles had been gutted by fire, the others had been abandoned relatively intact. They might contain valuable ammunition. But what Jacob hoped to discover was any sort of antitank weapon.

Faces smeared with burnt cork for camouflage, the two men crawled forward along the edge of the street. On knees and elbows, holding a pistol in his right hand, Jacob slithered past the burned-out remains of an armored car. Beside it lay the bodies of two Arab soldiers, caught in the cross fire.

What in daylight was no more than fifty yards became, in the menacing dark, a seemingly endless journey. A minute's pleasant stroll in another world was transformed into a creeping agony of apprehension.

Trying to take advantage of every scrap of cover, Jacob worked his way around a heap of shredded metal.

From somewhere up ahead came a sound like a footstep.

A hand clasped Jacob's ankle and squeezed it. Peter had also heard it.

Tense minutes of lying perfectly still followed. Jacob tried not to think about how close he had already come to being killed that day. The street ahead was partially blocked by the disintegrated front of the spice merchant's home. Jacob wondered how many more times he could challenge death with impunity.

No more sounds from the darkness. Was someone waiting out there? Had he gone? Perhaps it had been no more than the metallic click of metal cooling.

With the barest flick of his fingers at his waist, Jacob indicated to Peter that he was moving again.

The first relatively undamaged armored car loomed just ahead. From Jacob's vantage near the ground, it resembled a misshapen boulder in the gorge of St. George Road.

The driver's-side door was buckled and jammed shut. There was no other entry except the hatch on top of the turret. Jacob had to stand erect and climb up, then slip down inside it.

They reached the thirty-six-inch-tall front tire. Jacob passed his pistol to Peter. For a man going headfirst into the bowels of the car, a pistol would be of no use.

His hands slipped upward along the side of the car. Jacob found it took a struggle of will to make himself leave the shelter of the pavement and stand upright, although plastered against the car.

There was a running board on which he could step to reach the hatch.

One foot up.

Transfer your weight slowly, then wait to see if the thing groans.

Draw the other leg up.

Suspended off the ground, Jacob was overwhelmed with the urge to jump into the hatch. Surely that would be safe. Why not sacrifice quiet for speed?

The hatch was open. That was fortunate. Jacob did not want to have to deal with creaking hinges.

Levering himself upward and folding in the middle at the same time, Jacob imitated a snake as he skimmed the edge of the hatch.

Now all was done by feel. The darkness outside was enveloping. The blackness of the interior of the armored car was absolute.

Shells for the turret cannon. Useful, but not what he had come for.

Cartridge boxes.

The vehicle was a treasure trove for the impoverished Gadna Youth brigade.

Swinging left, Jacob lowered himself another level.

Putting out his hand he touched . . . hair!

Startled by the contact, Jacob fell on top of the dead driver.

Below the turret, clamped against the wall, was a cylindrical shape. The underside of the object sported a pistol grip handle.

*A bazooka! Were there shells?*

An oblong box, like an oversized egg carton, rested below the weapon.

Jacob shoved the bazooka out the hatch first.

He whistled for Peter. His dry lips would not work right. He made a sound more like a swimmer's gasp of air than a musical note.

Peter took the bazooka from him, lowered it noiselessly to the ground.

Jacob handed out the case of rockets.

It was going to work!

He located two cartridge boxes and handed one out.

Should he take the cannon shells? No, they already had as much as they could carry.

Would they have to make a second trip? Jacob could not even think of it.

Holding the remaining cartridge box above his head, Jacob began to climb through the hatch. But his left sleeve snagged a shard of metal. His wrist was wedged in the hinge of the hatch cover.

Jacob struggled to release himself without dropping the cartridge box.

Then he slipped, hanging by his trapped left arm.

Something snapped in his shoulder.

Gasping, Jacob released his hold on the ammo box. Crashing to the pavement, it burst open, scattering cartridges.

Gunfire and Arab shouts of warning followed!

Jacob dangled by his wrist.

A bullet clanged against the hatch lid and whined off.

Peter tried to help Jacob down.

Jacob groaned, "Caught!" His shoulder was dislocated.

Jumping up on the armored car, Peter freed Jacob's hand while more shots whizzed overhead.

"Can you run?" Peter asked.

"Give me the bazooka!" Jacob said grimly. "You take the shells."

His left arm dangling at his side, Jacob tucked the weapon under his right arm and ran for Mandelbaum House.

A row of slugs dug into the street at his heels.

Every jarring step was agony.

Stumbling over a block of stone, Peter swept him up from behind, propelling them both into the shelter of a doorway.

They reached Mandelbaum House as the first Legion flare lit the street. Jacob collapsed, retching from the pain.

■ ■ ■ ■

Though his skull was not fractured, Brandenburg had sustained a concussion of some severity. When he moved, the world spun around him. He did not protest when he was ordered by Dr. Baruch to lie still.

Brandenburg was moved to a bed in Ward A next to a young man who was blond, pale, extremely Aryan in appearance.

Brandenburg could not remember why everyone called him by the name of Wottrich, but he reasoned there must be a purpose in the deception. He would not question it until he remembered.

The youth next to him lay staring grimly at the flattened place beneath the sheet where his left foot should have been. Everyone else was sound asleep.

Brandenburg asked, "How did it happen?"

The boy scrutinized him. "You have the accent of someone from Dresden."

Brandenburg smiled. "Clever of you to notice."

"It is impossible to miss. I am also from Dresden, *ja?*" The young man brightened.

"An odd place for a reunion," Brandenburg remarked. "And yet it is not unpleasant to meet someone from one's home even so far away as this." He was hoping perhaps the boy would give him a clue as to why he was there. "What is your name, boy?"

"Daniel. And you are Wottrich," he said.

"So they tell me. But I don't remember much."

Daniel turned onto his side and propped himself on his elbow. "You told them you were a schoolteacher in Hamburg. You remember that?"

"No," Brandenburg replied honestly.

"Doesn't matter." Daniel scratched his ear. "But do you remember Dresden?"

Brandenburg did indeed. A charred pyre where sixty thousand

civilians were roasted alive in the inferno of Allied incendiary bombs in the last days of the war. His elderly mother and father had burned to death that night.

"When were you last there?"

Daniel replied, "I was just a kid. In 'thirty-nine."

"There is not much left, you know. The English and Americans bombed it because it was an easy target. No anti-aircraft guns. The Führer ordered all defenses withdrawn. No one thought they would bomb Dresden. Old people. Hospitals. They wanted to get even for London or maybe Coventry. And by then they knew what we were doing about the Jews."

"The Jews?" Daniel looked puzzled.

"You know. Everyone knows. So. Dresden, eh? Revenge bombing. It was a beautiful city. Where did you live?"

"Across from the big cathedral. On the market square. We had a flat above a little souvenir shop right where the trolley stopped."

"*Ja!* I remember that place. Very busy. Tourists in and out. Little plaster copies of the church . . ."

"That's it!" Daniel sounded overjoyed to meet someone who remembered.

". . . and religious medals. I rode the trolley past the shop every day. We had a joke about the place, you know. So strange. This shop full of Christian things and it was run by some Christ-killer Yid and his wife. You remember them?"

Daniel's eyes hardened as he scrutinized Brandenburg for a long, uneasy moment. His voice was flat and menacing as he asked, "What are you doing here?"

"I do not know," Brandenburg replied.

"Do you know where you are?"

"The Fräulein said Old City Jerusalem. The hospital. I suppose the Jews managed to hurt me and—"

"You are in the Jewish Quarter, Wottrich. The Yids? Christ-killers as you call them, in the shop at Dresden? They were my mother and father."

"*Mein Gott!*" Brandenburg blanched. Suddenly it all came back to him. "Wottrich. *Ja.* Dieter Wottrich."

Already Daniel had swung his legs out of the bed. He was going for help! The cry "Nazi!" was on his lips! Brandenburg had no choice. He lunged from his mattress and grabbed Daniel from behind.

It was easy for the heavier man to drag down a small crippled boy, but once on the floor Daniel surprised Brandenburg with the ferocity of his resistance.

While Brandenburg struggled to close his hands around Daniel's throat, the boy twisted and squirmed, croaking out a strangled "Nazi! Help!"

When Brandenburg clamped his hand over the boy's mouth to stifle the yells, Daniel used the freedom he gained to worm out from under. When Brandenburg tightened his clasp on Daniel's neck, the youth jabbed his thumbs into Brandenburg's eyes.

Someone could come at any time! Brandenburg needed to finish this immediately.

His own head swimming from the concussion and the exertion, Brandenburg was relieved when Daniel's eyes rolled back in his head and his resistance slowed. Another moment of squeezing the windpipe and then . . .

Someone was coming! The footsteps were already near the door.

"Help!" Brandenburg yelled loudly. "Someone help me! Hurry! The boy . . . he has had a seizure! Help!"

Esther Rheinhart and another nurse entered the room together. Brandenburg shook Daniel by the shoulders as if trying to revive him. "Get the doctor," he said again. "I'll lift him back onto the bed." He hoped they would both go so he could finish the job properly, but no, Esther stayed as the nurse bustled out.

"I'll fetch water!" Brandenburg said. Snatching a bathrobe from a chair, he hurried away.

■ ■ ■ ■

It was Dr. Baruch's urgent voice that Daniel heard first. "Come on, boy! Snap out of it! Daniel! Daniel!"

The room, the air pungent with the smell of chemicals, spun around him. It seemed as though a hundred faces gaped down at him. Who were they?

Mama! Papa! Suzannah! Asher!

Daniel worked his mouth, trying to warn them. "Nazi!" he gasped.

Dr. Baruch knelt beside him, his arm supporting him. Daniel's leg screamed with pain.

"Daniel, what is it, lad?" Then Baruch touched his neck. "This is no seizure. Someone . . . strangle . . . my God!"

Daniel said clearly, "Nazi! Wottrich is . . . he is a Nazi! He tried to—" Daniel's hand fluttered toward his neck then fell. He inhaled deeply at the doctor's command. His lungs and head began to clear.

"Where is Wottrich?" demanded Baruch.

One of the women replied, "He said he was going for water."

Baruch snapped, "He is not one of us."

"From Dresden," Daniel explained. "A Nazi. What's he want with us?"

Baruch helped him back to bed. "I don't know, but we will find him and get some answers!"

■ ■ ■ ■

Abe lay in Lori's arms. She held his head steady as Rachel spooned broth onto his parched tongue.

Patience! If too much liquid was given, it spilled out the corner of his mouth. And so it had to be served up drop by drop. Even then, too much, too fast, and he rejected the life being offered to him.

She pressed her cheek against his brow, willing him to live. *Sweet Jesus! Not this one! Please! Don't take him, Lord!*

Was it too late? Lori wondered. Too late for all of them? Even as her prayers ascended, her faith faded. She guarded herself against caring so desperately. She tried to restrain hope, deny the vision that she might make a difference in this one child's life. *You must stop believing! Believing only leads to heartache!*

Why did Baruch have confidence that she could pull Abe back from the brink? And, if she lost him? What then? Had she already resigned herself to his death?

*If he dies . . . if . . . I suppose there is nothing I cannot live with. . . .*

The words of Mother Superior spoke clearly in her memory.

*"Resignation is not acceptance. Nothing is something,* ma chérie. *Bitterness. Anger. We resign ourselves to live with such things. Sometimes, like weeds, they take over the garden. But would not life be better if we lived without them? Accepted pain without the bitterness? From our acceptance*

*of personal pain grows compassion for others who are hurting. That is what the Lord meant when He said, Blessed are those who mourn, for they shall be comforted. . . ."*

How long had it been since Lori allowed herself to feel compassion? Perhaps that ability had perished as she waited through the long, dark night beside the ruined house on Primrose Hill. The moment they laid the lifeless body of her son on the stretcher, the answer to survival had come to her. She had raised her fist in the face of heaven and vowed, *"I will not love again!"*

To love someone—anyone—admitted the certainty of pain. She did not mean the ache of loneliness. No. Loneliness was an easy burden to carry compared to the agony of losing one she cherished more than her own life. And death was but one way to have love torn away. . . . If he had lived to grow to manhood, would he not have left her one day also? Might he have looked at her and belittled the things she had done for him, as sons often did? Would he have despised her because her love had not been enough to make his life perfect? It was the way of it. Mother and child. No greater love. No greater pain.

Rachel spoke, interrupting Lori's reverie. "He takes the broth easier if it is on my finger." She placed her fingertip in the cup of liquid, then on his tongue. "See here, Lori. He swallows even though he does not wish to, I think."

Yes. Pale lips closed around Rachel's finger. The throat worked involuntarily, accepting the gift she offered.

Lori followed Rachel's example. Finger in the broth and then to his mouth. "That's it," Lori said. "I feel him take it." Then, "That's the way, little Abe. Not all at once. A bit at a time."

Rachel rocked back to sit cross-legged on the floor as Lori continued the process. After a time she said, "It is the burden Eve carried from the garden, is it not?"

Lori looked up sharply. Had Rachel been somehow listening in on her thoughts? "What burden?"

"It has always been so for us women, *nu?* We want to protect them and heal them and give them the perfect life. And when we cannot . . . how hard it is for us."

"I would change everything for this tiny bird if I could."

"He will need your love."

"And what if he will not take it?"

"Love is like chicken soup, *nu?* Maybe he will not accept it all at once, and so you give it to him one drop at a time. Maybe he will live because you did not give up. Maybe there really will be a happy ending for this one child because you cared. But, you must not quit hoping."

"You pretend to know about me," Lori replied resentfully.

"I know enough."

"How?"

"We are the same, you and I. All of us. Daughters of Eve. Some take the risk. Love in spite of what the end may be. Walk the Via Dolorosa as Mary did. Suffer because our children suffer and we cannot change anything for them . . . Mostly we learn to pray. And love them . . . love . . . one drop at a time, even when they do not seem to care. Even when they reject our love and . . . reject us."

"And if loving does not turn the tide?"

The words came to Rachel with difficulty. "There is a delicate balance, I think. I learned this when I was thirteen and . . . and I watched my mother . . . give her child away . . . to a stranger in a Warsaw train station. Mama knew she could not save him. She loved him so much she let go. Dear God! The desperation of that moment! Love so great it releases the child into the care of a loving God!" Rachel sat quietly with the memory. "My mother said good-bye forever. She prayed . . . and died . . . not knowing. That child is my brother, Yacov. God saved him. So . . . you see? Sometimes we must let go . . . offer them to God alone. Then leave it to Him . . . or our hearts will break and never mend."

From the hour of the bombing of London, Lori had never fully released little Al into the hands of God. She had mourned him, seen his broken body taken from the rubble, but she had never had the courage of Rachel's mother in Warsaw! She clung to his memory with regret and longing. Grief and bitterness had never given way to compassion because she had never entrusted the sweet soul of her baby to heaven.

"I am still holding on," Lori murmured. "Still longing. . . ."

Lori frowned and wished she could run from loving. But here he was. Little Abe. She had taken him from the arms of the mother who had died trying to shield him! Mrs. Kurtzman, beyond helping, somehow gave her child to Lori. *Life!* This little bird was in her hands. *Love him!* One drop at a time.

Rachel said, "If you run from loving, sweet friend, it means never knowing what miracle God might have done if we had stayed faithful to the end and believed."

The cannon boomed on.

Lori wondered if, after today, any of it would matter anymore.

■ ■ ■ ■

Jacob made light of his injury, but the greenish cast to his face betrayed him. He lay on the floor in the Hospice of Notre Dame. Putting his cheek against the cold paving stones helped him focus his eyes.

The bazooka rested between Uri's feet. Jacob tried to recall the elation that had come when he first grasped the weapon, but the emotion could not get past the pain. The fingers of his left hand were cold, numb, while the shoulder felt as if it were being stabbed repeatedly with a red-hot knife blade.

"We have to reduce the dislocation at once," Peter said apologetically. "If we wait and the muscles cramp, then it could be days." His sturdy farmer's fingers probed the joint, noting the proper alignment of the socket.

"Get on with it!" Jacob said through gritted teeth. He barely moved his lips as he spoke, and even that tiny effort caused him enormous distress.

Peter looked at Naomi and Uri. "Sit on him," he said softly.

Uri stretched himself across Jacob's chest while Naomi sat on his knees.

Standing over Jacob, Peter took the injured arm and rotated it until it reached the angle he sought. Planting his foot in Jacob's armpit, Peter tugged on the arm as if determined to tear if off Jacob's body.

Jacob screamed and there was an audible pop as the joint snapped back into place.

"He's fainted," Naomi observed.

"Good thing," Peter said. "Quickly, now! Prop him up while I bind the arm across his chest. It'll need support for a few days, but he'll be right as rain."

Naomi's eyes glowed with approval and devotion.

When Jacob came to, the pain in his arm was a dull ache and he had a roaring headache, but he could think again.

"Thanks," he said to Peter. "You saved my life, I think."

Peter brushed aside the gratitude. "Now we have a way to hold off the Legion's armor."

Jacob's face fell. "I can't possibly hold the bazooka steady enough to aim," he said.

"Uri," Peter responded instantly. "Uri can hold and fire the weapon. You will direct him. Naomi will be your spotter."

# CHAPTER 24

Saturday morning began for the defenders of Notre Dame with a thunderous crash. Just before dawn the Arab Legion unleashed a rain of two-inch mortar shells. Jacob awoke with a red-hot fire in his shoulder. The injury throbbed in time to the pulsing explosions.

Without warning an earthquake was added to the tempest. Jacob, Peter, and Uri were billeted in a top-story room named for the patron saint of France, St. Denis. They were thrown from their beds by a gigantic concussion on the roof.

Jacob bounced onto the wooden floor, landing on his wounded arm. The impact made him gasp in pain and sit doubled over.

"Artillery!" Jacob shouted.

Another detonation! The building shook again. Five floors of granite swayed as if made of timber and plaster!

Naomi rushed into the room. "Get away from this side of the building," she urged. When Peter did not move fast enough, she grabbed him by the hands and dragged him toward the corridor.

Jacob stumbled after them.

Naomi cried, "Our people on the roof . . . six of them . . . killed by the first explosion! All except Isaac. He says the shell came from beyond Damascus Gate. The Legion brought a big cannon down from the Mount of Olives. Twenty-five-pounder."

Peter said, "They know that the mortar rounds bounce off these walls. Now what?"

"There is nothing to do except huddle until the firing stops," Jacob said. Hugging his arm to his chest, he continued, "They can't send an attack forward until the barrage is lifted. Then we rush back and fight them off."

Another boom rocked them.

"But how long will it be before they batter us to pieces?" Uri wondered.

"Shells are falling on the roof. It means the angle of trajectory can't touch us lower down. We'll be all right, unless . . ."

"Unless what?" Peter asked.

"Unless they can get a big gun onto the Old City wall," Jacob said. "Then they can hammer us at point-blank range."

■ ■ ■ ■

Despite Jacob's prediction that the Arabs would have to lift the shelling, the incessant barrage continued. Machine-gun fire poured into the windows of Notre Dame, driving the defenders away. Mortar rounds and shells from the armored cars drummed against the walls.

Peter Wallich held up his ten fingers ten times, then shook his head to indicate he had stopped counting.

It was the cannon lobbing the larger projectiles that caused the Jewish soldiers the most worry. Already the rooftop positions had been destroyed and several rooms on the top floor were too full of fallen debris to be usable. One of these was the suite dedicated to St. Denis.

"Some saint!" Uri grumbled loudly as he, Jacob, Peter, and Naomi huddled in an interior hallway amid flying plaster dust. The wall against which Uri leaned bounced from the impact of another shell. "Even in this French-built holy place he cannot protect his own rooms."

"Saint Denis was killed by the ancient Romans," Naomi yelled in return. "He is famous because he was able to run while carrying his own head."

Glancing up at the brass plaque that bore the saint's name, Uri self-consciously scooted farther away from the doorway.

Dust-covered, deafened, and shaking, Jacob returned to his post beside the arched window in the room dedicated to St. Joan of Arc. A minute later the shelling stopped. What he saw up Suleiman Road toward Damascus Gate made him raise an alarm.

Six armored cars advanced in open formation toward the hospice. With them were two hundred Arab infantrymen. This time the Legion commander was taking no chances.

"Come on!" Jacob shouted to the others. Peter remained beside the detonator that would destroy the convent and block the road in case the vehicles got past Notre Dame.

One floor below, in a room named for St. Barbara—she who was invoked for help against lightning and explosion as well as being the patroness of firefighters, architects, and artillerymen—Jacob and Uri readied the tube of the bazooka.

Jacob cautioned, "Only seven rockets. You'll have to wait until you cannot miss."

Knowing that any movement would draw rifle fire or worse, Jacob and Uri crouched below the rim of the window.

Naomi shouted reports about enemy movements from nearby rooms. "Three cars have advanced beyond the others," she yelled. "Our machine guns are keeping the infantry away." Then, "One hundred fifty yards."

From his position to the rear and left of the bazooka, Jacob saw the sweat that trickled down Uri's neck. Curls of hair at the boy's collar dampened to soggy rings that lay plastered against his shirt. His shoulders were hunched with tension.

"We'll wait until the first car is one hundred yards away," Jacob said. He forced himself to sound unruffled, emphasizing the word *we*. He prayed Uri would not think about how critical this duty was.

"Stopped just beyond one hundred yards!" Naomi reported.

"Ease the tube onto the sill," Jacob instructed. "Don't fire until I give the order, or the rocket blast will burn my face off."

The tube of the weapon rattled against the window ledge.

"Two cars moving forward again. The one on the left is in front."

"We'll take the lead car first," Jacob said. "Here we go. Ease up onto your knees. Keep your finger off the trigger."

As he sighted along the tube, Jacob's first thought was that Naomi had misjudged the distance. Surely, these giant-seeming armored cars were much closer than one hundred yards away! But no, the girl was right. Uri was not the only one who was nervous.

Warning the boy first, Jacob nudged the weapon to the left, then sank back and turned aside. He covered his right ear against the blast. "When the car enters the ring of your sight, squeeze—don't jerk!—the trigger."

Seconds passed with the drag of interminable hours.

Instead of being overanxious, had Uri frozen in place? Was he unable to fire? Suddenly, Jacob was struck with an awful memory. He had seen the boy close his eyes when shooting a rifle. What if Uri's eyes were closed now?

"Uri?"

In reply, the rocket exploded from the forward end of the tube with a *whoosh*. A jet of flame passed within two feet of Jacob's head. An instant later the front of the leading armored car was ripped open. It bounded backwards as if hitting an invisible wall at full speed.

Jacob grabbed up another shell and inserted it. Working awkwardly with one hand, he made the connection that would let the weapon launch. Patting Uri on the head, he said, "Any time."

With a new confidence evident in the set of his jaw, Uri swung the tube to the right. "Get clear!" he ordered firmly.

Another rush, another gout of flame!

Another direct hit. The second armored car, angling across the street at the moment of impact, was struck behind the turret. It split in half as though cleaved by an ax.

"Well done!" Jacob exclaimed. "Let's move. They'll have us in their sights."

They crawled toward the door as machine-gun bullets from three directions sprayed the room, crisscrossing the ceiling with shattering effect.

■ ■ ■ ■

Mother Superior rose from her knees and held her Bible close to her heart.

It was too hot to keep the windows of her chamber closed, and so she threw the doors wide to the deserted courtyard below. The unrelenting bray of battle invaded her sanctuary. The once-clean sky of Jerusalem was smudged and discolored by plumes of smoke.

She winced, pained at the reality of her insignificance in the affairs of the Holy City. Her prayers had brought her no closer to an answer.

"What do You want of me, Lord? You know I will go where You command. I have no care for my life apart from serving Your Kingdom!"

She sighed and placed the well-worn volume of Scripture on the table beside a chair. When she returned her gaze to the shade of the courtyard, she saw the old man, kneeling, pulling weeds from among the overgrown rosebushes as though nothing existed beyond the walls of the sacred building. He did not flinch or cower when a loud explosion rattled the glass in the window frames.

Perhaps he was deaf, Mother Superior reasoned.

She said aloud, "It is a blessing from God to be deaf at such a time as this."

More blasts followed. At that, the old man raised his eyes from his task, saw her standing in the doorway, and waved heartily before returning to his work.

A slight breeze, smelling of roses, puffed the curtain and tossed the leaves of the nun's Bible back as though a hand had riffled through them.

As if speaking to herself, the old woman murmured the name by which she had been called as a child. "Espérance." She smiled at the sound of her name and her voice. It had been many years since she had thought of the meaning of the word *Espérance!*

Hope!

As she turned, her glance fell on the open page of Scripture: 2 Chronicles 20.

She began to read.

*"Do not be afraid or discouraged because of this vast army. For the battle is not yours, but God's. Tomorrow march down against them . . . You will not have to fight this battle. Take up your positions; stand firm and see the deliverance the* LORD *will give you, O Judah and Jerusalem. Do not be afraid; do not be discouraged. Go out to face them tomorrow, and the Lord will be with you."*

Looking up, she saw that the gardener was gone. He had left his tools behind—had he finished what he came to do?

Mother Superior closed her eyes and inhaled prayerfully. "Espérance thanks you," she said, certain of the answer.

■ ■ ■ ■

From the compound of the Latin Patriarchate, Daoud watched one side of the battle of Notre Dame.

Daoud came outside to escape the gloomy opulence of the hall in which the nuns prayed. Around the walls of the red-tapestried room, each sister knelt before a wooden-backed chair that substituted for her prayer station. The air of the hall hummed with prayers: constant, unceasing prayers.

He honored their devotion, but he needed to escape the continual litany of devotion and to think.

Daoud discovered it was not possible to think outside, either.

The sky over Jerusalem was crammed to capacity with the noise of war. Machine guns rattled, rifles popped, grenades exploded on Suleiman Street, at the far side of the Old City wall from where he stood.

Watching the Arabs lining the parapets, Daoud saw none of them get wounded or fall. Mechanically they worked the bolts of their weapons and yanked the triggers as if the battle's outcome would be decided by whichever side fired the most rounds.

That the shooting went on and on told Daoud the embattled Jews defending Notre Dame were not yet ready to concede.

Another sound was added to the mix, making Daoud look east, toward the lanes leading to Damascus Gate.

It was the sound of cheering, Arab voices loudly acclaiming victory. What did it mean?

Under the watchful eye of a squad of Legionnaires, twenty Jihad Moquades tugged on ropes. Drawn by these cables, bumping over the cobblestones like a recalcitrant camel, was a field cannon.

The teams of men hauling the artillery piece through the narrow streets were smiling. Behind the cannon were more Jihad Moquades struggling with pushcarts, but the wheelbarrows did not transport vegetables for the market: they were heaped with cannon shells, each of them half as tall as Daoud himself.

Daoud watched until he was certain of their destination: the cannon would somehow be heaved up to rest on the Old City wall, there to hurl unrestrainable death at the Jews a hundred feet away!

And at the convent of Soeurs Réparatrices next door to the hospice.

He ran to tell the Mother Superior. She could not go home! She would have to listen!

■ ■ ■ ■

At the south Jerusalem suburb of Beth Hakarem, women and children used wheelbarrows and pushcarts to haul stones. They built a barricade from which to defy an Egyptian column.

The nearby village of Ramat Rachel changed hands five times. Captured again and again by Arabs, it was recaptured over and over by Haganah troops when the Arabs stopped fighting in favor of looting.

In the port of Haifa, the Haganah received its first major arms shipment since the declaration of statehood. Machine guns, mortars, ammunition . . . but how to get it to where it was needed?

A resolution jointly supported by the U.S. and the USSR, calling for a Mideast cease-fire, was pushed through the United Nations Security Council.

Everyone knew Israel's existence was hanging by a thread.

Everyone also knew that this thread continued to exist only because the Arab Legion was pinned down in Jerusalem.

Following the Arab Legion assault on the Street of the Jews, a gloomy Old City defense council met in the corner room off Tipat Chalev's kitchen.

Moshe, Dov, Yehudit, and Ehud Schiff wore long faces. Rabbi Vultch had been a good friend: unflappable, reliable, brave.

Minutes were given to reflection and memories, then present demands drew them back to the crisis at hand.

"By the Eternal, he will be missed," Ehud summarized. "Now, Moshe, tell us plainly. How bad is it?"

A large-scale map of the Quarter lay spread in front of them. With the point of a pencil, Moshe marked the exact spot where the Legionnaires had dynamited their way into the Jewish Quarter. "Thanks to your quick action," he said, "it is not nearly as drastic as it could have been. The Legion hoped to exploit their opening while we were still confused. They wanted to push on through the heart of the district and split us in two in one attack."

"We cannot prevent them from repeating this method elsewhere," Dov pointed out. "What's to be done?"

"We must line the east side of the Street of the Jews with defenses so that wherever the Legion breaks in they will already face an obstacle. More than that, the key is our rooftop lookouts. Our sentries cannot stop the bombing, but they can give us early warning so we can fall back and catch the Legionnaires in a cross fire."

Yehudit leaned over and studied the map intently. "Fallback positions are well and good where we have a clear view up and down a straight road. It will work along the Street of the Jews, or along the wall at the south end of the Quarter, or along the Street of the Chain at the north. The real weakness is where the houses are a jumble and attack could come from any direction—like here, where there is just one truly defensible position." Her small finger identified the spot.

All of them saw where she was pointing; all of them knew what it meant. For a long time, no one spoke.

Finally Moshe said, "You are right, Yehudit. Nissan Bek . . . your father's synagogue . . . is the most important defensive anchor in that part of the Quarter. If we can see how essential it is, then so can the Legion. We must warn him."

Yehudit looked from face to face, ending with a tender gaze that remained on Dov. "He hates all of you," she said. "He believes you represent the source of the evil that has fallen on the Quarter. He would never listen to you."

Knowing what she was about to say, Dov interrupted. "I cannot allow you to go and be abused by him."

Gently she replied, "I know he believes that I have betrayed him. He struts and postures and proclaims that I am dead to him. But I am still his daughter, and I must try. God willing, I can reach him. . . . None of the rest of you would have any chance at all."

■ ■ ■ ■

Daoud was out of breath when he found Mother Superior in the library of the Latin Patriarchate. She and Sister Marie Claire were folding the yellow-and-white papal flag as though it were a bedsheet.

"Madame Mother, perfect and saintly woman!" Daoud panted in distress. "I have found you!"

"Yes, Daoud," the old woman replied, ignoring his excited prattle. "Sister Marie Claire and I are preparing to go home."

"But you cannot!" he bleated. "You have not seen what I have seen! You do not know what I know!"

Mother observed him reflectively. Did nothing ever ruffle the feathers of this hen? Daoud marveled.

"And you, dear child, do not yet know what I know. Nor have you seen what I have seen. But I trust one day you shall."

"A cannon! The Legion has brought a mighty cannon to perch upon the wall near New Gate! With this beast they will bring disaster to the Jews in Notre Dame. They will break down the walls and kill them!

No doubt your dear convent will also suffer much in this! You cannot go back there! You must not return to Soeurs Réparatrices. There is death and destruction for you if you go back."

Mother clasped the banner to her and patiently replied, "Sister Marie Claire and I have resolved to go. We have prayed to our Lord on the matter and we must return. Our presence may well put an end to the senseless slaughter. The Lord has spoken to our hearts, Daoud."

"If I take you, your blood will be on my head," the child pleaded.

"You must not go with us," Sister Marie Claire interjected. "We cannot put you in danger."

"But, but, but . . . ," Daoud stammered. This was not turning out the way he had expected.

Mother smiled kindly, irritatingly confident. "It is decided. Sister Marie Claire must go. You must stay, Daoud."

"You cannot go alone!" he protested hopelessly.

"We are never alone," Mother assured him as Sister Marie Claire agreed with a nod of her head.

"*Ya Allah!*" Daoud had such a headache. These crazy headstrong virgins! The reason they were virgins is that no sane man would have them! "I cannot let you go out. Soon they will have the cannon in place. Everyone will be watching. If you are with me, no one will look twice at you. We will walk out of New Gate and across the road . . . *Ya Allah.* Our own fellows may not shoot us, but the Jews will. And if we are in the convent, then the cannon will blow us to Paradise."

Mother Superior cupped her hand beneath his chin and said benignly, "Do not fear, child. Though I walk through the valley of the shadow of death I will fear no evil."

He shrugged and sat down to sulk and wait.

■ ■ ■ ■

Immediately after the Legion armored cars and infantry withdrew from the abortive attack on Notre Dame, the shelling began again.

Despite the incessant pounding, the hammering of the artillery rounds was a relief to the Gadna Youth. It meant that there was going to be an interval before another assault. There were minor wounds to be bandaged, handfuls of ammunition to be distributed, and consultations to be completed.

Jacob reported Uri's success with the bazooka to Peter. "He can do it on his own," Jacob said. "Assign Naomi to be his loader and you can use me somewhere else." Looking down at his bandaged arm, he added, "I can fire a Sten gun. Put me on one of the lower floors."

Peter disagreed. "And break up your team? No."

It was two in the afternoon when the shelling stopped and the Arab Legion advanced again.

Uri was back in St. Barbara's room. The boy was jaunty, even cocky, as he waited for the armored cars to roll closer. The first rocket already loaded, Naomi was once more acting as spotter.

"Six of them . . . coming three across this time," she called. "Maybe they know we only have one bazooka."

Jacob saw that the news rattled Uri, but the teenager steadied himself.

"The center one is leading," Naomi reported. "Approaching where you hit the first two."

Uri hunched forward and took aim. The rocket leapt from the tube as the target vehicle stopped.

Since Uri's aim led the armored car as it rolled, the projectile missed. Instead of striking the car, it hit the pavement in front. The Legion machine rocked backwards, its front axle bent by the concussion. When it moved forward again, its wheels wobbled, but continued to advance.

"Load! Load!" Uri said urgently.

"Stay calm," Jacob cautioned. Bullets smacked against the outside wall beside the window. "Let's move," he said.

"No time!" Uri retorted, flipping the tube of the bazooka onto the ledge.

A monstrous blast, greater than any they had yet felt, struck Notre Dame. The impact knocked Jacob onto his injured arm. It tossed Uri around and the bazooka misfired.

The missile sailed off in the direction of the Mount of Olives. It exploded on the onion-shaped dome of a Russian Orthodox Church.

No opportunity to wonder about the cause of the explosion.

"Load!"

The second and third Arab vehicles motored past the damaged car. Firing machine guns and cannons, they closed in on Notre Dame.

Uri braced the tube against the sill and aimed. As he did so, another enormous blast shook the building. The bazooka hit Uri in the mouth, knocking out a tooth, but he recovered himself and fired.

An armored car disappeared in a gout of flame.

"Load!"

Bullets were flying through the window. One chipped stone near Uri's face, but he shook his head and prepared to fire again.

The third armored car was almost too close to hit from the fifth floor. The angle was bad and rapidly closing to vertical.

Uri stood up in the window and fired downward.

The concussion of another Arab blast tossed the boy sideways. A bullet splintered on the casement. Fragments hit him in the cheek.

The rocket had already struck home. Hit in the rear deck, the third Legion armored car blew up, then disintegrated as the ammunition inside exploded.

"Load! Load!" Uri urged, wiping blood from his face.

"No need!" Naomi shouted. "Look!"

The Legion retreated again. The undamaged armored cars scurried away, leaving the crippled one to bumble backwards like a drunken elephant.

"Those giant bangs!" Uri asked. "What is hitting us now?"

The answer was not long in coming. The Legion had managed to heave a twenty-five-pound gun up on Suleiman's wall. It was firing into the south face of Notre Dame at point-blank range.

# CHAPTER 25

Her foot resting on the first step of the entrance to Nissan Bek, Yehudit drew in a deep breath and squared her shoulders. During her unmarried life in the Old City Jewish Quarter, the red stone pillars of this synagogue represented home. As the only child of a venerated rabbi, she had been pampered and praised until she believed that such cosseting was her due.

In her youth she associated the magnificent four-story-high dome—an 1869 gift of the Emperor Franz Joseph of Austria—with her family's honor. Just as the sanctuary was the preeminent structure in the district, so the offspring of Rabbi Akiva was first among the daughters of Zion.

That had changed, and Yehudit ducked her chin in chagrin at the memory. How arrogant she had been, how uncaring of others and without mercy!

How proud and stiff-necked her soul until . . . until she had seen the caring heart of the ransomed Rachel Sachar, until she had felt the love of Dov Avram, until she had seen the nobility of those willing to die to secure a homeland for those who would come after. . . .

Love had touched her and she was not the same person she had been.

It was compassion that drew her onward. Inwardly she quaked at facing rejection and denial, yet her sense of duty and love for her father compelled her to continue.

Her arrival at the triple-arched entry did not go unremarked. As soon as she was recognized, the glances she noted were hostile, the conversations guarded, except for pointedly loud comments like "How dare she show her face here?"

A matron, her head shaved, then covered with a black wig and a scarf, as was proper among the Hasidim, confronted Yehudit. "Have you come to drive another knife into your father's heart?" the woman demanded.

"I have come to see my father," Yehudit agreed. "Please tell him I am here."

Word of Yehudit's arrival had already reached the rabbi.

Chin up and chest thrust out, he strode across the marble floor toward her.

"Have you returned to your senses at last?" he said in a ringing tone. "Are you here to beg my forgiveness?"

"Is there nowhere we can talk privately?" she asked with her eyes downcast.

Akiva opened his arms as if to embrace the room as his words reached into its corners. "These are my children," he said. "You are the outsider. There is nothing you have to say to me that they may not hear."

Gulping back the tears that the knife of his words gouged from her, Yehudit said, "I have come to warn you. The pause in the shelling—"

"Which I personally arranged," Akiva interrupted proudly.

"It was a deceit . . . a ruse to make us let down our guard. The Legion—"

"Has Moshe Sachar put you up to this lie?" Akiva bellowed.

"Father," Yehudit pleaded, "please listen. The radio says the shelling stopped because the United Nations pressured King Abdullah not to harm the holy places. But the Legion is coming! They blew a hole into the Street of the Jews, and we think Nissan Bek may be the next target."

Akiva scoffed. "Haganah rabble are already on the roof despite my protests. What does Sachar want? Should we give them our beds as well?"

"You must—"

Akiva's eyes flashed at the word.

Yehudit tried again. "We will send reinforcements to help defend you . . . and the women and children and the elderly would be better off in the Hurva. We will make room for them. . . ."

"That is enough!" Akiva roared. "You came here to frighten my people. It is a low, shabby, and transparent trick of the Sachar *apikorsim* and we spit on it."

In the sanctuary of Nissan Bek he did not spit, but he made the sign against the evil eye, as if she were a prostitute or a witch.

Around her, black-coated Hasidim did the same. "Shame!" They said in a low but menacing tone. "Shame! Shame!"

Covering her face with her hands, Yehudit fled from the building.

■ ■ ■

Brandenburg, back on the Arab side of the lines, stood on the ramparts of Damascus Gate. He watched the Arab shelling of Notre Dame with pleasure. Exploding rounds lit up the skies above Jerusalem.

"An English cannon," he said. "The Führer would find it amusing."

Ahkmed al-Malik stood at his right, observing the action through field glasses he had taken from a dead Jew in Kfar Etzion. "Witness the will of Allah," he said. "English cannon, English officers, and Muslim soldiers who once fought for your Third Reich. They come together to destroy Jews. It is almost, perhaps, as if that war did not end. The Reich did not lose. Here is Germany in a new form. Soldiers fight to annihilate the killers of Christ, the defilers of the holy places of Islam. Allah is pleased."

Brandenburg did not reply. Did this buffoon think the war was about killing Christ-killers? Or . . . for Allah, was it? God in one form or another was always a convenient excuse to rid the world of some enemy, the SS commander thought.

But there were the secret and sinister accomplishments of Jewish political and economic leaders that finally convinced Brandenburg that Germany should dig a grave big enough to hold every Jew.

The SS lieutenant considered them a universal menace for practical reasons. They were a people without a country who had infiltrated the nations of the entire world. Brandenburg had read the secret Protocols of the Elders of Zion, the Zionist manifesto that decreed chaos upon the nations. It was well-known that Jews plunged Europe into financial disaster after the First World War for their own gains. They controlled the banks. They controlled the press. Their ultimate goal was to control the world and lead the *Volk* into Bolshevism as Lenin and Trotsky had done in Russia!

And so Brandenburg's commitment to rid the universe of *Juden* was simply common sense. Being an atheist, he did not hold to the Christian religious hatred that called Jews *Christ-killers* and thus applauded their extermination in Poland. Nor did he espouse the Muslim belief in *Jihad*: Holy War for the sake of Allah and his Prophet.

In spite of his contempt for religion, SS Lieutenant Brandenburg often stoked the fires of religious hatred to accomplish the correct philosophy of annihilation of an enemy.

Al-Malik's ignorant and fanatical religious dedication to the destruction of all Jews and all things Jewish made him a perfect servant of the now-fallen Nazi ideology that had trained him in the arts of slaughter. The Arab was proud of his brutality toward captured Jews and bragged openly to his men about his experiences with their women. In this, al-Malik reminded Brandenburg of minor Gestapo officers during the war who thought rape of women in occupied territories, followed by torture, interrogation, confession, and execution, was sport.

Brandenburg did not like al-Malik or his assistant Hassan el-Hassan, who was even more one-dimensional in his enjoyment of brutality for the sake of serving Allah!

The SS officer had served neither gods nor men, but his own sense of rightness. Ridding the world of these treacherous and clever Zionists was a service to humanity.

Perhaps, he thought, counting the volley of explosions upon the Jewish positions, Jerusalem would be the last stronghold and the final resting place of the Jews.

■ ■ ■ ■

The reality of what was shaping the Middle East was not found in council chambers anywhere.

Though diplomats harangued and deplored, Jewish Jerusalem continued to hold back the Arab Legion. Other Jewish forces continued to stave off the attacks of Egypt, Syria, and Iraq.

While the Legion struggled, five more disassembled Messerschmitts arrived in Israel. A rusty hulk of a ship limped into Haifa Harbor and two thousand refugees, after learning ten military commands in Hebrew, were prepared for battle.

With Moshe busy elsewhere in the Old City, Ehud and Dov were assigned to lead the reinforcements to Nissan Bek. Counting the newcomers, the Haganah contingent responsible for defending the vital post on the eastern perimeter of the Jewish Quarter consisted of fifteen men, five boys, and three teenage girls.

On the northern flank of the synagogue was an open square. It was bare, paved with stone, and contained nothing except two benches on which old people sunned themselves on mild winter days. Being in plain view of the rooftop sentries, it was not thought to represent a threat.

It was across this plaza that the Arab Legion attack on Nissan Bek began.

A reverberating detonation was followed by an alarmed cry from the post at the base of the dome. It brought Ehud running outside from the women's gallery. "There!" the sentry shouted, gesturing with his rifle.

An explosion ripped open the back wall of a house across the square.

"Shoot!" Ehud said. "Shoot!"

Five uniformed Legionnaires rushed across the plaza, accompanied by twenty Jihad Moquades. At the same time Arab snipers on top of the dynamited house fired at the synagogue's roof, wounding one defender.

Ehud stood upright and heaved a Players tin grenade. It exploded beside a bench. One of the Legion attackers dropped, clutching his leg, but the rest of the Arabs continued to advance.

Among the attackers, three Legionnaires lugged crates trailing fuses.

Dov shot one, but the others reached the base of the synagogue unharmed, then both were wounded as they retreated. Moments later the bomb exploded with a crash that made Nissan Bek's dome ring like a gigantic tolling bell.

Part of the east wall of the synagogue disappeared in a shower of stone fragments.

"Try to keep them back," Ehud barked to the other sentries. "Dov, you and I must go in through the windows." Gathering three more Haganah troopers, Ehud prepared to counterattack.

A screaming wave of terror-stricken Jewish men and women, including Rabbi Akiva, poured out of Nissan Bek and into the constricted alleyway leading west. "Go to the Hurva!" Dov yelled down to them. "The Hurva! You'll be protected there."

"What are we waiting for?" Ehud asked as Dov grabbed his arm and kept him from climbing through the window into the women's gallery. "From above we can shoot down on them before they attack the rest of the Quarter."

"Did you see that most of the attackers who made it to the building were the Mufti's Irregulars?"

"So? Does it not hurt the same to be shot by a Jihad Moquade as by a Legionnaire?"

"Wait," Dov said. During the pause, while Ehud chafed at the delay, gunfire popped sporadically across the square, but the interior of the synagogue grew quiet.

"What is happening in there?" Ehud muttered.

"What I hoped," Dov returned. "Grenades ready? Now we go!"

Bursting into the gallery from all five windows at once, Dov's men yanked the pins and tossed grenades into the hall.

The Jihad Moquades, their pockets stuffed with candlesticks and altar cloths, had laid aside their weapons in their eagerness for loot. Several were pawing through suitcases while two more attempted to carry away a steamer trunk.

The five hand grenades exploded within seconds of each other, killing or maiming the Holy Strugglers.

There were no Jewish bodies on the marble floor. The alarm raised by the Haganah sentry had given Rabbi Akiva's followers enough warning to escape.

Another wave of Arab attackers crossed the square. These were also driven back.

A third assault followed and a fourth. Each time, more Haganah defenders were wounded; each time, fewer could respond to the renewed challenge.

"This is bad," Ehud said after the fourth Jewish counterattack barely succeeded in dislodging the Arabs. "I have one grenade left and ten bullets. Out of the six men I was leading only one other besides me is unwounded."

The fifth wave of Arab troops again succeeded in entering the synagogue. These were all Legionnaires. Despite being sniped at from above, they placed a crate of explosives in each corner of the hall, then sprinted away.

"Get off the roof!" Dov yelled, blood streaming from his forehead, which had been grazed by a ricochet. "Get everybody off the roof!"

The dome of Nissan Bek jumped upward, then tilted eastward. A gigantic roar deafened attackers and defenders alike as two sides of the sanctuary blew out. The interior was choked with rubble and smoke.

Midnight found Ehud, Dov, and the remaining Haganah defenders withdrawing to the west, to the protection of a substitute barricade.

Nissan Bek, partially demolished and burning, had fallen.

■ ■ ■ ■

The British officer's assurance of safe transport did not spare David and Bobby Milkin from being spat on or having epithets hurled into their blindfolded faces. The endless jolting of the road was bad enough, but their guards delighted in tormenting them. Surreptitious blows were plentiful. Bound hand and foot and unable even to anticipate, let alone avoid, the strikes, David jerked away from every noise.

Even a supposed kindness, like being offered a drink of tepid, foul-smelling water, was accompanied by a jarring smack to the teeth with the rim of the tin cup.

No food was offered.

The convoy had traveled all day, and when the relentless sun heated the tarp-enclosed bed into an airless oven, the column continued to roll.

David reasoned that this was part of a big push to seize the road to the coast. If only the Messers were ready and he were in one! What a turkey shoot this would be!

Dozing, David imagined himself attacking the convoy with fifty-pound bombs and twenty-millimeter cannon fire. In his dream the Messerschmitt engine hummed perfectly, and every shot fired struck home.

The thrumming of an airplane engine grew louder. The buzzing in David's thoughts amplified into a menacing drone.

His eyes popped open beneath the blindfold. Was he still dreaming? *Bombing run!*

Lurching to the floor, David collided with Milkin, who had done the same. Both men braced for a racking explosion.

Instead there was loud excitement from the Arabs. The column of trucks did not even slow. The airplane's hum faded in the distance.

"What was it, Tin Man?" Milkin asked, the words muffled and indistinct.

"British bomber . . . Dakota, I think. Must be what the Gyppos use to beat up Tel Aviv. Showing off for his friends."

Ellie was in Tel Aviv! Another reason to be up in a fighter and not in the back of an Arab truck!

More uncountable time passed.

With a groan of springs and a whine of dust-laden brakes, the truck squealed to a halt at last.

Stiff from the beatings and enforced immobility, David and Milkin could not stand when ordered to get out of the truck. Their inability to walk was used as license to yank them roughly over the tailgate and drop them, face first, onto the dirt.

Hoisted up again, the two men were dragged into some kind of an enclosure.

David heard Major Burr speak, though the words were not directed at him.

"Tie them to the tent pole. Yes, leave them blindfolded. Post a guard outside. They aren't going anywhere. And lay out my maps. I'm expecting the commanders from Latrun and Deir Ayub at any minute.

■ ■ ■ ■

To the amazement of Daoud, the progress of the two nuns through the pitch-black night of the Old City was untroubled.

Twice Daoud heard the rattle of a wooden wheel on the stones of the street behind them. *The gardener?* But when he turned to look, he could see no one in the shadows.

Daoud whispered, "Everyone is gone to marvel at the field cannon. By now it will be ready to blow down the walls of Notre Dame."

The sentries at New Gate challenged them. Daoud responded that he was ordered to escort these two Catholic sisters outside the walls.

His claim went unquestioned. *Insh'Allah!* Amazing!

Within five minutes the trio entered the grounds of Soeurs Réparatrices Convent. The front door of the building was closed but unlocked. The flagstone floor of the foyer was littered with debris.

Mother Superior's voice was jubilant. "Glory to our Lord Jesus! We are home, Sister Marie Claire!"

# SUNDAY

*May 23, 1948*

*Show compassion to the righteous, to*
*the pious, to the leaders of your People,*
*the house of Israel, to the remnants of*
*their sages, to righteous converts, and to us,*
*Adonai our God. And give good reward to*
*all who truly trust in your name, and let our*
*lot be among them forever that we will not*
*be shamed, for we put our trust in you.*
*Blessed are you, Adonai, who is the support*
*and trust of the righteous.*

*The Amidah—The Thirteenth Prayer*
*"Tsadikim"*

*"Save us, Lord our God, and gather us together from the na-*
*tions, that we may proclaim your holy name and glory in your*
*praise."*

*Psalm 105:47*

*"And God shall wipe away all tears from their eyes; and there*
*shall be no more death, neither sorrow, nor crying, neither shall*
*there be any more pain: for the former things are passed away."*

*Revelation 21:4*

# CHAPTER 26

It remained oppressively hot. The Arab Legion column encamped somewhere between Latrun and Deir Ayub. The second village was unknown to David, but he recognized the name of Latrun and the strategic importance of the village. Ben-Gurion and Michael Stone had spoken of it.

Latrun was the key strong point on the road between Jerusalem and the seacoast. That highway was the lifeline of the Holy City. With Arab armies to the north, south, and east, there was no other supply route. For the Legion, possessing Latrun meant they could maintain the siege of Jerusalem until it capitulated or starved.

Unless the Jews were willing to abandon Jerusalem, Latrun was a crucial objective.

It was not surprising that the Legion moved men and equipment here from Galilee. This could be the climactic battle of the war.

David and Milkin were bound back-to-back, with a tent pole between them. Their ankles were tied with leather thongs. They had remained that way since detrucking from the convoy.

Sometime in the night a stooped Bedouin crone carrying a lantern brought them supper and removed their blindfolds.

Her chin was tattooed with faded blue lines and her skin was so wrinkled that her eyes almost disappeared in the folds. She did not speak, and when David tried to address her she rapped him on the head with a wooden spoon.

Nevertheless, she fed him a mixture of rice and mashed chickpeas. He lapped it up eagerly, as did Milkin. From a canvas bag she poured water into their mouths, letting them drink as much as they desired.

When the tin mess plates were empty she started to retie David's blindfold. At the mute appeal in his face, she drew back and left both men's eyes uncovered. Then she departed, taking the lantern with her.

His hunger and thirst eased at last, David dozed again. Questions played over and over in his mind.

*By now the Boss knows we didn't make it to Zorash. Wonder what they think happened to us. If they found the other bodies, do they think we died in the fire? Does Ellie know?*

David woke with a start, but did not know why. Apart from night birds and a distant rumble of thunder, there were no sounds.

A bent, robed figure stood in the doorway of the tent, outlined by the full moon.

*The old woman back again? Why?*

David's eyes were drawn to a movement by the enigmatic form. An arm thrust into the robe and withdrew something that gleamed in the moonlight.

A knife! They were going to be murdered after all!

With surprising speed, the apparition plunged across the tent and clamped a sinewy hand over David's mouth. In a rasping voice that made the hair on David's neck bristle, the man warned, "Do not speak."

The blade flashed, slicing through the leather straps and rope cords. Chaffing David's wrists and ankles, the unknown rescuer rubbed circulation back into his limbs, then did the same for Milkin.

"Go south. Two miles. You will come to a village—Beit Susin. Do not trust the villagers there. Turn west and you will find what you seek."

■ ■ ■ ■

The moon hanging over the Judean hills was a searchlight beaming down on David and Milkin. Every barren slope they had to cross seemed miles in breadth; every protective shadow into which they plunged no bigger than a handkerchief.

With every step, David expected an eruption of gunfire. How long could their escape go unnoticed? How many Legionnaires were on their track?

The descent into the gorge of Bab el Wad combined breathless waiting, followed by gasping sprints. The clatter of David's boots sounded to him like the clank of tank treads.

Approaching the highway, Milkin growled, "Look out! There's a truck there with its lights off."

The two men huddled together and watched. A spike of moonlight pinned the silhouette of a bus to the mountainside. No lights and no engine noise either.

David knew that night played tricks with his eyes, but this vehicle looked wrong somehow, twisted and deformed.

He slipped closer.

It was the burned-out hulk of a bus, victim of an earlier Jihad Moquade assault on the Jerusalem convoys. The front axle had been blasted loose and the wreck rested on its nose with its rear end up in the air. There was also a gaping hole in the roof.

"Come on!" he hissed to Milkin.

Lying in the shadow of the ruined vehicle, the two pilots planned their next move.

"We can't use the road," David said. "There are bound to be Arab patrols."

Milkin pointed to the shadows of the connecting wadis that hung about the gorge like tangled tentacles. "We can't wander around in that."

"The old man said if we went south and west, we'd find what we were looking for."

"Right now I'm lookin' for General Patton and a hundred tanks . . . But I'd settle for a couple Haganah guys with machine guns and a jeep."

"Let's move out."

As the two crawled forward, a bundle of dry sticks rattled beneath Milkin's hand. It was the charred remains of a human rib cage, proof of how fierce the battles had been for the pass of Bab el Wad.

They wasted no time in putting two rows of hills between them and the highway. Exactly as Milkin feared, there was no longer any clear direction leading toward safety. Four different canyons brought them to dead ends.

After they had followed another gully for ten minutes it looped around a horseshoe bend and led them back toward Bab el Wad.

Milkin remarked, "Let's point the nose west and go."

"We're on foot, Bobby. As the crow flies doesn't work."

Even backtracking proved impossible. Somehow they took a previously unseen branch canyon and wandered along it. "Great Boy Scouts, huh?" Milkin groused.

Against the dull grays and black, a silver beam illuminated a rounded white object about the size of a shoebox.

"A skull? Milkin hung back. "What's left of the last New Yorker who came this way?"

David bent to look closer. "It's a road marker—marble, I think."

"So?"

"Hold on." He brushed aside dirt that clung to an otherwise smooth surface. "There's carving on it." Tracing the engraving with his finger he added, "An X."

"X? Unless this is a code for Times Square, I ain't interested, y'know?

"Like the Roman numeral X. The Tenth Legion, maybe, or maybe it means ten miles from here to somewhere."

"You think some two-thousand-year-old dead guys are gonna come back and help us? And I hear they didn't like Jews any better than the Mufti does."

"It means," David interrupted in exasperation, "this trail was a Roman road. West to east. From the seaport into Jerusalem, maybe. *Now* we point the nose and fly west."

The road, seldom better than a goat trail at best and disappearing for a hundred yards a stretch, nevertheless led inexorably west. Skirting sheer precipices and switchbacking into and out of canyons, the trace emerged at last on a hilltop. Below the brow of this last knoll the ground dropped away toward the coastal plain . . . and the Mediterranean. The moon, having done its duty for the night, was sliding beneath the water.

■ ■ ■ ■

The cannon on the Old City wall pounded Notre Dame into the early hours of Sunday . . . Holy Trinity Sunday.

A gaping hole appeared in the south wall. A chasm was blasted in the granite, first one room wide, then two, and then three. It grew downward as well until the hole stretched three stories in height, as if an invisible knife slashed a wound deeper and deeper.

No defenders could remain in the south wing. A few of the Home Guardsmen tried, in rooms on the ground floor, below the level of the artillery. Deafened, ears trickling blood, they emerged after a half-dozen rounds were fired.

An urgent plea went out from Notre Dame to Haganah Headquarters: Do something to stop the unbearable detonations, or we cannot hold!

Peter said to Jacob, "If the Legion gets past the southeast corner of the building, then we have lost. There is no way we can occupy any of that part to fight back. They will surround us and finish us."

"Then we must keep them from reaching that spot," Jacob said. Each man saw terrible knowledge in the eyes of the other. With two rockets left for the bazooka, how could they hope to halt another assault? "It is more important than ever for one of us to be near the detonator," Jacob concluded. "No matter what else happens, blocking the road will prolong the defense of the New City even after . . ." He left the rest of the sentence unspoken.

■ ■ ■ ■

"Hello, Daniel." Alfie greeted his friend as he entered Ward B.

Daniel did not answer.

Alfie tried again. "I came to say hello. So . . . hello, Daniel."

Eleven other somber-faced men in the ward grumbled, "So say hello to him already!"

Daniel glanced at Alfie and then away. "Hello. I suppose."

Alfie sat on the table and swung his long legs as though he were perched on a garden fence. "I came to see how is your foot today, Daniel?"

"Which one?"

"The one which is not there."

"It has run off. Right off the end of my leg." Daniel turned away.

Alfie pondered this reply. No one smiled or hallooed to him like usual. He did not understand. "What is wrong with everybody today? You are gloomy."

"It's the kid," said the American at the far end of the room. "The Kurtzman kid."

"Little Abe. *Ja?*" Alfie queried. "He was okay. That is how you say it? Doctor Baruch says he is okay."

Daniel answered, "They say he is dying. Rachel Sachar came to fetch Lori Kalner. But the women in the hospital are talking about it. Doctor Baruch says there is nothing medical he can do . . . It is not a medical thing. And so . . ."

Alfie clasped his large hands together on his lap. He stared at his thumbs. "I have been praying," he said aloud and yet the comment was directed at no one. "What is it then you want me to do?"

"Go somewhere else if you must be cheerful," Daniel admonished.

"Where should I go?" Alfie murmured, his broad features sorrowful. And then, "The garden?"

"Right. The garden, why don't you?" Daniel did not look at him. "Back to Berlin . . . dummkopf . . ."

The American shouted at Daniel, "Shut up the bellyaching! It's bad enough. The dummy didn't do nothin'! He comes in here. Tries to give you a boost. Can it!"

Alfie slid off the table and turned around as though trying to remember which way was out. "What should I do?" he asked in a bewildered voice, and then he wandered away without his usual pleasant farewell.

■ ■ ■ ■

Moshe and Dov finished setting the charges to seal five tunnels which extended beneath the Hurva to the defensive perimeters of the Jewish Quarter. The cannon blasting Notre Dame would turn on the Old City soon enough. And since Nissan Bek had fallen, it was just a matter of time before the Jihad Moquades found their way into one of the underground passageways.

The radio message from New City Haganah Headquarters was clear. Moshe recognized the voice of Luke Thomas even before Yehudit shouted for Moshe to hurry to the radio room.

Luke, his tone laden with regret and exhaustion, explained, "You can hear it as well as we can. It's lobbing twenty-five-pound shells directly into the granite blocks of the hospice. Moshe, it must be stopped. We have nothing on this side of the wall to fire back."

"What about a plane?" Moshe asked hopefully. "A bomb? Strafing perhaps? Have our fighter planes and pilots arrived in Tel Aviv? David Meyer? Has he made it from Czechoslovakia?"

"Munitions are arriving hourly. But they're not through assembling the fighters. And . . . bad news I'm afraid . . . David Meyer is missing. Presumed killed. And Buzz Buerling, the Canadian fighter ace, was burned to death in a crash in Rome. Sabotage. We are almost certain of it. There's no help for Jerusalem from the skies, at least not today. Not against that cannon."

Moshe considered the information and the as-yet-unspoken request that was implied in this news.

Unless the artillery on the wall was put out of action, Notre Dame would fall. There was no way the cannon could be destroyed unless someone from inside the Old City Jewish Quarter came from behind and eliminated it.

Moshe said, "No help from the skies, Luke? It will take the help of heaven to accomplish what you are asking."

"I know that, Moshe. You must understand . . . there is no other way, or I would not have contacted you. If Notre Dame is lost, all of Jerusalem will fall. The cannon on the wall must be eliminated."

"Then we will do what we can and wait on heaven for the rest."

■ ■ ■ ■

Dawn on Sunday did not begin with the expected Arab Legion assault on Notre Dame. Instead, the gun on the wall continued to hurl twenty-five-pound projectiles into the hospice. The gap it created reached to the ground, forming a ramp of shattered blocks leading to the interior of the structure.

And the battering did not cease.

Mortar shells flew into rooms already so demolished that additional explosions merely rearranged the rubble.

Life for the defenders became one of catching a breath between detonations and holding it till after the next rumbling crash. Few had the energy for speech. Every face was drawn, clenched tight in anticipation of the next jarring outburst.

One day earlier the Gadna Youth had poked fun at the aged men of the Home Guard . . . fifty years old, some of them!

Now they looked at the hands of their seventeen-year-old comrades and saw uncontrollable trembling, as though all had been transformed into palsied octogenarians.

Artillery rounds continued to rain on the roof until the entire fifth floor was so cluttered with shattered slate tiles that it could not be occupied.

Jacob, Uri, and Naomi took up a different position on the fourth floor. St. Barbara's room was demolished, so they moved to one dedicated to Notre Dame de Lourdes.

With the supreme effort required to form the words, Uri asked Naomi, "What's this one mean?"

"Our Lady of . . . hopeless causes," she said.

■ ■ ■ ■

The thorny brush covering the hills turned from gray to dark green with the dawn. David and Milkin descended the last stretch of Roman road and then the trail disappeared entirely.

Directly ahead loomed a barbed-wire-enclosed settlement. The smoke of a breakfast fire drifted up on the first bit of breeze they had felt in days.

"So is this the place the old geezer warned us not to trust? Milkin asked skeptically.

"I don't think so," David replied, gesturing toward the flagpole in the center of the compound. The wind stirred the folds of a blue-and-white banner. In its center was a blue Star of David.

"Man, that is the prettiest thing I ever saw. What are we waiting for?"

The terrain eased from rolling hills to grassland to cultivated plain. Despite their aching feet, their speed increased with every step.

"First thing I'm gonna do is find somebody with a cigar to spare," Milkin declared.

"The first thing I want to do is let Ellie know I'm not dead."

"Yeah," Milkin concurred in a thoughtful tone.

A swale hid a rattling tractor from their view until they were almost on it. It emerged from the gully, dragging a heap of railroad ties wrapped in chains. Milkin waved to the driver, who did not wave back, but instead bailed off the machine and ran toward the compound.

"What's that about? Milkin said.

"Have you looked at yourself lately?"

"Hey, you ain't no garden-party prize yourself!"

"The robes. We look like Arabs."

A bell clanged insistently in the settlement. A trio of trucks, their cargo spaces barricaded with stock racks and boards, roared out of the compound. Rifle barrels bristled over the top of improvised armor.

Outside the gate the paths of the three vehicles diverged so that they encircled the flyers completely. A ring of men pointed their weapons at Milkin and David.

"Let me do the talking," David warned.

"*Hifsik!*" one of the settlers ordered. Then he rattled off a string of Hebrew words.

Tossing back the hood of the robe, David said, "Are we glad to see you." He advanced toward the speaker, extending his hand. "We're friends," he added confidently. "American flyers."

David was tackled by three men and Milkin by six. Despite the yells of "Hey, we're on your side!" the two Americans were thrown to the ground. An oily rag was thrust into David's mouth and the knotted end of a rope into Milkin's.

A hasty conference took place among the settlers. David caught the words for *shoot,* and *kill,* and others unknown but recognizable since they were accompanied by the brandishing of a noose.

"Wait!" David mumbled around the gag. "Speak English?"

Suddenly Milkin spat out the knotted cord. He bellowed, "*Shabbos! Gefilte fish! Briss! Macy's! Shabbos, you momzers!* Let me up!"

His babble parted the Red Sea. From murderous intent the villagers changed to solicitude and sympathy, hoisting David and Milkin to their feet, brushing them off, and escorting them into the compound.

The settlement, which was named Kfar Urriya, had no one who spoke English except an elderly physician, originally from Savannah, Georgia.

Dr. Miriam Gould explained the reason for the hostility of the kibbutzniks. "For now, at least, we're behind Israeli lines. But yesterday we were strafed by Egyptian planes. Then there was an Arab mortar attack last night at sundown," she said. "I have two critically wounded and two dead . . . all of them children."

# CHAPTER 27

From his post at Notre Dame, Jacob spotted the enormous yellow-and-white flag unfurled from the upper-story window of Soeurs Réparatrices Convent.

Whose banner was it? Syrian? A branch of the Arab Legion? Egyptian maybe?

Somehow, he reasoned, a Muslim force had sneaked around the Jewish defenses in the night and entered the convent! The explosives would all be disconnected and in their hands!

He leapt to his feet and raised the alarm, calling Uri and Peter as well as others in rooms on either side.

Peter peered cautiously through the sandbag slit and cursed softly.

"So much for blowing the convent!" remarked Uri.

"Whose flag is it?" Jacob asked.

"Whoever it is, you can bet they have heavier firepower than we have," Peter said bitterly. He exhaled loudly. "We'll have to attack. We can't have them at our backs."

As if to emphasize the point, Uri shouted, "I see movement in the window. Somebody! Quick! Shoot!"

In reply, six rifles opened up on the target, blasting holes in the flag and sending shards of wood flying from the window frame.

At the same moment, Arabs on the wall above New Gate also let loose with volley after volley, shredding the fabric of the yellow-and-white banner.

"Get the bazooka!" Peter commanded. "We'll wake them up. Hit one of the bundles of dynamite, eh?"

Again the patter of machine-gun fire reverberated from the Old City wall.

"Are they firing at us?" Jacob asked, puzzled that no bullets struck the sandbags.

As the roar of battle increased, Naomi Snow ran breathlessly into the room. She shouted in French and then in Hebrew, "Stop shooting! Idiots! Do you see the flag? *Mon Dieu!* The French nuns! This is the flag of the Catholic Pope! The nuns have reentered the convent!"

■ ■ ■ ■

The effect of the papal flag fluttering from the window was not what Mother Superior had expected.

Bullets slammed into the convent. She looked up, startled, as a slug whined past her head. "Sister Marie Claire," she said in a hurt and surprised tone, "they are shooting at the Holy Father's flag!"

"Where is their sense of propriety?" said the sister in wonder.

Daoud, his fingers dripping blasting caps plucked from the bundles of dynamite, ran into the room. Machine-gun bullets pocked the wall at Mother's right hand. He fell to his belly and shouted at her, "Fool! Get down! Stupid! They will blow your heads off!" Detonators, like tiny little bombs, spilled onto the carpet. *"Ya Allah!"* he cried.

Mother Superior dropped to the floor beside Sister Marie Claire. The women cast angry looks at Daoud. It had been a long time since anyone had dared to shout at the Mother Superior in such a manner!

Prostrate, she said in a too-calm, irritating voice, "The Lord shall preserve us, Daoud. Jesus our Lord and Savior is with us. He is our rock and our salvation. Fear not."

Sister Marie Claire sweetly and sadly asked, "Why would they shoot at the flag of the Holy Father?"

"Target practice," offered Mother Superior. "You know how they meant to intimidate us when we entered the Old City. It is the same. A game they play. They hope to terrorize us into giving up; make us leave."

Daoud looked at the explosive charges spread out on the Persian rug before him. This was no game. Any one of them could blow up and take hands or eyes or rip open the insides of a person. Not to mention enough dynamite in the convent to blow up the entire building. The intention of the Jews was clear. The rapid fire of Arabs on the walls was also not encouraging. Why was this crazy old woman talking nonsense?

His eyes bulged with fear. He was sweating. "Mother," he said in a rasping whisper. "I think the Jews will come back here! And soon!"

■ ■ ■ ■

"Catholic nuns!" Peter paced the room beside the useless detonator.

Jacob remarked, "Who would think a bunch of old ladies could make such short work of detonators and dynamite charges?"

"How did they do it?" Naomi asked.

"The detonators were pulled. They teach this sort of thing to nuns?"

"It doesn't matter how," Peter replied. "The point is they are there, and they have made our efforts a waste. We cannot blow Soeurs Réparatrices if they are inside. We'll have to get them out of there. Reconnect the charges."

"But what shall we do with them once we have them?" Naomi queried.

Their presence was a problem, Jacob agreed. "They are like pigeons, these sisters. Turn them out, and they come flying home. This time we can't have them coming back and plucking out the wires again."

Uri snapped. "Too many pigeons in the roost. The way to get rid of them is shoot them for the pests they are!"

At this comment everyone turned to glare at Uri.

"Just a joke." Uri held up his hands in surrender. "But you must admit the thought is appealing, no?"

Naomi growled at him. "These are good-hearted ladies. French. Like me. I survived the occupation of France in the care of sisters such as these. We must shelter them."

Peter shook his head. "Protect them from their own good intentions, is that it?"

"Let's drag them out of there, then," Jacob said. "Before the Arabs take them hostage. If they will listen to reason . . ."

Naomi gave a Gallic shrug. "Listen to reason? You are idiots, no? They will not listen to anything you have to say to them. You are a man. Men. Outside the confines of the church they will not speak to you at all. Except to say they cannot speak to you. You need a woman for this. Also I am French. I must go along."

■ ■ ■ ■

Daoud, Mother Superior, and Sister Marie Claire sat on the floor of the convent chapel with their backs against the stone pillar. This was, Daoud judged, the best place to be in case of shelling. Mother made him tie them to the stone column with a length of rope from the curtains. Like Joan of Arc, Sister Marie Claire declared, they were tied to a stake. They would die here if they had to, but they would not be budged.

Daoud was not so stupid as to join them in their determination to perish. He was not tied, but he stayed with them in case they changed their minds and wanted out.

Mother and Sister had taken to praying again, and the singing of joyful little songs in French and Latin.

Did they think their childish belief that all would be well would really make for a happy ending?

Daoud was certain their troubles had just begun. No doubt the Jews had already tried to blow up the convent. It was a good thing he had dis-armed the bundles and hidden the blasting caps in a toilet. But he had simply bought the nuns and their beloved convent a space of time.

He encouraged the ladies to wave a white flag, to return with him to the protection of the Latin Patriarchate. They refused. No doubt when the Legionnaires on the wall saw two nuns and a boy emerge from the building they would have a good laugh.

The Jews, on the other hand, would be furious that Daoud had ru-ined their work. They would pluck him up by the ears and torture him until he told where he had concealed the detonators.

He had already decided that he would tell them before they hurt him. They would find more, and what was the use of Daoud's suffering if the Jews would find a way to blow up the convent and block the road anyway?

Then the Jews arrived.

The *boom, boom, boom* against the garden door of the convent was more than someone knocking to be let in.

"They are coming!" he cried.

Mother sang, "*Tra-la-la*" and "*La-la-kyrie-la-tra-la!*"

The Jews' pounding became more fierce.

Daoud leapt to his feet. "Come on! Old woman! Kind, good, old woman," he pleaded. "Please let me untie you! We will escape!"

The Mother smiled at him the way a righteous martyr smiles at a silly weeping companion before she dies gloriously.

Daoud became enraged at her. She was not listening. She did not hear the crash of the door! The Jews were in the building!

He told her, "They have broken down the door! Come with me! We will hide! His heart was racing.

She stopped singing long enough to say, "You must hide, Daoud. In the cellar. Go on, child." Then she and Sister Marie Claire began again with their "*Tra-la-la-la*."

Maddening! Hopeless! Insane!

Daoud spun on his heel and dashed from the chapel, leaving the virgins to the fate they had chosen. He fled to the arched door that led down and down into the basement of the convent, where the belongings and baggage of the exiled population of Christian Jerusalem was stored.

There came ten shouts in as many languages.

"Where are they?"

"Look here! The nuns! They've taken out the detonators!"

"Here are the sisters! Come on, boys! They're in the chapel!"

The tramp of boots pounded the floorboards above his head. He clambered over piles of luggage and slipped into a space between a packing crate and a walnut headboard!

"*Ya Allah!*" he panted. "Allah, save me!"

■ ■ ■ ■

The bundles of dynamite at Soeurs Réparatrices Convent were reactivated. The nuns had cleverly hidden the original blasting caps, but it had done them no good. Within an hour the entire building was once again ready to disintegrate onto Suleiman Road if needed.

The electrical box that would blow up the convent was situated in the safest room in Notre Dame.

This was where Peter and Jacob placed the two nuns as well.

"The better to keep our eye on them," Jacob said.

Mother Superior and Sister Marie Claire were tied back-to-back in two plain wooden chairs by the same cord that had bound them to the pillar in the convent chapel.

As Naomi had predicted, the sisters refused to utter even one syllable since they had been thrown over the shoulders of the Jewish soldiers and hauled out of the chapel like sacks of flour.

The elder of the two, noble and martyr-like in her demeanor, refused even to glance at the men who hustled in and out of the chamber. At times, however, Jacob spotted her looking at the wires and the detonator in a cunning manner.

They rejected offers of food and water. This heaped guilt upon the fellows who had carried them here against their will and who would now destroy their home.

Jacob did not like the women. Peter was gruff and unintimidated. Uri was openly derisive.

Only Naomi was quiet and conciliatory. She accompanied them when they had to make a trip to the loo. Then Peter tied them up again. His face was a scowl as he looped the cord around their wrists with the deftness of a man who knew how to tie sheep for the slaughter.

■ ■ ■ ■

The air pulsed with the ominous bellow of the Muslim weapon demolishing the Jewish position in Notre Dame.

"There is nothing else to do," Moshe said. "I'll need Arab clothing."

Dov, who with Yehudit heard every word of the exchange between Moshe and Luke Thomas, remarked caustically, "In Warsaw we held back the German panzers for over fifty days. This is but one cannon. Why are they so afraid?"

"Nobody wants to die, eh?" Moshe replied.

"Sometimes it is necessary, *nu?*"

"You managed to survive," Moshe declared.

"Most of us did not. But we kept Hitler's army busy long enough for good people to gather their wits about them and do something."

Yehudit asked in a weak voice, "Is that what we are about? Slowing them down?"

"It is enough." Dov put his arm around her.

Yehudit leaned heavily against him. "Then you must go, also."

Dov nodded. "Yes, my love. I must."

■ ■ ■ ■

"How is little Abe?" Moshe asked Rachel, pulling her gently from the room.

"He will not be comforted," she replied.

He masked his true intentions with questions about the boy, but even before Moshe explained that he was leaving, Rachel knew he was going. Perhaps he was not coming back.

He took her hand and led her up to the fortifications on the roof of the synagogue. The sky above Jerusalem was thick with dust and smoke from the shelling of the hospice. The incessant roaring from the north was punctuated by the gush of flames and the distant shimmer of fire-bursts as each shell hit its mark.

What he said to her, he said without speaking. It was there in his eyes. He would have to do what he could to bring an end to the destruction. Each rumble meant that the chance for Jerusalem's survival was crumbling.

Between salvos she asked, "How will you go out?"

"The tunnel."

"How will the thing be done?"

"We have explosives, Dov and I. . . ."

He waited as the mouth of the cannon spouted death once again.

"But how will you get close enough?"

He had no answer for her but this: "This morning Alfie Halder came to me. He said . . . he had a word for me . . . a word from the Lord, he said. 2 Chronicles 20:15. 'This is what the LORD says to you: "Do not be afraid or discouraged because of this vast army. For the battle is not yours, but God's."'" Again the air was shattered. Moshe put his hand over her head protectively. "If this is the hour of Israel's deliverance, then I will go out as He says I must. And though I don't know what the next hour of my life will bring, we will see His hand fight for us. I cannot say how . . . but . . . He has promised."

He kissed her, a lingering kiss of farewell. She held him, not wanting him to leave her, but knowing he must. "I will pray for you, Moshe. I will pray for God's shield to guard you and a sword in the hand of a mighty angel to fight for you." Her words were drowned by the roaring of the thunder over Jerusalem.

Did he hear her plea?

*"Come back to me, my dearest heart!"*

■ ■ ■ ■

The thunder of the cannon on the Old City wall continued for hours.

Daoud wondered about the people in Notre Dame. He hoped the stubborn old nun and Sister Marie Claire had not been blasted to Paradise.

So far, the Arab cannon had not fired on the convent. Why should it? There was nothing here but Daoud hiding from perhaps a few Jewish sentries who paced the floor above him.

Certainly, Daoud reasoned, the Jewish defenders had repaired the damage Daoud had inflicted on their dynamite. Daoud would listen for their exit. When they left, the end of the convent would be near. He had already worked out his escape. He would leave through the garden entrance; the side where there were no charges. The Jews meant for the broken body of the convent to fall upon Suleiman Road and block it.

Even a child could see this, Daoud thought.

Meanwhile it was cool in the basement of Soeurs Réparatrices. Daoud had not been so cool in many days. He was also weary. The nuns had worn him out.

Daoud could hear the footfall of the Jewish soldier directly overhead.

He closed his eyes and counted the boom of shells to twenty before he fell asleep.

It was the clacking of shoes upon the steps that finally awakened him.

*Ya Allah!* Had the Jews come to search him out and kill him? Had they tortured the old Mother and Sister Marie Claire until they confessed Daoud's hiding place?

The footfall was certain! Heading directly toward him!

He cowered in the baggage, covering his head with his arms against blows he was sure would follow his discovery. His blood roared in his ears!

*Cr-r-r-rump! Cr-r-r-r-ump!*

Daoud was certain the Jews would take their revenge on Daoud! He would call out the name of Dr. Baruch. Perhaps they would spare him.

"Daoud!" A voice proclaimed knowledge of his whereabouts. All was lost!"

The boy shuddered with the certainty of his own death.

The voice said again, more urgently, "Daoud! Why are you hiding here in the baggage?"

Daoud was not so stupid that he would fall for such a trick. Did the idiot think Daoud would answer?

"Daoud." The voice was gentle but compelling. "Do not be afraid."

Daoud peered from between his fingers. Smiling down at his hiding place was the old gardener. "You!" Daoud shouted. "What are you doing here?"

"I told you I would follow you."

"Why?"

"Come out, boy," the old man urged with an amused shake of his head. "Mother needs your help."

"How do you know this?" Daoud got up slowly and looked to see if the old vagabond had brought a troop of Jews with him.

"I have seen where they carried her."

"Have they killed her?"

"She and Sister Marie Claire are tied to chairs. They are waiting for you to come to them."

"Me?"

"Who else?"

"You."

"This is for you to do."

"But where are they?" Daoud flicked his gaze to the ceiling. "Are they here in the convent?"

"No. They were taken to Notre Dame."

"You want me to go into the Jewish stronghold while my own fellows are blasting it to sand? If the Jews do not kill me, then the cannon of King Abdullah will!"

"You are afraid?" The old man extended his hand to Daoud.

There was a fierce gash in the old fellow's palm.

Daoud, distracted, said, "You are hurt."

"It is an old wound."

"It looks fresh."

The leathery face of the old man wrinkled in a compassionate smile, as though he saw how frightened Daoud was. "Fear not, Daoud." The voice deepened, becoming young and strong in its command. The old man turned from the boy and began to climb the steps up and out of the cellar. Daoud was certain the old fellow meant that Daoud should follow him to destruction. The boy hung back.

"Is anybody else up there? Besides you?"

From above him a voice resonated. "Fear not, Daoud! Do not be discouraged! The battle is not for you. It is the Lord's. Follow the wires from here to there, and you will find what you are looking for."

Resenting the command of one so aged and ignorant as an ordinary gardener when the Holy City was packed with proud commanders, Daoud reluctantly trudged up the steps.

"Where are you, old man?" he called when he reached the landing. The gardener had vanished.

# CHAPTER 28

It was on the stroke of twelve noon that the artillery stopped firing and the Arab Legion attack on Notre Dame was renewed.

The defenders were so stupefied by what they had experienced that they did not immediately react.

"Come on!" Jacob urged. "Uri, Naomi, get ready."

Three armored cars motored toward the hospice. Around them were three hundred Arab infantrymen.

It was clear the Legion intended this to be an all-out assault and had unleashed overwhelming force.

"Two rockets left," Jacob reminded Uri. "Have to make them count; block the road if we can."

Uri nodded curtly.

"One hundred fifty yards," Naomi reported. "Three across and coming on together."

The armored vehicles moved faster this time than ever before.

The cannon on the wall roared again, battering the south end of the hospice, keeping the defenders from reinforcing that weakest point.

"Now!"

Uri raised the bazooka . . . squinted along the sight . . . fired!

The left-hand car in the front rank was blown into the air, wheels still spinning, machine gun still firing.

It crashed, upside down, on top of the center vehicle.

The middle car shook from side to side as if trying to throw off the sudden weight, then ground to a halt.

The Arab gun crashed again.

One rocket left!

■ ■ ■ ■

After cautiously listening behind the panel concealing the tunnel, Moshe beckoned to Dov. The men entered Rabbi Lebowitz's deserted basement.

Moshe wondered if they would be able to return by the same route. Around the perimeter of the Jewish Quarter dynamited rubble sealed the underground passages. Like breaking the spokes of a wheel, the tunnels leading from the center outward to the shrinking rim were blocked to prevent the Arabs from using them. Even this one, leading back to a point below the Hurva, was guarded by Ehud Schiff. Ehud had strict orders to blow the passageway if he was attacked, or if Moshe and Dov did not return after a specified time.

There was also an instant for Moshe to wonder if he would make it back to Rachel at all.

The two men were dressed in the robes of dead Jihad Moquades.

With mercenaries gathered in Jerusalem from Saudi Arabia, Iraq, Syria, Lebanon, Yemen, and Egypt, Moshe had no worry that they could pass as Arabs, provided Dov did not speak.

Raised in the Old City, Moshe was fluent in Arabic. Dov's Polish accent mangled whatever simple phrases he attempted.

The street onto which they emerged was bustling with excited Muslims, waving rifles and shooting into the air. The alley rang with cries of "*Ya Allah,*" punctuated by the boom of the cannon on the wall.

With every round fired, renewed cheering broke out, adding to the atmosphere of celebration.

"The cannon is blasting apart the Haganah position!" exulted one Holy Struggler. "Soon we shall carve a lane into the New City through the bodies of the Jews!"

"Why aren't you on the wall, shooting bullets at Jews instead of wasting them in the air?" queried a man in the uniform of a Legionnaire sergeant.

A squad of Legionnaires pushed the crowd, driving them northward. "Get to the wall!" the sergeant repeated. "Save your rejoicing for after the battle."

Moshe and Dov were swept up in the mob.

A lumpy Jihad Moquade, his bright-blue eyes an oasis in the desolation of his scarred face, spotted a Players cigarette tin protruding from Dov's pocket.

"Give us a smoke, brother!" he demanded.

Dov scowled and shook his head, remembering to keep silent. The tin was full of explosives, like the others strapped in leather pouches under his robes.

"What ails you, you greedy—"

"Your pardon," Moshe interrupted. "My friend is grieving for his cousin, killed yesterday. The cigarettes he received from his kinsman just before the death, and he wishes to send the box home to the family."

"A thousand apologies, then! Let him stuff it with the ears of Jews! That is the proper way to grieve, eh?

■ ■ ■ ■

Alfie stepped carefully over the people and piles of belongings that littered the cellar floor of the Hurva. The people of Nissan Bek mingled with the people of the Hurva. They did not like one another, that was plain. How unhappy and scared were their faces! Mothers clung to children and looked up at the domed roof as though it would fall on them at any moment and kill them as Mrs. Kurtzman had been killed. The council of Nissan Bek rabbis sat in a knot with their heads together. Rabbi Akiva was furious.

And the children, who had played before, also sat silently, fearfully. The roar of the cannon on the Old City wall tore apart Notre Dame and blasted away the last defense of Jewish Jerusalem.

But these things were unimportant matters to Alfie. They were like birds flying high overhead across the sky. They were there, but he did not look at them for long. There was something so much more important. The little boy, Abe.

Alfie found Hannah Cohen with old Shoshanna and a crew of volunteer cooks. Hannah had returned to her cooking and organizing. She gestured broadly with her hands as she spoke and seemed angry about the doubling of the population in her soup kitchen.

Twice the mouths to feed! How would it be done? She had measured everything, figured how long the food would last to the day. Had the people of Nissan Bek brought no rations with them? They ran away from their food and water without even considering what it would mean to the congregation of the Hurva? They would make do. Somehow, they would manage. And blast the Jerusalem High Command for not keeping the corridor opened to the outside. And blast Ben-Gurion and the rest for not smashing through the Arab forces at Bab el Wad and opening the road! Where were the airplanes? Where were the convoys they had promised? How could the Jewish Quarter hold out? Would those who died defending this place have died in vain?

Alfie waited until she was finished with this. She rounded on him. "And I suppose you want something to eat?"

Alfie was indeed hungry, but so was everyone. "No, please," Alfie replied, not wanting to cross her. "I come looking for the little boy. For Abe Kurtzman, please."

At this request the fury of the woman collapsed. Her eyes clouded and her shoulders slumped. "Two bouillon cubes for chicken broth I have saved. They are for him. But he will not eat a bite." For a moment Alfie thought she would cry, but she did not. Jerking her chin up, she barked, "They have him in there. Away from the Nissan Bek rabble who drove his mother out." A look toward a pantry door. "It is quiet."

Alfie wanted to pat her back and tell her he was so sorry about her grandson dying. But he did not. She was busy complaining, and he did not want to remind her that she had any reason to be sad. It was better she should worry about strangers in her kitchen than about the death of young Nathan.

Alfie thanked her. She said he was big and that it would take a lot of rations to feed him. He did not tell her that he expected he could live a long time without food and so he had not eaten in some time.

He knocked on the door of the pantry, then opened it on groaning hinges. The room smelled musty like potatoes. A single candle flickered above the chair where Lori sat with little Abe in her arms. Rachel sat on the floor and hugged her knees. The room was cramped and even with the candle it seemed dark and close. Alfie had to duck his head as he entered because the door frame was low.

"Where is the windows?" he asked.

"No windows, Alfie," Lori said. Then, "Close the door."

The child seemed dead already. "Has he eat yet?"

"A few drops," Rachel answered.

"A bit," Lori said.

Alfie sank to his knees and tried to put his thick finger into the clenched fists of Abe. "He won't let go his blanket, huh?"

"No," Lori said. "It needs washing."

"Not when he's so scared. I had a flannel bunny once." Alfie tried to explain that little boys sometimes have things that are soft and smooth and comforting to rub against their cheeks. Abe had worn out this blanket with loving. "He thinks you want to take it," Alfie admonished, "Don't say you will wash it no more. He don't care it's dirty. He's scared, see?"

Lori said Abe was not scared but something else. He did not want to live.

"He needs windows." Alfie stroked the child's hair. "Hey, Abe. They won't take your blue blanket. Come on. Remember how I give you a ride once on my shoulder?"

No response. The roar of cannon blasts permeated the silence.

Lori dipped her finger in a cup of Hannah's chicken broth and then put it in Abe's mouth. He did not care. He was like the small kitten Alfie had found in the graveyard. Eyes closed, shivering and wet, it wanted to die too. Alfie had fed it until it decided to live. "But Abe's not a kitten, Lori," Alfie blurted. "His eyes is open, see? He is looking for light. See? Last time he saw his mama it was dark and close and things was bad. He needs to see sunlight. See?"

Lori pursed her lips, impatient with Alfie. "Can you hear the shelling? We can't go out."

Alfie ignored her. He said to Abe the way he used to say to Werner, "I can carry you to the garden. I can carry you on my shoulder if you like."

No flicker of acknowledgment in the boy's eyes.

Lori explained, "Today we stay here in the shelter, Alfie. No one can go out there."

Alfie smiled vacantly at Lori. She did not understand. "He will die if I don't carry him out."

"There is shooting," Lori repeated. "You can't take a child out in this—"

"Then you do it. You take him," he suggested. "He will die here if you don't."

"What garden?" Lori asked desperately.

Rachel Sachar stood up. She said, "I think he means the roses on Gal'ed Road."

"The grave?" Lori queried.

"The roses. The garden. Sure," Alfie said brightly. "He brung them for Abe. We will go together to see them." Alfie took the boy from Lori's arms. "Then we will come back, and he will eat Hannah Cohen's soup."

■ ■ ■ ■

The route followed by the shouting Arab throng surged along a crooked lane, then turned beside the Wailing Wall.

To Moshe it seemed every other Jihad Moquade made the same quip: "Today the Jews will have a new reason to wail!"

Like a cramped canyon, the massive blocks of the wall crowded out all but a scrap of sky glimpsed high overhead. Crevices in the stones contained painstakingly written prayers, placed there before the constricted alley was too dangerous to visit. Arab snipers on the Temple Mount picked off the unwary, or dropped rocks on their heads.

What would happen to this holy space if the Jewish Quarter fell? Haj Amin Husseini had used rumors to inspire riots here numerous times. If the district were lost, when would Jewish worshippers ever again be allowed to touch the timeless stones that connected them to the glory of the temple?

The crowd flowing north joined an even larger stream in El Wad Street. Jihad Moquades who fled from the Haganah a few days before returned with the Arab Legionnaires so as to be part of the glorious victory when Notre Dame fell.

Like the thumping of a giant drum, the echoing clangor of the artillery pounding Notre Dame drew them onward. The cannonfire called them to witness the destruction of the last obstacle between the Arabs and the conquest of Jerusalem.

■ ■ ■ ■

"They are coming," Peter said to Mother Superior and Sister Marie Claire, who remained bound in their chairs. "I'm sorry, but there may soon be no other choice but to blow up the convent."

Neither of the Catholic sisters spoke. There was reproach in their eyes.

Peter said fiercely, "We are fighting for our lives . . . a scrap of earth . . . bare, scorched earth, if need be . . . but a place to raise children without fear."

■ ■ ■ ■

The advance of the Arab Legion forces toward Notre Dame was relentless.

"Load, load!"

Jacob's shaking fingers and the awkwardness of the sling combined to make him clumsy. He inserted the missile but could not rig the connection for the bazooka.

"Hurry!" Naomi urged. "The third car is almost below us!"

"Now!" Jacob said.

Uri stood in the window, heedless of his own life. He swung the tube, sighted along it . . . as the rear of the third vehicle disappeared from view below. "Too close!" he shouted. "Now what?"

"Down! We go down! Hit it from the ground floor!"

Grabbing his Sten gun, Jacob ran for the door. Uri, carrying the loaded bazooka, followed. Naomi dashed ahead of them down the steps.

The cannon bellowed again.

■ ■ ■ ■

Past the timeless healing spring of Hammam esh-Shifa, which some archaeologists connected with the biblical Pool of Bethesda, through the medieval cotton bazaar known as Suq el Kattanin, down King Solomon Street, flowed the jubilant crowd of Muslims and two very worried Jews.

Drawing Dov aside into a doorway Moshe whispered, "We have to turn off here. This mob is heading straight for the Damascus Gate."

"They aren't fools," Dov returned. "Until Notre Dame is ripe to be looted they won't go too near the actual fighting."

It was when Moshe and Dov neared Suleiman's wall—that stretch of crenellated stonework that marked the northern boundary of the Old City—that they saw how the Legion had managed to get its weapon into position. The steep steps leading to the ramparts were smoothed and gentled by sandbags. The cannon, its nearby roar now punishing their ears, had been muscled into place up onto the battlements. The snout of the artillery piece protruded from a sixteenth-century embrasure, designed to resist the bolts of crossbows. The muzzle pointing at the Hospice of Notre Dame delivered its explosive messages from across the mere width of Suleiman Road.

The cannon itself was sheltered by ramparts of sandbags and oper-ated by a crew of Legionnaires. Every time it fired, the parapet on which it perched shook.

"No way can we get up there," Dov noted. "We could never get close enough to throw a grenade, let alone destroy that monster."

"Maybe we don't have to," Moshe said, pointing to a spot below the artillery position. "Look!"

Though the men firing the cannon were trained artillerymen in Le-gion uniforms, a tramping loop of Jihad Moquades carried shells from the magazine at the base of the wall. In an arched chamber on the ground level directly beneath the cannon was a heap of twenty-five-pound shells.

"If we can get a bomb inside that," Moshe suggested, "it will elimi-nate Notre Dame's problem."

■ ■ ■ ■

Peter heard the shouts of warning.

"The Legion is at the base of the hospice! Everyone downstairs, quickly!"

He was torn. How could he remain in safety while teenagers—his teenagers—went hand-to-hand with hardened Legionnaires?

He checked the connections to the detonator. All intact, the electric message of destruction ready to be sent.

He checked the cords that imprisoned the nuns. They were secure and the women could not interfere.

He made up his mind. Peter would go into battle with his troops. If all was lost, he would race back here and dynamite the convent.

He sprinted out of the room.

■ ■ ■ ■

The remaining armored car halted around the southeast corner of the building. As the twenty-five-pounder continued to blast away almost overhead, the armored car added its puny-sounding cannonfire to bat-ter down the entry doors.

"Stop here!" Jacob said to Uri on the second-floor landing. "Wait until you cannot miss. Knock out that last car!" Then he and Naomi continued downward.

Legion infantrymen were around the base of the hospice. Shooting rifles and machine guns, they closed in on the Jewish stronghold.

Uri joined a group of Gadna Youth gathered beside the second-floor windows. From these they hurled Molotov cocktails and grenades at the Legionnaires, driving them back.

The armored car shifted its aim to the windows, shattering three teenage defenders with machine-gun bullets, and the Arab infantry advanced again.

Jacob, Naomi, and ten others emerged from a side entrance. Their Sten-gun fire took the Arab foot soldiers in the flank.

Caught between grenades and bullets, the Legionnaires drew back away from the building.

The snout of the armored car pivoted toward the new threat.

"Get the armored car!" someone urged Uri. "Before it turns back toward us."

Uri drew a bead on the armored car, then saw a pair of Legionnaires hidden from Naomi's view by a set of steps. One of them pointed his rifle toward the girl.

Without stopping to think that it was a bazooka he carried . . . or that this was the last rocket . . . Uri pivoted the tube, aimed, and fired.

The missile caught the Legionnaire in the chest, passed through him and exploded against the steps. The explosion killed the second Arab as well.

Uri flung the empty bazooka down and grabbed a rifle.

He never saw the muzzle of the armored car swivel toward him, never heard the burst of gunfire that killed him.

■ ■ ■ ■

Peter emerged behind Jacob.

The cannon on the wall altered its aim. The next round that hammered Notre Dame struck one floor above the windows from which the grenades were thrown.

A bullet whizzed past Jacob, smacked the building behind him. He fired a shot burst from the Sten gun, spotted a trio of Legionnaires in the garden, and fired another stream of shots that made them dive for the ground.

He heard Naomi cry out, "The Arabs are in the building!"

Using the heap of shattered stones as a ramp, a dozen Legion foot soldiers swarmed upward. Jacob and Peter fired into them, saw two fall, and the others ducked.

Huddling with Peter and Naomi, Jacob said, "Between the cannon on the wall and the armored car we cannot hold them off much longer! Go, Peter! Blow the convent!"

Naomi grasped Peter's hand, looked into his eyes, then nodded.

■ ■ ■ ■

Daoud emerged from the corridor and entered the room with the detonator. "Mère!" he said when he saw the bound women.

"Daoud! Hurry, child! Untie me!"

The loops of rope that secured the Mother Superior did not bind her tightly, but the cord crisscrossed her body in such a way that she could not be freed without undoing the knots.

Daoud plucked at the first, started it, then freed an end of the cable. He turned to the second of the knots that held her.

"My hands first, child," she said. "Then I can help as well!"

■ ■ ■ ■

Moshe and Dov crouched behind the counter in a deserted candle-maker's shop around the corner of Bab el Jadid from the artillery piece.

The clock of the Franciscan church tolled the hour, to which the cannon added an emphatic concluding stroke.

Tying together a bundle of explosives, Moshe secured the timing device made by Dov. "We join the line of carriers," he said. "When we reach the magazine, we plant the device inside. Then less than a minute to get clear, and—"

"Good-bye, cannon!" Dov concluded.

■ ■ ■ ■

Peter raced toward the detonator. Why had he ever left that room? He had accomplished nothing of value. What if the Legion surged forward, past Notre Dame, before he could ignite the charges?

The defensive line would be lost, and with it Jerusalem!

Outside, in the garden, an Arab infantryman raised his rifle, looking for a target. Through a window he saw Peter charging along a corridor. The Legionnaire shifted his aim to the next window over and waited.

The bullet slammed into Peter's thigh.

Crying out, he managed two more steps before the leg failed him. He fell, landing face first on the floor.

The Legionnaire followed up his shot with two more that missed because Peter remained sprawled below his sight picture.

Peter scrambled to shelter. The bullet had not struck bone and had exited cleanly.

There was a lot of blood.

No time to think about that. Ripping off his shirt, Peter wrapped it around the wound, tying it in place with his belt.

Why had he ever left the detonator?

# CHAPTER 29

The Gadna Youth and the Home Guard managed to keep the front of Notre Dame clear of Legionnaires. It was the south face and the rear that were threatened. Unless something was done soon, more Arab foot soldiers would slip around the back of the hospice, protected by the guns of the armored car. Then all would truly be lost.

Leaving Naomi with two Sten guns and the ammunition, Jacob sprinted back into the building. On the way to the street level he had passed a storage room where Molotov cocktails and grenades were assembled. Tucking grenades into his sling and the crook of his injured arm, Jacob also grabbed two glass bottles containing petrol. These he carried in one hand by their long necks.

As he exited the hospice once more, a bullet struck one of the petrol bombs between Jacob's grip and the bottle. As it fell and splintered on the steps, a shower of petrol sprayed from it.

Jacob was covered with gasoline.

"You can't light that!" Naomi said.

The armored car's cannon fired, shattering part of a window casement above their heads.

The twenty-five-pound gun also bellowed, collapsing two rooms into one and crushing two more Gadna defenders.

"I'll go," Naomi said, passing back the Sten and taking the last petrol bomb.

"I'll distract them!"

Jacob bounded up, waving his bandaged arm at the armored car like a matador's cape to a bull. He ran toward it from a side angle. Firing the Sten gun, Jacob saw the slugs bounce off the iron hide of the vehicle, so he discarded it and plucked a grenade from his sling.

Releasing the pin with his teeth, he tossed the bomb toward the armored car, then dashed himself flat. Jarring his shoulder made his eye-sight flicker. He could not keep this up for long.

The grenade exploded short of its target, causing no damage.

But the crew had seen him, knew he was a threat.

Trundling backwards, the Arab machine swung in an arc to bring its machine gun to bear on him.

Jacob, stumbling, slipping, circled with it barely ahead of the spray of bullets.

He drew another grenade, armed it, threw it.

It bounced on the turret, exploding on the other side.

Jacob lay on the ground, panting. He was almost spent.

The car continued to rotate. Another foot and its weapon would be trained on him.

Where was Naomi? What was she waiting for?

■ ■ ■ ■

Naomi spotted the cigarette lighter in the breast pocket of a dead Legionnaire. Plucking it out, she ignited the wick of the Molotov cock-tail.

The crew of the armored car were so focused on Jacob that they did not perceive the threat from the other side.

But other Arab soldiers spotted the girl as she rose from conceal-ment. Despite the shouts of warning and the bullets whizzing past, Naomi ran straight toward the vehicle as if she would climb in.

The concussion of a nearby mortar round knocked her off her feet.

She landed with her hand between the smoking petrol bomb and the cobblestones. Partly stunned, she watched the bottle roll from her fingers.

Jacob lay on the ground in front of the armored car. Bullets kicked up dirt beyond his head. He was too low and too near for the car's ma-chine gun to touch him.

The engine raced.

They were going to run over him.

Snatching up the Molotov cocktail, Naomi rushed forward. From ten feet distant she dashed it against the front of the armored car, over the visor slits.

The front half of the machine was engulfed in flames leaping sky-ward.

The hatch popped open. The Legionnaires wasted no time jumping clear.

Naomi passed two of them as she ran to help Jacob. They did no more than glance at her as they ran toward their own lines.

■ ■ ■ ■

Alfie cradled little Abe in his arms as Rachel and Lori followed him out into daylight. The child was unaware of anything. Breathing his last. At least, Lori thought, he would not die in the gloom of the cellar room.

Tears streamed from her eyes. Not the smoke. *Oh God! We are lost! Jacob! Moshe! This little boy! My boy! All of us! Lost, unless You save us!*

The ground beneath their feet quaked. The sky fulminated with thick clouds lowering over the city where Christ had suffered and died and risen. Jerusalem's dust and stones, glutted with ancient blood, opened to swallow more.

Lori's thoughts clung to the image of Jacob. Where was he? Was he alive?

Lori held Rachel's hand, also keenly aware that Moshe was somewhere on the other side of safety. Every moment the cannon bellowed meant that he had not yet succeeded. That perhaps he had died, and all was lost.

Rachel, her eyes moist with emotion, inclined her head briefly against Lori's shoulder. "Do not be afraid," Rachel said calmly.

Lori looked at her in wonder. Not to fear?

Alfie brushed his lips on the forehead of little Abe. He explained to unhearing ears, "I will carry you. See, Werner? See, Daniel? See, Abe? The sky is blue behind the clouds. Do not be afraid. No. It is only thunder. I will carry you. Carry you to the garden, and you will see everything. . . ."

■ ■ ■ ■

The line of Jihad Moquades feeding the cannon moved forward in a series of pauses and jerks. Each man ducked to enter the arched alcove, then emerged a moment later, hefting a twenty-five-pound projectile.

A flight of stone steps gave access to the parapet above, where a Legionnaire received each shell. The carrier then rejoined the end of the line.

A score of Arabs were ahead of Moshe and Dov as they attached themselves to the queue. But no one paid any attention to them. The Jihad Moquades covered their ears as the cannon blasted, eliminating any attempt at conversation.

Moshe, carrying the rigged grenade, was in front. That way Dov would shield him from view as he planted it.

A smoking shell case fell from the ledge above, landing a few feet away. Moshe glanced up at the gun emplacement.

Dieter Wottrich!

Whatever his real name, the German mercenary was on the wall!

Moshe looked quickly down at his sandals, then turned his back to the parapet. "Keep your face hidden," he hissed to Dov. "Wottrich is on the wall!"

Moshe touched the pistol hidden under his robes, but there was nothing to do except move forward.

The third Arab ahead of them in the line tripped as he came out of the magazine. Stumbling, he almost dropped the shell he was carrying.

"Idiot!" someone upbraided him. "Are you trying to kill us?"

From the corner of his eye, Moshe saw the man known as *Wottrich* peer at the commotion below, then away.

When Moshe was outside the cache of shells, he partially withdrew the grenade from the folds of his robe.

The man in front of him lifted a shell, grunted, and walked past.

Moshe entered the grotto. Perfect! The artillery ammunition was stacked on wooden pallets. There was a space behind the heap where the grenade would not be seen.

As Dov shielded him from sight, he started the timer and tucked the grenade in place.

■ ■ ■ ■

At the same second that Moshe placed the grenade behind the pallets of cannon shells, another brass shell casing tumbled off the wall above.

Idly watching it fall, Robert Brandenburg looked directly into Dov's face.

Both men's eyes widened with recognition.

Dov grabbed Moshe's arm. No time for deception and blending in. Run!.

"Jews!" Brandenburg bellowed. "They—"

The cannon roared, drowning out his words. The concussion startled him, made him stumble. Where had Dov gone?

"Jews!" Brandenburg yelled again. He brandished a pistol, shaking it into the upturned countenances of the Jihad Moquades. Shrugging, his audience gestured to their ears. Thinking he was haranguing them about the destruction being wreaked on Notre Dame by the cannon, they smiled and waved their own weapons back at him. The cannon was killing many Jews, *Ya Allah!*

The line of men moved forward, picking up more shells.

The cannon boomed again.

There! Two men in striped robes were at the edges of the crowd, hurrying toward the Jewish Quarter. It had to be them!

Brandenburg extended the arm holding the pistol. He let the muzzle drop smoothly toward the taller of the two running figures.

His grip tightened on the trigger.

Suddenly Brandenburg had the inexplicable sensation that the stones beneath his feet were lifting up, flying into the sky.

Then as Moshe and Dov rounded the corner of Beit Jadid, Brandenburg and thirty-five Jihad Moquades and Legionnaires disintegrated, together with the cannon and a sizable stretch of Suleiman's wall.

■ ■ ■ ■

Mother Superior stood and ran to the detonator.

"Do you know how this works?" she asked Daoud.

"These two wires," Daoud said, indicating the connections to the detonating cable. "If we unscrew these, the weapon cannot be exploded." He tested the first threaded bolt. "It is stuck," he said with a grunt.

"Don't!" groaned an agonized voice from the door.

Peter Wallich lay on his side. His pant leg from crotch to ankle was dyed red. A trail of smeared liquid led back to the hallway. He had crawled as far as the entry, but now, dizzy and nearly unconscious from loss of blood, he could go no farther.

Daoud stared at the stricken Jew. "Mère," he said. "He bleeds like a goat at the butcher's."

"Just one place in the world . . ." Peter panted. "One scrap of earth . . ."

Mother Superior looked out the window. There, no more than a stone's throw away, was Soeurs Réparatrices. It was stately, dignified, hallowed by generations of prayer and worship.

"Mère," Daoud repeated. "This man . . . he will die if we do not help him."

"Yes," the Mother Superior agreed. "They may all die if we do not . . ." She looked at Daoud. "Hurry."

She yanked the plunger up to its furthest point. Hesitating an instant, she forced it down with all her strength.

A bellowing reverberation, louder than any detonation yet heard, shattered Jerusalem. Soeurs Réparatrices lifted as if it would ascend into the heavens, then split into a million fragments, blocking Suleiman Road.

■ ■ ■ ■

They knelt beside the roses of Gal'ed as the earth and sky erupted in a conflagration to the north. The concussion knocked Lori to her face and bleached the color from the world.

In a shimmer of white light she saw Alfie, unmoved by the blast, shielding Abe and smiling into the face of the child. The giant man reached out to touch a rosebud with his finger as the boom and whine of shells gone wild distorted the sky of the Old City.

Grief commingled with joy on the face of Rachel as she dug her fingers into the earth of the garden. "Moshe! Moshe!" she cried.

Had Moshe survived his victory over the Arab field cannon?

Lori covered her head as the rain of debris began. Solid chunks of stone and bits of metal fell from the sky to pock the garden of Gal'ed.

Alfie continued to talk to Abe above the clatter and the din. What was he saying?

And then, suddenly . . . silence. Bits of dirt continued to patter around them. But the raucous chatter of battle had stopped.

Lori, eyes squeezed shut and her face in the dirt, lay unmoving, waiting for the noise of the battle for Jerusalem to resume.

It did not.

There was just Alfie's voice crooning softly to Abe. "You see? Huh? See Abe? It is only thunder. It is only rain."

Rachel, eyes full, nudged her to look and to believe.

And then a child's voice replied, "I was scared."

Alfie nodded seriously at Abe's remark. "Sometimes, me too. *Ja.* But we don't got to be scared no more, Abe. It was only thunder, see? Now we are in the garden, like I promised. God sent you roses. Smell them. Nice, huh? Look at the roses, Abe."

"Hmmmm. Pretty." Fingers of Abe's tiny square hand stretched to touch a bloom.

"Careful of thorns. Like I said, the roses wasn't on His crown. Just thorns, see? Roses grew after. Where He planted the crown. Here, Abe. He planted it here deep inside Jerusalem's heart."

"Will He come back to get it?"

"Soon."

"I will like to see it on Him."

"Someday. But . . . just look at the roses till then. A promise, see? Do you know your colors yet? We got to wash your blue blanket, you know."

"Sure."

# EPILOGUE

*You are forever mighty, Adonai: giving*
*life to the dead, You are a mighty savior . . .*
*You sustain life with kindness, giving life*
*to the dead with great mercy, supporting*
*the fallen, healing the sick, and freeing*
*the captive, and keeping faith with sleepers*
*in the dust. . . .*

*The Amidah—G'vurot*
*The Second Prayer*

*. . . Then they took away the stone from the place where the*
*dead was laid. And Jesus lifted up his eyes, and said, Father, I*
*thank you that you have heard me . . . And . . . he cried in a*
*loud voice, Lazarus, come forth!*

*from John 11:1–45*

Sir John Glubb's armored car was under fire from the moment it came over the rise at Herod's Gate at the northeast corner of the Old City. Machine-gun bullets clanged off the metal sheeting. With each hammer blow the Legion driver jerked the vehicle to the side as if he were running from wolves nipping at his heels.

There were three hundred yards of exposed road to traverse and the Jewish gunners in Notre Dame made good use of the opening. Over and over, the driver muttered, "Allah keep me! Allah keep me!" until Glubb told the man to be quiet.

With a final yank of the steering that almost wrecked them, the armored car lunged into Damascus Gate and out of sight of the Haganah defenders.

Major Tariq Athani met his superior as Glubb exited the vehicle.

Despite the presence of the two highest-ranking Arab Legion officers in Jerusalem, the Legionnaire guards slumped against the wall of Athani's command post. Their faces dirty, downcast, unshaven, they neither saluted nor looked up.

Inside the hotel Athani had commandeered were more glum, weary soldiers. Though the floor was littered with stone fragments and shards of window glass, fifteen Legionnaires sat . . . or slept . . . there.

The windows in Athani's office—those facing Notre Dame—were solidly blocked with sandbags. Athani offered Glubb a packing crate on which to sit, then took another for himself.

"We must make one more attempt on the hospice," Athani urged. "We came so close last time. Give us another cannon and three more armored cars and I promise the building will be yours tomorrow."

Glubb was already shaking his head before Athani finished speaking. "Suleiman Road is totally blocked by the demolished convent. We are withdrawing from this battle," he said flatly. "I have told . . . I have *propose* to His Majesty that we concentrate on seizing the road to the coast and strangling Jerusalem into submission."

"But the Jews must be nearly finished!"

"Ask my driver's opinion of that statement," Glubb suggested dryly. "No, the Jews are holding on to the Old City *and* the hospice." Leaning forward, he confided, "The Jews have stopped the Syrians in the north. The Egyptians still have not taken the settlement of Yad Mordechai. And we . . . we have wasted days, equipment, and *lives* trying to capture Jerusalem. It may have cost us the war!" Recollecting that he should not be so candid with a subordinate, Glubb said, "The Jews do not know how battered we are or how reduced our ranks are. If they did, then *they* would attack *us* . . . and we could not stop them from overrunning us . . . perhaps even capturing the King's palace in Amman. No," Glubb concluded. "We must content ourselves with holding them here . . . and we will take Jerusalem another day."

■ ■ ■ ■

The jeep, driven by Dr. Gould, bumped and rattled down the dirt track leading from the kibbutz to Tel Aviv. A pair of Egyptian Dakota bombers roared past overhead as the jeep veered off the road and under the sheltering branches of a tamarack tree.

"Didn't even bother to strafe us," David observed.

"Yeah," Bobby said. "Must not have known what an important target they passed up here."

"They are going to Tel Aviv to bomb the docks," said Dr. Gould, maneuvering onto the road again. "They have been coming every day."

As the jeep neared an intersection where another gravel route branched off, David touched the doctor's shoulder.

"Doesn't that lead to the Haganah airstrip?" he asked.

The affirmative reply caused Bobby and David to look into each other's dirty, unshaven, bruised and battered faces.

"We really oughta report in," Bobby said. "The Boss prob'ly thinks we're playin' hooky."

"Yeah," David agreed. "I really should go see Els. Let her know I made it."

In unison the two flyers demanded, "Turn here!"

A C-46 transport plane was drawn up beside one of the tin sheds.

Czech mechanics were helping it give birth to an engine cowling and a landing gear.

But David's attention was elsewhere.

Inside the hangar nearest the end of the dirt runway stood a fully assembled ME-109 fighter.

Its windshield gleamed. The Czech mechanic, Zoltan, threaded a belt of ammo in the machine-gun housing. "Hey," he said to David with an exuberant wave. "You not too dead, eh?"

David shook his head. "Fueled up?" he asked. "Ammo, too?"

"Full to the brim."

A pair of black dots in the sky resolved themselves into the Egyptian bombers returning toward Cairo.

David patted the side of the 109 before reaching for the goggles and helmet Bobby extended to him.

"My turn," David said. "My turn."

From the next installment in the *Zion Legacy Series*
# JERUSALEM'S HEART

In the superheated atmosphere of the Old City the measured boom of mortar shells resounded through the narrow streets. One explosion took on the voice of ten. The brittle echo of a single rifle became a fusillade.

"The Arabs are attacking! They have rallied! More defenders to the north perimeter!"

Amid the shouts of alarm from the Jewish defenders of the Old City, Alfie returned to the garden of Galed. Now it was time to get back to the safety of the Hurva shelter. Alfie gathered little Abe into his massive arms. The child perched on Alfie's shoulder fearlessly, as though he could not hear the thunder of explosions, the screams of the injured, and the resonant pop of small arms.

It was, Lori thought, an image like the giant Saint Christopher bearing the Christ Child and the weight of the world through the deep waters of Jerusalem.

Abe's gaze fixed on the roses of Galed that crowned the graves of his brothers and sisters. "Where we going?" he asked Lori in a piping voice.

"The Hurva," she explained, quickening her pace as a shell exploded and dust bloomed over the tops of domed roofs.

"Flowers"— Abe stretched his fingers toward the receding rose garden—"sister sleeping there."

"We'll come back to visit the roses soon. Visit sister. You need to eat a little something. The soup kitchen," Lori replied patiently, trying to master her sense of panic. "You see, Abe." She gestured toward the billowing smoke as though she were making all things clear.

"Alfie too?" Abe smiled and patted the big man on the shoulder as if he were a dray horse trotting over the cobbles of a narrow village street in the Cotswolds.

"No. You be a good boy. Eat something. I got to go now, see?" Alfie explained, rounding the corner and coming within sight of the entrance to the courtyard of the Hurva. Five Haganah soldiers ran past, headed for the northern barricade. Two others, supporting a wounded comrade, hobbled down the steep steps of an alleyway. "I got to carry other good chaps. Big fellows. Hurt fellows can't walk—see, Abe? I got to carry them 'cause they can't walk."

Abe frowned and shook his head fiercely. "I can carry good chaps too."

Lori ignored Abe's protestations and instructed Alfie, "Those explosions. They are coming from the perimeter beyond the hospital. You will be needed. Tell Dr. Baruch that Abe and I will be in the shelter at the Hurva. When he goes to sleep I will come to the hospital." Lori reached up to take Abe from Alfie. The child resisted, entwining Alfie's hair in his fingers.

Abe's wail competed with the cacophony of the battle. "Not the dark place! No! Not in the dark place no more! Mama's down in the dark place. I want the garden! Flowers! The garden!"

Alfie leaned down. Lori pried Abe's small hands free and pulled him away from Alfie.

"No! Not the dark place! Not the crying place! I can carry good chaps!"

Lori wrapped her arms around his middle to restrain him.

Alfie laid a benign paw on the struggling boy's head. "Be good, huh? I'll come see you." This assurance made no difference. The pitch of hysteria increased. Alfie scanned the sky and said to Lori, "He's scared, you know? That bomb on his house, see? No wonder. The sky is blue outside."

Lori looked up at the pall of smoke and dust that washed all color from the day. "He's got to eat."

"Maybe so." Alfie nodded as Abe kicked. "But he's awful scared. Not much light in there. In the cellar. Real hot, too. Lots of people in there. People crying. Maybe out here is better?" He pointed across the square toward the arched open portico of the Yeshiva school. Several dozen refugees huddled there. Heaps of meager belongings provided no real protection from danger. If an Arab shell hit in the open courtyard there would be no escaping the shrapnel.

Just then a geyser of debris spewed up outside the walls of the Hurva compound.

Could she let a child's tantrum dictate where they took refuge? Without looking back she embraced Abe and dashed toward the sandbags that protected the portal of the Hurva.

Abe's once-chubby little frame was skeletal from months of privation. Like a small bird caught in a paroxysm of grief, he had refused all nourishment since the night his family perished beneath the shell that destroyed their home.

"Hannah Cohen will have a good meal for you." Her words were lost as they entered the sanctuary beneath the dome of the great Hurva. Soldiers on the scaffolding took aim through lattice-covered windows. Arab snipers on the minaret beyond the wall pumped bullets into the compound.

## FOR THE BEST IN PAPERBACKS, LOOK FOR THE

In every corner of the world, on every subject under the sun, Penguin represents quality and variety—the very best in publishing today.

For complete information about books available from Penguin—including Puffins, Penguin Classics, and Compass—and how to order them, write to us at the appropriate address below. Please note that for copyright reasons the selection of books varies from country to country.

**In the United Kingdom:** Please write to *Dept. EP, Penguin Books Ltd, Bath Road, Harmondsworth, West Drayton, Middlesex UB7 0DA.*

**In the United States:** Please write to *Penguin Putnam Inc., P.O. Box 12289 Dept. B, Newark, New Jersey 07101-5289* or call 1-800-788-6262.

**In Canada:** Please write to *Penguin Books Canada Ltd, 10 Alcorn Avenue, Suite 300, Toronto, Ontario M4V 3B2.*

**In Australia:** Please write to *Penguin Books Australia Ltd, P.O. Box 257, Ringwood, Victoria 3134.*

**In New Zealand:** Please write to *Penguin Books (NZ) Ltd, Private Bag 102902, North Shore Mail Centre, Auckland 10.*

**In India:** Please write to *Penguin Books India Pvt Ltd, 11 Panchsheel Shopping Centre, Panchsheel Park, New Delhi 110 017.*

**In the Netherlands:** Please write to *Penguin Books Netherlands bv, Postbus 3507, NL-1001 AH Amsterdam.*

**In Germany:** Please write to *Penguin Books Deutschland GmbH, Metzlerstrasse 26, 60594 Frankfurt am Main.*

**In Spain:** Please write to *Penguin Books S. A., Bravo Murillo 19, 1° B, 28015 Madrid.*

**In Italy:** Please write to *Penguin Italia s.r.l., Via Benedetto Croce 2, 20094 Corsico, Milano.*

**In France:** Please write to *Penguin France, Le Carré Wilson, 62 rue Benjamin Baillaud, 31500 Toulouse.*

**In Japan:** Please write to *Penguin Books Japan Ltd, Kaneko Building, 2-3-25 Koraku, Bunkyo-Ku, Tokyo 112.*

**In South Africa:** Please write to *Penguin Books South Africa (Pty) Ltd, Private Bag X14, Parkview, 2122 Johannesburg.*